GODDESS FOUND

MORE BY THE AUTHOR

Hunter Ascendant
A *Goddess Found* prequel novelette available for free to
my newsletter subscribers.
Visit www.CalantheColt.com for more info.

GODDESS FOUND

CALANTHE COLT

CENTAURI PUBLISHING

Published by Centauri Publishing.

ISBN (paperback): 978-0-473-66797-9
ISBN (Kindle): 978-0-473-66799-3
ISBN (Apple Books): 978-0-473-66800-6
ISBN (generic ePub): 978-0-473-66798-6

A catalogue record of this book is available from the National Library of New Zealand Te Puna Mātauranga o Aotearoa.

Cover design © Stefanie Saw, SeventhStarArt.com — cover uses stock images purchased by the designer.

Typesetting © Centauri Publishing Services.

Map created with WonderDraft under a commercial license.

Rider Waite Tarot images are in the Public Domain.

To everyone who has ever felt invisible.
I see you, and I believe in you.

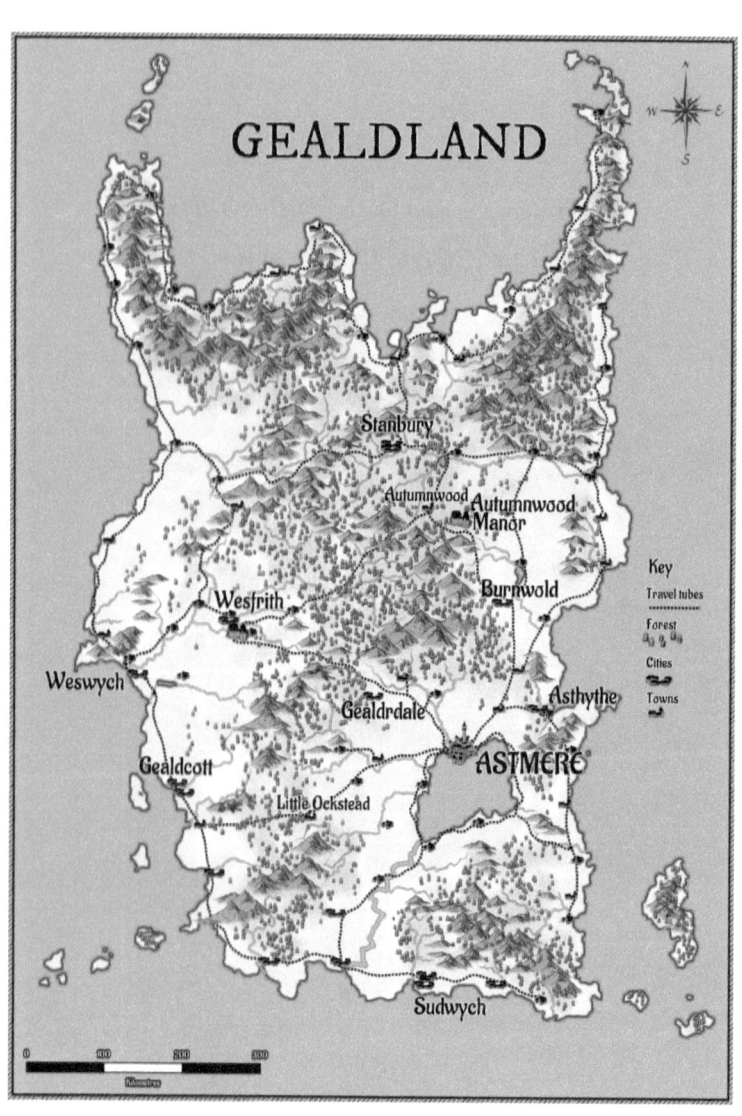

THE FOOL
UPRIGHT

Let go of your expectations. Be ready to approach new experiences with an open mind. Follow your heart.

To Marcus,

I need to take a personal leave of absence for one day and evening. I will return to Autumnwood Manor tomorrow morning. I hope my absence does not cause too much trouble. May I perform a reading for you before young Jack arrives, perhaps tomorrow? You never took me up on my offer last year.

Sincerely,
Mirabelle

Leta lost herself in the rhythm of her kitchen: the scone dough that needed mixing, the stew that needed seasoning. The total lack of jobs which needed no magic that she'd found on the aetherweb globe that day…

Nope, not thinking about that.

Her mum kept saying, 'there used to be lots of non-magical jobs around before; there will be again.' But these days, all employers wanted their employees to 'add value', and 'value' meant magic. That's why Leta wanted to study something that would let her be her own boss, so her lack of magic wouldn't be an issue. But to study, she needed money. It was a classic catch-22.

Not thinking about it! Leta reminded herself to just focus on dinner.

Her mother had sent her a message on her aether-voicer asking her to make an extra portion as they'd be having a guest. Who knows which distant relative or old friend her mother had run into during her work as Little Ockstead's travel tube catcher? But Leta, the household cook, was used to fluctuating numbers at the dinner table. What she wasn't used to was distant cousins asking what happened to her job at the bakery (business failure), when she would be starting that pâtisserie course she wanted to do (when she could find the money for course fees), and sidling around the elephant in the room: that in a nation of mages, Leta had no usable magic, and therefore was someone to be pitied.

Well, her mum never thought less of her, even if the school bullies and the busybodies in the supermarket had.

As if summoned by Leta's stray thoughts, her mum chose that moment to stomp through the front door. Leta peered down the hallway to see who she'd brought home. Her mum unwound her scarf and took off her woolly hat. She scrubbed her short dark hair into a semblance of order, hair that was so different from Leta's own long, reddish mop. "Please, come in," she said, and waved someone into the hallway. There was a note of excitement in her mum's voice that piqued Leta's attention.

Leta put the tray of scones into the oven, wiped her hands, and stepped into the hallway. In the entryway, wrapped in a fashionable woollen coat and fur hat and leaning on a gold-topped cane, stood an older woman. She looked familiar to Leta, but she couldn't place where she'd seen her before.

The woman took a moment to slip off her shiny court shoes and place them on the rack, hang up her coat, and remove her hat, revealing short, curled steel-grey hair. Her sharp green eyes honed straight in on Leta. "Hello, you must be the younger Ms Wildwinter. My name is Mirabelle Crowlea. A pleasure to make your acquaintance." She held out her slim hand. Her nails were sharp and painted an unusual navy blue.

Leta took the woman's hand on instinct. "Lovely to meet you." She gave her mother a quizzical look. She had no context for who this guest was.

"You know that aethercast I was watching last year? The one where they're looking for the new Goddess Incarnate?"

How could Leta have forgotten? The 'cast had taken Gealdland by storm. Instead of letting the country's newly ascended God Incarnate search for his Goddess Incarnate by travelling around as was traditional, some company had got a hold of him. They had turned it all into a reality aethercast with hopeful contestants and whatnot. Leta had found the whole thing distasteful. "Yeah, I remember."

"This is Seer Mirabelle from the aethercast!"

With the right context, Leta remembered seeing this older lady on the aetherweb. She'd performed readings and divinations for the contestants and for God Incarnate Jack. But what was she doing in their entryway?

"I ran into her at the travel tube station," explained Leta's mum. "Seer Mirabelle wasn't aware of how, uh, quiet the village is in the evening. She has accommodation for the evening, but..."

But there was no restaurant in the village, only a noisy pub.

"So I offered her a seat at our table."

"I am so sorry to intrude on such short notice," said Seer Mirabelle.

"Not at all," said Leta. "Would you like a cup of tea?"

Before long, the three of them sat around the kitchen table.

"So, what brings you to Little Ockstead?" asked Leta's mum. "We're a bit off the beaten trail here. Thankfully for me: I wouldn't want too much of a workload!" Leta's mum caught and sent every travel capsule to and from Little Ockstead. When she left work for the evening, that was the end of local long-distance travel, and people had to take a transport to get around instead.

"I am looking for something in preparation for the next season of our aethercast. Are you aware of *Goddess Found*?"

"I'm a fan of the 'cast!" said Leta's mum. "It's great."

Mirabelle smiled. "Thank you so much for saying so, Ms Wildwinter."

"Call me Carol."

Mirabelle acknowledged Leta's mum with a stately nod. "Do you watch our aethercast, Leta?"

Leta jumped. "Oh, um, a bit." A change in the scent of dinner caught her attention. She rose and removed the scones from the oven, stirred the stew, and set about serving dinner while she listened to the seer.

Mirabelle put her teacup down on the table. "I could beat about the bush for a while, I suppose, but perhaps it is best if I am forthright. While performing a series of readings preparing for the next season of our aethercast, I had a vision that contained a portent. That vision brought me to your village. I did not know what I was looking for until I arrived, but sitting here at your table, I have a theory."

"A vision… brought you here," said Leta's mum in wonder.

Leta's stomach flipped at the seer's words. "What kind of portent?"

There must have been something accusatory about her voice because her mum made a shushing motion, but Mirabelle just smiled. "My job is to find those slight changes in circumstances that will weight fate one way or another. Sometimes the change can be tiny. Choosing a certain breakfast. Taking one route to work rather than another. I advise people of the slight changes they can make to increase the likelihood of achieving their goals. And I think I may find one of those slight changes here, one that will make it more likely for us to find the goddess on our aethercast this season."

Leta and her mum looked at one another. Leta found her own confusion mirrored on her mum's face. "How can we help?" said her mum.

"Does one of you need a job?" asked Mirabelle.

"Oh! My daughter does! Terrible thing, but the bakery she was working at shut up shop. She's even had to move back in with her boring old mum, poor thing."

In truth, Leta's attempt at going out flatting had only lasted eighteen months until she'd been back at her mum's again. And she'd been back home all the time anyway, since she'd only been living around the corner.

"Well, Leta," said Mirabelle, "I think we can help each other. I need an assistant for the aethercast this year, and since my vision brought me here, I am sure it is you I am supposed to offer the job to. Would you like to come work for me?"

Leta gaped. "It's a kind offer, but I don't like the idea of being on an aethercast," she said. "I'd feel very nervous about everyone looking at me."

Mirabelle smiled. "The role would be behind the scenes. You wouldn't appear in the aethercast itself."

Her mum was making an encouraging face and nodding, the excitement near vibrating off her.

Work behind the scenes on an aethercast? A trashy reality aethercast that she didn't enjoy watching? Was her mum serious? But then again, a season of an aethercast wouldn't take that long to capture, so she could stick it out. Also, maybe before turning it down, she should check if the pay would cover the course costs...

And then there was that hopeful look in her mum's eyes. She couldn't bludge off her mother forever. She was already twenty-four! She had to stand on her own two feet.

"What would be my responsibilities? And may I ask about the pay?"

Mirabelle beamed. "Good lady. Let me explain..."

A SENSE OF FOREBODING chilled Jack's spine as the car approached Autumnwood Manor. A hive of activity swarmed the grounds. Late though it was, people were

6

testing floodlights around one of the manor's follies, a faux mini castle. No doubt it would be a location for one of those forced dates he'd hated last season. Since he hadn't found his goddess yet, and the contract he signed with AllAether when he was broke and fresh back from his travels was still in effect, he had no choice but to do it all again. It was a magically binding contract, of course. The network owned his damned soul.

Tyres crunched on gravel as the car circled a fountain and stopped by the grand manor entrance. At least the one waiting for him was a friend. Marcus was the host of the aethercast; he was also a producer at AllAether. They'd bonded when he'd given Jack welcome advice on how to handle his sudden fame.

Jack stepped into unseasonably chilly air that smelled of pine sap. "Jack!" called Marcus, the light of the foyer turning his blond hair into a halo. "Welcome to the manor!"

The two men clasped hands. "Great to see you, Marcus. Are you doing well?"

"Can't complain, can't complain." His sharp grin showed off aether-ready dental work. "Come in out of the cold. I'll show you to your suite."

Jack turned to get his suitcase, but found the driver standing behind him, suitcase in hand. Threads of light visible only to him showed Jack that the driver was hefting the suitcase with his kinetic magic. Jack still felt uneasy in such situations: he was a kinetic mage, damn it! He should be the one carrying things for people. But that wasn't his life anymore. Instead, he followed Marcus into the manor.

"How are you doing?" asked Marcus as they climbed the stairs and passed through the arched entranceway. "I heard you had a busy second Blessings tour."

"That was a few months back now." Jack had spent spring and early summer travelling the width and breadth of Gealdland. The number one most important job of the God Incarnate was to act as the focal point for the energy of the Hunter to flow into the land and boost its productivity. During the Blessings tours, Jack had to get as close as he could to as much of the land as he could. The rest happened naturally. There was a whole route that the officials from the head temple took him on. It would work better when the goddess ascended; the Harvester was more important in that regard. But Jack was doing his best in the meantime. It was why they were capturing the aethercast in autumn, as Jack's Blessings tour was too important and time sensitive to postpone. "I've heard this year's harvest had a boost."

"Excellent. I bought stocks in farming a few years back, so thanks. Bet you got some nice donations out of it too."

They'd paid him a stipend, sure. But the bulk of the money paid for Blessings rites went towards temple upkeep, not into his own pocket. People always assumed he was rich now, but it didn't work that way. Jack shrugged. "A bit," he said.

"A bit. Right." Marcus paused and gestured expansively. "What do you think, God Incarnate?"

Jack craned his neck to look around. Any refurbishment of the foyer over the years had retained its character. The dark wood bannister of the double staircase shone, and the marble floor tiles glistened. Ancient well-maintained furniture filled the air with the scent of wood polish. Distant voices echoed from deeper in the manor, the words indistinguishable.

"Very nice," he said. In truth, he found the manor to have a repressive atmosphere, but he doubted that's what Marcus wanted to hear.

A large portrait in prime position caught Jack's attention. Its presence confused him until he noticed the darker strip of wall just visible beneath. A different portrait usually hung there; this one was for the 'cast. It was his previous life, the former God Incarnate Archibald Sudbury. Beside him stood the previous Goddess Incarnate, Julia Sudbury. Jack gazed up at himself who was not himself. Archibald's eyes had been blue and his hair a light brown, and he hadn't been able to tan to save his life. He'd also tended to carry a bit of extra weight. Jack had brown eyes, dark hair, and a slimmer, taller build. He also tanned easily, courtesy of his grandmother who had hailed from the continent. Even so, he felt like he ought to remember being Archibald, but he couldn't. He just had… impressions, from time to time. Like forgotten dreams.

The image of Julia Sudbury, as always, engendered a complicated mix of feelings. She represented what he was looking for and he couldn't help but imagine his goddess having her dark curls and dark, soulful eyes. Which was silly, because if Jack differed from his previous life, his goddess would too. Who knew what she looked like? He wanted to know, though. Every fibre of his being wanted to find her. It was like hunger, or the need for air.

"C'mon, Jack," called Marcus from the stairs, jolting Jack out of his reverie. "Let's get you settled."

Marcus led Jack to what had once been a family suite. Antique or replica furniture crowded the sitting room. Over-stuffed chairs brushed knees with ottomans. Heavy red draperies obscured the windows like sheets of blood. An air-freshening aetherdevice sat in a corner, its threads of magic twisting around the edges of the room, but the mustiness of the ancient furniture persisted.

Jack stepped into the bedroom. It featured a four-poster bed draped in more red and surrounded by more horsehair stuffed armchairs. The bathroom contained a claw-footed bath and lots of marble. Gold accents were everywhere. The entire suite was too much. Too much of *everything*.

"The aethercast has upped its production quality, as you can see," said Marcus. "Isn't it divine? Better than that industrial-style holiday home we used last season."

Jack had preferred the clean lines of the industrial-style place, even if it had felt cold and soulless, but he nodded as if he agreed with Marcus, anyway.

"Are there any modern conveniences?"

Marcus lifted the hatch of an escritoire to reveal a large aetherweb globe within. "Of course. We're not cutting you off entirely."

Jack walked over and tapped the glass. It lit up, ready for his credentials. Threads of magic light spun up around it. When he had first ascended and began to see magic in action, he had found sights like this bewildering. He was now accustomed to it. Mostly. "Thanks," he said to Marcus. "I'll check in with a few people, tell them I've arrived. What do I need to know about this season of the aethercast?"

Marcus tsked. "We'll have a full house meeting on Saturday where we'll update everyone. Just get settled in for now. Take a rest. Put your feet up."

"Thanks," said Jack. "Is there a Singing Grove on the property?"

Marcus shrugged. "Probably, but why do you ask? We've picked the contestants for their magical expertise, among other things. They won't need the protection of a ring of magical trees. And it's not as if you need to practise magic, eh? You've got new innate powers now! Lucky you!"

Jack held in a sigh. Sure, he'd received the ability to see magic. But what about his kinetic magic? "I want to practise my own magic, the one I had before. I don't get much of a chance anymore, and I think I'm getting sloppy."

Marcus smiled and shook his head. "Jack, you need to accept what a big deal you are now. You don't need to exhaust your magic being a labourer to make ends meet. The whole of Gealdland is going to be paying you money to, like, bless their tilled fields and their milking herds, and kiss their babies for good luck and whatnot."

Jack tried not to show how disappointed he was. He thought Marcus, who had held onto his own magic despite not needing it for aethercasting, would have understood. "OK," he said instead.

Marcus clapped Jack on the shoulder. "Good man. I know it's a big adjustment, but it's for the best. I'll let you get settled in then." He backed towards the door, shooting finger-guns at Jack. "You're going to be great. We're going to have a great season!"

Jack sighed after Marcus left. He ought to be more positive about the aethercast, like Marcus was. Yes, he found it restrictive. Yes, he had his concerns. But there were reasons he'd thought it was a good idea to sign on in the first place. The aethercast might well introduce him to the goddess and let her ascend. That would be fantastic. Also, he'd had a rocky start to being a God Incarnate because by the time he had ascended many people had already become disillusioned with the process, and convinced that the magic he fed back into the land and the people was just an old fable and not real at all. There were even protesters, convinced he was a fake and taking attention away from the real issues of Gealdland. Maybe, just maybe, the aethercast could convince those people that it was real, that he wasn't faking it for attention from the Geald Council.

Maybe this aethercast would have a positive outcome, if only he stuck with it. Then all this fuss would be worth it.

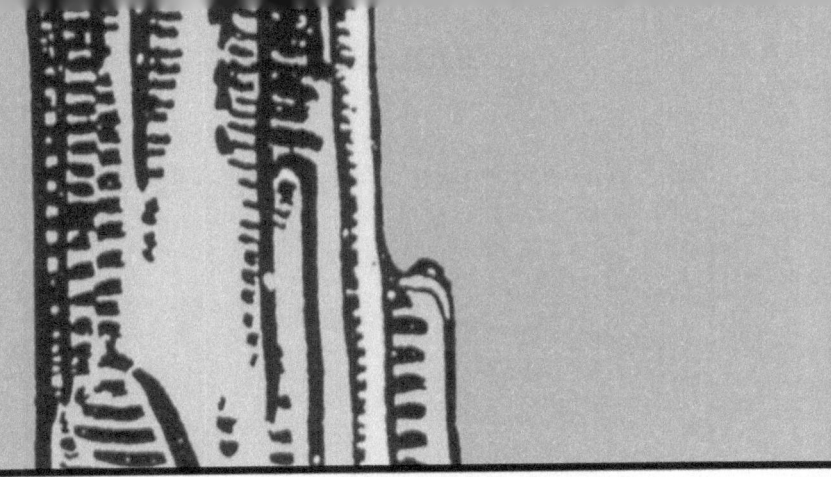

THE HERMIT
REVERSED

Your penchant for keeping yourself at a distance is causing you trouble. Reach out!

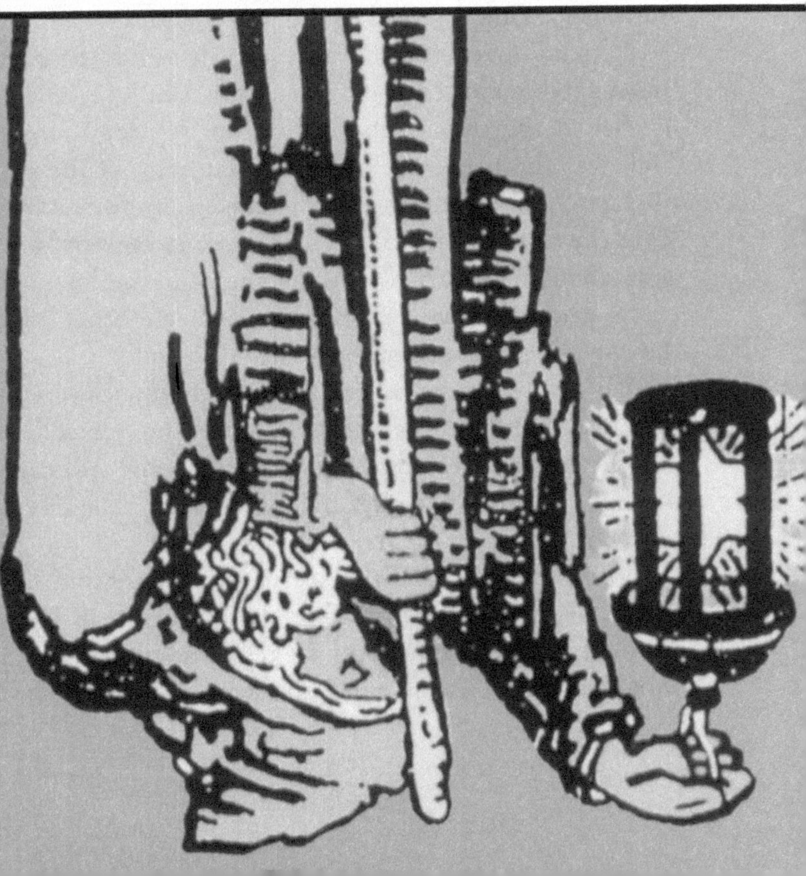

GODDESS FOUND

G,

I found our butterfly. Have you found the net?

One day only: Leta had one day to prepare to join the crew of *Goddess Found* on location for a six-week contract, signed directly to Mirabelle. Leta's mum had been so excited. Leta, not so much. But she was looking forward to the pay cheques.

Leta had packed a suitcase, left a list of tasks to ready the vegetable garden for winter, and then farewelled her mother at the travel tube station on Saturday morning. That was the benefit of being the daughter of the village tube catcher. Whenever she travelled, her mother was always the last one she saw before leaving, the first one she saw when she returned, and as she rode the lines of the travel grid, the magical presence of her mother cradled the capsule and made sure she travelled safe.

Mirabelle met her at Autumnwood Tube Station. The seer was bundled up against the unseasonable cold snap in a fur collar coat, her green eyes cold gems in the morning light. "Good morning, Ms Wildwinter. The day suits you, no?"

Leta wasn't sure if the seer was commenting on her name or her style of dress. Leta always prioritised comfort in her clothing, and she'd had no time to buy anything smarter. That morning she wore the smartest warm outfit she could scrape together: a woolly jersey over a collared shirt, a corduroy skirt, thick woolly tights, and ankle boots. Over it all, she wore the only winter coat she owned, a puffer coat, and a hand-knitted hat and scarf combo. She had stuffed her suitcase with similar fare.

"I suppose it does," she answered, hoping that covered the interaction no matter what Mirabelle had meant.

They stepped out of the small station and into the crisp morning air. A group of people of various genders and ages loitered beside the exit. One smoked a cigarette, and several others were having a loud conversation. Leta at first pegged them as locals waiting for a transport, but then did a double-take when she saw placards.

Say no to fake gods
The future is more important than the past
We choose our own path
No more fake gods stealing the health of our land!

One placard just had a picture of God Incarnate Jack's face with a big cross over it.

Anti-Incarnation protesters.

Leta had seen people like this on the news. It hadn't occurred to her they would be here protesting the aethercast. How did they even know to come to Autumnwood? It wasn't common knowledge yet where the aethercast would be this season.

"Do you think they'll cause trouble?"

Mirabelle raised an eyebrow as she appraised the gaggle of protesters. "Hm. Interesting." She then smiled at Leta. "Do not fret. I know a few people I could contact to increase security if need be. I would be surprised if I were the only one on set with such connections."

"Connections?"

"One benefit of my profession is I have many people who feel like they owe me a debt of gratitude. I dislike taking advantage, but keeping others safe is a time when I would consider using my influence."

Good for some, thought Leta. Mirabelle moved in circles that Leta would never have access to.

One protester, a young sweaty-looking man with blond hair, shouted "Shame on you!" in their direction. But no one joined in, as Leta and Mirabelle were not the target the protesters were waiting for. They increased their walking speed as much as Mirabelle's cane allowed.

No, these protesters would be waiting for God Incarnate Jack. The thing that got on Leta's wick about the protesters was how they were drawn into the scene because of Gealdland's recent troubles. The farming sector, in particular, had a rough time of it as yields declined, and lots of people lost their jobs and livelihoods. For some reason, these people were now blaming their misfortune on the gods and their incarnations.

But the land had idled for the last few decades *because* there had been no ascended incarnation to channel the blessings of the Hunter and Harvester into the land, ever since Archibald and Julia Sudbury had passed. But Jack was here now, and his goddess would be soon too. That power was flowing again. These idiots were protesting the one who was here to fix everything.

They should have been protesting the Geald Council, who hadn't carried the weight during the interim like they were supposed to. That's a cause Leta could have sympathised with.

They kept their heads down as they passed the group and then took a taxi to the manor. The local taxi driver was looking tired, but happy. No doubt he had lots of business, with all the people arriving for the aethercast.

"Up to the manor, ladies?" the driver asked.

"Yes, please, my good man," said Mirabelle.

Autumnwood Manor was bigger and busier than Leta had imagined. Porters and messengers ran hither and thither, setting up equipment and carrying notes. Thankfully, a few security personnel stood about here and there too. They would keep any protesters away.

As Leta and Mirabelle passed through the grand hall, they had to circumnavigate a man with shaggy greying hair who was setting up a veritable fleet of small devices. Each device had a shiny silver body, four propellers, and a curved scrying mirror like a large, shiny eye on the front.

"Auto-aethercasters," said Mirabelle. "Most aethercasts use the traditional method of employing multiple aethercasters for the 'natural' look. On *Goddess Found* we have so many people to follow, who aren't following a script, that our aethercaster Fogarty uses auto-aethercaster drones instead. He collects their 'casts and sends them to head office for processing. They're usually used for nature documentaries. Fitting, no?"

Leta suppressed a snort of laughter, remembering all the posturing and tense group dynamics of the first season. "I had no idea all of this was going on when I was watching the 'cast."

"It's a big operation. Lots of people are involved. We're all hoping to find the goddess."

Leta wondered about that. Did they? Or did they want to find her in a few years, after they had milked the aethercast for all they could? Or maybe she was just being cynical.

"Careful where you're putting your feet, ladies!" cried Fogarty. Leta and Mirabelle looked at him in surprise, then at their feet. Neither of them was close to standing on an auto-aethercaster.

"Don't mind him," said Mirabelle. "He's famously grumpy." She continued along the hall, her cane tapping louder on the floor than it had before. Leta nodded to the grumpy man, who ignored her, then followed in the seer's wake.

Mirabelle led Leta to the old servants' quarters. There, she was taken to a small office and 'processed', i.e. they did a background check. Mirabelle presented her with the official copy of the work contract to sign, and she also signed a non-disclosure agreement. The official processing her documents was a blood mage, who took a tiny drop of her blood and wove it into the documents, making the contract and NDA magically binding. *Mum will be devastated when I tell her I literally can't say what's been happening on the 'cast and she'll have to make do without spoilers.*

Leta was issued a lodging room high in the servants' wing, a small stark room painted white with a modern bed, particle board modular wardrobe, and grey blinds, all added much more recently than the furniture in the rest of the manor. She dropped off her suitcase, locked up, and followed Mirabelle to her own rooms, a guest suite in period styling with a sitting room all in blue and cream.

"I'm embarrassed to have such grand rooms," said Mirabelle, "but part of my role on the aethercast involves receiving Jack and the contestants for private consultations and viewings to help guide them, so I need this sitting room, which just so happens to come with a ridiculously lavish bedroom as well."

"Enjoy it while you can, I suppose." Leta settled onto a sofa. The upholstery was hard yet smooth under her hands. She didn't begrudge the seer for being given the use of this extravagant suite when Leta was in a dorm room. Leta would have been terrified of ruining something expensive if she had to live with antique furniture.

Mirabelle fussed at a cabinet that had probably once held liquor; now it housed a tea and coffee station. She brought over two cups of tea and sat in a vast brocade armchair, dwarfed by it.

"As I outlined the other night," she began, "the reason I have hired you is that I had to do a lot of running back and forth last season delivering the daily readings, which made it difficult for people to catch me in my suite for private viewings and consultations. Also, my knees aren't quite what they used to be," she motioned to her cane that was leaning by the door, "and this manor has more stairs than the holiday home we used last time. Your job will be to deliver the dailies to the cast and bring back any responses they give to me. Also, it will be your role to manage my schedule and go to the cast to make those bookings. There will also be several 'public viewing' events where I read divinations for Jack and the contestants in front of the auto-aethercasters. On those days, I will need you to help set up and to usher the contestants through, carry more messages, that sort of thing. The first one will happen on Tuesday. It is a bit of a basic role, I am sorry to say, but I hope you will also be exposed to other happenings on set and you may even find something in this job that you didn't know you were seeking. That's the ideal, isn't it?"

Leta nodded. "That sounds fair. And I'm not going to end up on the aethercast at all, am I? I mean, people viewing it won't see me?" Mirabelle had said she wouldn't be that first night, and again before Leta signed the contract, but she couldn't help but ask again. The thought of being on an aethercast, even in the background, terrified her. Or rather, it was the thought of those high school bullies seeing her that made her stomach turn sour. She could imagine the jibes: "Look, it's that fat Mundane from school! Didn't we say she would be good for nothing but grunt work?"

"They shouldn't need to include you, no. They do like to capture me doing my general readings from time to time because the footage can increase the tension and give the audience a mystery to wonder about, but I'll give you warning so you can make yourself scarce if you would like."

Leta very much would like, yes. If she had been told now that she would be on the aethercast after all, she didn't know what she would do. Cry, perhaps. "I'm grateful to be given this opportunity, Seer Mirabelle. There aren't many opportunities back home in the village at the moment." She fidgeted in her seat. "You said, though, that a vision brought you to me. Is there anything I need to do to make whatever change you saw?"

Mirabelle smiled. "Not a thing, dear. Maybe you are fated to say something to someone else that will make them think about some aspect of their life in a new way. You are likely to be the proverbial butterfly's wings, causing a ripple effect, not a landslide of change. Therefore, you need be nothing but yourself. Put it out of your mind. In my long career, if I've learned anything at all, it is that fretting about these things is pointless. No matter what, you will do the thing, or not do the thing, as the universe sees fit. Just being in the right place at the right time and going about your life suffices for fate to take effect."

Leta nodded, hearing Mirabelle's words, but still daunted. "OK, I'll try."

When they finished their teas, they went to the all-staff meeting. It was held in a drawing room that was set up as the executive office for the 'cast. Period furniture stood at the periphery of the room — bookshelves of leather-bound books and aged armchairs, overhung by portraits of long-dead Magelords — but in the middle of the room a modern boardroom table hunched like a great, unwelcome beast. Many extra chairs flocked around the table to accommodate the influx.

"I'll sit down the back," said Leta when she saw Mirabelle head to the boardroom table where the important people were sitting.

"OK, dear."

Leta perched on a creaky folding chair and tried to look like she wasn't looking at everyone who came in. It turned out that she needn't have worried about dressing smart. Some people were, but many others were wearing basic worn jeans, hoodies, and trainers; or high-vis vests; or other random assortments of comfortable clothes. Most people were dressed for practicality, assuming that they would not be included in the aethercast.

The room was full of the hubbub of people catching up with one another after a significant break apart and the odour of a coffee cart that perhaps needed a bit of refreshing. As well as Mirabelle, Leta recognised the counsellor, the Incarnation historian, and the etiquette expert from their segments last season. She couldn't remember any of their names. The star himself wasn't in the room. Surely he would have stood out. Gods Incarnate were known to have presences that no one could ignore.

Leta wasn't used to sitting in a room with so many people she didn't know. She slipped her hand into the pocket of her skirt and ran her fingers over her worry stone, which she had picked up at a beach long ago and had taken to keeping in her pocket at all times. She had a habit of doing so when she felt overwhelmed.

Beside her, two people, a dark-skinned woman with a Gealdland accent and a red-headed man with a foreign twang Leta couldn't identify, were whispering, but not low enough to keep Leta from eavesdropping.

"The Gealdr Mentorship Programme?" asked the red-haired man.

"Yeah," said his companion. "It's supposed to be, like, a philanthropic thing to let strong mages get better connections and access to high-placed careers and stuff. But it's a way for people with connections to toady themselves and get their kids even better connections with the Geald families."

"What's that got to do with the aethercast?"

Even Leta knew the answer to that one: the rumour mill had been rife with it last year. AllAether had timed

Goddess Found so that it would happen during the selection process, hoping strong mages would apply to be contestants, to show off their skills.

The woman explained as such to the man. "The contestants don't even mind if they are the goddess or not," she added. "It's win/win. Either they raise their profile and increase their chances of being selected for the programme, or they're the goddess and they'll be famous."

The man shook his head. "Nice for those who have a lot of power, eh? All the opportunities they have."

Struck by the man's words, and the reminder she had no magic to speak of, Leta snorted aloud. The conversing couple looked at her. Leta blushed to be caught eavesdropping, and looked away, hoping they wouldn't call her out.

"Hello, are you new?" said the woman.

Leta flinched. "Uh, yeah. I'm here to assist Seer Mirabelle. Sorry, I didn't mean to overhear."

The woman made a dismissive gesture, as if to say, 'No big deal.' "Are you a seer too?"

Leta blushed even further. "Oh, no, I'm just here to run messages."

"Ah, a light mage, huh?" said the woman, naming the mage school that took care of magical messaging.

Leta ought to have corrected the woman, but she would have had to out herself as a Mundane. She couldn't bring herself to be ostracised on the first day. "Do you think the contestants are here because of the Gealdr Mentorship Programme rather than because they think they might be the goddess, then?"

The woman shrugged. "Last season, I think at least some women hoped they might be, but all of them seemed aware that getting the notice of the Gealdr was no shabby consolation prize."

Leta nodded. It all made sense. Each family had one representative on the Geald Council that ruled the country, and that representative changed with intra-family political shifting. The council was supposed to be more adaptable than a monarchy would be, but it led to a lot of time and energy being wasted on political manoeuvring. Though getting the notice of any Geald family member could win major political power and mage tenure opportunities in the future. It was the traditional manner of upward social mobility in Gealdland and had been for centuries. Millenia, even. All of this… it was just the modern iteration of an age-old game. One that Leta could never play.

She wondered, though, how all of this was supposed to mesh with attempting to trigger an ascension. Last season, the aethercast had been an odd mix of the contestants trying to prove that they had good etiquette and magical abilities, while the aethercast events tried to make them squabble like children. Of all the known methods of triggering an ascension, emotional instability in the presence of another incarnate was the easiest to arrange. Manufacturing a meeting with a god's true essence in a sacred place and hoping that god would spill the beans was next to impossible to achieve. And putting the women in mortal peril wouldn't pass the ethics in media code.

The sound level in the room shifted, and Leta returned her attention to the front. A blond man in the kind of casual clothes that scream 'I cost ten times what I should have cost' entered the room and stood at the head of the table. Leta had taken little notice last year, but she thought he looked like the host of *Goddess Found*. He waited while the hubbub died down and then flashed a bleached white grin. "Welcome everyone. Thank you for being here, and for being ready to put your all into bringing the second season of *Goddess Found* to life. For those who are new here, I'm Marcus Yewgrove. I'm the host of the aethercast, and I also act as a producer here on location. The higher-ups have entrusted me with their vision for the aethercast."

Something about the way he introduced himself sounded patronising. *He doesn't expect that anyone wouldn't know who he is*, thought Leta. *He would hate it if he knew I hadn't known his name until he introduced himself!*

"This year we'll put together the most exciting reality aethercast this country has ever seen!" said Marcus.

A ripple of applause ran around the room. Leta didn't agree with Marcus' words. How could *Goddess Found* be as exciting as *Extreme Baking: Battle Royale*?

"We have an exciting new set of challenges designed to expose the goddess's powers, if she's in attendance. We have a charismatic and charming set of hand-picked contestants demonstrating the best of Gealdland. And of course, we have the dashing Jack Fairholme as our hero!" Marcus gestured to the door as Jack entered the room.

If anything, he was more handsome than he seemed on the aetherweb. He was tall and broad-shouldered, with dark hair that swooped in interesting ways and warm, light brown eyes. The length of his eyelashes, a length wasted on a man, was visible at a distance, and to add insult to injury, he had a hint of a dimple in one cheek. Leta now understood what people meant by the presence of a God Incarnate. He almost seemed to shine, but it wasn't her eyes she saw his shine with; it was whatever small portion of magic she possessed. She wondered if people with more magic perceived that glow more than she did.

She expected swagger, or some other 'I'm better than you' attitude, similar to Marcus. After all, he was very famous. Instead, there seemed to be a tension to him, a stiffness in his back, taut muscles around his jaw. Leta got the distinct impression that he was not comfortable being at the front of the room. But no one else seemed to notice.

They clapped for him, and smiled, and no one at all gave Jack a worried look. Perhaps Leta was imagining it. She didn't know the guy, after all. She was probably just projecting.

"Thank you, everyone," said Jack in a deep but soft voice. "Thank you for having me."

Leta's eyebrows rose. That was a self-effacing welcome. Was he *really* the God Incarnate? The guy who had agreed to sully the search for the Goddess Incarnate with a reality aethercast?

Marcus clapped Jack on the back. "Come on, Jack. We wouldn't be here if not for you. All right, let's move on. Today I want to give a brief run-down of the contestants and the main events planned for the season, and then please partake of afternoon tea and have a mingle."

Leta settled into her chair, ready to soak up the information she needed to do well at her new job.

JACK TRIED HIS BEST to focus on the list of contestants, but the details slipped through his mind like tiny slivers of soap in a bath. He was supposed to be meeting the contestants blind for the aethercast, as far as the audience was concerned. Would it matter if he knew as little as he was pretending? The list of important dates and events he committed to memory, though.

By the time the catering staff wheeled afternoon tea into the drawing room, he was famished. So far at Autumnwood he'd had salad and steamed chicken breasts, and other 'healthy' food — the 'aethercast star' diet. His stomach grumbled at the sight of normal food.

He eyed up a plate of mini savouries, and as soon as Marcus announced tea time, made a beeline for the food. Or tried to. Person after person waylaid him to make small talk, to ask questions. The divine aroma of the savouries tormented him. He left each conversation as soon as he could, but when he got to the carts, the savouries were all gone. Only egg and cress sandwiches and a few half walnut muffins remained.

"Jack! Good to see you! How are you doing?"

The latest person to greet him was Seer Mirabelle. She was as fashionably dressed as always. She was being shadowed by someone Jack had never met, a young woman with silky reddish hair tied up in a bun and a cute dusting of freckles across her cheeks. The unknown woman clutched a plate of snacks as if it was a lifeline and gave him a wary, uncomfortable look, her storm-grey eyes large behind brown-framed glasses. She wore a heavy jersey and a thick corduroy skirt, but her curvy figure showed through the layers, making a crass, naughty part of Jack's mind supply the errant thought: *Ooh! Sexy librarian!* He squashed that thought down as best he could. It wasn't the time for that kind of thinking.

He dragged his gaze back to Mirabelle. "I'm doing well. Yourself?"

"I'm well, thank you. I look forward to the event on Tuesday."

Tuesday? Ah, the first public divinations. "Yes, me too."

"I'd like you to meet my new assistant, Leta. She will run the dailies. Leta, this is Jack."

Jack held out a hand. "Nice to meet you, Leta." Leta fumbled her plate as she dithered somewhere between taking his hand and dropping a curtsey. "Oops!" said Jack as he reached out with a flick of kinetic magic and tilted her plate upright, saving her snacks.

"Oh!" said Leta. She chuckled in surprise.

Jack liked the lack of guile in her face and her clear laugh laden with no ulterior motive, just surprise. He chuckled too. "Got to save the savouries. They're a rare commodity."

Leta looked at the empty plate behind him; her eyes widened in understanding. Wordlessly, she handed one of her two savouries to Jack.

"You don't have to…"

"Yes, I do. Take it."

He grinned at her. Saved by the sexy librarian!

He remembered Mirabelle's presence. Even though she was the one who had addressed him, she waited patiently with a smile on her face.

"Ah, may I arrange a time for a private viewing before we start capturing on Monday?" he said to Mirabelle. "I'd appreciate your guidance."

"Of course. I am free after this gathering, if you like." She opened her mouth to say more, but Marcus interrupted them, a toothy grin on his face.

"There you are, Jack." His eyes looked past Leta, and even Mirabelle, as he steered Jack away.

"I was just scheduling a private viewing with Seer Mirabelle," said Jack, digging in his heels.

"Plenty of time for that later. Simon's over here. He's dying for a word with you…"

Jack gave Mirabelle and Leta an apologetic look over his shoulder.

"I'll send Leta to you to book a time later!" called Mirabelle as Marcus led Jack away.

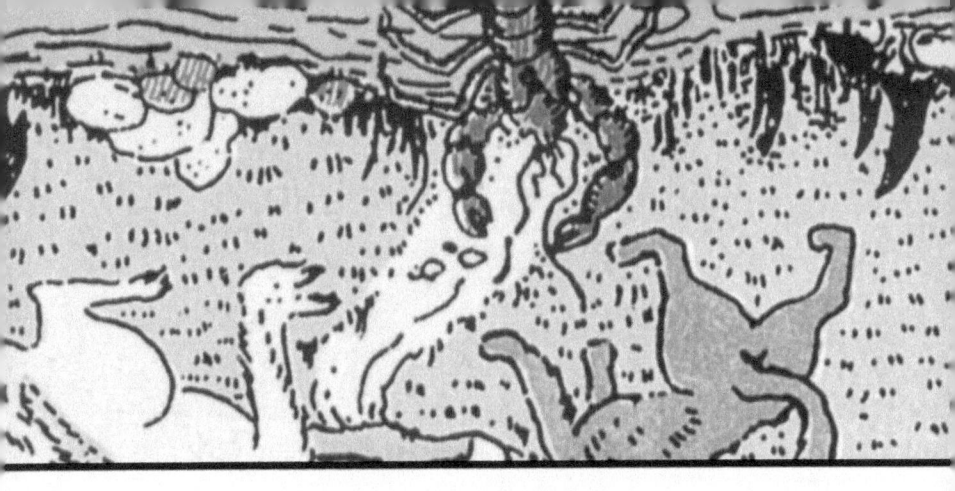

THE MOON
REVERSED

Pay close attention to your dreams and visions. Your subconscious has an important message for you.

GODDESS FOUND

Mum, Dad
  I'm at Autumnwood. Have met the new crew.
Room's flash, food is paltry, as per usual.
        Take care
        Jack

The hallway outside Jack's suite was quiet, although the sounds of the busy crew echoed from elsewhere in the manor. Leta checked her hair was tidy one last time before knocking on the door. She carried a clipboard she didn't need to make it clear she had Important Business and was not some random person who had snuck into the manor. Her heart thudded in her chest. She was pretty sure she'd made a bad impression on Jack the day before, or at least an awkward one, and she was not ready yet to try again. Not that she'd even been intending to leave impressions on the God Incarnate, of course.

Jack answered the door wearing far more casual clothes than he'd been wearing the day before: jeans, a t-shirt and a baggy cream cardigan with a shawl collar and wood toggles. Leta preferred this look over the suits and tailored semi-casual clothes she'd always seen him wearing for the aethercast. "Hello. It's Leta, right?"

His warm voice sent tingles along her spine. *Stop that!* she told her spine. *No tingles!* "Yes," she said, surprised he remembered her name. "Seer Mirabelle sent me to let you know she's free for the rest of the afternoon, if you would like a private viewing. At your convenience, of course."

30

Jack smiled. "No time like the present," he said and emerged from the suite, closing the door behind him. "Shall we go?"

I have to walk through the manor with him? Where people will see? Leta didn't want that sort of scrutiny, but it would be rude not to walk with him. As they set off, Leta tried to drop behind and trail along behind, as she often did when walking with people, but frustratingly, he slowed down to let her catch up. *How does one walk beside another person without knocking their arm with your own? How do people do this?* She was so preoccupied with not walking in the swaying gait that her traitorous body suddenly decided it wanted to try that it took her a moment to notice he was talking to her. "I beg your pardon."

"I said, how did you get the job as Seer Mirabelle's assistant? Are you a seer too?"

"Oh, no, no. Mirabelle said a vision told her to hire me. I'm a butterfly's wings, or something like that." *Ugh, Leta! Why say that? It sounds so self-aggrandising!*

Jack whistled. "Interesting. I wonder what you'll set in motion."

"Mirabelle said it may never be clear. She told me not to worry about it, but I can't help but see it as a burden."

"I understand," said Jack. "I'm not supposed to worry about my message as God Incarnate. My mere existence is meant to convey it, so long as I'm being true to myself." There was an odd catch to his voice.

"Are you true to yourself?" she asked, and regretted it immediately, because the look he gave her was tinged with sadness. Leta hunched her shoulders against the sudden tension. In a mere minute, she'd tripped over his most sore point. Of course.

For the sake of the Hunter and the Harvester, Leta, don't get yourself fired right away! Think of the money! The money! Even so, her conversational stumble made her feel more favourably towards God Incarnate Jack. If he was happy with this farce of a reality aethercast, it wouldn't have been his sore point, would it?

They were half-way there, walking side-by-side down a staircase, when Leta's boot slipped on the smooth wooden stair. She yelped as she grabbed for the bannister. Then, to her horror, she over-corrected and tilted forward.

Somehow, in that split-second, she had time to imagine the bruises. The snapped glasses. A broken arm...

Something warm wrapped around her and pulled her back. Her knees gave out, and she flopped down to sit on the steps. The scent of coffee and petrichor surrounded her. Legs pressed at her sides, and an arm snaked around her chest from the right to grip her left upper arm.

Jack's breath puffed in her ear. "Are you OK?"

The sound of his voice in her ear and his chest against her back made her heart flutter, among other things. He was so close she thought she could feel his pulse. She scrambled to her feet, clinging onto the bannister. "I'm fine!" she squeaked. "I'm so sorry!"

She glanced at him. He still sat on the stairs, a flush creeping up his cheeks, his eyes wide.

"You nearly fell," he said, as if still processing what happened.

"Yeah. Silly me. Why didn't you use your kinetic magic to catch me? You have kinetic magic, right?" *Why did you catch me with your body? So much of your body?*

Jack flushed even redder. "I do. But my magic has been slow off the mark since I ascended. The magic of the Hunter keeps sort of getting in the way, if that makes sense. I guess I didn't trust it in the split-second I had."

Leta tried to imagine what it would feel like if, say, her mother couldn't trust that she could access her magic immediately. She wouldn't even be able to do her job anymore if that happened. Time was often critical in kinetic magic. "That sounds frustrating," she said. "I'm so sorry."

He looked up at her again, his gaze earnest. "Don't tell anyone, please. I'm still trying to see if I can adjust. It might be a non-issue in time."

Leta nodded. "Of course. If nothing else, because you just saved me from having to fork out for a new pair of glasses." She gave a strained huff of a laugh, trying her best to lighten the mood. If she'd needed to replace her glasses, then there would be no way she could afford study fees as well.

Jack smiled and stood, brushing off the seat of his trousers. "Thanks. Shall we get going?"

Leta looked around. Thankfully, no one had spotted them scrambling around on the stairs. "This way, please."

They continued the rest of the way to Mirabelle's suite in silence, though Leta's heart rate didn't slow down one bit, the adrenaline not letting up at all.

When they got there, Jack looked like he would hold the door open for her, so she sped up to get there first and open it for him. She was the assistant here! He didn't protest at all, just thanked her and walked through. Leta was glad; she hated it when men tried to take the door from her again, thereby shoving their armpits at her.

"Jack! Hello," said Mirabelle from her favoured arm-chair. "Leta, dear, you're free to take a break now. Tour the gardens if you like, or take a rest."

Leta smiled into the room. "Thank you. When would you like me back here?"

"In about an hour, if you please."

"Of course." Maybe she could look at the gardens? She always enjoyed walking in nature whenever she was off-kilter. She missed her own garden terribly, and it had only been a day. But first, she would drop by the kitchens. The variety of food coming out of there from the caterers intrigued her, and she wanted to learn more about it, out of professional curiosity. As she began shutting the door, already preoccupied with thoughts of greenery and pastries, Jack gave her a smile and a wave. Her cheeks flushed again.

She left the wing at a rapid pace, shaking her head. She was grateful that he had saved her and was still inclined to smile at her instead of looking at her like she was a weirdo. But he ought to know the effect his divinity-powered smile had on people and be more cautious of using it.

MIRABELLE'S PARAPHERNALIA SAT neatly stacked on a side table beside her. "Since this is your first viewing, I thought we might try all my methods to see whatever there is to see. Is that all right?"

Jack nodded. "Sure, that sounds fine." He rolled his right wrist. His arm still tingled where he'd grabbed onto Leta to stop her from falling. Her curves had been soft and warm under his arm, between his thighs, in a way that had distracted him ever since. Her breath had heaved with the adrenaline rush in a way that made him think other naughty thoughts he was still trying to banish.

"Would you like to start with the crystal ball, the cards, or the bones?" asked Mirabelle, drawing his attention back to the present.

Jack pointed at the bones. They always freaked him out, the tiny rabbit and snake bones tumbling together into the tray, so he wanted to get that augury out of the way as soon as possible.

Mirabelle balanced the velvet tray on her lap and untied the small purse. She tipped the tiny bones into her palm and closed her eyes. Jack saw the glow of her magic collect around them on her palm as she prepared to read the probabilities of the universe.

He hadn't been able to see such things before he ascended that fateful night he'd gone to a party in a foreign temple with some fellow backpackers. When he'd woke up seeing auras and flashes of light everywhere, he had almost hoped that he'd contracted a magical illness, because the alternative scared him more. But his fears were confirmed when he returned home to be met by a delegation of the Geald Houses at the airport, and his ashen-faced parents standing with them.

His own magic had been paltry before he ascended. In a way, it still was: he could do very little. Just move small things with his kinetic magic. But he could see what everyone else was doing, and that was a valuable skill. If only he had a decent opportunity to use it. Couldn't he help with stopping crime or something? Couldn't he be useful?

As Mirabelle shook the bones in her cupped palms, their small clinks sent ripples of magic out into the world around them. The world leaned in to watch. Just as the tension became unbearable, she tossed the bones into the tray. When she opened her eyes to read them, they glowed in his sight just as the bones did.

She spent a long minute carefully noting the position of every tiny bone, reading their message. Jack tried not to let his knee jiggle while she did so. Did she have any good news for him? Would this damned aethercast be over soon?

"The message is forked," said Mirabelle. "There are two large possibilities looming for you this season. Either great success or great tragedy."

Jack's heart leapt. "By great success, do you mean I might find my goddess?"

"Perhaps. But is that the only possibility that you would consider a success?"

Jack thought of finding a way out of his contract and being free to search for the goddess on his own terms. "No, it isn't." He frowned. "What about the great tragedy?"

"A similar situation. Not being able to achieve your goals would be a tragedy, no?"

"I hate to say it, Mirabelle, but this augury is less useful than normal."

"Not so. I mean *tragedy*, Jack. If you find your goddess, protect her." Mirabelle looked deep into his eyes as she said those words. He gulped. If he found his goddess, something might happen to her.

"I'll keep your words close to my heart," he said.

Mirabelle nodded as she put away the bones. "I know you will. What would you like to try next?"

"The cards?"

Mirabelle took her cards out of their gilt leather case. The backs were a deep blue, the same colour as her nails, and decorated with an intricate red rosebush pattern with prominent thorns. It was the same set that she'd used the year before. Jack remembered the illustrations as being moody, abstract, and intimidating, with characters that seemed to stare at him. "Last year we used the Page of Swords as your significator. Do you think you have changed enough to re-evaluate which we use?"

Jack sighed. "No. I think I've gone nowhere fast over the last year."

Mirabelle didn't comment. She just searched for the Page of Swords in the deck and placed it face-up on the coffee table. She took the rest of the deck and shuffled the pliable, well-used cards with deft fingers, and placed the stack on the table beside the Page. "Cut the deck into three, please."

Jack did as instructed. The edges of the cards buzzed under his fingers. He could almost feel the place where they wanted to be cut, but couldn't pinpoint it. He had to rely on luck, after all.

"Please pick a pile."

Jack pointed to the one farthest away from him, which Mirabelle then inverted before shuffling the cards again. This time she engaged her magic as she shuffled, and the edges glowed just as the bones had. He saw small pings as certain cards brought themselves to the attention of her fingers and asked to be shuffled to the top. How long had it taken Mirabelle to learn to shuffle the cards into the places where they wanted to be? He should never play a mundane card game against her. No doubt the skill allowed her to cheat horrendously.

"I will use the cross and wand spread." It was a spread that she had used often with him the previous year: a cross and wand using ten cards that is useful when looking for love. Which he undeniably was. Very publicly.

She placed a card over the significator. "This is your inner situation. Five of Swords upright. You are in conflict with yourself."

Jack nodded. "I'll bet."

"Maybe self-focussed too. Remember, there are others with you." Then she dealt a card sidewards, crossed over the first. "This is your outer situation. Four of Cups reversed. Withdrawal. I noticed this myself yesterday. It shows."

He supposed it did.

"Open up to others." Then she dealt a card above the existing pile of three. "This is your goal. Ten of Cups upright. What a surprise."

"It's always there for me."

"As it should be. Do you need me to tell you that you should try to find your Divine Love?"

"Nope. I feel that need in here." He touched his chest with a finger.

Then she dealt a card below the others. "This is your foundation. Six of Wands reversed."

"That's different."

"Yes. It tended to turn upright for you last year, which meant success and public recognition."

"Are things getting worse for me?"

"No, I like this change for you. For this card, reversing it means having an internal, self-guided sense of success. But it comes at a price. This is a harder road, but a more rewarding one." She dealt another card to the left. "This is your past. The Tower upright."

"Revelation and awakening. Or rather, ascension to God Incarnate."

"Yes." She dealt another to the right. "Your immediate future. Seven... of Swords upright." There was an odd tension in Mirabelle's face.

"What?"

"This card *can* mean acting strategically or alone."

"You don't think it does. What else does it mean?"

She looked up at him, her glowing green eyes piercing through him. "Betrayal."

Jack huffed. "Forewarned is forearmed, I guess."

"I hope it is not a great betrayal, Jack."

"Thank you."

Mirabelle began dealing the cards of the wand, starting with the bottom one. "Your fears. The Lovers reversed. As discussed last year, the meaning of this reading is rather more literal for you than it is for most."

"I'm afraid I won't find the goddess."

Mirabelle nodded. She dealt the next card up the wand. "What others think of you. The Hierophant upright. Spiritual guidance, but also tradition. Or, of course, an indicator of the God Incarnate."

"Yet again. That one is also consistent."

Mirabelle sat back, and the glow in her eyes faded. "Did you ever have a reading like this before you ascended? Did The Hierophant ever come up for you? Any clues at all?"

"I never had a card reading before I ascended. At least not as myself. I kind of remember having readings like this often some time ago."

"When you were Archibald Sudbury?"

"Before that, I think. Harold Brightborne, maybe? He was a Geald family member and was used to such things. Oh, but I did once have a palm reading that told me I have a strong love line."

Mirabelle chortled. "Palm readings aren't one of the true divinations. That person was lying. And yet, they were right."

"It's a 50/50 type situation."

Mirabelle sat forward again and dealt the second-to-last card. "Your wishes and dreams. Queen of Cups upright. Hm."

"Hm?"

"I think this position is showing something different from the usual. Considering your unique situation, I think this card is attempting to give us a description of the goddess."

Jack leaned forward. "This didn't happen in any of my readings last year."

Mirabelle smiled. "Perhaps you are closer to finding her. This card, when used as a significator, means a nurturing, warm, compassionate person who is in touch with their feelings. She has a rich inner world and does well in loving relationships. She needs someone to attend to her needs, because she is the type of person who gives too much of herself."

Jack's heart thumped in his chest. This was the first hint he'd had of his counterpart. He liked the description. Even though he didn't know her yet, he already wanted to care for her kind heart and shore it up for more giving to the world.

Mirabelle dealt the last card. "This is the overall message of this reading, and a hint of the outcome. Six of Swords upright. Change, a rite of passage, healing. This reading indicates tumultuous times ahead for you. It is heavy in Arcana, as expected of you. It is heavy in Cups, as expected of someone seeking love. It is heavy in Swords. That's the tumultuous times. But out of tumult comes change, and out of change comes something new.

The Swords make people nervous, but the world would be a boring place without them. This is a reading with some caution and some hope. Take with you what you will."

Jack took a long moment to look at the final spread. The magic in the reading was fading away, the merest glimmer now. He appreciated Mirabelle's no-nonsense style of reading the cards. It felt more like a conversation. But that glow meant he couldn't ignore the deeper meaning.

This was his fate.

"OK. Thank you, Seer Mirabelle."

"Would you like me to help you see in the crystal ball as well?"

"Sure; why not?"

She put her cards away. Then she placed the ball on the table on its plinth. She ran her hands over the crystal, bringing it to light. This light wasn't just visible to his magic; it was a true glow. As with the bones, Mirabelle's eyes glowed as she looked into the ball, and the world leaned in to watch. "Something is here for your eyes only. Look into the ball. Don't tell me what you see. Keep it to yourself and reflect on the vision."

Jack leaned forward. Clouds billowed inside the crystal. The clouds parted and revealed... emerald green satin. A flash of light. A piercing scream. A rush of adrenaline. He opened his mouth to ask about what he saw, but Mirabelle shushed him.

"With this kind of vision, if I know what the crystal showed you, the threads of fate may become tangled."

"OK." He sighed and hung his head. "Wow."

"You have a heavy burden on your shoulders, Jack," said Mirabelle. She sounded puffed and tired. She'd used a lot of her magic during the viewing. "Please don't hesitate to ask for guidance. Leta can schedule you in for another private viewing whenever you like."

"Thank you," he said, moving to the tea station to make her a restorative cup of tea, knowing from the previous year that she would need one. "I will."

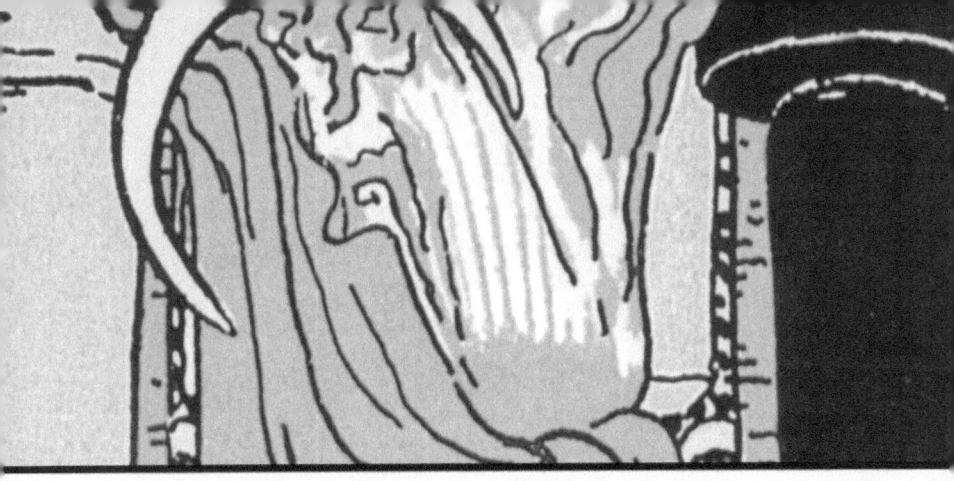

THE HIGH PRIESTESS
REVERSED

Ignore the drama and the gossip. Focus on what is right in front of you.

Marcus,
Our boy had an auspicious reading, indicative of
both success and drama along the way. In my expert
opinion, this season is going to be interesting.
Mirabelle

F inally, yet too soon for Leta's liking, the first day of capturing *Goddess Found* arrived. Leta milled with a bunch of other idle crew members in the second drawing room, which had a view of the drive. A few people gave Leta friendly smiles, but everyone seemed to have their friend groups and conversations that she didn't want to interrupt, so she kept to herself. She'd already made a spectacle of herself in front of the God Incarnate of all people. It was time for her to be on her very best behaviour. She took up position at a window and waited.

The the contestants' arrival was preceded by the arrival of the auto-aethercasters. They hovered in formation by the entry, waiting for the action. Minutes later, a line of cars drove up the driveway, the discordant hums of the drivers' respective magics audible even through the windows. They parked in an arc around the fountain. Then nothing happened for a moment. After a long pause, a car door popped open and a slender brunette woman in a fine red wool coat stepped out onto the gravel. An auto-aethercaster swooped down to focus on her, and then remained near her, ready to record her every move.

Soon after, another woman stepped out of her own car, this one with dark hair and mid-brown skin. Then another contestant emerged, then another. The last two women held out for several minutes: a tall red-head and a shorter woman with a choppy haircut and a blue-dyed fringe. Each of the eight women had an attendant auto-aethercaster. Some stood ramrod straight by their cars, while some took a step forward, looked at the other stationary women, and second-guessed themselves.

"Just let them in," someone whispered over by another window. "They must be freezing."

Leta rubbed her own arms, thinking of how cold it must be out there. AllAether was playing games with the contestants in the very moment they arrived at the manor. The previous Goddess Incarnate had come from humble beginnings, and so Leta guessed a humble demeanour might be a clue about the identity of the goddess. They were being tested for their humility right from the get-go. The two hold-outs had failed the first challenge. Which seemed unfair considering the scuttlebutt about the 'cast being used to inform the upcoming Gealdr Mentorship Programme. Because 'humble' wouldn't cut it for the Geald Families. Leta, for the first time, saw beyond her jealousy of those with powerful magic and understood that it wasn't any defence against being stuck between a rock and a hard place.

"Porters, go," sounded a magically amplified voice from the floor below. Eight people in neat suits streamed out the front door of the manor. Each one went to the boot of a car and took charge of the luggage of one woman. Some poor porters had to carry more than others. They all seemed to have some level of kinetic magic to assist them.

Once all the luggage was off-loaded and the cars had driven away, Marcus emerged from the manor, two auto-aethercasters following him. He wore a light grey suit. He marched down to stand before the women and their porters.

"Here we go," said someone in the room.

Marcus talked to the women, giving them some directions or information and probably also talking to the audience, but his words were not audible to those watching from the drawing room.

Leta wondered if Jack would appear soon too, but then the women filed into the manor, each tailed by their porter.

"Contestants incoming in 5, 4, 3, 2, 1," said the amplified voice from afar.

That was it for now: they were in. The next hour would involve the auto-aethercasters following the women as they marvelled at the architecture (or pretended to) and as they saw their suites; two contestants to each suite, of course, with the worst possible combinations selected, to foster drama.

And so it begins, she thought. Leta would deliver letters from Mirabelle to each of the hopeful contestants in two hours. Until then, all she had to do was keep her head down, and do her best to forget about the sound of God Incarnate Jack's voice rumbling in her ear on the stairs. Those women were the ones who would have his attention now.

MARCUS CLAPPED JACK on the shoulder. "Try to look 'mysterious' and 'impenetrable'. Give that patented intense God Incarnate gaze. Intimidate them, if you can."

"From up here?" scoffed Jack. How intimidating did he think he was? They stood on the landing above the grand entrance, far from where the women would be walking.

Marcus did his finger-gun thing, winked, then started down the stairs, throwing, "You're going to be great!" over his shoulder as he left to welcome the contestants.

Jack stood for several long minutes, trying to seem confident rather than awkward.

Eventually, the contestants and their porters entered the manor below. Each porter paused, giving the contestants time to examine the room and spot Jack standing on the landing above. Then they led the contestants through a side door away from him and on a roundabout path to their rooms.

The gaze of the auto-aethercasters lay heavy on Jack's skin. He would get used to them soon, but in that moment, for the first scene of the new season, they were an uncomfortable imposition. He hoped he was schooling his features well.

Jack watched the procession of incoming candidates with a sinking feeling. He looked closely at each one, hoping to feel some spark of recognition, some hint of a connection. Would one of them look up at him just so, and trigger one of those odd echoes of a past life he got from time to time? But none of them did. There was nothing in looks or manner that felt familiar to him about any of them. Though it was too soon. He was being impatient. He should give the contestants a chance. Not just because one may be the goddess, but also because they may be nice people who he could make friends with.

The executives who selected the contestants must have been thinking along the same lines as they had the previous year, despite how wide a net they had cast for applications across the aetherweb. They were a similar age as him or younger, which was a fair call, as the goddess had to be born after the previous Goddess Incarnate had died. But otherwise, there was no excuse for how similar they seemed. They were all pretty, and he could appreciate their looks objectively, but subjectively none of them seemed like his type.

His goddess should be the kind of woman he'd always favoured, and Jack had always been drawn to women you'd curl up on the sofa and read books with. The contestants were all slimmer than the kind of woman his eyes had always gravitated towards, except for one who was, at most, 'average weight'. They dressed in expensive clothes and carried themselves with the poise of those brought up in or on the periphery of Geald family society. The network claimed they were hand-selecting the 'most likely candidates from across the land,' but their definition of likely was classist. *What about me?* Jack thought to himself. *I wasn't brought up among those people. Dad's a farm accountant!*

Once the contestants had gone deeper into the manor and a caller shouted out, "Contestants in 5, 4, 3, 2, 1," Marcus returned and shoulder-bumped Jack.

"Some lovely ladies this year."

"Yes, lovely," said Jack. "It's not about who's lovely, though. It's about compatibility, and I don't know if that will happen."

Marcus made a shushing motion and surreptitiously pointed at the closest auto-aethercaster. "Don't sound so morose," he said in a low voice. "You signed a contract, and AllAether wants an appealing aethercast star, not a sad sack. You can do it, Jack. You did it last year. It'll all turn out for the best. I promise."

Jack hoped so. He really hoped so. Because if he got disillusioned enough to break his contract, he would pay a hefty price. His own magic was on the line, and that wasn't a price he wanted to pay. "OK, thanks for the pep talk."

"You're welcome." Marcus clapped him on the shoulder again and went further into the manor, leaving Jack alone. Jack sighed and rested his elbows on the railing. He just wasn't feeling it. Whatever 'it' was. Enthusiasm? Hope? Something was missing this season. He had to have faith that something good would still come of the aethercast, that he might find the goddess, or improve public opinion of himself and incarnates in general. Something. Because if there wasn't a benefit…

Before leaving for Autumnwood, Jack had pored over his contract, looking for a way to bend the aethercast to his will and make it what he needed it to be. Scrying the endless clauses looking for hope. Something. Anything. As far as he could tell, though, it was watertight. The network agreed to pay him a salary so long as he conducted his search for his goddess on their network for a period of at least five years. If he broke the contract, he would have to pay them all the money back.

The contract was magically binding, so if he couldn't repay with money, his magic, his original kinetic magic, would be syphoned off to pay the debt. 'It's no big deal,' they'd said. 'You're the God Incarnate now. You don't need that magic anymore.' So, foolishly, he'd signed, somehow expecting his God Incarnate powers to be more useful than they were. He didn't have all that money anymore. It had gone on rent, food, clothes. He hadn't even been frivolous. Everyone had expected him to live in the city close to AllAether's headquarters, and to keep up appearances with branded clothes in his downtime for 'professionalism'. AllAether covered his clothes and accommodation during aethercasting, of course, but not for the rest of the year. It was an expensive lifestyle.

He hoped he wasn't wasting time. He should be out there, meeting more people, lots of people. The contract forbade that too. They had slipped in a clause about 'a place of the network's choosing'. He had been a lamb led to slaughter. A recent returnee from an exciting overseas holiday he'd taken as a break before university, with little money in his accounts and no fixed abode. He'd tried meeting more people between the seasons, just going out, like a normal person. But he wasn't a normal person any more: he was a celebrity. It wasn't possible to make real human connections in amongst whatever Blessing-seeking scrum that developed around him whenever he was in public. And AllAether kept him busy anyway, with magazine and aether interviews, speeches, presenting at awards ceremonies, publicised Blessing ceremonies…. It was a lot.

He sighed again and stood up straight. The only way out of his troubles was through them, so he'd best get to it. He had a season of an aethercast to play his part in, and he had better do it well so that no one could say that he was shirking his duties. He was, after all, the representative of a god.

LETA CARRIED THE STACK of dailies through the manor, each addressed in gold ink in Mirabelle's swooping calligraphy. This was the part of Leta's job that made her most nervous. She'd been assured the aethercast wouldn't need to include her handing the dailies to the contestants; if so, they would have used one of the impeccably dressed porters to deliver them. Even so, there was still the chance that small glimpses of her would end up on the aethercast. All she could do now was cross her fingers and hope for the best. Oh, and avoid the auto-aethercasters if possible.

Leta arrived at the East Wing first floor, which had been given over to the four contestant suites. Each door along the hall had two names on laminated labels taped to the wall nearby. All Leta had to do was push the letters under the correct doors and leave. The auto-aethercast footage would focus on the contestants finding the letters and reading them, no doubt with an excess of drama. Some shocked hands over faces. Some advertisement breaks. That sort of thing.

It wasn't a difficult task. Not at first.

She had delivered four dailies and was about to deliver the other four when a group of three women in exercise gear rounded the corner into the hallway. They were attended, of course, by their auto-aethercasters. Leta's stomach dropped. She neither wanted to talk to the women, nor did she want to be caught on their feeds. She still didn't know which woman was which, so she hoped they were all staying in the rooms that she had already delivered to, which were closer to them than she was. She had no such luck.

The three women paused their conversation as they spied Leta ahead of them in the hallway. One was the red-haired woman who was one of the two hold-outs when disembarking the cars. Another was the very first woman who had exited her car, the brunette in the red coat. The third was a blonde woman who had been giggling through the conversation until it paused. All three of them wore exercise gear, the type that wouldn't come in Leta's size. They had flushed cheeks, as if they had just finished a workout.

She tried to stand unobtrusively to the side to let the women pass, but the leader of the trio, the red-headed woman, stopped and arched an eyebrow at her.

"Somehow I think you're lost. This is the contestant wing." There was a note in her voice that Leta remembered her bullies using at school.

"I know," said Leta, brandishing her diminished pile of letters. "I'm working. Please ignore me."

The woman looked Leta up and down. For a moment, Leta expected that the woman was judging her figure; Leta was larger than average, and often expected people to judge her because of it. But instead, the woman said, "In those clothes? Oh, don't worry. I will." The blonde woman giggled again. That was also a sound Leta remembered from school.

The red-haired woman then read the name on the envelope on the top of Leta's stack and ripped it out of Leta's hand. "That one's mine. Thank you." The last was delivered in a sing-song voice. The name on the envelope was Destiny, the most Geald family-sounding name Leta had ever heard.

"Ah, I'm supposed to post that under your door so you find it afterwards. Let me do so, and then you can act all surprised to find it for the auto-aethercaster."

"It's not *my* fault you were tardy delivering it," she said, and turned to enter her room.

Leta's first instinct was to defend herself — she wasn't tardy; they just interrupted her — but it wasn't worth it. She had no intention of causing drama that the network would be tempted to include in the 'cast — the nightmare she'd had the night before about all her old school bullies laughing at her frumpy figure in amongst all these pretty people made her sure of that. So she bit her tongue and let the other two (Tiffany and Chrissie) take their letters too. Tiffany, at least, said 'thank you' in a normal tone of voice, with no hint of mocking.

She delivered the last of the contestant dailies, then set out across the manor to Jack's door to post his one. As she walked, she felt the shame of an ill-handled social interaction roil in her belly. Not that she wanted to get to know the contestants or anything like that, but it still rankled that she was so bad at people.

She reached Jack's door and slipped the letter underneath. When she had done so in the contestant wing, no one had opened their doors to see where the letter came from. This time, Jack's door opened a crack, and he smiled out at Leta. He was wearing a suit again, rather than the comfy clothes he had worn the day before.

"Thanks; I was waiting for this."

Leta smiled in return. "Don't mention it."

Maybe this job wasn't so bad after all.

STRENGTH
UPRIGHT

Your well of inner strength is deeper than you know.
You can persevere.

To all staff:
   Please keep an eye out for any suspicious people or activity on the premises. If you see anything of note, please let security staff or your section manager know.

                              AllAether Executive Team

A navy velvet backdrop hung from a frame at the head of the ballroom. Two gold embroidered chairs sat in front of it, with a table between. *The set suits Mirabelle well,* thought Jack. *Somehow she fits in here.*

Jack stood back and watched the setup for the Divinations event. Runners ran, auto-aethercasters aethercasted, and caterers catered. He edged towards the craft table at the rear of the hall. Maybe he could purloin a sandwich...

A hand clapped Jack on the shoulder. "There you are," said Marcus.

"Here I am," said Jack as he turned to his smiling friend.

"You ready? Set up is almost complete."

"Yes." All he had to do was watch the contestants have their viewings, react for the auto-aethercasters, and have his own viewing with Mirabelle.

"Yeah, just sit there and smoulder."

Jack raised an eyebrow. "'Smoulder'?"

Marcus chuckled. "Look handsome and brooding. Dampen some knickers."

Jack shook his head. Marcus could be crude at times. Jack looked to the craft table again: a caterer was delivering a platter of mini muffins. Jack wanted one, but he didn't think he'd get away with it in front of Marcus.

"What divination method will Mirabelle be using today?" he asked instead.

"Just her crystal ball. Her cards were too fiddly and time-consuming last season. And the bones are fucking creepy." He shuddered.

"They work."

Marcus hummed.

"You don't think they do?" Marcus had expressed scepticism about seers before. "The magic is real, I can assure you."

"Oh, I know it's real," said Marcus, waving off his words. "I just don't like how open to interpretation divination and clairvoyance are. I can't trust how accurate my understanding of the message is. Give me something concrete any day."

As far as reasons to distrust divination went, it wasn't a bad one. At least he wasn't claiming it was all a sham, like some people did.

"Do we have any contestants whose magic might clash with Mirabelle's?"

"One contestant is a clairvoyant. Mirabelle'll have to be careful with that one. And you, of course. The others are fine. We're still going to get them to demonstrate their magics, though. It makes for good viewing."

Jack watched in silence for a minute as a light mage, a woman with a long dark braid down her back, lit up the velvet backdrop with sparkles. He hadn't appreciated until he ascended how deft and complicated a light mage's work was. It must be exhausting for them to control. It was one of the first magics he had ever seen with his new sight, and the criss-crossing of intricate lines of magic required to create even simple light shows had bewildered him ever since. His own kinetic magic only needed to be shoved at things to do something useful.

"Speaking of the contestants," said Jack once the display was alight, "how did the selection process go?"

Marcus sighed. "We had three hundred and seventeen applicants that made it past the first 'weeding out' — you know, looking for weirdos and fake applications, and those who didn't meet the criteria. Then we had to whittle it down to forty people to interview. We spent days arguing over who would make the cut."

"Sounds like a pain."

"Well, I got paid for it." Marcus laughed.

"What do you think of the contestants? How do they compare with last season's?"

Marcus wagged a finger in Jack's direction. "Tsk. You're supposed to form your own opinion."

Jack raised his eyebrows at Marcus and waited. He knew his friend wanted to chat.

Marcus eased closer and lowered his voice. "Well, they're all hot, for starters. Not all my personal taste, of course."

Jack made a 'continue' gesture. AllAether's casting criteria in that arena were patently obvious. "How about who they are, what they want out of all of this? Last year, even though we didn't find the goddess, there were a few 'winners' anyway. I heard a couple of them got Gealdr Mentorship Programme placements."

"Becca got a placement with some Moonwater guy who's expected to be on the Council in about ten years. I think they're already dating, so she's probably bagged her politician husband. And Sarah got a placement with the Gealdwards."

"Another marriage in the making?"

"Nah. He's a sponsor of her university or something. She'll be a Dean in a decade."

"Wow. And the Gealdwards are always cosy with the Hallowbornes."

"Yup, you got it."

The Hallowborne mage family was the closest thing Gealdland had to a monarchy, as they usually held the Chair of the Council position. Plus, some of the most powerful multi-talent mages in the country were Hallowbornes. Sarah, a demure contestant was the 'winner' of the first season, if such a thing existed. "So the contestants this year..."

Marcus nudged Jack's shoulder. "I'm sure some of them are at least wondering if they're the goddess. And, Hunter and Harvester, our ratings were phenomenal! So that was a draw, of course. But, yeah, most of them are looking to follow in either Sarah or Becca's path and get some of that sweet, sweet Geald upper echelon action. Whether of the influence or of the matrimony persuasion."

Jack sighed. It was as he expected. He couldn't blame the contestants, either. It was a good opportunity. But it meant he wasn't here to find his own match. He was here to help the women find theirs. And to help the Geald families find fresh blood. That was why so many of them had financial stakes in the aethercast.

But it would work out for him too, right? Right?

Marcus nudged Jack with an elbow. "Chin up, Jack. We'll find her, I promise. I mean, it might not be this season. But we'll keep looking until we do. It'll come out all right in the end."

Jack smiled. "Thanks, Marcus."

Marcus shot his finger guns at Jack. "Gotta go. It's about time for me to herd the women." He strode towards the hallway, taking a moment to clap the light mage on the shoulder and praise her work.

Jack sidled up to the craft table and snagged a muffin, then stood against the wall to eat it.

Mirabelle entered the ballroom, her cane tapping on the floor. Jack's eyes flicked to the side, looking for her assistant, Leta. There she was, following in Mirabelle's wake and carrying a large wooden case with the utmost care.

The two women were an unlikely pair. Mirabelle was small, heading toward frail, and dressed in expensive clothes. Jack had once heard a rumour that she was a Gealdr Mentorship Programme alumnus, and she sure looked the part. Leta, meanwhile, looked like a regular person. Not in a bad way. In a very good way. The best way. She looked like a girl he would have approached at a bar or a party in his pre-incarnate days, interested in who she was, sure, but also lured in by her curvy figure.

Leta carried the box to the small table in front of the backdrop, and the two women together unpackaged Mirabelle's crystal ball. Then Mirabelle took a seat in a chair, and spoke to Leta, who gave a last nod, and went to the craft table.

Jack couldn't help but watch in envy as Leta loaded up a plate with several sandwiches and a muffin. She turned and looked around. For a moment, her eyes caught on him, a flush staining her cheeks, and he straightened under her perusal, wondering if she would come to stand by him. But no; she walked to the opposite side of the ballroom and took up a position tucked in behind a pillar to eat her snack.

Before long, it was time to capture the day's activity. Jack had to forget about Leta for the moment as he was briefed, briefed again, and escorted to his mark. Then it was all go.

Marcus entered the ballroom, preceded by his auto-aethercasters, flying backward. "Hello everyone, and welcome to *Goddess Found*. I'm your host, Marcus. We have a special treat for you today…"

Marcus introduced the contestants, who each walked through the ballroom to sit in a double row of tiered seats. It wouldn't be the first time the viewers at home would have seen the contestants as they'd captured a first introduction the previous day. But this was the episode where the viewers — and Jack — would get a first good look at who they were.

"And last, but not least, please welcome our God Incarnate, Jack Fairholme!"

Jack walked to his next mark, gave a bow, and took the remaining seat.

Marcus had a scripted chit-chat with Mirabelle about the role of a seer and their wishes for the season.

Jack peeked to either side. To his right sat a petite blonde woman called Purity. She had a Geald family name — Fernheart. She sat so still she looked carved from marble. To his left sat a statuesque red-haired woman called Destiny. She also bore a Geald family name — Brightborne. The third Geald family contestant, Constance Geldwright, also sat in the front row. The back row women had more common family names. Was it coincidence? Not likely.

"So, how will you be proceeding today?" Marcus asked Mirabelle.

"First, I will ask each contestant to demonstrate their magic so that I may assess whether I need to take precautions to avoid magical clashes. Then I will perform a reading on my crystal ball."

"And we'll get to hear your divination."

"Yes. I will avoid revealing any intimate details that come to my attention, of course. Even so, I expect that the audience at home will find my readings most illuminating about our guests for the season."

"Well then, without further ado, let's get started."

Marcus rose and approached Jack and the contestants. "Who would like to go first?" he asked.

The order had been determined out in the hallway. Constance, at the end of the front row, raised a hand. "I volunteer," she said, "because my magic will interfere with Seer Mirabelle's, so let's get it out of the way."

Marcus gave a fake laugh. "That's as good a reason as any. Come on down."

Constance walked to the middle of the ballroom. She looked stiff and awkward standing there, but she was wearing a fashionable pink dress and she had an eye-catching high-fashion hairdo, mostly blonde but with a blue forelock.

"Please demonstrate your magic for Mirabelle," said Marcus.

"Could you come here, please, Marcus?" asked Constance. "I need a volunteer. I'm a clairvoyant, and I need someone to read."

Marcus's smile seemed a bit more strained. Even so, he stood before her.

Constance squinted at Marcus, leaning forward. In Jack's vision, her eyes glowed a blinding white. She soon relaxed, and the light in her eyes disappeared. "I see two dogs," she said. "If you are humble, they will stay, but you will miss out on another opportunity."

Marcus's throat bobbed, and he nodded. "Ah, thank you, Constance. Please take a seat by Mirabelle."

Once she had done so, Mirabelle smiled at her. "Thank you for your demonstration, Constance," she said. "I see how you read the probabilities, and I can shift my magic to the side, so to speak, to avoid yours. My reading may not be as accurate for you as for others." She waved a hand over the crystal ball. It and her eyes glowed in Jack's sight as she engaged her magic. "There are two visions here. I see a ring of three overlapping hands. You will make friends on this aethercast. There is a vision for your eyes, too. Please look and keep what you see to yourself."

Constance leaned forward. Her eyes flicked back and forth, watching only she knew what. Then she sat back. "I thank you for the message," she said.

"Best of luck this season, Constance."

The rest of the contestants followed the same pattern. In many instances, they needed something to help demonstrate their magic, and each time, Marcus brought the object required over from a table.

Destiny demonstrated fire magic by weaving the flame of a candle into intricate patterns. "Think carefully about why you are here," said Mirabelle as she read the crystal ball. "Are your choices the right ones for you in the moment or in the long term?"

A tall, dark-haired woman called Tiffany demonstrated light magic. She made a shower of stars rain around her in a complicated pattern that mimicked well-known festival dances. "You are not here for the reason you think you are," said Mirabelle as she gazed into the ball.

"Are you saying I'm definitely not the goddess?" Tiffany asked.

"Were you sure you were?"

"No."

"Then I suppose you still could be. Or you will get something else important out of appearing on this aethercast."

Tiffany looked intrigued as she returned to her seat.

The event proceeded past a woodcraft mage, a kinetic mage, and a stone mage, all of whom received cryptic messages from Mirabelle that would surely make sense in time. Jack hadn't seen stone magic performed since his ascension. He was fascinated to see that the stone mage vibrated the stone to make it turn into sand that she could manipulate and then put back together. It took her a fair bit of effort, though: a sheen of sweat beaded on her brow.

Then a blonde woman called Chrissie Merriweather was called up. She looked a little embarrassed as she approached Marcus.

"What magic will you be demonstrating for us today?" Marcus asked.

"Uh, light magic."

Oh, thought Jack. *Poor woman. Being the second light mage wouldn't be fun.*

In the end, Chrissie did fine. She demonstrated a different trick than Tiffany had, making columns of light ascend from the floor to the ceiling. Her trick may not have been as delicate as Tiffany's, but it was bold.

"Not everyone who helps you is doing so in your best interest," said Mirabelle after scrying for Chrissie. "Beware who you trust."

Finally, the last contestant was called up. She had long black hair, dark eyes, and olive skin. At least AllAether had included one person not fully Gealdr in ancestry. He knew the Geald families had certain expectations of who the goddess would be, and in the first season, everyone had been white. As if it hadn't been proven by other countries' incarnates that 'pure' blood, whatever that even means, was of no concern to the Gods.

Jess asked Marcus for a glass of water. She nearly fumbled it when Marcus handed it to her. She blushed, and Marcus grinned at her, the corners of his eyes crinkling. Jess stepped back and then twisted the water in the glass up into a thread that wound around her in a circle. She manipulated the water further, creating intricate patterns. Splashes broke free and shaped themselves into tiny birds that flew around her head.

Marcus gave a slow clap as Jess gathered the water back into the glass and drank it. She handed the empty glass to him before taking a seat beside Mirabelle.

"There are two paths before you," said Mirabelle. "The path with a better end has a trickier beginning. If you take it, you will have hardships to overcome. You will need to choose before the end of this aethercast."

"Wow, uh. OK."

"There's more," said Mirabelle. "A private vision for you."

Jess leaned forward and frowned into the glass. She blushed, and look away.

That would make for fascinating viewing for the audience at home. Jack had no doubt that when this episode 'casted, the whole country would be dying to know what Jess had seen.

"All right," said Marcus. "We have one more person here with us today. God Incarnate Jack, please step up."

Jack took his mark. He spent a moment looking back at the contestants, as he had been instructed to do. As with the day before, none of them leapt out at him as a potential goddess any more than the others. But then again, would he know this early? An un-ascended incarnate could meet their other half several times, or even repeatedly, without triggering, until something brought on the awareness. That's what this aethercast had been built upon: the idea that throwing Jack together with a bunch of people in a variety of situations might eventually trigger an ascension in the goddess if she was there.

But for now, he felt nothing other than the normal mild interest one had in new acquaintances.

Jack turned to Marcus and smiled. "Hello," he said.

"I won't get you to demonstrate your magic because, as we found last year, it's hard to demonstrate. But we know you can see the invisible threads of magic in use."

"That's right, Marcus."

"And you couldn't see that before you ascended?"

"Not at all."

"And what did you see just now as the contestants demonstrated their magics?"

"It was very interesting to see them at work," he said. "They're all very talented, and I suspect a few were holding themselves back."

"Interesting insight. I wonder who was being polite and trying not to show the others up?" Marcus grinned. "Ok, then. I'm sure Mirabelle is dying to read your fate."

Jack took the seat beside Mirabelle. She gave him a fond smile. "Welcome, God Incarnate," she said.

"Thank you, Seer Mirabelle."

"Now, as per usual, my reading for you might take a little longer than for the others. For the viewers at home who don't know, reading an incarnate can be tricky because the visions come through thick and fast. I usually read Jack with multiple methods to help tease out the message. So please bear with me while I see what I can in the crystal ball."

Jack flinched from the glow in her eyes and the crystal. He looked instead at the contestants. Most of them wore polite waiting faces, but Constance and Destiny leaned forward, eager to hear the reading. Why were those two in particular keen?

Despite himself, Jack also glanced to where Leta had hidden herself. She was biting her lip in thought, and he could almost feel her teeth in his own lip. He looked away before anything weird showed on his face. Ogling an assistant while on the job! Hunter and Harvester, what was wrong with him?

"I see confusion," said Mirabelle. "The road ahead is hazy."

Jack laughed nervously, aware of the auto-aethercasters recording everything. "I hope that doesn't indicate an inauspicious start to the season."

"Not necessarily. I often see confusion before a breakthrough. Whether you find the goddess this year, you will find something more about yourself. You are soon to come into your full identity as God Incarnate of Gealdland. We will see a substantial change in you this year, Jack."

He nodded along. Until he saw whatever change she meant, he couldn't imagine it. Unless she meant a contestant was the goddess. He looked up at them. They all seemed interested now.

"There is a private message for you here, Jack. Please look into the crystal ball, and keep what you see to yourself. It is a message just for you."

Jack leaned forward, wincing against the glow of the crystal ball. Just as with his private viewing the other day, the same emerald silk billowed up from the depths. Or no; satin, maybe? This time, he saw more detail in the fabric: fine green embroidery in the same hue, with a leafy pattern. A sense of danger, a flash of light. The need to push, as hard as he could, with his kinetic magic. A voice in his ear. *NOW*. It sounded like God-Voice.

The Hunter wanted him to do something. But he didn't know what. Or when. Green fabric, danger, push. He filed the warning away for later. He could only wait for the right moment.

Jack shook the lingering vision away.

"Thank you, Mirabelle."

As he stood to return to his seat, he wondered what emotions had shown on his face.

What the country would think of his fear.

"HUNTER AND HARVESTER!" Leta swore.

After the divinations, most people stayed in the ballroom, chatting and socialising. Mirabelle sent Leta to a small hidden kitchen to get her a cup of coffee. A coffee machine sat on the incongruously modern bench top, but the damned thing wasn't working for her. It was one of those units with an aura trigger instead of a depressible button, one that was calibrated for a higher rating of magic than Leta had access to. She had nothing to flare under the sensor to let it know she was there.

She hated it when this happened. Why did manufacturers only test their products on people with active, usable magic? Why? And why was it vending machines and public loo hand towels that gave her grief? Everyone needed to use those!

Leta looked out into the ballroom, and tapped on the worry stone in her pocket. She needed help, but she also didn't want to ask for help. Because whoever she asked would then know she had no magic.

Jack was framed in the doorway, surrounded and distracted by the gaggle of contestants vying for his attention. The sight made Leta more irritable. Why did everyone else have to be having a great time while she was struggling?

"Did you see any of the anti-incarnation protesters at the station?" she could just hear Chrissie asking Jack.

"No, I didn't. Were they there?"

"Out the front. They totally got in my way. I was really scared. There were placards and everything." Chrissie shook her head.

"Don't worry," said Jack. "It's only me they have a problem with."

"They aren't happy with us for testing to see if we're the goddess, either," said Tiffany.

"You're important, Jack," said Purity, "no matter what those people say. My family owns farmland, and we haven't seen a truly excellent crop or calving since the last time God Incarnate Archibald did a Blessings tour. The magic is real. You did your second tour this spring, didn't you? The entire farming industry is thrilled you've ascended."

Jack grinned. "I'm sure they will be even happier once the goddess is found. The spring tours work better with the Goddess Incarnate."

Leta accidentally made eye contact with Destiny, the tall red-headed contestant. Destiny was frowning at her, and with a start, Leta realised she was staring and eavesdropping on their conversation. Leta turned back to the coffee machine and tried again to get the coffee to flow. The machine paid as much attention to her as it had previously. "Blast it!" She looked back over her shoulder, only to see Destiny smirking in her direction. Leta flushed and looked away. She began looking through the cupboards for instant coffee.

Being around these perfect, powerful women was already giving her self-esteem a knock, and it had only been a day. How would she be feeling in six weeks? It wasn't just that they had powerful magic. They were so beautiful, and Leta was freckled and frumpy. She knew she shouldn't compare herself with those women out there, because comparisons got a person nowhere. But it was so hard not to. What was she next to them?

Leta heard footsteps behind her, and she expected Destiny had come into the kitchenette to mock her. But when she turned, she found Jack. "Are you OK?" he asked. "You've been in here a while."

Leta flushed and nodded at the coffee machine. How could she explain herself without revealing her weakness?

"Is it out of coffee beans?"

"Uh, no. Um."

Then his eyes lit up in recognition. "Oh. *Right*. Say no more." He stepped forward. "Which one?"

Leta edged into his personal space and pointed at the sensor she'd been trying to trigger. Jack waved his hand under it, and the machine rumbled to life and began grinding the beans.

"Don't tell anyone," Jack said in a low voice, "but before I ascended, I had this problem with a vending machine at my old gym." He smiled and then slipped back out of the kitchenette, casually leaving her with one more secret to keep.

Why was he so sure she was trustworthy? Around him, several of the contestants gave her cool looks. Why? She didn't call him over. He came of his own accord!

Leta took the now-full coffee mug into the ballroom. Destiny had left the nearby group, thankfully, but Marcus had attached himself in her place. There was something brittle about his smile as he watched Jack talking to the contestants. What was that look? Impatience? Boredom? Jealousy? She wasn't sure.

She approached Mirabelle, who was engaged in a heated conversation with a light mage.

"Oh, thank you, dear," said Mirabelle as she took the mug. "Why don't you take a break?"

Leta nodded. "I'll do that."

She knew where she wanted to be right now, and it was not in this ballroom with its glitterati and their eye daggers. She missed her garden — the grounding and the solace. So she slipped outside and went for a quick walk in the manor gardens.

It was a cold, cloudy day, so she hugged her arms around herself and walked briskly. She intended to walk once around the manor through the nearby sculpted, though dormant, gardens and then straight back inside to where it was warmer.

She was alone along the first two sides of the building. Rosehips brightened the rose garden against the backdrop of deep green hedges. The bright flame of autumn leaves overhung all.

On the third side, tall hedges broke the gardens up into private grottoes, with cobbled paths wending between and stone benches nestled in green alcoves. Leta stepped along, both enjoying the crisp green-scented air in her lungs and chilled by it on her skin. Just before she stepped around a hedge, nearby whispers broke her peace. She stopped, unwilling to interrupt who it was, lest they think she was eavesdropping.

She idled for a moment, trying to decide if she would wait, go far enough around that she wouldn't bother the people, or retrace her steps.

"We need something more concrete than that!" hissed a man's voice.

"Don't talk to me in that tone," a woman's voice replied. "You're the one who wants something. I'm just going about my business."

The man scoffed. "If you don't want something, then why are you even talking to me? You types are all the same. You think you can take and take but never give back. Well, if you want our support, we need something in return. Get us some dirt."

Leta leaned closer to the hedge, listening.

"I'll speak to you later," said the woman. "I don't want to see you until half-way through the capturing, OK?"

"Fine, whatever. But you *will* see me again."

With a stab of panic, Leta realised the conversation was over and one of the participants could come around the corner at any moment. She turned and hurried back the way she had come, trying not to step loudly on the cobbled path.

"Oi! You, Mundane girl!"

Leta spun around, her heart beating at the insult. Mundane, what all the mean kids at school had called her because she had no magic. It was Destiny who had thrown the insult at her this time. With a sinking feeling, Leta realised Destiny had caught onto Leta's lack of magic in the kitchenette. Of all people...

"Are you spying on me?" demanded Destiny.

"No, I'm going for a walk. Forget I was here."

Destiny gave Leta a slow look down and up, an eyebrow quirked disbelievingly. Rude. "If you're going to report on my actions, at least get the story straight," said Destiny. "I caught a reporter sneaking around. He tried to get some gossip, but I sent him on his way."

Right. Because Destiny offering an explanation without being asked was so believable. "You don't have an auto-aethercaster with you."

Destiny looked up. "Oh, so I don't. I guess I lost it in one of the turns." She stalked off. "I'd better go find it."

Leta stood still for a minute. Having that insult thrown at her had rattled her. Was Destiny telling the truth?

Another figure stepped out around the corner and walked off in a different direction. He was a nondescript sort of middle-aged guy in a dark rain jacket and jeans. The person Destiny had been arguing with. Leta looked at him, considering. He looked like he could be a reporter. Perhaps. He looked like he could be pretty much anything else, though, too.

Except an associate of a young Geald family mage born with a silver spoon in her mouth.

THE HERMIT
UPRIGHT

It's time for a journey of self-discovery. You have deep wisdom within you, and it is time to find it.

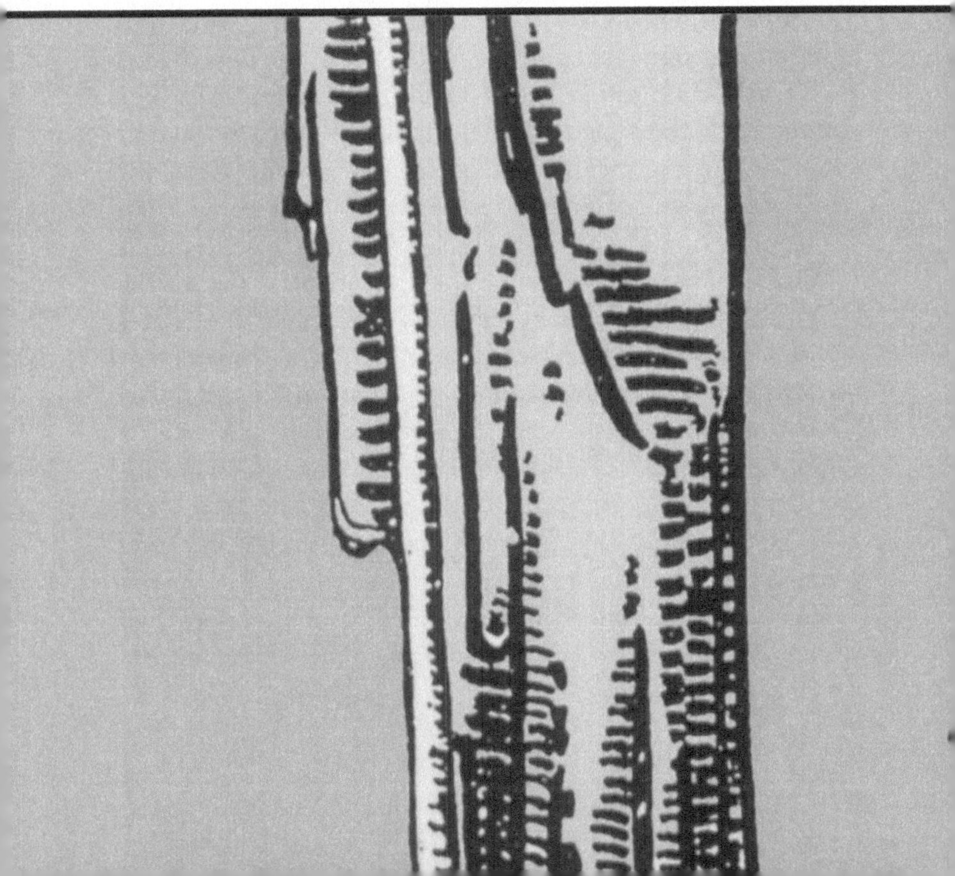

Hey babe,

Contestants are here. Jack didn't seem into anyone in particular. Which way are we leaning at the moment? Good or bad thing?

This manor is draughty as fuck. You sure you're too busy to join us? I want someone to keep my toes warm at night.

Three days in, and Jack was exhausted. Since Monday afternoon, he had been capturing the acclimatisation week for the contestants. He had dinner in the dining room with them every evening, sitting in the head seat with a different pair of women to his left and right each meal. For the rest of the day, he had a series of 'dates' to get to know the contestants. The dates each took place at a different folly in the manor garden. He also received dailies from Mirabelle. Each one included words of encouragement and hints about what the goddess might be like, which had come from readings Mirabelle was doing using the Queen of Cups as the significator. So far, none of the women he'd had dates with seemed to fit the description.

Mirabelle's dailies hadn't been very illuminating. The most useful one had been, *Be wary of causing problems for others while being focussed on your own.* That was good life advice.

He was now having green tea in a pagoda on a tiny constructed lake with a curly-haired, freckled kinetic mage called Nellie. She was more approachable than many of the women he'd spoken to so far. However, she was obsessed, truly obsessed, with furniture. It was all she wanted to talk about. The furniture in the manor. The furniture she had seen on last year's aethercast. The furniture in her house. The furniture she wanted to buy. Jack wondered what she was doing on this aethercast when she ought to be studying interior design. She had a true calling. But she too came from a prestigious enough family that working a job, providing a service to people, was seen as beneath her. When he had asked her what she wanted to be, she had answered 'philanthropist.'

They were kneeling at a small table in the pagoda. Jack's feet were going to sleep, and the weather was frigid, so he was having a tough time keeping warm. Heat radiated off Nellie, who was wearing a short-sleeved dress. She must be using magic to manipulate heat, an ability that either weather mages or, more rarely, some kinetic mages possessed. Alas, Jack didn't have the knack. In fact, Jack wondered if she was stealing his warmth for herself. He tried to look engaged, but he just wanted to go back to his rooms and have a large mug of hot chocolate.

At least this was his sixth 'first date,' so he only had two more to go.

"What kind of house do you want to have in the future?" asked Nellie, keeping the conversation firmly within her own sphere of interest.

"A warm house," he said. That was a top priority to him at that moment. "One that smells of delicious food, with a fireplace and comfy chairs. And plants inside and out."

"You like outdoor living? What sort of outdoor furniture would it have?"

There it was; a furniture question. "Something practical and weather appropriate."

Nellie nodded. "So, a country mansion."

He was actually thinking along the lines of 'country cottage.' So many people assumed that as God Incarnate, he wanted to be rich and famous. He knew he had a duty to the people, but he didn't want it to be more than that. He didn't want fame or fortune.

After some further inanities, the production assistant gave Jack a 'thumb's up,' letting him know he could wrap up the date. He gave some pleasantries, expressed a desire to spend time with her again, and made a show of handing her down off the pagoda onto the grass. He made it seem to the auto-aethercasters like he might escort her back to the manor. Instead, he escorted her to the gaggle of crew who were milling nearby.

"I think we got a good capture," said the production assistant. "Thanks, both of you."

Nellie made a face. "I don't like green tea. Is there something I can wash the taste away with?"

One of the second assistants offered her a cup of milk tea, poured from a flask.

"Would you like a cup too, sir?"

"No thanks," said Jack. "I'm freezing and I want to go back inside. You want me to carry any of this equipment?"

"No, no, don't worry about that sort of thing," said a grip. "You head on inside, sir."

Jack waved to them all. Nellie looked torn for a moment between following him and having her tea, but she must really have disliked the taste of the green tea because she chose the beverage.

Jack walked towards the manor. At least, until he was out of view of the crew. He had won himself about a half hour of free time, with no one but the auto-aethercasters following him. There was an itch between his shoulder blades, something telling him to use this time productively, despite how cold he was. So he took a left-turn through the rose garden and headed for the dense copse of the Singing Grove.

The trees of Autumnwood Manor's Singing Grove were ancient yews, far beyond their youthful, upright growth habit. It may have been there before the manor, though Jack didn't know yews well enough to be sure. The trunks no longer looked like trunks, but rather thickets of branches all grown together. Someone kept the ground around them well-swept.

Jack swung a leg over a lateral branch to climb into the Singing Grove. The bare circle of the grove contained only a few practice rocks for kinetic and stone magic practise and a stone pit for water and fire magic practise. The yews blocked almost all sound from the surroundings and left only a small circle of sky visible above. Jack shivered and rubbed his hands together.

"Well, this is hardly my first time in a Singing Grove," he muttered to himself. But the grove he'd practised his magic in at high school had been new, a tidy ring of ash trees. It had kept stray magic inside, sure, but it hadn't loomed the way this grove did.

Jack rolled his shoulders and walked over to the rocks. He reached deep within to find his pool of kinetic magic. It used to be just there, the first thing he came to in that place in his mind. But now he had to push past the shimmering aura of his incarnation magic to find his darker blue kinetic magic. The incarnation magic clung, wanting to be used, but that's not what Jack was there for. He didn't need to look at magic from others — he wouldn't be able to see anything beyond the yews, no matter what. He wanted to make sure that he was still himself, somewhere below that shimmer.

At last, he grabbed a decent hold of his kinetic magic. It had only taken him a few seconds, but that was a few seconds he didn't previously need. He wanted to get faster at this switch. The other day was a good case in point. What if he hadn't been close enough to grab Leta, and his magic eluded his grasp? She would have fallen down the stairs right there in front of him. Panic rose within him at the thought. That wasn't good enough.

One by one, he manipulated the rounded lichen-covered practice rocks, shunting them back and forth across the Grove, warming up with the effort until he no longer felt the cold. He started at the smallest and went about half-way through the line until he reached a rock that was too heavy for him to move. Not bad. He had thought he might have lost strength over the last few years, but if anything, he'd been able to move one more rock than normal. It was hard to say for sure, though: this was the first time he had used this particular set, of course, and these were too old to be standardised weights.

All too soon, Jack's time at the Singing Grove ran out. If he stayed any longer, he would be missed. So, promising himself he would continue to slip practice in whenever he could, he left the grove and headed back to the manor.

He strode through the gardens at a brisk pace, his hands deep in his pockets to keep them warm, and took the stairs up to one of the side doors two at a time. He had to pass the parlour that was being used as a common room. Conversation and laughter spilled out into the hallway. Just then, Leta came down the stairs from the floor where the contestants were staying. She had her hair tied up in a strict bun, and she wore a knee-length skirt and a blue jersey. She was holding on to the bannister as she descended; she had learned her lesson. She smiled when she saw him and then seemed to cut the smile off half-way and replace it with a serious expression. "Ah, God Incarnate Jack," she said. "I was about to deliver this to your rooms." She held a letter out to him with Mirabelle's familiar handwriting on it: his daily. "Would you like me to slide it under the door like normal, or would you like to have it now?"

Jack took the envelope. "I'll take it with me and save you the walk. Thank you very much."

Leta gave a small bow and looked like she was about

to leave, but he waylaid her. "How are you settling in?" he asked. "And the job: how is it going?"

"Oh, very good. No complaints." She blushed, and Jack found the look to be cute.

"Good, good. Let me know if you have any problems and I'll see what I can do."

"Thank you. Um, actually." She motioned for Jack to step closer. When he did, she said in a low voice, "Yesterday, I saw Destiny having a weird conversation in the gardens with a mystery man. Middle-aged, nondescript clothes. She said he was a reporter nosing around. I just thought you should know."

Jack raised his eyebrows. That was well worth being aware of. He wasn't keen on unknown people being on the estate. If a reporter could sneak in, then an anti-incarnation protester could too. Most of them were just loud, but occasionally they could get violent. "Thank you. Have you told anyone else?"

"I mentioned it to Mirabelle. She said she would tell security."

"That's great. Thank you," he said.

"No problem. I should be getting back to Mirabelle."

"See you later." He continued on his way, smiling a bit about how Leta treated him. She wasn't trying to curry favour or anything. She was just pleasant and helpful. How refreshing.

He went back to his rooms, made himself a hot chocolate, and sat in a chair to read the daily.

Dear Jack,

The one who is kept down should stick up for themselves.

Also, I see the gardens in my viewings of you. I believe spending some free time in the outdoors may bring you luck.

Mirabelle

Jack shivered. Was Mirabelle's reference to the gardens an encouragement to hone his magic? Even though he knew of her abilities, it still shocked him whenever she was so on point. He decided to take the advice as he saw it, and do his best to get more magic practice in.

And as for sticking up for himself, he could try.

LETA JOLTED UPRIGHT in bed and clutched her ears. It was pitch-black, well before dawn. A screeching sound melded with the last shreds of her troubled dreams, and for a moment she thought she was dying under the piercing magic of battle mages.

"It's the fire alarm, fool. Get moving!" she said aloud. She couldn't hear her own words over the din.

She grabbed only her puffer coat on the way out of her small room. Everyone else on the floor threw their own doors open about the same time.

"Along the hallway, down the stairs, through the kitchen and out into the courtyard!" called a woman with a dark plait hanging down her back over flannel pyjamas, the light mage who had decorated the set for the Divinations event. Her voice cut across the din. She took a moment to use her light magic to make a glowing green sign over her head before adding, "And no running!" Leta supposed the sign said 'fire warden', but she hadn't picked up her glasses on the way out so it was blurry to her eyes.

The fire warden started checking rooms along the hallway. Leta paused for a moment, wondering if she should offer help, but the woman pushed Leta between the shoulder blades. "No dilly-dallying!"

Leta followed the other crew members down the stairs. She threw her coat on as she went and then covered her ears with her hands. She now remembered the evacuation route being drilled into her on her first day, but she appreciated the fire warden's prompt. Leta was not the only person who would have dithered in her doorway for twenty seconds, trying to remember what she was supposed to do. It felt like it was in the small hours of the morning, far too early for Leta's brain to be working at full efficiency.

By the time she had fumbled her way to the door and out into the courtyard, there was no longer a stream of people ahead of her. She knew she was supposed to line up with the others from her hallway, but where were they? She could make out half a dozen different groups of people standing around, some with their fire wardens — obvious to her by the glowing green signs above them — and some without. Which of the three groups whose fire wardens were still inside was she supposed to go to? She couldn't make out the details of anyone's faces, despite the floodlights over the courtyard.

Panic welled up in her. Everyone must be looking at her standing in the doorway. Seeing her not knowing what to do. Judging her. She had to fight with all her might not to flee back into the building. There could be a fire in there. Her legs moved of their own accord, carrying her along the outside wall, looking for a dark corner like a frightened cockroach.

She collided with something firm… and warm. "Sorry, excuse me!" she squeaked. *Hunter and Harvester! Just come for me now, fire. Put me out of my misery.*

Hands held her upper arms to steady her, and another presence steadied her in the small of her back, one that felt an awful lot like when her mum had used her kinetic magic to catch her when she was running too close to the road as a child. "Are you OK?"

Leta froze. She knew that voice. She was close enough that when she looked up, past a chest clad only in a singlet, past distractingly toned shoulders, she could see Jack's polite but perplexed expression clear as day. His petrichor-like scent, as if the very land was embedded within him, surrounded her. Everyone would certainly be looking at her now! *Hurry, fire! Please!*

"I'm so sorry. I forgot my glasses." She gazed up into the light caught in his eyelashes, shining in his eyes, which seemed darker at night. He blinked, frowned at her. Struck by the force of his direct gaze, she lowered her eyes. But then she was just looking at his mouth. He licked his lips.

"Oh," he said. He gestured towards the gathered people in the courtyard. "Uh. I think you need to go over—"

"I'll take her, God Incarnate Jack." The fire warden from Leta's floor had emerged from the kitchen door at some point and walked over to fetch Leta.

Jack relinquished his hold on Leta's arms as the fire warden led her away.

"Sorry!" Leta called out over her shoulder to Jack. Then, in a quieter voice, she said to the fire warden, "I'm sorry about this. I wouldn't usually have forgotten my glasses."

"That's OK. It's what I'm here for. They shouldn't have done this at 3 am when everyone would have been deeply asleep."

Leta stumbled as she walked. "'Done'?"

"It's just a drill. It's part of the 'cast. For drama."

Leta's stomach dropped to somewhere near the core of the planet. For the 'cast... that meant the auto-aethercasters would have been capturing when she ran into Jack. She was going to be on the aethercast. In front of the entire nation. In her pyjamas.

And worst of all, there wasn't even a real fire to come and end her miserable existence.

THE HIEROPHANT
REVERSED

THINK ABOUT THE RULES THAT ARE ACCEPTED AROUND YOU.
DO THEY ALIGN WITH YOUR VALUES? IS IT TIME TO GO YOUR OWN WAY?

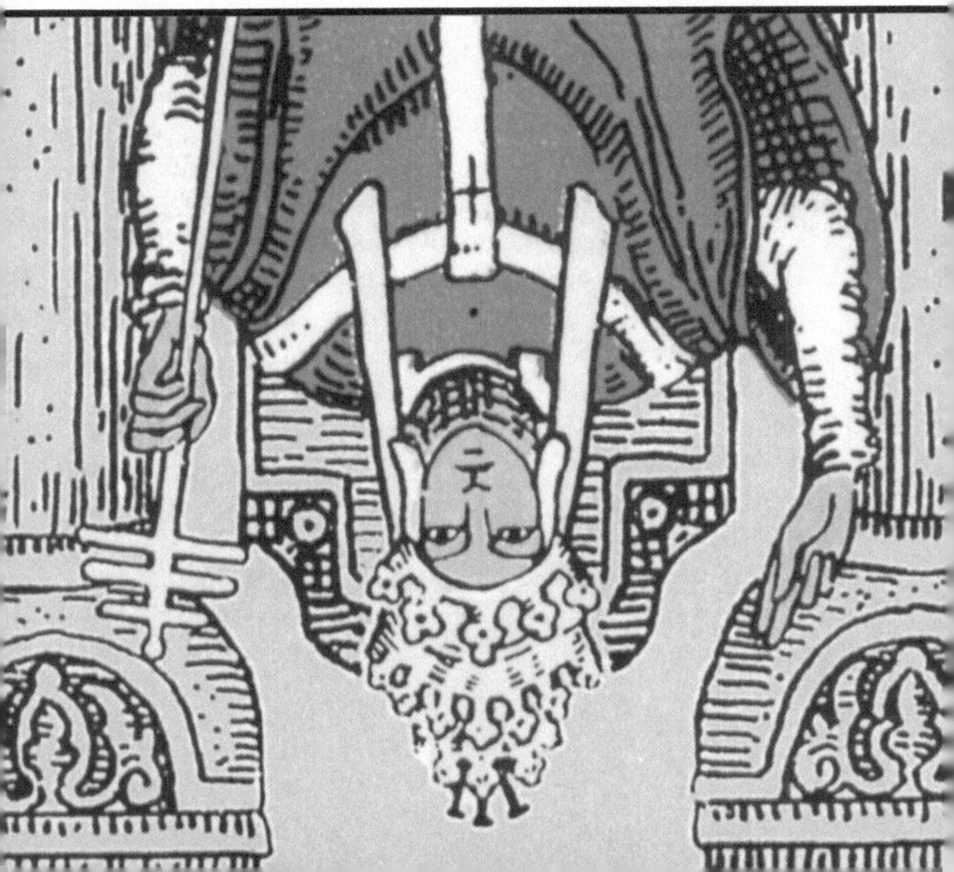

MARCUS

What the actual fuck was that? What is going on there??? Who's the fat chick, and was Jack drooling over her? We need her name. New crew member?

The team's going over the capture to see what we can salvage. We'll get back to you with a plan once we've seen her contract.

Evelyn

J ack knocked on the door to the executive suite. A young man, one of the assistants, answered his knock.

"Is Marcus there?" asked Jack. "He asked me to drop by for something."

"Just a moment," said the young man and disappeared back into the suite. A few moments later, he opened the door wide and ushered Jack in.

Marcus stood by the window, his face showing no emotion. "Jack, good to see you! Take a seat, take a seat." He waved to a table in the middle of the room. "Kenneth, two coffees, please, and then have a break."

Jack and Marcus waited until the young man had delivered their coffees and left before talking.

"Are you an idiot?" Marcus asked.

Jack blinked. "I beg your pardon?"

"We gave you the perfect setup. Fire drill, your evacuation route leading you out to stand right in front of everyone, all chiselled and handsome…"

"Thanks for stealing my dressing gown, coat, *and* cardigan to arrange that. I mean, I would have preferred not to freeze my balls off, but I'm sure the optics were great."

"You're welcome. But back to the source of my ire. Yes, we caught you by surprise, but it doesn't take a *gealдwright* to figure out you were supposed to greet the contestants who were *right there in front of you*, waiting to fall at your feet and tell you about how scared they were. But no, instead you catch the swooning mole wearing a *sleeping bag with arms*."

Jack tutted at the unflattering description. He'd been envious of Leta's coat. "She walked right into me. What was I supposed to do: let her bounce off me and then step over her? Is that the kind of behaviour AllAether wants me to display?"

"You could have just steadied her. I don't know what it felt like you were doing, but to all of us watching, it looked like you were clinging to her arms and gazing into her eyes for, I guess, ten seconds? Which is a *really long time* to look at someone. It was *super* awkward to watch."

"I was just checking that she was OK."

"Uh-huh. You know she can't be the Goddess Incarnate, right? We surreptitiously tested all the crew for their magical speciality as they came in for processing. She doesn't have one, as far as the tester could see. She doesn't have enough magic to support ascension."

A stab of disappointment took Jack by surprise. But he couldn't expect to find his goddess that easily. "That's someone's confidential information you're telling me."

Marcus held up his hands in a surrendering gesture. "Sorry, my bad. But it's probably something you need to know, considering what comes next." Marcus sighed. "If you were going to have some silly meet-cute with one of the crew, couldn't you have at least chosen a pretty one? This is going to be a little harder to set up than it would be otherwise."

"Set up what? What comes next?"

A knock sounded at the door. "Hold that thought," said Marcus as he rose to answer it. "Welcome, ladies."

He ushered Leta and Mirabelle into the room. Mirabelle held her head high, but Leta hunched in on herself. She wore a jersey in a pale green that looked great on her. When she noticed Jack at the table, she flushed red and then looked as if she was going to be sick. Jack's self-confidence sufficed to realise that it wasn't him who had upset her, but rather the reminder that AllAether had put her into the aethercast with no warning. In her pyjamas. He winced in sympathy. The poor woman.

"Thanks for coming," said Marcus as the women took their seats. "Let's get down to business. The producers back at the studio reviewed the capture from last night. While it really wasn't what we were going for, we can work with it."

"I'm really sorry," interrupted a blushing Leta. "I forgot my glasses and…"

When she paused, lost for words, Marcus waved her silent. "It's fine. What's done is done."

"Am I going to be on the aethercast? Will people see my mistake?"

"Yes."

Leta looked horrified.

"C'mon, Marcus," said Jack. "Isn't that cruel? She didn't sign up for this. She's an assistant."

Marcus leaned over to his desk and snagged a file. He opened it and turned it around. It was Leta's contract.

"Marcus, she signed a contract with me," said Mirabelle. "Not with AllAether."

"I know," said Marcus. "But you used a template provided by AllAether, didn't you? Consulted with the lawyer on staff?"

"I—"

Marcus flicked to the third page, on which a clause had been highlighted. "Let me read that for those who have poor eyesight." Leta winced as Marcus picked up the folder again and read the clause aloud. "'The consultant, while undertaking tasks for Seer Crowlea, may be required to perform tasks for Seer Crowlea's employer AllAether, as required.'" He paused for a moment to let them ponder the clause. "I've been reliably informed that this does indeed allow us to require Leta to participate in the aethercast."

"Why am I not fucking surprised?" said Jack. "It's so open-ended it's basically a blank cheque. Pardon my language," he added, giving the women an apologetic look.

Mirabelle inclined her head gracefully, but Leta missed the swearing, or perhaps she didn't care. She looked at Mirabelle, her eyes pleading. "You said when you hired me I wouldn't be a part of the actual aethercast."

Mirabelle held a hand out to Marcus. "May I see?"

She took her time reading it over. Then she sighed. "I'm awfully sorry, Leta. I should have been more careful. When I saw that clause, I thought it regarded delivering notes and the like."

"Speaking of delivering notes," said Marcus.

"What are you planning?" asked Jack, trying to put a warning in his voice.

"Not me: don't shoot the messenger." Marcus settled his elbows on the table. "What we were intending to set up last night was strife and anxiety among the contestants. It's a well-known trigger of ascension in Incarnations. The fire alarm was supposed to get them riled up, and then you, Jack, were supposed to come along and console them, except you can only console one person at a time, so perhaps there would've bean jealousy, another powerful known trigger... you see what I'm saying?"

Mirabelle nodded along. Jack sighed. He remembered all these shenanigans from the previous season.

"What's that got to do with me and my contract, though?" asked Leta. "Or delivering notes? I'm sorry I messed the plan up, but can't it be done again?"

Marcus grinned. "*Jealousy*. The contestants are angry."

Leta shrank in her seat. "At me."

"Yup. They are super jealous, and that's *good*. We were intending a contestant to be the target, but a crew member could work too."

Leta shook her head. "Oh, no."

"C'mon, it won't be that bad. You just have to deliver the dailies a little more publicly than intended. Timed to run into the contestants rather than avoid them. And we'll give you more messages to deliver as well, since you don't seem so busy. Oh, and Jack, when she delivers yours, you invite her into your rooms, OK? Shut the door for a minute?"

"I don't want to ruin her reputation for the sake of this aethercast," he said. "Because you're intending to catch some of her comings and goings on the auto-aethercasters, right?"

Marcus shrugged. Leta inhaled sharply.

"It'll be fine," said Marcus. "We'll focus on how the contestants feel about there being a crew member who Jack spends a lot of time with. 'Who is most angry?', 'Who is most jealous?', that sort of thing. You're not becoming a contestant, OK? Don't get your hopes up. There might be a few shots of you with papers or a clipboard, but we'll move on to how the contestants react to you, not you yourself, OK?"

Leta didn't look OK, but she didn't protest. Probably because she was frozen in fear, but Marcus seemed to take Leta's lack of a response as acquiescence. "Hm, just had a thought," he mused. "You dress plain. And you're not exactly model material. What do you think, Mirabelle? Can she be dressed up a bit?"

Jack expected Mirabelle to stick up for Leta against Marcus's unflattering descriptions, as she'd seemed supportive so far, but instead the older woman said, "I'll see what I can do."

"Mirabelle," whispered Leta. "I'm not comfortable with this."

"A butterfly's wings, remember, Leta? This might have been what I foresaw."

"Oh?" asked Marcus, leaning forward.

"I thought you didn't believe in the accuracy of my readings," said Mirabelle.

Marcus shrugged. "Suit yourself. Just get her dressing nicer. We'll have a new schedule for you tomorrow," he said, looking at Leta again. "Similar to before, but with a few more people to go get messages from. You two are dismissed. Jack, stay a minute?"

Both women walked stiffly out of the room, even though only one had a disability to explain the gait. Leta just seemed in shock.

When they had closed the door, Marcus stretched and linked his hands behind his neck. "See what I mean, Jack? It would have been better if you ran into a pretty girl. Since the network wants you to feign some interest in that frumpy one now instead. Can you do it?"

Jack thought about the time he'd caught her when she nearly fell down the stairs, how he'd been affected by the feel of her, by the green, leafy scent of her. "I'll be fine," he said. "She's the one you should worry about."

Marcus snorted. "You think she wouldn't like you? She's probably never been this close to hot guys like us before. She seemed star-struck." Then Marcus clicked his tongue. "Ah, you think she bats for the other team?"

"That's not it. Marcus, she's clearly terrified. Do we have to use an assistant on a temporary contract, one new to this industry, for this? It doesn't seem fair."

Marcus stood and clapped Jack on the shoulder. "Life's not fair, Jack. You should know that by now."

LETA WENT THROUGH the motions that day, delivering dailies in numb shock and jumping every time she caught sight of an auto-aethercaster. Thankfully, she didn't see many people around. Jack and the contestants were busy outside with something or other. Leta was sure she had been told about the day's schedule at some point, but with all the excitement, she'd somehow forgotten. To make herself scarce, whenever she had downtime she visited the kitchens. She'd already introduced herself to the catering staff and talked about her interest in the field. Naturally, the chef was eager to put an experienced but idle person to work, and a batch of spiced apple muffins made by Leta had gone out to the dining room for lunch.

Later that afternoon, Leta led Mirabelle to her own small room, where the older woman inspected the contents of Leta's suitcase. Mirabelle then perched on the edge of the bed and had Leta hold various pieces of clothing up to herself. Mirabelle didn't let her thoughts about Leta's clothes slip, but since her own clothes always looked so fancy, Leta imagined that Mirabelle found them to be lacking.

Eventually, Mirabelle had all the information she needed. "We can work with your skirts. All you need is some more flattering blouses and a blazer to keep you warm. The jerseys are fine for your downtime, but a classic blazer will look better on the aethercast. There isn't a suitable boutique in Autumnwood, so I will order them in." She took a measuring tape out of her purse. "May I take your measurements?"

Leta reluctantly let Mirabelle measure her.

"Thank you, dear. I will procure your wardrobe upgrade. It will be a business expense, so you needn't pay. It's always exciting to get fancy new clothes, isn't it? Oh, and do book an appointment with one of the makeup artists. They can give you tips on how to apply makeup to look your best on an aethercast. It's not quite the same as applying makeup for being seen in person." Mirabelle picked up her cane. "Please take a break for now and relax before dinner. You must be overwhelmed."

"Very. Thank you for everything."

"Not at all, dear." Mirabelle then left Leta to her own devices.

The sudden silence and alone time were both jarring and a relief. She curled up with a blanket on the bed, intending to take a quick nap. No sooner had she done so than a call came in on her aethervoicer. She dug the old scratched slice of glass out of her pocket.

Leta smiled when she saw her mother's face flicker into motion within the crystal. She bet her mother had been hanging out for details. "Hi, Mum. How are you doing?"

"Don't worry about me, love. How's it going? I'm dying to know! You can talk to me, right? I'm not getting you in trouble?"

"I'll only be in trouble if I say something I'm not supposed to. Which I won't." She didn't want to tell her mother she *couldn't*. She wouldn't be happy that AllAether had bound her with a blood oath.

"...I won't get anything meaningful out of you about the aethercast, will I?"

Leta grinned. "No."

Her mum huffed and pouted. "How about you? Is your room OK? Are they feeding you well enough?"

Leta worried at the blanket around her legs. If only she could talk about what had happened! But her mum would see it when the episode 'casted in a few days. "The room's small but comfortable enough. No complaints. The food is very 'caterers for uninspired corporate meetings,' if you know what I mean. At the bakery, we used to put together lunches like these for clients who wanted to feed lots of people without paying a fortune. Filling enough, but nothing special."

"So, no venison steaks at the manor?"

Leta laughed. "Not for me, at least. More egg and cress sandwiches and sausage rolls. And salads that are mostly lettuce."

"Oh, right."

"I had a poached egg for breakfast."

"You're talking round something. What's the matter?"

What was the matter? Many, many things! But Leta couldn't talk about them. But could she talk around some issues?

"Just a moment," Leta said as she went to check outside her door and make sure no one was eavesdropping. "OK," she said, returning to her blanket nest on the bed. "I just don't understand a lot of these people. Their priorities."

"Is Seer Mirabelle treating you well?"

"Yes, she is. She's been very kind. But some people —" *like Marcus* "—are so cutthroat. It makes me uncomfortable."

Her mum sighed. "I bet. We've all heard rumours about nasty people involved in the media. Is there truth to that?"

Leta hummed.

"The contestants?"

Leta winced. She didn't want to think about them, and how she would soon be set up to bear the brunt of their ire. "I haven't talked to many of them yet. Some seem fine, but some... well."

"They hire them for the drama and the ratings."

"But I thought it would be manufactured drama, you know? That they would make the contestants look more bitchy than they are in real life."

"Are the ones who are more troublesome members of the Geald families?"

"I can't tell you that. It's not general enough for me to say." Though her mother was right. Destiny was from a Geald family.

"Then I'm going to assume they are. Those girls would've been normal if they'd been born to normal families. Power corrupts, and the Geald families have had too much power for too long. As if they were the only ones with magic! They may have been once upon a time, but they sowed so many wild oats over the generations that they're not special anymore. They act the way they do because their families taught them to, so they can hold on to power as much as they can, all because they feel the tides changing and their specialty slipping away."

"I guess so."

"There's no one as greedy as someone who already has nearly everything."

Leta shook her head. It was a simplistic view, but she felt the nuggets of truth in her mother's words. "Well, not all the contestants have been nice to me so far, but does it matter? Most people have either been nice or have ignored me, which suits me fine."

"Most, hm? How about the God Incarnate? Have you met him? Is he in the 'nice' category or the 'ignored me' category?"

"Why assume someone as lowly as me would have much to do with him at all?" She'd never hear the end of it if she said that she'd already talked to Jack several times. And walked straight into him while wearing her pyjamas. Oh, Hunter and Harvester! Her mother would want to hear everything if she got the merest hint of that.

"True," said her mum with a sigh. "True, true. He'd be a 'high and lofty' sort too."

Leta wanted to defend him — he hadn't come across that way to her — but doing such a thing when speaking to her mother would be unwise.

"Anyway, thanks for checking in, Mum. Things are going as fine as can be expected. I know what my role is here—" *alas* "—I can do it, and there are nice people. All good. I'll be back in about five weeks, with some new money in my account that'll tide me over the next phase of my true job hunt." Because this job wasn't a career. Even if she got her course money, she would need to find something else after this contract was over. The thought of looking again filled her with dread. She didn't have faith that she would find something good soon.

"OK, Honey. I won't keep you longer. Have a lovely evening, and best of luck!"

"Bye, Mum. Talk to you later."

Leta cut the call and flopped over sidewards onto the bed. She did at least feel better after talking to her mother, who was right about the contestants. If any of them began behaving nastily towards her over the next few weeks, it would be because someone had taught them to be that way. That didn't mean she was going to be happy to put up with it, but it was still sad, anyway.

THE EMPEROR
UPRIGHT

Look out for those who are important to you! They are counting on you, but do not feel alarmed: you are up to the challenge.

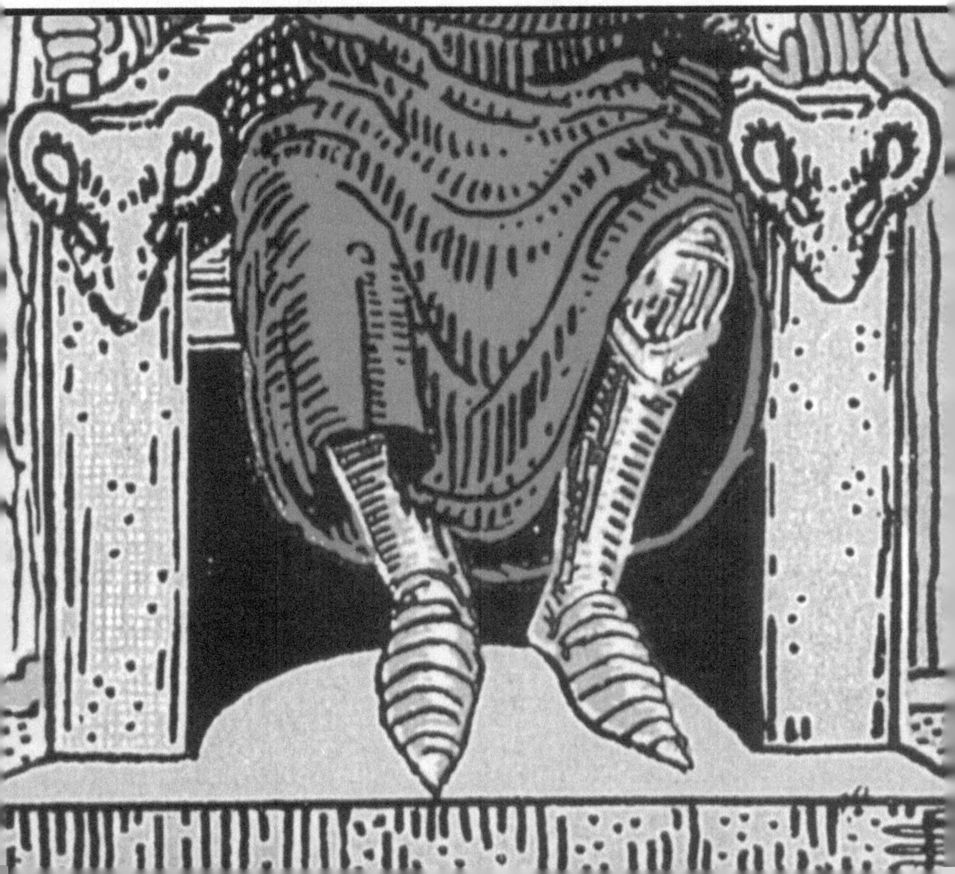

To Constance,

I hope I do not step on your toes this season. I am well aware of your talents. However, I have been tasked by AllAether to perform daily readings for each contestant.

The cards were excited to read for you. The High Priestess was adamant I should pay it special attention. All indications are that your talents will be called upon soon. If I may hazard a guess, the Goddess Incarnate may call upon your help one day.

All the best
Mirabelle

For all that the aethercast chafed Jack's spirit, on the odd occasion, it was pure genius.

He had finished the last of the 'first dates' with the contestants the day before. Now he was in the kitchens to capture the first of the 'shared dates', during which he would do a group activity with four of the contestants. The activity for the morning? Grinding meat and making sausages. The four contestants selected? The most high-born of the lot, those who would never have done such a thing before in their lives.

The point was to push the contestants outside their comfort zones, as that was a known trigger of ascension, particularly if there was another incarnation around.

He'd been allowed to dress more casually than usual. His wardrobe for the aethercast usually involved a suit of some kind, but he was wearing slacks and a fine blue jersey pushed up to his elbows. He felt, if not quite himself, at least half-way there.

Jack entered the kitchen early. He waited in a corner out of the way. The previous season, he had offered help in situations like this, but he had always been met by horrified or embarrassed faces. This year he was trying to remember not to bother people while they worked.

Several assistants bustled around, setting up meat grinders on the long work surface in the middle of the industrial-sized kitchen. They also brought out bowls, chopping boards, aprons, and knives. By the time they were done, there were six near identical work stations.

"Just this way," he heard Marcus's voice outside. A moment later, he led in a woman whose face was familiar, although he couldn't figure out why. Then he felt foolish: he knew her because she was a celebrity. Cinthia Crawcoombs, celebrity chef, often appeared in AllAether's aethercasts. Her trademark blonde bob was just as shiny as it seemed on the globe, but she was smaller than he would have guessed, both in stature and around. She was known for her voluptuous curves, but despite her clothes being chosen to accentuate such a figure, she was slender. Crow's feet were more obvious around her eyes in person, but she still looked nothing like her 50-ish years.

Cinthia walked straight to Jack and held out a hand. "God Incarnate Jack!" she cried in a loud yet smooth contralto. "How lovely to meet you!"

Jack took the proffered hand. "The pleasure is mine."

Cinthia stood beside him and nudged him with an elbow. "So, stuffing sausages, eh? Risqué on AllAether's part, don't you think?"

Jack gaped at her. She'd just met him and she was jumping straight to dick jokes? Sure, she had a reputation for phrasing things saucily, but straight away? Really?

Cinthia looked up at his face and then chortled. "Oh, bless, what a pet you are." She patted him on the arm and then went to check the work stations, still chortling. But as he watched her work, he realised Cinthia was right. Stuffing sausages, indeed. The entire event was a dick joke. Hunter and Harvester!

Marcus took the vacated spot beside Jack. "She's a hoot, isn't she? I've worked with her before and any set she's on has a certain vibe to it."

"I can guess what vibe."

"Is that censure I'm hearing?"

"No," said Jack. "Not at all. The contestants are going to get bulldozed, though, and I don't think they'll be used to it."

"That's the plan, Jack." Marcus cleared his throat. "Speaking of plans, we're going to have that assistant bring you a dummy note. Just give her a flirty smile, read the note, put it in your pocket, and thank her warmly, OK? Let the contestants and their imaginations do the rest of the work."

"Is this really necessary?"

Marcus clapped Jack on the shoulder. "You're a good man, but yes, it is."

Fogarty visited to scope out the layout and add a few specially programmed auto-aethercasters to the fleet in the kitchen. Then everything was in place. Cinthia waited in the large pantry and Jack waited at one of the two middle work stations. Jack and Cinthia knew their cues, and it was time to capture the event.

When Marcus led the contestants into the kitchen, they seemed surprised by what they saw. Some of them hid it better than others. Marcus led each of the contestants to a workstation, two at one end of the bench and two at the other. The first contestant to take her place was Purity. She looked at the cooking implements and package of meat in front of her with a calm, if icy, look. Jack's first 'date' with her had been a walk through the woods, on which she'd been sure-footed and comfortable; not surprising, since the Fernhearts had a huge wooded estate and were renowned for continuing the hunting party tradition, but her woodcraft magic was apparent in the way she stepped silently through the forest. In another life, she would have been a hunter or a tracker. She had been inscrutable, and Jack had learned nothing else about her.

The second contestant was Georgina, a tall stone mage with brown hair and blue eyes. Her family wasn't one of the Geald families, but from what Jack had heard, they often married into them — professional hangers-on. Jack's date with her had been a chilly boat ride on the lake. They had talked about moving to Astmere as adults, which they had both done. She wrinkled her nose when she saw the meat laid out at her workstation.

The third contestant was Constance, the clairvoyant. Jack's first date with her had been cocktails served in a small terrace garden, during which he'd felt like a bug under her scrutiny. He wasn't sure if it was her attitude or her magic that cause the sensation.

The fourth contestant was Destiny. The statuesque redhead had acted sweet and friendly on their lawn croquet date. Destiny paid little attention to the workstation before her, instead smiling and waving at Jack.

When they were all in place, Marcus stood before them and flashed his 'host of an aethercast' grin. "Welcome ladies, God Incarnate Jack. You are here today to get to know one another better, and what better way to do so than through a group activity? Can anyone guess what we're doing today?"

For a moment, no one said anything.

"I believe we are cooking," said Jack, pretending he didn't know what they would be making.

Georgina raised a hand. "Excuse me, but I'm vegetarian."

"Ah," said Marcus. It sounded to Jack like Marcus was well aware of that. "You don't have to eat what you'll make today. You could feed Jack. After all, they say the way to a man's heart is through his stomach."

Jack, plagued with a sudden vision of needing to eat a dozen sausages, said, "Huh?"

Marcus laughed. "Don't worry: we won't force-feed you." Then he held out his hand towards the pantry door.

"We have a special guest with us today to help you with the challenge. Please welcome Cinthia Crawcoombs!"

Cinthia sashayed out of the pantry to stand beside Marcus. "Thank you for having me! I am so excited to be here and take part in this special work you are all doing: looking for the Goddess Incarnate."

Jack was thankful for the reminder of why they were there. Their purpose tended to get lost in the day-to-day bustle of capturing the aethercast.

Cinthia took a further step towards them, so that she could lower her volume. "I'm sure you're all dying to know what we're doing today. I thought we would get back to basics and learn how to make a most humble food, one that no one these days makes for themselves. After all, our goddess was last incarnated in a different time, when different expectations were upon the house-wives of our land." Her airy delivery hinted at disapproval of the attitudes of the past, but Jack rather thought people would only notice it if they were inclined to do so. "Back when we didn't have supermarkets and aetherpod delivery, it was of vital importance," she raised her eyebrows suggestively, "that wives knew how to stuff a sausage for their husbands."

There was shocked silence, and then a small titter of laughter.

"I doubt Julia Sudbury spent time in the kitchen stuffing sausages," said Constance. Had... she not noticed the double entendre? Or was she just ignoring it like Jack?

"Not after she ascended, to be sure," said Cinthia after a brief startled pause and the briefest eyebrow waggle. "But remember, she was a commoner before that. Which is why I have chosen a commoner task. I understand that none of you young ladies would have done this before; am I correct? I wonder if we can shake free any memories from past lives today?"

That was a good point. Natural talents that didn't align with a person's upbringing could indicate a strong connection to a past life.

"All right, everyone: aprons on!" For the next half hour, Cinthia demonstrated making sausages at her station. She made several flavours of sausage, each time talking as if it was the first demonstration, to give the aethercast lots of options to choose from. Jack watched in interest as she cut up both pork shoulder and pork fat; mixed in herbs, spices, and a surprising amount of salt; and ran it through the grinder. She kneaded the resulting mince like it was a bread dough before running it through the stuffer into the casing. It was a hands-on, messy process.

Jack looked around at the contestants. Purity paid close attention. Constance surreptitiously shifted from foot to foot, perhaps tired of standing and waiting. Destiny looked bored. Georgina was green around the gills.

Before long, they were all washing their hands and getting ready to try making sausages for themselves. Then Jack unwrapped his cut of meat and started chopping it. Safest to look busy, and encourage the contestants to get to it as well, so that they wouldn't need to be here all day.

Jack chopped and mixed his ingredients, trying to do as Cinthia had done. It was rather soothing, making something with his hands. For the first time in he wasn't sure how long, he felt useful. It was just sausages, but it felt important somehow in a way that all the aethercast capturing and the publicity never did.

Cinthia paused on the other side of the bench and looked at his work. She raised her eyebrows and nodded. "You don't need to cut things that small for high quality grinders like these, but otherwise, very good, God Incarnate Jack. Have you done this before?"

Something whispered in Jack's mind, something from long ago. Earlier than Archibald. "Not in this life."

Cinthia raised an eyebrow, but made no reply.

Jack paused his work once he had everything mixed ready for the grinder, and washed his hands so that he could take a glass of water. As he did so, he watched the contestants. If this exercise had been planned to bring out any memories of past lives, it had failed miserably. None of the contestants looked comfortable with what they were doing. Cinthia was busy giving them basic instructions and making sure they didn't cut their fingers off. Poor Georgina looked like she was going to be sick. Several auto-aethercasters were pointed in her direction. No doubt her discomfort would be milked for all it was worth in the final aethercast.

"Excuse me, Jack," said Destiny with a smile. "Cinthia is busy down the other end, and you're doing so well. Would you please help me for a moment? I'm a bit confused."

Jack didn't mind helping. "Sure," he said, and walked to her workstation. "What's the problem?"

She pointed at the dish of fat. "This white stuff goes in too, doesn't it?"

"It's pig fat. And yes it does."

"Do I cut it smaller or larger than the meat, or what?"

"About the same will be fine," said Jack.

Destiny gave him a relieved smile. "Thank you, God Incarnate Jack. I'm out of my depth here, but I'm learning quickly, with your help." Destiny glanced up, checking the position of the nearby auto-aethercasters.

Jack plastered a polite smile on his face. She had been doing so well until that moment. He had developed a sense for when people were preparing to play power games, and Destiny's sudden bout of coquettishness was giving him that impression. There were worse power games that could be played than Weaponised Flirtatiousness, of course, but even so. "You're welcome," he said politely but with no additional warmth, and stepped back to his own station. As he turned, he saw Leta in the doorway.

She looked like a mannequin, frozen with fear. She gulped and glanced from person to person, her eyes wide above cheeks with enough pink in them to subdue her freckles. Her hair was loose for once, and makeup accentuated her full lips and storm-grey eyes. Jack recognised the hand of the makeup department in her new look. Her clothes had changed too. She still wore a knee-length skirt, this one of dark green, but she also wore a wraparound v-neck blouse in spring green and a grey blazer the same colour as her eyes. She looked smart, but by the way she had her arms crossed over her front, a folded paper clutched in one hand, she was uncomfortable.

If she were just a messenger, there wouldn't be any reason for Jack to assume the message was for him. But he knew it was, and he knew she hadn't found the courage to enter the kitchens, so he took pity on her. He walked over to meet her in the doorway, the gazes of the contestants behind him so intense they were palpable. Leta watched him approach as if he were her doom.

"May I help you?" he asked when he stopped a few paces from her. Any closer and he feared he would have trouble stopping himself from peeking down the v-neck of her blouse. Which had no doubt been the effect intended by whoever had chosen the blouse for her. He kept his eyes higher, but found himself staring as she worried her plush lip with her teeth. Damn, but he'd like to bite that lip himself. *No! No thoughts like that! Be good!*

Leta flushed crimson under his gaze. She shoved the paper in his direction. "Message for you, God Incarnate, sir." Her voice was small, perhaps too quiet to be heard by the contestants in the room. Jack was uneasy about that. He wanted them to be clear that she was a messenger, not someone who was here for personal reasons. This would all be worse for Leta if they got that impression.

He took the note and opened it.

Don't forget to look happy to see her. Look flirty.
M

Jack held in a sigh, then folded the note and put it in the pocket on his apron. He deliberated: Should he play the part the aethercast had given him and give Leta a flirty smile? Or should he go against what he had been told to do to spare her some of the scrutiny?

"I don't need to send a response. Thank you." In the end, the smile he gave her was neither the flirty leer he had been instructed to give her, nor the more polite, formal smile he had been considering. He wasn't sure how he had smiled at her, but it had been a natural smile that popped out, one unconsidered and brought forth merely by seeing her expectant face. A smile just for her and not for the aethercast at all. In the end, he'd had no power to choose how to react to her.

Leta blinked, surprised. Then she inclined her head and left. Jack leaned out the doorway for a moment to see her scurrying down the hallway as if the Hounds of the Hunter were after her. Then he turned back to the event in the kitchen.

He froze in the doorway, just as Leta had. He was not expecting four sets of eyes focussed on him with such laser intensity. The contestants stared at him with a mix of surprise, suspicion, and puzzlement. He flinched, not only from their regard, but from the sharp glint of magic in Constance's eyes as she activated her clairvoyance while looking at him.

Jack turned to Cinthia instead, hoping for a friendlier visage, but the incorrigible chef gave him an arch look and a small smirk.

WHEEL OF FORTUNE
UPRIGHT

IF YOU ARE KIND TO OTHERS, YOUR GOOD LUCK WILL RETURN SOON.
BE OPEN TO ACCEPTING HELP.

Tiffany,

Take the time to listen to others and learn where they are coming from.

If you reach out, you may make friends on this aethercast.

Mirabelle

p.s. You haven't yet visited for a full reading. I can provide you more advice in person, and I assure you what I read will be confidential.

A yawn overcame Leta. She'd had trouble getting to sleep the night before. Her thoughts had travelled in circles of anxiety, playing over the events of the day. Some part of her had, in retrospect, been won over by Jack's apparent kindness, and she'd expected him to go easy on her when she'd delivered the fake note yesterday. But he hadn't. He'd done exactly what he'd been told to, and treated her with special interest. She'd seen the way the contestants had stiffened with surprise, how the auto-aethercasters had focussed on his reaction to her presence. What a talented actor he was! He'd looked sincerely interested in her. She knew now to take anything she saw from him with a grain of salt. There was now no way of escaping being a part of the aethercast. What would the people back home think when they saw her?

Her only option now was to keep her chin up and pretend it didn't affect her. Never let them see how she was withering under the scrutiny. She could lick her wounds later, when she was home again and her bank account was flush. She could cut her hair, dye it dark, get contacts. She would be fine. She would be forgotten. In five weeks.

She hoped.

Mirabelle was already in the middle of a card reading when Leta reported for duty. Rose-scented incense smoke from an agate burner hazed the air in the coral beams of morning light from the window. "Make yourself a hot drink, dear," said Mirabelle. "You look like you need it."

"Thank you. Can I get you something?"

"No, thank you. Not yet. I like to finish my first readings of the day before I caffeinate."

Leta made herself a coffee and watched Mirabelle at work. She knew better than to disrupt the seer more than was necessary while she was reading the cards.

Mirabelle turned cards over one by one, jotting notes in a spiral-bound notebook. When she finished her reading, she scooped up the cards with a practised flourish and shuffled them back into the deck without even watching her hands.

"Would you be a dear and take my schedule over to Jack and see if you can get him to agree to another private viewing? The cards say he needs it."

Leta hesitated a moment.

"Is there a problem, Leta?"

"No, no, not at all," she said. *Other than the awkwardness of seeing the God Incarnate so soon after he threw me to the wolves.*

She downed the dregs of her coffee, gathered up the schedule book, and headed out to Jack's rooms, hoping that he was a morning person and she wouldn't catch him in his pyjamas. Everything about their brief acquaintance was complicated enough already.

When she got there, she made sure her blazer and scarf covered her blouse, as she wasn't comfortable with the cut Mirabelle had chosen for her. She wasn't used to showing any cleavage. Then she gave the door a light rap. She was about to knock harder when the door swung open. Jack peered out. It didn't look like she'd caught him too early. He'd combed his hair already, at the very least. He blinked at her in surprise. "Good morning?"

Leta brandished the schedule book like a shield. "Mirabelle asked me to schedule another private viewing with her. She said she thinks you might need one."

Jack's eyes widened. "I'm always surprised when seers manage that, even though I know what they do for a living." He pushed the door open and gestured for her to enter. "Come on in."

Leta hesitated at the threshold.

Jack's eyes showed understanding. "This isn't an aethercast-related request. I think the auto-aethercasters are still in night mode. It's just that the hallway's chilly and I'm not enjoying the draught." He gestured more expansively for her to come in.

Leta looked around and spied an auto-aethercaster resting on a hall table, its globe dark. Leta eased past it through the doorway, expecting at any moment to see its soulless lens swing in her direction. But it didn't react to their conversation or her movement.

Jack's rooms were a similar size and style of furnishings as Mirabelle's, but in red and gold rather than blue and cream. The air smelled of coffee and furniture polish. Jack looked more out of place than the ever-pristine Mirabelle. He was wearing track pants and the same woolly cardigan he had been wearing the other day. He looked very comfortable, though. Even his hair was more at ease, with bits flopping down over his forehead. *Oh no*, thought Leta. *It's a good look. Don't think about his looks, Leta! No getting flustered!*

He waved her to a chair. "Tea? Coffee?"

"No thanks, I just had one." She took a seat.

"All right." He fetched a schedule book of his own.

They spent a few moments looking it over until they discovered a common gap later in the day. "I'll report back to Mirabelle," said Leta.

"Thank you." He escorted Leta to the door. "Uh, sorry for yesterday," he said. "I know you weren't comfortable with what Marcus was asking of us. I wasn't sure how to play it."

"So you just did as you were told?" Leta asked, then winced. That was rude of her. She shouldn't let on how upset she was. So much for keeping her chin up. She needed more practise. "Sorry, God Incarnate, sir. That was out of line. I'll get going now."

He looked at her, puzzled. "Did as I was told... uh... I'm sorry." He ran a hand through his hair. "I didn't mean to cause you grief. We're both in a bit of an awkward position here, aren't we?"

Leta pursed her lips. She couldn't see how the God Incarnate could be as helpless as her, who was just an assistant. But she'd let him play his game. She was, after all, only going to be working this job for a few weeks, and then she would be off doing what she really wanted to be doing. "As you say, sir. I should go now."

Jack sighed. "All right."

Leta slipped out the door. Jack closed it behind her.

Leta was so occupied with her puzzlement and discomfort that she nearly ran into someone — one of the contestants, the brunette called Tiffany, who she'd had a run-in the other day with two others while delivering the dailies. Tiffany put her hands on her hips. "What in the High Hunt? Destiny was right. You are some flirt trying to get your hooks into Jack!"

"I beg your pardon?" said Leta, flushing at the implications. She glanced up and spied the auto-aethercaster nearby. It was no longer in night mode, but instead swung to focus on them. Just what she didn't want!

"Oh, come on," said Tiffany, her eyebrow raised. "Coming out of his rooms in the morning?"

Leta hefted the schedule book. "I'm working, that's all. For Mirabelle. I was in there for only a few minutes."

"A likely story."

Leta sighed. This was all playing out according to her fears. She could dump Jack in it, she supposed, and claim that he was unprofessional. He'd certainly seemed so yesterday, giving her, an assistant, flirty looks. But this aethercast, this task they all shared, was for a bigger purpose, whether anyone else remembered. This was all for the Goddess Incarnate, whoever she was. She had to do right by her goddess, if no one else. "I don't mind if you believe me. Believe that *he's* taking things seriously, though. He's looking for his goddess. He won't get distracted by anyone who isn't her." Leta looked around. "Why are you over in this wing, by the way?"

"N-nothing at all. Just going for a morning stroll."

Leta glanced at the auto-aethercaster. She was tempted to leave Tiffany to it, but she wasn't sure that her conscience would sit well with her doing nothing. She leaned towards the other woman for a quieter word. "That auto-aethercaster there won't even bother recording me because I'm not important enough." Leta gulped, remembering that wasn't really true anymore, but she didn't want any of the contestants getting wind of that. "But you could be causing drama, so it'll be recording you. You do anything to cause a sensation, and it will make the final capture of the aethercast. Do you want that? Really? Because you don't have any control over how the network spins it."

Tiffany flicked her eyes up to the auto-aethercaster, but said nothing.

"Or do you perhaps want to come with me and we do something innocuous like schedule you in for a private viewing with Mirabelle?" Leta continued. She held up the schedule book. "You were on your way to find *me*, right? Because you want to see Mirabelle?"

The other woman's eyes hardened. "I don't need your help." She pointed up at the auto-aethercaster, and only then did Leta notice it wasn't pointing its lens down at them as it had been a moment before; it was pointing up at the ceiling. "How—?"

Tiffany shrugged and gave a smug grin.

Leta's eyebrows shot up. "You're a multi-talent?" she whispered. She must be, because Tiffany had already demonstrated light magic, and the auto-aethercasters ran on aether magic. "Does the network know?" It was considered bad form for a multi-talent to keep magic types hidden, because hidden magics were often used for crime. Though of course, many multi-talents did.

Tiffany shrugged. "It's on my school record. Up to them to check, no?"

Leta sighed. It irked her that this woman had more than one magic while Leta had none, but she didn't want to let on that she was bothered. Chin up and all that. "I bet that thing can still hear, though," she said instead. "And what about others? My help is still available." She started walking along the hallway, leaving Tiffany to make up her own mind. A moment later, she heard footsteps as Tiffany rushed to catch up. She led the woman to a bench seat further along the corridor, where they pencilled Tiffany in for a viewing on Sunday afternoon.

"Have you had one of these yet?"

"No. I was told to, but I hadn't got around to it yet."

"Seer Mirabelle is very good at what she does. She'll give you good advice and guidance." Leta stood and snapped the schedule book shut. "I'd better get back to Mirabelle. And you had better get back to the contestant wing."

Tiffany nodded, though she gave the corridor to Jack's room another speculative glance. "Hey, uh, for the record," she said, not looking at Leta. "I just wanted a quick word with him. It's difficult to even tell if there's a connection there, if I could even be the goddess, with all of this scheduling and whatnot. How are we even supposed to get to know him if there's no time for a humble chat?"

It was a valid point. How were they supposed to tell? It wasn't clear. "The network doesn't know what will set off the goddess's ascension. They're just guessing. So I guess I see where you're coming from. But maybe try talking to him at meals times or something?"

Tiffany shrugged. "I try. But there's eight of us." She stood. "See you later."

Leta shook her head as she watched the other woman walk away. Why had she meddled? It wasn't her problem if a contestant caused drama and scandal. But she couldn't help but feel camaraderie now, even if it wasn't returned. They were all being manipulated into telling a ratings-worthy story. Leta looked towards Jack's suite. Him too, of course. Leta wondered if she'd been too harsh. She didn't know how much pressure he was under.

Leta sighed. At least AllAether didn't seem to know everything. Had the higher-ups realised they'd brought in a contestant with aethercast magic, one who could circumvent their auto-aethercasters?

JACK WAITED IN THE manor ballroom, preparing himself for another few hours of being 'on' for the auto-aethercasters while they captured the other group activity. He wasn't alone; a dance instructor and Marcus were talking on the other side of the ballroom, something about the music choices and the order in which the contestants should be called upon. The dance instructor was a middle-aged woman in a flowing dress and worn black dance shoes, who wore golden hoops on her ears and lots of tinkling bracelets.

The four contestants were heralded by their auto-aethercasters swooping into the room. The four women who would be joining him for ballroom dancing were Jess, Chrissie, Nellie, and Tiffany. All the women were wearing dresses, though there was a mix of casual and more formal dresses between them. Perhaps that was a test. Would the audience judge the 'formal' dressers as the winners or the 'casual' dressers?

The contestants stood in a line once they were in the ballroom. Some waited patiently, and some with furtive glances at Jack to one side and the instructor to the other.

The instructor moved to the middle of the room and commanded attention with a flourish and a chiming of her bangles. "My name is Geraldine, and I will be your instructor," she said. "We're going to learn some common ballroom dances, and of course, have a lot of fun!"

Jack had a crash course in ballroom dancing a few years prior when the Geald families who had snapped him up when he returned to the country — those families with financial ties to the network who had decided to make a profit off him — panicked when they saw how common he was and arranged etiquette lessons. He wasn't worried about performing this segment.

Tiffany looked very confident, of course. It was hard to tell with her if her confidence had a basis, though. Nellie, as always, seemed to be a million miles away; Jess looked excited; and Chrissie looked faintly ill.

Geraldine pointed at an amused-faced Marcus. "Hit it," she said. He turned the music on; it was a tango. She waved Jack over. "Here, please let me demonstrate. Do you know how to tango?"

"Yes, I do."

"Excellent. You may lead. Girls, watch me closely."

Jack danced a basic tango with the instructor. For all she said he was leading, she still corrected his form with subtle guidance. "Good, good. You'll do fine." She then pointed at Marcus. "You, do you know how to tango?"

"Me?" he said in surprise. "I'm the host. Ignore me."

"We need another man or we'll be here all day. Come on over."

Marcus made a big show of caving in and jogging over to demonstrate that he could also tango.

"Good, good," said Geraldine. "You, and you, pick a man." She pointed at Tiffany and Nellie.

Surprising no one, Tiffany strode straight over to Jack. Nellie was left to approach Marcus. While they sorted out the pairs, Geraldine returned to the audio player and restarted the music, then stood with the two contestants who were waiting their turn. "Let's critique them, shall we?"

For the next hour, Jack danced with each of the contestants. Of all of them, Nellie was the best dancer, and Chrissie had no idea what she was doing.

He fought the entire time to give equal attention to all the contestants. Tiffany wasn't shy about approaching him. On the other hand, Jess was difficult to give enough attention to because she was hogging Marcus's attention instead. That was interesting, but none of his business. It wouldn't go well, though.

Although it was a secret from the public, Marcus already had a partner: an older girlfriend who had financed his breakthrough into the entertainment industry. Jack hadn't met her, but he had spied Marcus on a dinner date in a private restaurant back room once. Marcus's partner had turned away from Jack in such a way that he suspected he should know who she was, and he even suspected who, based on the haircut, but it was all hush-hush.

Jack was almost enjoying himself. Or maybe he was just proud of himself for doing OK with the dancing and not messing up. It was a nice boost to his ego after the day before. Cinthia had announced he had a 'heavy hand' on the spice, and declared Purity's sausages to be the winners of the day.

Maybe hubris was his downfall, but eventually he did mess up. While dancing with Tiffany again, he spotted a furtive Leta in the doorway, trying to flag down Marcus, a sheaf of paper in her hands. He looked at her a moment too long, waiting for a hailing that never came, so sure that the message would be for him. He stood on Tiffany's foot, and then nearly tripped over when he backed off in a hurry.

"Are you all right?" he asked Tiffany.

"Yes, fine," she said, though she looked like she was wincing.

Marcus guffawed. He'd been watching. Jack rose an eyebrow at him and pointed to Leta in the doorway. "I think you have a message from Seer Mirabelle."

Jack watched out the corner of his eye as Marcus took some papers from Leta, scanned them, and stuffed them into a folder by the door. Marcus smiled and patted Leta on the shoulder as if they were friends. Leta froze, clearly uncomfortable, and Marcus flicked his eyes to Jack to see his reaction. Then he must have dismissed Leta, because she bowed and stepped into the hallway. As she left, she looked over at Jack, and her eyes widened when she caught him looking. With a jolt of embarrassment, Jack returned his attention to his dance partner. Tiffany was giving him a speculative look.

"Shall we continue?" he asked.

"Sure, unless there's someone else you'd rather dance with?"

Bloody hell, Jack. Get a hold of yourself! he despaired, wondering what they had captured of his reaction, how it would be spun in the aethercast. Jack sighed and held his hands out to Tiffany, forcing himself to be ready to dance again.

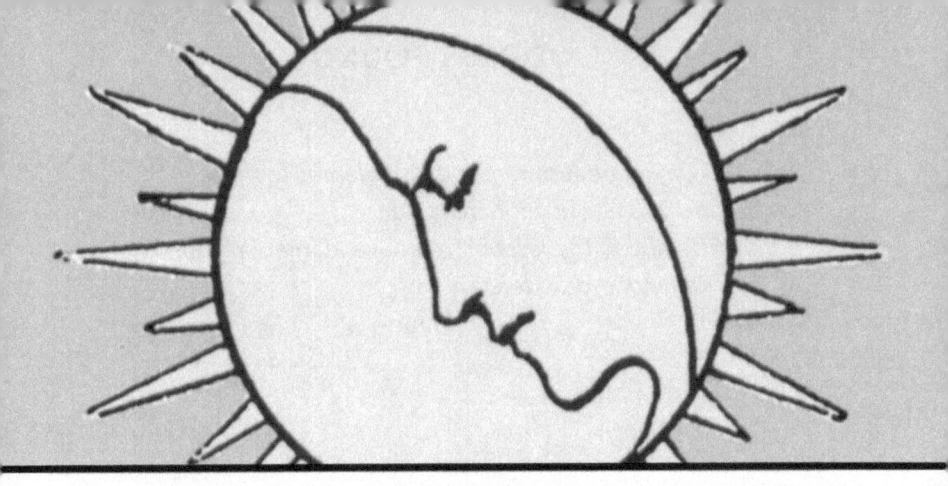

THE MOON
UPRIGHT

THE WOUNDS OF THE PAST CUT DEEPER THAN YOU REALISED.
IT'S TIME TO ADDRESS THOSE OLD WOUNDS SO YOU CAN MOVE ON.

Destiny,
How you treat others speaks volumes to those
around you about your character.
Rise above the lessons you have learned in your
life. Be kind and understanding.
Mirabelle

Leta stayed well clear of Mirabelle's rooms while Jack had his private viewing. Interacting with him where other people could observe felt awkward after the morning with Tiffany. And then she had seen Jack and Tiffany dancing together...

Perhaps Mirabelle had noticed her avoidance when she said she wanted to get some fresh air, but she hesitated to ask Mirabelle what she had intuited.

She dallied in the gardens longer than intended, and returned well after Jack left. "There you are, dear," said Mirabelle. "We have been asked to attend a staff meeting. It will be a catch-up session to make sure we're all still on the same page, so to speak."

"Me too?"

"Why not? If anyone questions it, say you are there to take minutes for me. Actually, could you do so? And I'd love to hear your observations on the people at the meeting. I think that... I shouldn't say anything. But I would love your insight."

The fact that Mirabelle was concerned about the crew of the aethercast right after talking to Jack... that was surely related. "I'm not sure how valuable my insight would be, but I'll do what I can."

They headed to the boardroom. "Has the aethercast begun 'casting to the public yet?" asked Leta on the way. "I'm not sure about the schedule."

"Not yet," said Mirabelle, as the click of her cane echoed off the panelled walls around them. "The aethercast lags behind the capture, to give AllAether time to process the footage and weave a narrative. By the time the 'cast starts, we will only have about one more week at this location before we move to the hotel in Astmere."

The aethercast would use a different location for the second half of the season, some ultramodern, fancy hotel that Leta would never have had a chance of staying in otherwise.

"Good," said Leta, scuffing her feet on the dense wool runner rug she walked on. "Good, good. I'm not looking forward to a certain episode being released, is all."

Mirabelle patted her on the shoulder. "All will be well, I assure you. I have a friend outside the production who will watch the 'cast. We're in regular contact, even now. Shall I ask him to keep an eye out for how you are portrayed, and let me know so I may tell you?"

Leta chewed her lip. "I'm not sure I want to know. Maybe if it's not too bad?"

"Understood."

They arrived at the boardroom. Just as on the first day, Mirabelle sat at the table while Leta took a seat down the back. The room wasn't as full as last time, because only the more important people and those assisting them were present. At the table sat people like Fogarty the aethercaster, Marcus, and other production staff and heads of departments. Jack was absent. At the head of the table sat a woman Leta hadn't seen before. She had steel grey hair and wore a light grey pantsuit and pearl earrings.

When everyone had arrived, Marcus stood. "Good afternoon. Thank you for coming. For those of you who are newer, may I present Evelyn Windrift, the chair of the board. Evelyn is interested in how the aethercast is progressing."

Evelyn steepled her fingers. "Thank you for having me. Please, act as if I'm not here."

As if we could forget you're here with that sort of aura! thought Leta. The woman's presence was intimidating in a way that didn't make sense to Leta; it was more than just her position above the company, or her family name, which was one of the Geald family names. She felt dangerous, like a shark. *I wonder what her magic is. Is she a natural battle mage? Maybe that's why she is involved in an aethercasting network. We haven't needed battle mages for decades.*

"Ok," said Marcus. "Fogarty; your area is the most critical. How is the auto-aethercaster fleet going?"

"We're getting great captures," said the grizzled man. "Just like last year, the contestants sometimes forget about them and we've been getting some candid stuff." He talked for about 10 minutes about the minutiae of his week's work. Leta took some notes, mostly for herself, because she was sure Mirabelle knew how all of this worked. But to Leta the details were interesting, and now relevant to herself — may the High Hunt take Marcus for making it so. Evelyn had the look about her of a woman listening closely to every word.

"Thanks, Fogarty, for that detailed account," said Marcus. He flicked his eyes to Leta. "And I can report that we've set a few things in motion to heighten tension among the contestants."

Leta's stomach flipped. Was she being brought up as a topic of conversation in the meeting? No! She forced her shoulders back. She would keep her chin up, no matter what.

But Marcus didn't elaborate. Evelyn gave Leta a close look, then turned to Marcus. "That one? Really?" she murmured, but her voice reached the entire room, any-way.

Marcus shrugged and murmured something back that Leta didn't catch, but he made the universal 'big boobs' gesture, which made Evelyn smirk and look at Leta's chest. Leta flushed red and crossed her arms. The perusal made her feel squirmy and violated. Her bust size was not relevant!

Thankfully, Marcus left the topic there. "Mirabelle? How are things on your end?"

Mirabelle sat up straight in her seat. "Very interesting this year; very interesting indeed. I've had one private reading with each of the contestants except one who I will see tomorrow. I've also had two private viewings with Jack. All of my divination methods have much to say this year, particularly when reading for Jack. I think some-thing exciting may happen."

Marcus grinned, and Evelyn raised an eyebrow.

"Excellent," said Marcus. "Now…"

"I haven't quite finished, Marcus," said Mirabelle. "I believe Jack feels the aethercast is losing its purpose. We need to reassure him we are all looking for the Goddess Incarnate. We have nothing if we don't have him."

Leta started. Was that a possibility? For Jack to leave the aethercast?

"Have you been encouraging such thoughts with your divinations?" asked Marcus.

"Of course not. I don't encourage; I reveal. If the cards or the bones have said anything along those lines, it is because that is the truth of the matter. And as for what he sees in the crystal ball, I don't even know what that is. You should come to me for a reading of your own, Marcus, so you can see how I operate. I made you such an offer last year, but you declined." She folded her hands on the table in front of her with an air of 'I've said my piece.'

"Jack won't be leaving the aethercast," said Marcus. "The penalties of his contract are too high. All of you," he added, pointing his finger in a sweep of the room, "don't speak or act like you think that could be a possibility. We don't want the public to lose confidence in us because of baseless rumours. He will stay, and he will stick to the schedule."

"But shouldn't our schedule be structured around finding the goddess, wherever she may be?" asked Mirabelle.

"May I interrupt here?" said Evelyn in a way that made it clear she was not asking a question. "We think the strategy we have put forth for the show will find the goddess, if not this year, then within the next few seasons. Jack himself has come from within the commoners. Therefore, it is likely that the goddess will come from within or near the Geald families. All we have to do is throw him in with all the young women of about the right age and status until we try the right one, and she ascends within his presence when they interact enough. Short of finding the right resonant string within the ley lines, which we know from other countries' searches is challenging to predict, we have no more reliable way of doing it than in these longer periods of dates and conversations."

"I am well aware of the ley line research, and that it has not yet yielded a result. I understand why ascension takes a while," said Mirabelle. "But why do we think she must be among the families?"

"Simon?" Evelyn said to a spectacled man, the Incarnation Historian employed by the aethercast. "Your work was part of our decision-making process. Can you elaborate?"

Simon cleared his throat and adjusted his collar. "Well, I could give you a detailed account of the history of the Gods and Goddesses Incarnate..."

"…Please don't," said Evelyn.

"Then, suffice it to say, at least one of them is always of the families or closely related lines, even if the other is not; at least within our own country. The Gods and Goddesses Incarnate of other regions don't all follow this pattern. But ours do."

"It could be coincidence," said Mirabelle. "We have a responsibility to consider that."

"We have a responsibility to entertain our audience," said Evelyn. "This aethercast is a moneymaker for our shareholders. That is our top priority. What do you want to do: follow Jack around as he talks to every waitress and bank teller or whatever in the land to see if he hits it off with one? No one would want to watch that!"

Leta wondered if the 'she must come from the families' line was just an excuse for them to structure the show the way they wanted to. After all, despite what they liked to think, the blood of the families *was* everywhere. That's why magic was now everywhere too. It's what thousands of years of Geald men who couldn't keep it in their trousers had wrought.

"Listen, Mirabelle," said Marcus. "I know you mean well, but if you muddle Jack's head, you're just going to stress him. Let's just focus on one thing at a time, eh?"

Mirabelle pursed her lips. "Yes, one thing at a time," she said in a measured voice.

"Good." He looked down at the page of notes in front of him. "And if you don't do the right thing, I'm sure we can find another seer."

Leta gaped. Had he just threatened to fire Mirabelle for bringing up valid concerns?

When the meeting moved on to the next item, Mirabelle gave Leta a long look. *Did you hear that? Heed it well*, her expression seemed to say.

Leta wished she hadn't needed to sign away her ability to talk to family about the details of the aethercast to get this job because she really wanted to talk to her mother about it.

THE CONVERSATIONS AROUND the table were bad enough, but it was the sharp clink of cutlery on fine porcelain that got into Jack's head. He sat at the head of the table in the dining room, partaking of his daily 'social meal'. The contestants sat at the long table, though their seating positions changed each day.

That evening, to his left sat Jess and to his right, Destiny. Jess spent the meal talking to Georgina, who sat on her other side. Meanwhile, Destiny was polite and friendly, but she never seemed to remember that he might be eating instead of paying her undivided attention. He bore Destiny's conversation with as much grace as he could, and told himself she was probably a nice person — it was just the way she had been raised. She had big only child energy, which, to be honest, Jack probably had too, as he was also an only child.

Leta hadn't yet delivered the daily divinations. A knot of worry squirmed in Jack's belly. He was sure that Marcus had arranged for Leta to deliver them at dinner, for maximum chaos. Leta hadn't been around when he'd had a private viewing the day before, which both relieved and annoyed him. He wasn't examining why; he was too busy. Then he'd had a frustrating reading with Mirabelle. Nothing had changed from the week before, and it had all felt rather pointless, which was not how he usually felt about her viewings. He even saw the same vision in the crystal ball. Perhaps the emerald green fabric was clearer, the screams more urgent. But that told him nothing more than he already knew. After so much experience being guided by Mirabelle's viewings, it seemed strange to feel cut adrift from what the bones and cards could tell him.

As if summoned by his musings, Leta edged into the dining room, a tight expression on her face and her chin held high as she looked at the hovering auto-aethercasters. Jack was used to them, but still felt uncomfortable. Their presence must be torture for Leta, who hadn't consented to being used by AllAether this way, or at least hadn't intended to. It wasn't something that she could ask other members of the crew for advice about, either. Usually, people were either a part of the aethercast, such as the contestants, Jack, Mirabelle, or Marcus; or they weren't, such as the rest of the crew. AllAether liked to pretend that the aethercast just 'happened' and hide the people who did all the important work. Poor Leta now occupied a liminal space, supposedly a part of the background, but one who was 'accidentally on purpose' being slipped into the edges of the foreground, all to cause tension and boost ratings.

Leta murmured, "Pardon me," as she approached the table with her usual stack of dailies. Someone had divested Leta of her blazer to reveal one of her new blouses that was cut to show her figure. It didn't seem like a choice she'd made for herself. Jack tried not to look at her curves that were on display, but he couldn't keep his forearm from tingling, remembering what those curves felt like in his arms.

Leta started delivering the dailies to the contestants, placing them on their napkins. At first, the others ignored her. Then Tiffany saw her and said, "Oh, it's you."

"Don't mind me," she said. "I'll be out of the way soon."

"Take your time; don't hurry," said Jack, hoping to avoid stressing her. Apparently, it was the wrong move.

Destiny looked up at Leta, her eyes sharpening. "Oh, look; a *Mundane*. That really brings down the quality of the company."

There were a few muffled gasps along the table. Leta froze. Her face turned first ashen, then red. She kept her chin up and continued her task, but there was now a tightness in her movements and her jaw that was painful to watch.

Marcus had already spilled the beans about Leta's magical status to Jack, but he was sure it was something she would want kept secret. She must be horrified by what Destiny had just revealed to everyone. There weren't many people with too little magic to have a specialty anymore, and they usually tried to avoid drawing attention to the fact.

Jack turned to Destiny. She'd been nice to Jack so far; belatedly he realised that, like many others, how she treated him wouldn't be at all indicative of how she treated people who weren't a God Incarnate. That was a lesson he was having trouble wrapping his head around. What Destiny had done, outing her like that, was rude. It was also exactly the sort of thing AllAether would build upon for the drama. He wondered how Destiny had even known about Leta's status. But it didn't matter. All he could do was to take charge of the situation.

"On this aethercast, we treat the crew with respect, thank you," he said.

There were murmurs along the length of the table. None of the contestants had seen him put his foot down before. He supposed his behaviour would seem out of place. But those who had known him before he ascended would know that he didn't suffer fools. He'd always called people out when they were being dicks, and done his best to put them on the right path. Maybe it was time to reclaim more of who he had been before AllAether tried to change him.

A frown marked Destiny's brow, and spots of colour appeared on her cheeks. "Is that what you were doing the other day, when you left us during the group activity to flirt with her? Don't let people like that drag you down to their level, God Incarnate Jack. You have a responsibility to rise above such things."

Jack looked at Destiny for a long moment, considering how this all looked. He'd defended Leta on instinct, and because he thought it was the right thing to do, but by Destiny's reaction and Leta's tense shoulders, it hadn't been the right choice. It had just made Destiny blurt everything out and play into Marcus's hands. He looked along the table. Everyone was looking at either Jack or Leta, some looking surprised, some looking angry.

Jack returned his attention to Destiny. If he was to do what Marcus wanted, he'd say something that would keep their suspicions up. But he couldn't bring himself to do so. "That's a bold claim. I wonder why you said that?" Some of the other contestants gave Destiny questioning looks.

Leta was still working her way around the table despite the tension, her mouth a grim line. She paused by his shoulder to deliver his daily. "It's all right," she murmured when she was near his shoulder.

"What are you whispering to him?" said Destiny. She ripped her own daily out of Leta's hand as she passed.

Leta didn't react to Destiny's words, and Jack didn't intervene either, though he wanted to. He made a mental note to avoid Destiny as much as possible.

"You're far too nice, Jack," said Destiny, leaning towards him and lowering her voice so it wouldn't carry to the auto-aethercasters. "You don't need to be nice to people who don't have your best interests in mind, not in your position. In fact, it's better if you aren't because otherwise you'll encourage people to take advantage of you. It's sad, but it's true. I've seen it all too often. People like that are always trying to get a leg up using people like us."

Was she trying to imply she was only saying those things for his benefit, while cruelly tearing down a person with less status than her? What a piece of work. Jack gave her a cool look and then opened his daily, needing the distraction.

Jack,

   The bones are concerned about your wellbeing today. How are you holding up? Currents swirl throughout our land, indicating that you are distressed. I will try to speak on your behalf, but alas, I cannot make promises.

   I know that we will speak later today, and so this note is but brief. I fear that my daily divination for you portends emotional strife and interpersonal conflict. But something great will happen soon to balance it out.

   Be cautious of your words.

   Mirabelle

Jack sighed. She'd done this reading before holding his private reading earlier that afternoon. If it had been delivered on time, rather than held up for dramatic effect, it would have been more useful. He might have held his tongue. Jack glanced up at Leta, who was already leaving, her shoulders hunched. The announcement that she was a Mundane would go out to the nation. He'd made a right mess of things for her. She may never want to speak to him again.

He looked around the room to see how the contestants would take the altercation. Following his lead, many of them were perusing their daily readings. Destiny humphed, but flicked guilty eyes in Jack's direction. Had she, too, received a belated warning?

Jack returned to his meal. While he ate, he pondered. He shouldn't barge around like a bull in a crockery shop. Marcus had made him an integral part of another person's wellbeing during her job. He had to do better. In fact, it would be better for Leta if he didn't pay her any attention at all, despite what AllAether wanted. Maybe then contestants like Destiny would leave her alone.

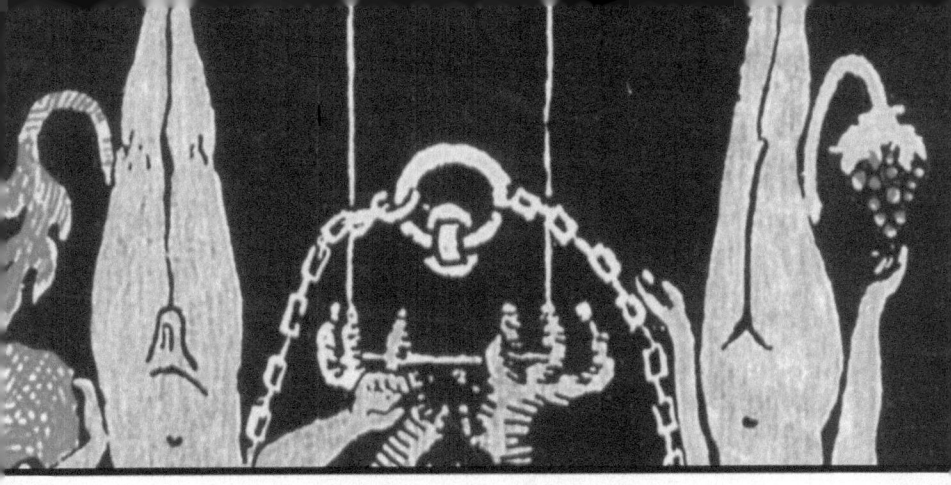

THE DEVIL
REVERSED

What are you anxious about? What are you scared of? What is the worst that can happen? It's OK to feel these things. You will be fine, so long as you don't let these fears rule you.

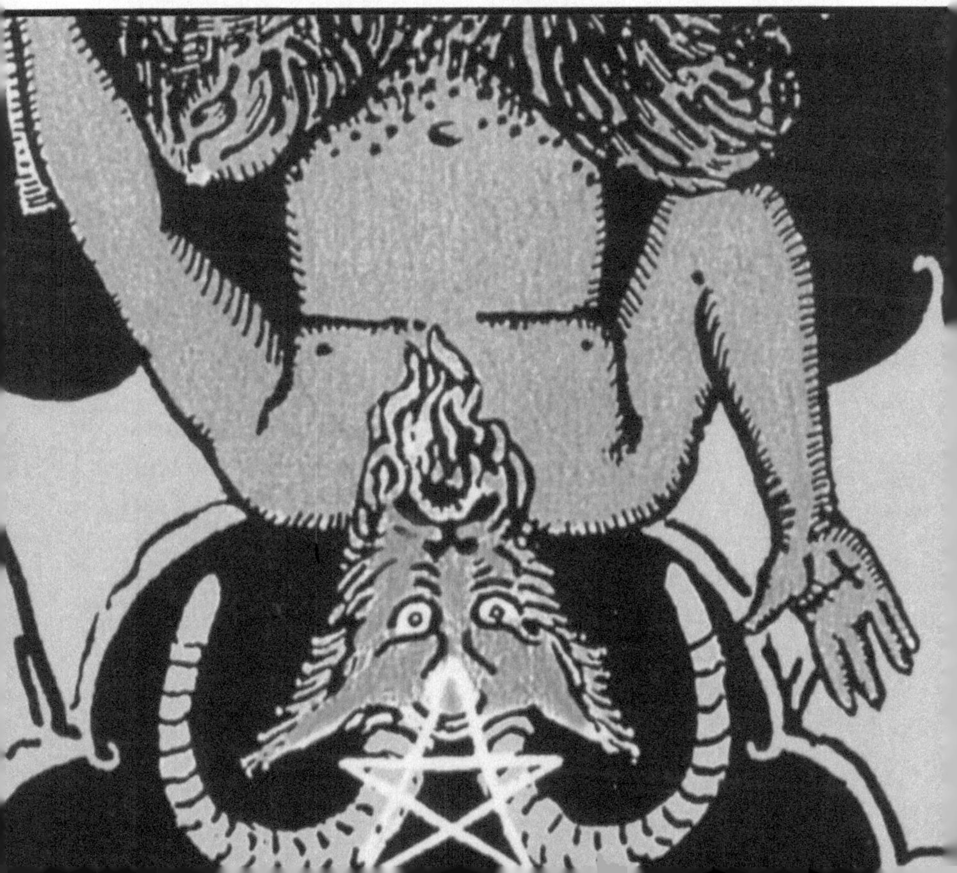

Marcus,

OK, yeah, I see it now. Capture's getting some good moments: Caught J having a sneaky peek down her cleavage. Contestants look pissed.

We're still not getting a good capture of the girl, though. She looks scared. This plot line won't have legs if that's all we get from her. Can you get some female drooling or whatever? At least some blushes. We want the audience at home to wonder if they're banging.

Evelyn

So, it had happened. Someone had outed her as having no magic. In front of all the contestants. In front of all the auto-aethercasters, and therefore in front of the nation. And worst of all: in front of Jack.

What had she done to earn such ire from Destiny, other than exist? And OK, be set up by AllAether to be the enemy of the contestants. Oh, and catch Destiny having a weird conversation with a shady person?

OK, it made sense.

Fuck my life, she thought to herself for the thousandth time. No matter what, there would be no way now that she'd be getting a decent job after the aethercast finished. She'd better come out of this experience with enough money to get herself a small business where she could hire herself, or she'd be bludging off her mother forever.

She'd lain low since the altercation, or at least as low as she could while doing her job. Everyone at the manor now knew she was a Mundane. Everyone. Some looked at her with pity, some with quizzical looks like they were not sure why she was even there. It was uncomfortable, but at least better than the sneers she had received at high school. Her worry stone got heavy use, though, as she worked through her feelings.

Leta had been so embarrassed by Jack hearing Destiny's cruel words that for the next few days, she had begged another messenger to deliver his dailies. Until she had to see him because the network pushed her into it, she wanted to stay clear. Jack had stood up for her, but that too had embarrassed her, especially because she knew how Destiny would spin it. Exactly how AllAether wanted her to spin it.

On Tuesday she'd been braver and had delivered his daily under the door like normal. Now on Wednesday, she had to find more bravery, because Marcus had told them that right now was the perfect time for Mirabelle to make an appointment for a private viewing with him again. Like, right now. She clutched the schedule book to her chest as she walked, afraid to her bones of what was brewing.

There was no answer when she knocked on the door of Jack's suite. She went looking for him, first in the dining room, then in the common room that the contestants were using, then in the executive suite. She was about to start searching the manor from top to bottom when a grip took pity on her.

"You look lost," he said. "Can I help?"

"I've been asked to find Jack for something. He was scheduled for downtime, but I can't find him."

"I think I saw him in exercise clothes not so long ago. Have you checked the gym?"

"No; where's that?"

"In that big outbuilding round the back. It used to be the stables."

Leta held in a sigh. Why had Marcus deemed it so important to make sure Leta ran into Jack while he was busy exercising? "Thank you," she said to the grip.

Leta found the building easily enough. The whir of cardio machines and the clink of weights sounded from within. It wasn't her favourite of environments. She much preferred gardening and brisk walking for maintaining health. She pushed through the double doors into the foyer and peeked through the frosted glass doors into the gym proper.

A handful of people were working out. Two of the contestants — Chrissie, the giggly blonde, and Georgina, whose long brown hair was tied up in a bun for exercise — were on the ellipticals; a man Leta wasn't familiar with was lifting dumbbells; a female grip Leta did recognise was using the leg press; and Jack was using the pully-downy-thing — what was it called? *The lat pull-down*, Leta reminded herself. She had learnt them all during PE at school. She hadn't expected to remember them. Even here, in the gym, auto-aethercasters spun in the air, on the lookout for drama.

She watched Jack for a long moment. She hadn't appreciated until she saw him working out in a tank top how broad across the shoulders he was. Every time he reached up to release the weight of the machine, the muscles of his shoulders, back, and sides expanded and contracted in a well-practised rhythm.

He hadn't noticed her yet. She tip-toed into the room, keeping herself small so that she wouldn't snag her clothes on any of the equipment. She wasn't dressed for an environment like this. When she came far enough into Jack's field of view that he noticed her, his eyes widened and he set his weight machine at rest. He didn't smile like he had in the past, just waited.

"Sorry to bother you, but Mirabelle sent me to pencil you in for another private viewing."

"Sure," he said. "Is there a gap in her schedule on Saturday morning?"

She flicked through the book. "Yes, there is. At ten am."

"That sounds great. Thank you." His tone made his words sound like a dismissal.

"Ah, OK," said Leta as she wrote the booking in. "Thank you. Enjoy your workout."

As she turned to leave, she saw the two contestants on the ellipticals watching their interaction and whispering among themselves. Chrissie giggled. Points of heat flaming on her cheeks, Leta hurried out of the gym, her shoulders back and her chin high.

She took a moment to gather her thoughts outside. Jack seemed so less friendly than normal. Was that a part of why Marcus had sent her? Was this a game? Something to further increase tension in the aethercast? It took all of her self-control to keep in a holler of anger. She hated being manipulated, being used. How dare they? She was a person with wants and needs, not a prop to be moved around the set at the producer's whim!

Leta couldn't bring herself to go back into the manor with her feelings roiling the way they were. Mirabelle wouldn't need her again for a little while. She briefly considered going into the kitchens again and helping with the catering, but her feet moved of their own accord down a garden path, around a formal garden, and towards a more wooded part of the grounds.

She found a path that led into a copse. Oak leaves lay thick on the path, rustling as she slid her boots through the piles. Overhead, the branches still bore some orange and brown leaves, providing enough shade to make her feel protected and hidden, but not enough to rob what remained of the warmth of autumn from the air. Leta breathed deep of the loamy smell of nature, subtly different from home but close enough to provide comfort. A tight sensation in her chest that she hadn't even noticed eased away. Her shoulders relaxed, and she smiled for what felt like the first time in an age.

Hunter and Harvester, I missed this!

Not this copse, of course, because she'd never been there. But just getting out, taking a walk in the fresh air, amongst nature. She was used to taking rambling walks around her village for exercise and to clear her mind. She hadn't had a chance since arriving at the manor.

The copse turned out to be more of a small wood. The path carried on for a while, twisting around vast, sprawling oaks that must have been there since before the manor. As she rounded one such venerable oak, a small wooden building came into view at the end of the path. No, not a building. A temple.

Leta stood at the antlered arch for a moment, eyeing up the size of the lichen growing on the standing stones. The arch, if not the temple itself, was ancient. The wooden temple beyond, though newer, likely outdated the manor. It was probably a registered Historic Location. Leta looked around, but with only trees to observe, she saw no problem in stepping through the archway.

The stone aetherpool beyond the archway was filled with leaf litter and loam — no one had cleared it out and filled it with magic for a mage test in many years. Of course. Magic ability could be tested with a simple blood test these days. Leta hadn't gone through an embarrassing failed dip in front of her village to find out she had no usable magic. She'd found out at her doctor's surgery in her preschool health checkup while the doctor explained the results to her mother, noting how there were no pings on any of the standard swatches, not even the kinetic swatch they had expected Leta to register on. Her mother had held her on her lap, playing with her hair and trying her best to hide how disappointed she was from four-year-old Leta.

Beyond the pool, the wooden temple crouched, its thatched roof unsound and green with moss, and its paint long gone. The carved depictions of the Hunter to either side of the door had been worn smooth by time, the features hard to distinguish.

Leta didn't dare open the door. The altar would be inside, but also Leta's doom if the roof came down. Instead, she knelt outside the temple to make her offering. She rummaged through her pockets, looking for something suitable. Under normal circumstances, she would have come prepared. She found very little. Just her aether-voicer, which she wasn't willing to part with, a sticky plaster in a crumpled wrapper, and her worry stone. She took the stone out of her pocket and looked one last time on the familiar crooked line that bisected it. She felt a pang at the thought of losing the stone, but there was no way the Hunter would be happy with an offering of an ageing sticky plaster that was destined to be worn on her heel or finger for a few hours. With as much reverence as she could muster, she placed the stone on the front step of the temple.

Leta wasn't hugely devout — she didn't go to temple every week. But she wasn't stupid, either. The proof of the Hunter's existence was in every mage in Gealdland, and most especially in Jack, his incarnation. So she knew that the Hunter in his godly aspect would hear her, and would even know something of her situation through Jack. At least, that was the common understanding of how this all worked. It made her unsure of how to start. How did one ask advice of a God who wouldn't respond about a topic that in a way they were already in mid-conversation about?

"Was it my imagination, or was he a bit of a dick back there?" She paused, and bit her lip. "Sorry for not being polite, but you're kind of him, in a way, and I'm already in the thick of things with him."

She heard no response but the breeze in the trees.

"I'm sorry to bother you with my minor concerns, Hunter. I'm just…" she sighed. "This is all getting to my head. Being told I'm needed here, but not having any idea what for, and having everyone's conflicting interests all piling up around me like rumpled carpets, ready to trip me. Being used by AllAether. I'm not even sure why I was mad that Jack ignored me today. It's pretty much exactly what I wanted. Did you have to pick such a handsome incarnation? It's inconvenient."

The wind through the trees again was the only answer, but this time it had the cadence of laughter, and a scent of petrichor, just like Jack's scent.

"You're right," said Leta. "I'm being silly. My concerns are small, and temporary anyway. I'm just here for a few weeks, and then I'll be gone. I know I can stick it out. I'm just griping." She said the words before she knew they were true. But she *could* stick it out. It wouldn't be easy, but she could do it. She smiled. "I thank you for the boost of confidence, Hunter. I appreciate it."

She felt a breeze brush her cheek like the light graze of knuckles. *Stay strong*, the wind seemed to say.

"I will."

JACK HAD BEEN DOING his best to ignore Leta for a few days. Every time he did so, she made such a hurt face, and he felt like the world's worst villain. He'd been in an escalating bad mood all week. It had culminated that day in him barely being able to bite his tongue during a full-complement contestant event, an archery competition out on the wider fields of the manor's grounds. The competition had worked up to impossible shots, designed to tease out if one contestant was better at archery than she ought to be. All it had teased out was interpersonal conflicts between the contestants.

He went via the Singing Grove again after the event to work out some of his stress. Afterwards, he decided to talk to Marcus about how things weren't working for him. He ran into Jess on the way to Marcus's suite. She gave him a guilty look and scuttled away. Jack stood watching her go. Had she been laying a complaint about him? How badly had he been treating the contestants? He took a deep breath and knocked on the door.

Marcus opened the door a crack and peered out. "Jack! Just a moment." He closed the door, and a minute later, opened it wide enough for Jack to enter. He looked flushed. *Oh. Oh no.* Jack realised why Jess had scuttled away. He did not want that information. He pretended ignorance. "You're not busy, are you?" he asked as if he hadn't seen a pretty young someone exiting the suite.

"No, not at all, man. At least, not more than usual. What can I do for you?" He waved Jack into an armchair.

"I'm not sure about how the 'cast is playing out. Between the shape of the season and how you've been creating tension… I feel like I should do something different. My purpose as the God Incarnate is at odds with what we're doing here. Is there anything that could be done?"

Marcus sat down and crossed his arms. "It's quite early in the season, though," he said. "Are you sure you won't settle in?"

"I don't think I will," said Jack. "Something is niggling away in the back of my head, telling me I'm making a mistake, or at least going about things wrong. Do you understand what I mean?"

"Well, I'm not God Incarnate, so no, not really. Maybe it's modern technology conflicting with your role. We all feel that way sometimes. No aethercast has ever relied on auto technology to this extent. Who made you think this was a big problem? Has anyone been saying anything to you? How about Mirabelle? I've always wondered about her influence. She has a position where she could sway people's thinking and they wouldn't even notice. And she might've been miffed that we're stealing some of her assistant's time."

Jack shook his head. "She's legit, you know. I can sense that now, as God Incarnate. She wouldn't be able to fool me with a false reading. I'd know."

"Is it someone else? The girl? She wasn't happy when we made use of her. More fool her for signing that contract. Has she been saying anything to you to get herself out of it?"

"No, she's said nothing. I've barely talked to her all week."

"Yeah, we noticed. We didn't get a good capture from when we sent her to the gym. We wanted, I don't know..." Marcus waved a hand about, searching for words. "Some drooling, perhaps? Some preening from you? Anything at all. But it was all very boring. She's just uncomfortable around you. Also, far more to the point, Destiny outing her as a Mundane makes it harder for us to imply what we were hoping to."

"And what was that?" Wasn't implying an affair enough?

"We were hoping some of the audience would wonder if she was the Goddess Incarnate, of course. But it's now clear she isn't. All they would be wondering now is if you're shagging her. Which, also, you clearly aren't if she seems scared of you. If the girl asks you about it, say the pressure's off. We'll keep her on the back-burner, of course, but AllAether's looking at new ways of increasing the tension, since she doesn't seem to be into you enough to make it work." Marcus shook his head and chortled. "You look disappointed. That's hilarious. Maybe she bats for the other team after all, eh? Don't let it get you down."

Jack tamped down an unexpected pang of disappointment. Wasn't that the outcome he'd wanted for Leta, anyway? That they would leave her alone? "Shouldn't you be telling her yourself? It's not my job to run your errands."

"Oh, finally learning to be high and mighty, are you? About time." Marcus snorted. "So if it's not Mirabelle, and it's not her assistant, who's put ants in your pants?"

Jack paused for a moment, the memory of his vision of emerald fabric flashing through his mind. The sharp tang of fear, a calamity that was yet to happen. But he knew Marcus didn't trust such visions. Would anyone believe that Jack's fears were justified? "It's me," he said. "I'm not the right shape for this aethercast this year. It's going against my nature, what I'm supposed to be."

Marcus leaned forward. "Don't forget the terms of your contract. Could you bear with it until the end of the season? Then we could review our strategy. Maybe you'll get back into the swing of things."

Jack sighed. He didn't think he was going to get through to Marcus. "OK."

"Oh! I'm not supposed to tell you, but we have a surprise planned for you tomorrow. You'll meet someone who can give you some advice and reassurance. So look out for that."

Jack nodded, intrigued, but still disappointed overall. "OK, will do. Thanks for your time," he said.

"Hey, don't mention it."

Jack left the executive suite with even more concerns than he'd arrived with.

CURIOSITY GOT THE BETTER of her. Leta hadn't been sent on any false errands for a while, and she wanted to know why. Mirabelle also seemed to be out of the loop, so her choice was between Jack and Marcus. Which wasn't a choice at all. She would take the awkwardness of talking to Jack again over the distastefulness of talking to Marcus any day.

Leta returned to Mirabelle's suite early enough to run in to Jack after his private viewing. Though she had avoided him before, now that she wanted to run into him, he was avoiding her. Just her luck. But she could change her luck. She got her timing right — or rather, she lurked to make sure she would.

"Oh, hello," she said, making it look like she was about to knock on the door. "I didn't realise you were still here. How did it go?"

He blinked when he saw her, then looked around for his personal auto-aethercaster that had waited outside the suite while he had his private viewing. The auto-aethercaster was still idling on a nearby side table. When he saw that, his face opened.

"Nothing new to guide me. The cards have been consistent for me for a while. I guess that means the message is real, but somehow it's still disappointing when you need guidance."

Leta shrugged. "I know little about these things, but maybe you already have everything you need; you just don't know it yet."

Jack gave a wan smile. "That's pretty much what Mirabelle said." He then slapped himself on the forehead. "Oh, I was meant to give you a message. Marcus said that they won't use you to cause tension in the aethercast anymore. He said that you'll be on the back-burner, whatever that means."

At his words, tension eased out of Leta's shoulders. "Thank you. No one told me, though I had wondered." She cleared her throat. "I guess it's because of what Destiny said, right? It's now obvious I'm not useful." She couldn't meet his eyes.

Jack sighed. "I think so. But they're wrong about your worth. And also wrong to think about you in terms of usefulness."

Leta flushed, unsure if there was a compliment in there for her. She didn't want to read more into his words than he said. She plucked at the blazer she wore. "I wonder if being off the hook means I can wear my own clothes again."

"Go for it, I say. Those blouses, while they look nice on you, seem to make you uncomfortable. There's no point dressing up if you don't feel like yourself when you do it." Jack sighed and plucked at his own suit, and Leta knew for sure that the suits were not to his taste; that the cardigan and casual trousers she'd spied him in before were the real him.

Nearby, the auto-aethercaster whirred to life and took up position near Jack. His face closed down again. "Excuse me," he said and stepped around Leta, then strode away without looking back.

Leta watched him go. He didn't want anyone to know he still talked to her beyond her brief role in the aethercast, not even the editors back at the head office. That realisation hurt. It's not as if she was ever expecting to make friends with important people. But he had seemed so nice at first, and now he didn't, or at least not always.

Leta entered Mirabelle's suite without knocking, lost in thought. "Hello, dear," said Mirabelle. "Is everything all right?"

"Hm?" Leta looked up in surprise at the worried look in Mirabelle's sharp green eyes. "I'm fine."

Mirabelle raised an eyebrow and then pointed to the chair opposite. "Cards, bones, or crystal ball?"

"I don't need a reading."

"I want to do one for you. You seem troubled and I am responsible for you here. If I can help, I will." She pointed at the chair again.

"Let me at least make us some drinks first."

While she prepared a pair of teas, Leta thought about the divination methods. "The cards," she said as she set Mirabelle's tea down. "But just a simple spread for me, please. Don't trouble yourself."

"All right, dear." Mirabelle took out her cards and shuffled them; asked Leta to do the cutting and turning; and shuffled them again. Then she dealt three cards, face down on the table. "This is the most simple spread, but I can do something more elaborate for you later if you like."

She pointed to the card on the left. "This one is your past, the one in the middle is your present, and the last one is your future. Shall we see what the cards wish to say?"

"OK."

Mirabelle turned over the first card. "Five of Cups upright. Do you feel you've been a failure until this point, Leta? Do you regret what has come before?"

Leta smoothed her skirt. "I don't have any magic. That's hard in today's world. People don't trust me even to do things that don't need magic. It's not just me. There're a lot of us. And we all struggle to find jobs at the moment. Mum has a lot of magic. She catches transport pods for a living! She should've had a stronger daughter than me."

"I can see why you feel that way, although it is very unfair that the world did this to you." She turned over the next card. "Seven of Swords reversed. You are plagued by self-doubt. You have impostor syndrome."

"Because of what I just said, right? I know you explained why when you hired me, but I still wonder if I fit in here. And I have a plan for the future, but I'm not sure I can achieve it."

"I think the tasks I set you are well within your abilities. Have I done wrong by you?"

"No, not at all."

"Have other people said anything?"

"You mean other than that arsehole, Marcus?" Leta nodded. "The contestants took to Marcus's plan quickly. Some of them were mean."

"They have been taught to look down on those with little magic."

Leta frowned. "If only Destiny hadn't figured out I have no magic."

"I am so sorry that a contestant was awful to you, Leta. I haven't seen the capture, but from all accounts, she was cruel. Do you know what brought it about?"

Leta hunched in on herself. Did Mirabelle think Leta brought the bullying on herself? She wouldn't be the first to say so. Some of her teachers at school had implied the same. "She did exactly what AllAether was hoping: interpreted the manufactured situation in the worst way and lashed out because of it."

Mirabelle sighed. "That's the bad side of aethercasts like this, I'm afraid. They encourage drama and bring out the worst in people. In their normal lives, outside of a competitive environment, the contestants would be nicer people. Most of them, anyway."

Leta's shoulders hunched inwards. "Jack's avoiding me now too."

Mirabelle smiled. "Did he see the contestants being mean to you?"

"Yes."

"And was he not against the idea of involving you in the first place?"

"I guess he said that."

"Then he's probably trying to avoid causing more problems for you. He's been through all of this before. He knows about how the setup of the aethercast spikes jealousy."

"Even when there's no one else around?"

"No one but the auto-aethercaster."

Leta took Mirabelle's point, but even so, she shook her head. "It's more than that, with everyone. I'm a frumpy, boring girl with no magic. I don't fit in here. I know that a vision brought you to me, but maybe I've already done the thing I was supposed to. I couldn't even be manipulated by the network properly. They found the drama I caused to be too boring. I don't even know why that's upsetting in any way at all, but it somehow makes me feel even more like a failure. Maybe I'm not cut out for this environment and I should go home. I'll find money for my course fees somewhere else." She wrapped her arms around her knees. The admission of her failure was inevitable, but painful.

"You're getting ahead of yourself, Leta." Mirabelle pointed down at the table. "There is one more card to read. Your future." She turned the card over. "The World upright." She said the name of the card with a note of wonder. "This is a very auspicious reading, Leta. Everything will come together for you. You will accomplish something great. You will go on a journey, whether in reality or within yourself. Don't give up hope, Leta. You will find your place."

Leta took in a deep breath and let it out with a huff. "Really? Really, really? Are you sure?"

Mirabelle smiled. "Yes. You will. All will be well. Now, I have an idea. I gather that one card reading is not enough to cheer you up on its own, even if it is The World. And it seems I've been neglecting your emotional needs." When Leta tried to protest, Mirabelle held up a hand to forestall her. "I forgot how emotionally draining it is to be running around with auto-aethercasters capturing everyone's movements. I'm sheltered here in these rooms, but I send you all over the place running errands for me, as was Marcus for a while. I have nothing to do this evening. How about we have dinner in the village tonight, away from the manor, the stress, the scrutiny? There are few options, but there is a traditional-style pub. We should see what it is like before the aethercast relocates to Astmere for the second half. Would you like to go?"

Leta tried to imagine demure and impeccably dressed Mirabelle in a pub, rubbing shoulders with local farmers who were there for their evening pint, and nearly giggled aloud. "That sounds lovely."

THE HIEROPHANT
UPRIGHT

You will take great comfort in listening to the advice and guidance of those who have been where you are now in life. Heed their words!

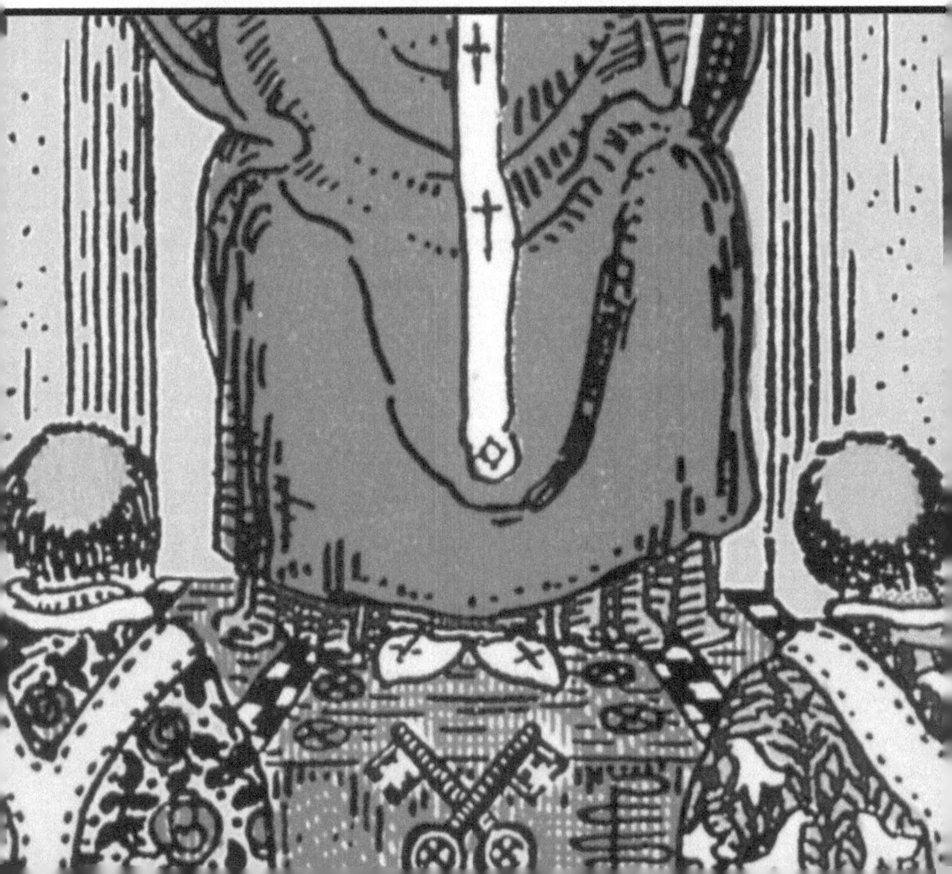

G,

*   May I make use of your network? There's
someone I need to get in contact with regarding the
current matter.*

J ack's calendar had always been booked out for that afternoon for a 'special event,' and Marcus's words the day before had clued him in that a guest would visit the manor. He couldn't guess who. *It would be far too much to hope that they've found the goddess for me elsewhere, wouldn't it?*

A harried-looking young man delivered Jack a message asking him to wait in the foyer. When he arrived, groomed and dressed for the aethercast, Marcus was already there. "You ready for a surprise?"

Outside, a car pulled up the drive, the hum of its driver's magic loud in the still afternoon. The car parked in front of the door and the passenger bounded out, not waiting to be handed. At first, Jack saw a normal man with a tan, not recognising who it was. He was no one he had met before. But then recognition shot through him. He'd seen him on aethercasts, and more importantly, in previous lives. The recognition was deep, with hints of past feelings caught up in it. *Is this what meeting my goddess will be like?* Jack wondered.

The visitor was Ander Palomo, God Incarnate of the Agrani. He who had in previous lives been Jack's friend, his foe, his mentor, his apprentice. What he was growing to be. Ander had ascended a good decade before Jack, and was famous in his lands and abroad.

This larger-than-life VIP bounded up the stairs, his longish brown hair flapping about in the wind of his passage, near skidded to a halt and looked at Jack with wonder in his dark eyes. "Amazing!" yelled Ander. "How amazing it is to see again someone from a past life! I never get used to this!" He swept Jack up in a hug, as if he were not half a head shorter, and pounded him on the back. "So good to see you, my friend! Last time I saw you, you were an old, fat man! Now you are young and handsome!" Ander's Gealdrspeak was accented but easy to understand, reminding him of a friend he once made on his travels, one who had been there the night he had ascended.

"I can say the same for you," said Jack, bringing his thoughts back to the present. "I'm sure I last saw you bald and with a walking stick. Or was that the life before?"

"I can't remember. It comes and goes in flashes. And only when we meet each other. In between, it's gone, no?"

They were talking like old friends, excited to see each other after a long break. Which was the truth, in a way. How strange this must look to others! It was strange to Jack if he thought about it, but as natural as anything if he didn't.

Marcus was shepherding them along a hallway, but Jack took no notice. "Is this what it always feels like to meet another of our kind? This is my first time. I *saw* a Goddess Incarnate once, but I wasn't close enough to talk to her. Is this what it would be like to find my goddess?"

Ander shook a hand in front of his face. "Only if she is ascended. It only happens with those of us who have our powers, our connection to the divine. I met my wife *four times* without knowing it was her. One day, something clicked, she realised who she was. Poof! Amazing! Like now, but more, so much more. I'm excited for you. You get to feel that soon."

"Maybe."

Ander gave him a side-long look, but didn't ask what Jack meant.

Marcus ushered them into the billiards room along with half a dozen auto-aethercasters ready to capture their interaction. He handed them cues. "Here; why don't you have a game and get reacquainted? This game was popular the last time you two knew each other. Ander, if you have any advice for young Jack, please give it to him." Marcus raised an eyebrow at Ander, who must have already been briefed about the kinds of things he was allowed to say to Jack.

"Sure, I will do so," said Ander.

Marcus stepped back and watched them from the edge of the room. He was guiding this segment more than he usually controlled the aethercast.

Jack somehow expected a triangle of many balls, thinking of bar pool, the only cue game he'd played before, but when Ander set up a red ball on the table and held out two white balls in his hand, one with a red dot on, confidence welled up from within. He knew this. He took the one with the red dot. "Toss a coin for us, Marcus?" he said.

Marcus took out a coin and flipped it onto the back of his hand, keeping it covered with his palm. "OK. Heads or tails?"

"Tails."

Marcus revealed heads, and Ander crowed.

They started their game, dashing through the turns. The cue felt natural in Jack's hands, more than it ever had when he had played bar pool. He hadn't played since his ascension. What a shame. If only he had known, he could have made a killing between when he ascended and he returned to Gealdland.

As they played, they talked. Ander asked about Jack's ascension and offered his story. They talked about how

their powers had manifested — Ander leaned more towards being able to nullify other people's magic. Then
Jack asked Ander about a topic closer to his heart.

"Can you tell me what it's like to find your counterpart?"

Ander leaned on his cue and smiled, his eyes distant
and introspective. "I thought she was cute straight away.
My type was always like her. But I didn't feel the fire-
works in here that I expected to if she were the Goddess
Incarnate." He tapped his chest. "I was disappointed. But
I kept running into her, somehow. Fate brought us closer.
It didn't let us miss each other. One day, someone tried to
hurt me. We have anti-incarnation protesters at home.
Some of them, they tried to hurt me. She saw it happen.
She protected me with more magic than she usually had.
And she ascended. We didn't notice people around us,
people being arrested. We looked at each other, and
looked, and looked. And my heart felt like this." He threw
his hands out as if mimicking an explosion. "I don't know
a big enough word in your language. I don't know one in
my own. And we got married a month later."

"Wow," said Jack. "I want that experience. I want to
find my goddess."

"Of course. It's like air, no?"

"Like air."

"You will find her."

"Maybe."

Marcus stirred by the door, and Ander noticed. He
raised his eyebrows at Jack and returned to the game.

They played in near silence for a while. Jack was desperate to ask about Ander's opinion of how the aethercast
was doing, and whether they were going about it all
wrong. But he didn't want to ask that question in front of
Marcus.

While they played, a messenger came into the room
and whispered to Marcus, who said, "What?" He turned

to Jack and Ander. "I'll be back in a moment. Keep enjoy-ing your game." He hurried from the room, messenger in tow.

Ander wiggled his eyebrows at Jack. "Now is our *chance*. Let's go."

"Go where?"

"Come on. I did some bribery." Ander left his cue on the table and strode from the room. Jack remembered the private viewing he'd had with Mirabelle earlier that day: *Don't be afraid to follow*, she had said. Jack put his cue down and followed Ander along the hall, back to the en-trance.

"Excuse me!" called a voice from behind. It was the porter who hadn't had a chance to escort Ander inside. "You must stay here."

Ander ignored the man at first and kept walking. When the porter caught up, Ander stopped, and Jack nearly ran into him. Ander turned on the porter. "I am God Incarnate of the Agrani. You going to stop me? Cause a diplomatic incident?"

The young porter went very pale and froze.

Ander didn't give him a chance to find his bravery. He skipped down the steps of the manor and to the car that was still waiting. Flinging the door open, he waved Jack in. He piled in after, and said, "To the town!"

"Sure thing, sir," said the driver as he started the aetherengine. "Wherever you like."

Ah, thought Jack. *The aforementioned bribery.*

While the car whirred to life and crunched its way down the drive, Ander pulled a duffle bag up from the footwell and rummaged around in it. "Here," he said and offered Jack a zip-neck wool jersey. "Get that fussy blazer off. We're going to a country village." Jack com-plied, holding in a sneeze at the smell of unfamiliar laun-dry liquid. While he did so, Ander also changed into a more casual top. "Is the size OK?" asked Ander.

The jersey was tight around Jack's shoulders, but not enough to hinder him. "It's fine."

Ander passed him a woolly hat and put another hat on his own head. "I heard there's some anti-incarnation protesters here too. Let's go *incognito*."

Jack pulled his hat down over his ears. "Where are we going?"

"Drinking, just us, none of those flying things. You need to talk some shit out, my friend, without that company listening."

Jack gaped. He'd only just met Ander (in this life, anyway), but the man was already going to extreme lengths for him. It was touching. "I… don't know what to say."

"You will. Let's talk."

"No, it's a turn of phrase. I mean… thank you."

"No problem, my friend. I understand how it is."

The car soon entered Autumnwood, a stereotypical country village with rows of stone houses and businesses adapted from older services: an aethercanister refill station in what had been a blacksmith; a corner shop in an ageing shop building that had once sold clothes or furniture; a doctor's surgery in an adapted house. But the car dropped them off in front of a business that had surely not changed much in several hundred years — the pub. A sign hanging over the door depicted a red unicorn, and as in times past, they hadn't bothered labelling it in words.

Ander led Jack inside the dark building. Jack had to duck under some smoke-stained beams in the entryway, but further in, the ceiling was high enough that he wasn't in danger of hurting himself. The pub's interior was a mix of original features, such as the beams, the cavernous fireplace, and some ancient wall units; and more modern fare, like laminate tables with pleather chairs. The bar, too, was a plasticised replica with an inbuilt tap system. There was an odour of stale beer, most probably from the short-pile carpets that had once been green all over but now had khaki areas as well. It was a warm and cheery pub, though, despite being desperate for a refresh, and half the tables had patrons sitting at them.

Ander bought two pints of beer and waved Jack over to a table out of view of the main door. They both took a moment to take long pulls of their beverages; it wasn't the best beer Jack ever had, but neither was it the worst.

"I needed this," said Ander. "I bet you did too, my friend."

"Yeah, I think I did," said Jack as he slouched further into his chair. He looked around at the other patrons. Were any of them the anti-incarnation protesters he'd heard about?

Ander plonked his pint glass on the table. "So, how's it really going?"

Jack reflexively looked around for auto-aethercasters, but the ones following him hadn't made it into the car and were probably still milling about in Autumnwood Manor's driveway. "Pretty poor. I don't have any confidence that we're doing the right thing. How am I supposed to find my goddess when I'm forced to spend weeks at a time only meeting women that the network has sent my way? They keep picking only women from certain social circles. The goddess could be anywhere. I'm desperate to get out there and find her!"

Ander nodded. "Yeah, I hear you. That must annoy you very much. You feel trapped?"

"So trapped. But I signed a contract. I can't get out of it for several more years."

"It's so hard when you haven't found your other half. I was very impatient. You must be too."

Jack nodded.

"I didn't find my goddess for four years. It felt like eternity. I used to wish that she had ascended first, that I was the one who had to be looked for. But when I found her, I forgot about those lonely years. They were unimportant. My advice is even if you can't find her for some years more, from then until your dying day you will be together. You will have many, many years. It will be OK."

"I hope so. But I feel so *used* right now. I'm entertainment. The aethercast is a way for the already influential to make their daughters famous. I just... I hate it." Jack took a long drink of his beer and sighed. Something niggled at his mind. What was it?

"I know, Jack. I've been worried. We get your aethercast at my country. I see it. It's not healthy for you. It is popular, though. I think half the women in my country are in love with you. Your escapades make the news."

Jack groaned. That was the last thing he wanted!

"There's even a woman who goes on chat aethercasts claiming she knows you and was there when you ascended."

Jack leaned back in his chair. "If she's a water mage called Ileana, she's telling the truth. She was there."

"Huh. I thought for sure she was lying. Is she telling the truth about having had a steamy affair with you too?"

Jack groaned again. "No! Hunter and Harvester, why would she say that?"

Ander shrugged. "Probably to clear student debt or something?" He raised a finger and frowned. "Just a moment." He drummed his fingers on the tabletop. "Someone was using their magic to eavesdrop. I stopped them. No need to worry."

"Someone from the aethercast?"

"I don't think so. Someone over there." He pointed at a table of drinkers at the far end of the room.

Jack didn't see any familiar faces, but one nondescript man in a dark anorak had the fading remnants of magic around him. "They look like locals to me."

"Yeah, busybodies. Hopefully, they don't know who we are and they just are being nosy."

Jack looked at the table out of the corner of his eye. He did his best to commit the faces of the patrons to memory, in case they turned up again as anti-incarnation protesters. As well as the man in the anorak, there was a woman with dyed red hair and a man with stringy blond hair who was looking in the other direction.

He turned back to Ander. "Your ability to nullify others' magic must be so useful. I felt something, I think, but I wouldn't have been able to do anything about it. If anyone was in trouble around me, I'm not sure I could do anything." He shivered, remembering the vision in the crystal ball.

Ander shrugged. "Yeah, it's good. But I bet you could do something. Don't forget your innate magic. Who you were before you ascended still counts."

Jack grinned. "Thank you for saying so. Everyone keeps telling me the opposite, saying only who I am now counts."

"Those people are insensitive jerks, and I give you permission to ignore them."

Jack laughed. "Thanks for listening. I needed to grump. I know there's no fix for these problems until my contract runs out and I can choose not to sign up any longer, but it helps so much to talk to someone who understands all of this."

"No problem."

"What about you? How are things going for you? Do you have pressures like this?"

"Some, although I get better at controlling my public persona every year. It's mostly about the Awakening and the Thankful Time for me. I love those trips. Love seeing the people and the land."

The Awakening and the Thankful Time were rough translations of the equivalents of his own Blessings Tours. Once Jack's goddess ascended, she too would go on two tours per year. Jack hadn't done so yet because the

Hunter was not useful in autumn in a farming society. He was much more useful in spring to help the lambs and calves be born strong. But the god that Ander was a representative of wasn't a hunting god; he was a direct agricultural god.

Ander grinned and looked around to make sure no one was close enough to hear with their naked ears. "Can you keep secrets?"

"Sure," said Jack. "I owe you a lot already."

Ander leaned forward to whisper, his dark eyes twinkling with excitement. "Carla, my wife, she was going to be here too, but she cancelled. You know why?"

Jack shook his head.

"Too much morning sickness to travel!"

Jack blinked, and his jaw dropped. "Congratulations!" he whispered. "That's so great! How far along is she?"

"A few months. We won't announce until she is round in the belly."

"I'm so happy for you. Please give her my congratulations as well."

"Oh, I will. Thank you, friend Jack."

They talked for a long while, stopping now and then to get more rounds of beer. Ander talked about his life and his hopes for his child, and Jack talked more about what it was like behind the scenes of the aethercast. He still felt uneasy about his escape. He kept looking towards the front door, half-expecting Marcus or someone else from Autumnwood Manor to come looking for him and drag him back to the manor.

When he saw someone from the manor, it was not who he was expecting. Mirabelle peeked around the corner at them, looking out of place in the pub. Ander looked up when she did and gave a small salute. Mirabelle returned the salute and went to the bar to order.

"Did she just...?" said Jack.

Ander grinned. "Friend of mine knows a friend of hers." He snorted with mirth. "Well, a researcher who studies me and Carla like we are experiments. He wants to isolate 'ascendant energy', or whatever. That one there may or may not have been behind the note your producer got." He jutted his chin in Mirabelle's direction.

Jack remembered Marcus getting a message and running off in a hurry. "Huh."

A few minutes later, Mirabelle took a table in their view but out of earshot. From where she was sitting, she could monitor them and see the door at the same time. Moments later, she was joined by Leta, who was carrying both their drinks. Leta saw Jack at the same moment he saw her, and from the way her eyes widened, she was not in on the evening's shenanigans. Leta flushed and gave Mirabelle her drink, taking a seat of her own. Then she jumped up again, saying "Oh, sorry, just a moment!" loud enough for Jack to hear and near ran over to the bar again, returning a moment later with a bowl of fries. She thumped herself on the forehead as she did so. Jack smiled. There was something so endearing about her, but also he wished he could convince her to be more confident in herself.

"Hm," said Ander. "Am I boring you?"

Jack whipped his head around to look at his companion. "No, no, not at all. I was thinking about all the plotting you did to get me out of the manor for the evening."

"Were you? I think you were looking at that young lady?" There was a knowing smile on his face.

"Well, I glanced, surely."

"My friend, you were looking at her for a whole minute with a silly grin on your face."

"Don't exaggerate."

"I'm not exaggerating. I'm preparing to give you advice. If you ever do that with any woman. Or anyone who could be your goddess; no transphobia here. If you ever do that, try to find more time with the person. Either they could be your goddess, or maybe they are like your goddess in some way, so to know them gives you clues."

"I *was* talking to her," he said. Ander raised his eyebrows, but let Jack continue. "The producers got wind of it and used her to cause jealousy with the contestants. They starting bullying her. They made comments about her magical ability. I backed off so I wouldn't cause her trouble."

Ander shook his head. "I understand that thinking. You are in a strange situation with those women on your aethercast. They'll be competitive. But what if you miss out on finding your goddess? To find you would improve her life too."

Jack looked over at Leta, who turned her head away quickly enough that he was sure she had been looking at him. "You think she could be my goddess?"

"I don't know; do you?"

Jack shrugged. "I don't know. I've talked to her many times and didn't get the feeling that she was." He twisted that right wrist again: he knew he was attracted to her, though.

"Remember how I said I met Carla four times before we knew? Don't rule anyone out who piques your interest, my friend."

Jack felt sure he would think long and hard about this. Because he knew women like Leta weren't popular at the moment, more's the pity; she was larger than many and wore glasses and cosy clothes. But she was cute to him. More than cute. She was sexy. He'd always liked women like her. Nice. Honest. Warm-hearted. But with a sharp tongue if annoyed, a tendency he could see Leta needing to tamp down from time to time. If women like her opened up to a person, they meant it. If they let you into their heart, or their bed, then they truly wanted you there. No power games. Plus, he had to admit that he was shallow enough to appreciate her curves, to want to kiss those plush lips, to be turned on by the thought of losing himself in her soft, warm embrace.

Ander was right. She was a very clear clue about who his goddess was and what he should look for. No one else had ever described that to him so clearly.

"You've just given me the best advice anyone has given me," he said to Ander.

"That's what I'm here for."

TEMPERANCE
REVERSED

Is something 'off' in your life? Attend to it now before the
molehill becomes the mountain.

GODDESS FOUND

To Seer Mirabelle,
I well understand the problem. Thank you for
contacting me. I'll talk to him.
Kind regards
Ander Palomo

The taxi ride had been brief, but even so, the warmth of the pub had been a relief against the chill that had soaked into Leta's bones on the way. Alas, a chill of a different kind soon chased away the warmth: one borne of surprise.

Leta had not expected to see Jack drinking with another God Incarnate, Ander Palomo, in the pub. There weren't any auto-aethercasters around. How had they gained permission to escape the aethercast for the evening? She had thought Jack's every movement was being recorded. She looked at Mirabelle wondering if the older woman was also surprised, only to see a cheeky twinkle in her eyes. "Did you... do something?" asked Leta.

"I don't know what you mean. Did we forget to order the snacks?"

"Oh, sorry, just a moment!" she cried in an embarrassingly loud voice. *Why so loud?* She chastised herself as she fetched their fries. She didn't want to draw attention to herself, particularly not Jack's attention. *Why so* loud?

When she returned to the table, she tried her best to ignore Jack on the other side of the room. He looked out of place here. He was dressed down in a plain jersey and a woollen hat, but even so, he and his companion shone in the gloom. Their presences were remarkable. Interestingly, Ander seemed to glow a different colour than Jack, more gold than silver. Or maybe it was more accurate to say the temperature of their glow was different? The essence? It was strange. Maybe she would have understood better what she was perceiving if she had more magic and was therefore more used to using it.

Mirabelle waited until their meals had arrived before ambushing Leta with tricky questions. Leta had a mouthful of steak and ale pie when Mirabelle asked, "What do you think of Jack?"

Leta spluttered and reflexively looked at the man in question. She thought for a moment he had been looking at her until she turned her head, but that seemed unlikely. And the flush on his cheeks was likely because he was on, by the number of glasses on the table, his third pint. "What do you mean?" asked Leta when she had swallowed her mouthful.

"Do you like him?" Mirabelle took a dainty bite of her chicken breast.

Leta dabbed at her mouth with her napkin. "He seems like a good sort," she murmured, hoping Jack wouldn't hear they were talking about him.

"Hm?"

Leta frowned as she considered how to answer the question. "He seems out of his depth sometimes."

Mirabelle nodded. "You're looking at him on a different level than most people."

"Is that bad? Is it rude? What's the etiquette with Gods Incarnate?"

Mirabelle chuckled. "It is good. I suspect he needs friends. I would imagine he feels alone." They both looked over at Jack and Ander, who were laughing about something. "Well, not *right* at this moment," Mirabelle amended. "But the other God Incarnate is only visiting briefly; he will go home. Do talk to Jack whenever you have the chance. It may help."

Leta applied herself to her meal to avoid looking at Jack. She had never considered that she could help him. She hadn't thought of herself as important enough to the aethercast for that. But maybe she didn't need to be important. She just needed to be there.

"I'll see what I can do," she said.

When she finished her meal, she excused herself to visit the ladies', which were off a small dim side corridor that also sported the gents' and a cleaning closet. It was not the most pleasant of facilities that she'd ever used. She hovered, trying to breathe shallow, and dried her hands on the inside of her jersey because the cloth hand towel had reached the end of its track and had been used in the same place over and over for a while. When she emerged into the small side hallway, she nearly ran into someone in the gloom. "Excuse me!" she said. A familiar scent of petrichor caught her attention.

"Leta."

She looked up at her name. She had nearly run into Jack. His lips were parted and his light brown eyes seemed deeper and more mysterious in the corridor's gloom.

"Fancy seeing you here," she said, then immediately cursed her awkwardness. What kind of ridiculous cliché was that?

"Oh. I thought you'd already seen me here." He scratched the back of his neck.

"Yes. I did. I'm not sure why I said that. Please ignore me." She tried to push past him, but he caught her forearm. She looked down at his strong, long-fingered hand on her arm. He frowned for a long moment, and he seemed unsteady on his feet.

"My apologies. I wanted to say sorry for avoiding you." He ran his thumb back and forth on her arm, bringing up goose bumps as he did so. "I saw how the contestants were treating you and it was all my fault. I didn't want to cause you any more problems."

"Oh," said Leta, her voice breathy at his touch. "I thought I'd insulted you."

His eyes went wide. "No, no, no, not at all," he said, waving his free hand about as if warding off her words. He looked around at the room behind him and pulled her over towards the cleaning closet. He opened the door and tucked them both in behind it, not quite in the closet, but out of view of the other patrons. They stood so close that Leta felt the heat radiating off him. "Leta, I'm so sorry if I made you think that."

She took a deep breath. Dizziness was creeping up on her. Fumes from cleaning fluids, perhaps? "That's all right," she said. "Some contestants were mean to me before the fire drill incident, so it's not that. I've always had trouble with 'popular' girls, you know? I'm a bit of a target for a certain type of person."

"Is there anything I can do?"

Leta shook her head. "I don't think intervention from men helps all that much. But thank you."

He smiled. "For what it's worth, I think you're interesting." He brushed at a lock of her hair. She looked up into his earnest eyes. His throat bobbed as he swallowed down some feeling or words. For a moment, it seemed as if he was leaning closer, as if he was going to kiss her. She almost closed her eyes and let him. She steadied herself against him with one hand on his chest. But he glanced around again, took stock of their location. He cleared his throat. "I'm, ah…" he pointed towards the gents'.

"Sorry, yes, go break the seal." She stepped away and let him escape. He must have been trying to push past her for half the conversation. Anything else she thought he was going to do must have been her imagination.

161

As soon as Jack had disappeared, Leta banged her head on the back of the cleaning cupboard door. *Break the seal?* "Please, Hunter, could you perhaps ride through this hallway right now and sweep me up into the High Hunt, never to be seen again?" Which was a stupid prayer to make, since the incarnation of the Hunter was the person she wanted to escape from, and who she knew was busy that instant dealing with a call of nature of another kind. She reached for her worry stone to settle her mind, but she didn't have it anymore. She whimpered and stepped out of the cupboard. A woman with heavy eyeliner and red hair dye that was growing out paused in the archway, looking at Leta like she was mad. She edged around Leta and disappeared into the loos. "Great," said Leta. "The locals think I'm weird too."

She slunk back to the table. "I think I just made a fool of myself," said Leta to Mirabelle. "Actually, I know I did. Are we staying for dessert?"

Mirabelle smiled. "I'm quite full. Shall we call a taxi and head back to the manor?"

"Yes, please."

It wasn't until Mirabelle had paid their account (despite Leta's protests) and they were outside in the cold waiting for the taxi that it registered in Leta's mind that Jack had called her interesting. That wasn't a word that Leta was used to having applied to herself. She half-believed that it was a back-handed compliment of sorts, perhaps implying she was weird. But he hadn't seemed mean at all when he said it. Just sincere. And there was the way he'd touched her hair… Leta didn't even know how to process the encounter.

MARCUS WAS WAITING for Jack and Ander in front of the manor entry way, his arms crossed and a thunderous look on his face. Other people peered down out of the windows — no doubt nosy onlookers.

"Chin up," said Ander. Jack squared his shoulders and forced himself to look casual, even as the auto-aether-casters swooped down to start capturing his image again.

"So good of you to return," said Marcus, his voice tight. "Thank you, Mr Palomo, for visiting the aethercast. I wish you a pleasant trip back to your country."

Jack winced at the clear dismissal. Marcus was push-ing the bounds of diplomacy between their nations with his tone. Ander, however, shrugged. "Sure, no problem." He turned to Jack and clapped him on both shoulders. "You'll do fine, my friend. Send me a message any time." With a jaunty wave, he headed back to the car. Jack waved and smiled. He would see Ander again. Maybe next time he would meet his family too.

"May I have a word with you in the executive suite?" Marcus said to Jack.

"Sure." *Here it comes.*

Jack followed Marcus up the staircase and through the dim corridors of the manor. The smell of wood polish and old carpets was more oppressive than it had seemed before. Nosy people peered at him around corners or doorframes as he walked. He pretended they were auto-aethercasters. There, but OK to ignore.

Marcus ushered him into the executive suite and closed the door behind them. "What were you thinking?"

Jack took a seat in an armchair uninvited. "I had God Incarnate things to discuss with Ander."

"You were supposed to talk to him *here*. Where the auto-aethercasters can record you. We had a whole spe-cial episode planned. We've now only got ten minutes of capture to use for it! He was supposed to talk to you about god things, then you'd dine with the contestants, then there would be a special challenge with a quiz. We spent ages writing that quiz! It was educational!"

"I'm sure you could have still done the quiz if you hadn't sent him away. And don't tell me you didn't record

163

the 'where's Jack gone' drama. I'm sure you can do something with that."

Marcus rubbed his temples as if he had a headache. "Something, sure. But this was supposed to be the main event here at this location. We're moving to Astmere in a few days, remember? We don't have time now to organise another good 'Autumnwood Manor finale' event. You've screwed with the season arc." He sighed. "Jack, buddy. You were in breach of contract this evening. I have no option but to serve you a written warning."

"Some things are more important than a silly aethercast, Marcus."

Marcus leaned forward and jabbed a finger in Jack's direction. "Tell that to the contract *you* signed. Do you want to be financially ruined? And remember, it's magically binding. If you can't pay, AllAether will syphon off your kinetic magic to recoup the loss. I've noticed you sneaking off and trying to build it up to prepare for paying the penalty. It doesn't work that way, Jack. No matter how strong you get, it'll all be gone. It'll take you years to build it back up. Just do yourself a favour and do as you're told from now on. And if you feel the urge to pull a stunt like this again, for goodness' sake, we have a counsellor on staff. Go talk to Kellan first before doing something stupid. He'll get you sorted out."

Jack was half-way back to his rooms when he realised Marcus hadn't even tried to be friendly. He had just been like any other bloody executive.

THE HANGED MAN
REVERSED

You are lost in the woods of life. You need to make room for
yourself before you burn out.

Tiffany,
  Don't be afraid to lend a hand when asked.
         Mirabelle

The High Hunt did not come for Leta.

She had intended to take Mirabelle's advice to heart and be friendly with Jack, despite feeling awkward about how strange she must have sounded at the pub. However, Jack was kept busy for the next few days, as was everyone else. The rumour mill had it that Jack and Ander running off to the pub that evening had thrown out the schedule, and the extra work was to round out their time at the manor, and that Jack was in a lot of trouble. He wasn't in his rooms when Leta delivered his dailies. She hoped he was getting useful hints out of what Mirabelle was preparing for him. The seer was doing extra readings on Jack's behalf, trying to find any useful hints. Though, from the furrowed brow she sported after her readings, perhaps she wasn't finding anything new to report. Leta supposed these viewings could only change so much when taken daily.

The only time Leta saw Jack was at a large last-minute outdoor dinner. Much of the crew went out to observe the capture (and be ready to graze the leftover food). Leta tagged along, now certain she wouldn't be forced into the aethercast again, and stood to one side of the crowd.

They had dressed the contestants and Jack up in medieval clothes. The table, too, bore old-fashioned decorations, although it was under a marquee. Mage lighting lit the marquee, and the space was heated by the efforts of a tired-looking weather mage. Good thing, too, since the contestants were wearing dresses that left their shoulders and large parts of their cleavage bare. Marcus also looked tired, and he occasionally checked in with the weather mage and rested a hand on his shoulder. Leta suspected he might be a weather mage too.

Jack wore a silver fabric doublet and, amusingly, a crown with sapphire-coloured paste gems. Leta wondered if they were going to enhance the look of the crown in post-production because in person it looked like a child's costume piece. Jack, though, looked as handsome as ever. He smiled and small-talked, and sat as if he wasn't wearing embarrassing and likely uncomfortable clothes. But when someone else was the centre of attention, and he must have felt that no one was looking at him, his smile faltered and he looked drawn. Now that Mirabelle had alerted her to it, she saw his loneliness. It wasn't fair what the aethercast was doing to him. He was too important for this silly charade. Couldn't they see that? He had things to do, places to be, but he was stuck being the entertainment of the nation.

Maybe there was some way she could help. She just had to think of one.

Some contestants spotted Leta's presence, and the weight of their gazes made her wonder if she should have come. Curse the lure of free fancy food.

There were a few unfriendly looks, a few puzzled looks. Tiffany and Constance raised eyebrows at each other after seeing her. They may have figured out she was just a pawn, then.

Leta retreated as soon as she'd snagged a quince pastry, seeking the quiet and solitude of her own assigned room. As she climbed the stairs, her aethervoicer rang. She answered straight away, seeing her mother's indicator on the glass. "Hi, Mum; can you wait a sec? I'm just on my way back to my room."

Her mum made a tense noise of affirmation. Leta's stomach flipped. Had something happened back home? She hurried along the corridor and shut the door behind her.

"Mum? Is everything OK?"

"LETA," said her mum in a voice Leta had never heard her utter before. "LETA." She seemed unable to utter anything else.

"Ah. I can guess which episode was on this evening. The fire drill?"

"LETA. Are you shagging the God Incarnate?"

Leta's face flushed boiler-hot. "No!"

"Are you trying to shag him?"

"No, of course not!"

"That's what they're implying. You know that, right? They lingered on you and Jack running into each other, then made it look like you were staring into each other's eyes. There's even speculation on the gossip aethers wondering if you could be the Goddess Incarnate." Leta's mum waited, and Leta took a deep breath in the awkward silence. She couldn't, *wouldn't*, admit that she had got lost in his presence, that they hadn't needed to edit the capture as much as her mum was assuming. And as for being speculated about by national gossips, the mere thought terrified her. "What happened?" asked her mum. "Why am I suddenly seeing you on my globe? That's not what you went away for."

"I *know*." Leta was ashamed of how much anguish there was in her voice. She knew she should rein it in for her mum's sake, but it tumbled out anyway.

"Oh, Honey," said her mum. "Do you want to come home?"

"Not going to lie to you, Mum. Of course I do. But I signed a contract, which had loopholes in so the aethercast could use me in this way if 'necessary'. Also, I want the money. It'll cover that course I showed you. All the course fees. I'm an adult, so I'll just put my big girl trews on and keep going. I'll be done in a matter of weeks, anyway."

"Will I see more of this kind of stuff over the next episodes?"

Leta sighed. "I can't say."

"Oh, right. Great galloping goddesses. How will I be able to do the grocery shopping? The entire village is going to want to talk about every detail." Leta's mum sighed. "Beans on toast for the next few nights, it is."

"I'm sorry, Mum. I didn't mean to cause you trouble." Leta's voice came out small and weak.

"It's not your fault, Honey. I'm going to be *so glad* when you get home, though."

"Yeah, me too, Mum. Me too."

IN HIS WAKE, Ander left Jack with the high of an evening well spent with a good friend, all manner of work stress, and several burning questions. He needed more advice, more information. He'd considered asking Mirabelle, but after multiple readings she'd already given him as much advice as a seer could.

Should he be circumspect? Or should he be bold and take advantage of the connections available to him?

He was tiring of circumspection. Bold it was.

He found Constance sitting with Tiffany in the same terraced garden in which he'd had his first 'date' with her. She didn't look surprised to see him, which boded well. It seemed he understood her magic, and she'd known he would come to talk to her.

Constance nodded to Tiffany. "Please, go ahead," she said.

Tiffany grinned. "See you later," she said. "I'm taking a walk around the grounds. I'm going stir-crazy in this manor!" She then walked down the wide steps to the lawn and, to Jack's immense surprise, all the auto-aethercasters followed her, including those allocated to Jack and Constance. Each one was, to his eyes, tethered to Tiffany by a thin crimson thread of magic.

He stood and watched in amazement for a long moment.

"Sit down, please," said Constance, tucking her blue and blonde hair behind her ears. "Mr Myrtlewood will come to fix the 'error' soon enough."

"She's an aethercaster," he said as he took a seat at the patio table. "Does AllAether know? I thought she was just a light mage. I never heard about her being a multi-talent."

"I doubt they know," said Constance. "They didn't test us for our specialties in person, just asked for our certifications during the casting process. I think a few of the girls can do more than they let on. It's pretty common for multi-talents from well-connected families to hide magics that are not seen as seemly for their stations. While Tiffany is registered as a light mage, just like Chrissie, she has other skills. Not that I'm convinced aethercasting differs from light magic, anyway. It's all electromagnetic. It seems logical to me they would be the same thing."

Jack hadn't been expecting a philosophical discussion on the classification of magic, but oh well; here they were. "And you? Did you fudge the truth?"

Constance gave him one of her intense stares. "Clairvoyance is seemly for my station."

He huffed. Yes, it would be. It was one of the magics the Geald families valued.

"You need advice beyond what Seer Mirabelle can provide," said Constance. It was an explicit statement of fact, not a question.

"Yes."

Constance nodded, and her eyes glowed in his mage-sight.

"Do, uh, do you need to know what I have questions about?"

"No." She squinted. "You're tricky to read because you shine so bright as soon as I turn my clairvoyance on you, but I can still see what I need to." She looked away from him and stared out over the lawns, to where Tiffany was a red-clad blob by the far tree line. "The seer's assistant."

"Leta? Yes, I suppose she was part of what I was going to ask you about."

"I see you and her in a travel tube capsule. If she ever asks you to go somewhere with her, take her up on the offer."

"OK. But why? And does this relate to —"

Constance held up a hand to him. "My magic is not like Seer Mirabelle's, God Incarnate Jack. I have neither reasoning nor pandering to give. I see two paths ahead of you: one where you go somewhere with the assistant, and one where you don't. The one where you go is harder in the short-term, but with a better long-term outcome. It's up to you which path you choose."

"Do you suspect something?" asked Jack, his belly clenching with worry that Constance may read the intent behind his question, but unable to keep himself from asking. "I saw you reading Leta."

"What I saw in her future is not for me to say to you. My apologies. I've given you all I can. The rest is in your hands."

"Why are you helping me?" he asked.

"Because, unlike the seer, I can read myself using a mirror. I saw two paths for myself: one on which I asked Tiffany for help to give you a private consult, and one on which I left fate to go its own way. It looks like by coming here I will put us all — you, me, Tiffany, the assistant — on paths where we learn something about ourselves. And that sounds preferable to me over not learning."

Her words sounded like the truth to him. "Thank you for the consult, Soothsayer Constance."

"You're welcome, God Incarnate Jack. I hope these events lead to you finding your goddess." She stood, wrapped her wool coat more tightly around herself, and went back into the manor.

Jack stood too. Constance's advice hadn't been clear. Or comforting. He suddenly appreciated Mirabelle's approach more.

He wandered down the path towards the far gardens. Perhaps he should sneak in another training session at the Singing Grove before his auto-aethercasters returned. He wouldn't have another chance before they left for Astmere. But his feet carried him around a formal garden and onto a path that led to a small wood. He followed the path between twisting oaks. A thread of silver magic wafted in his sight before him, drawing him on. He didn't think it would be visible to anyone else. He had a feeling he knew where the thread was taking him.

Sure enough, he soon stood before an ancient horned arch. He stepped through, and then around a crumbling old aetherpool to stand before a mouldering ancient temple. "Hello, old chap," he said. "Fancy finding this here, and right before I leave too. I should have figured."

You should have come earlier, little one, said a voice on the wind. He didn't hear that voice every time he visited a temple, but often enough that it wasn't a shock anymore.

"I'm sorry," he said. He dug in his pockets, looking for an offering, as he'd always done before his ascension. But a breeze held his wrist, and he stilled.

No need for that, little one. Not any more. I did like that custard square you left me when you were seven, though. It was much appreciated.

Jack laughed. "Well, I'm glad someone got to appreciate it."

You need advice.

Jack sighed. "I just don't know if I'm on the right path."

When two paths pass through a wood in parallel, it is not inevitable that you would remain on the same path the whole time. It is a risk, but you can go in search of the other.

"No human would ever advise me to go off the path in a forest."

We are not human, little one. The forest is our domain. We may take the chance and survive.

"But what if taking the chance puts someone else at risk?"

I see what troubles you, said the voice. *But she is a strong one. You don't need to worry. Also, she is faster than you. She has already been here.* A breeze blew a leaf across the ground until it skittered over a small stone sitting on the step of the temple. Jack squatted down to take a closer look. It was a pale grey pebble like one would find on a beach, with a white thread running through its middle. The stone was shiny, as if someone had turned it over and over in their hand for a long time. *It was left for me,* said the voice, *and I accepted it as an offering. I would like you to hold on to it for me.*

Jack hesitated. He was accepting offerings on behalf of the Hunter now? But, of course, he was. When would he learn?

He reached out and picked it up. The stone felt warm in his hand. There was no explanation for the warmth; it ought to be icy to the touch. If he had followed the thread of the conversation right, then this stone had been left here by Leta. A little prickle of excitement niggled at him. Could it be? But he didn't want to jump to conclusions. There could be another reason the Hunter wanted him to hold on to the stone.

Jack put the stone in his pocket. "I take it that one day I'll figure out why you want me to have this in my possession."

No doubt. Go well, little one.

Jack walked back to the manor. Half-way there, the auto-aethercasters returned. He had hoped for answers. Instead, he had found more questions.

THE EMPRESS
REVERSED

Today is a 'treat yourself' kind of day. You need some 'me time' to reconnect with your self-love.

Jess,

The cards hold a warning for you today. You have been offered temptation. How will your choices affect others, and how will their choices affect you? Take the time afforded by our change in location to consider your options.

Mirabelle

The aethercast crew started packing up at Autumnwood Manor. They would move in several stages over the next few days to Emerald Marquise Tower, one of the biggest and fanciest modern hotels in the capital, Astmere. They had picked a very different venue for the second half of the season. Leta packed her sparse belongings and boarded a travel capsule with Mirabelle and a few others at Autumnwood Tube Station. She reached out with the small amount of magic available to her. It was disorienting to feel her mother as neither the thrower nor the catcher of the capsule. Somehow, it felt less safe than usual, even though Leta was sure the travel tube catchers responsible for their relocation were just as professional as her mother.

They alighted at North Central Tube Station and boarded hired cars bound for the hotel. Leta marvelled anew at the size of the production surrounding the aethercast. She was part of only the first wave of the relocation; all the contestants, the lighting crew, and Fogarty with his auto-aethercasters were still at the manor. And yet they had ushers and a line of cars.

Although it wasn't far to the hotel, it took them a long time to drive there because of the traffic. Leta had visited

Astmere a few times before, but not long enough to become used to the sheer over-stimulation of her senses. Even through the windows of the car and under the hum of the driver's magic, the city was just so *loud*. There were people everywhere, streaming along the pavements, stepping in between the crawling traffic, entering and exiting the shops that lined the streets. A quarter of the entire nation lived in this sprawling metropolis.

Leta breathed a sigh of relief when her car approached the hotel. Most of the cars in their convoy drove into the underground car park, but one peeled off and pulled up past a group of people waving placards to the grand entrance instead. Leta supposed that was the car carrying Jack, although her car was well within the dark car park before she could see who stepped out. She hoped the security guards holding back the protesters did their job well, because the crowd was no doubt anti-incarnation protesters. Again, how had they known where to protest? AllAether hadn't announced the second location yet.

A lady with a clipboard and a box of keys met them as they disembarked. Leta hefted her own bag and Mirabelle's from the trunk and stood with the seer as she waited to be ticked off the list and assigned a room key.

"1024," she said to Mirabelle, reading her room number.

"I am in 1032, presumably not far away."

"Shouldn't I be in a small room away from the fancy rooms?"

Mirabelle smiled. "This hotel has no small rooms, Leta."

They rode the elevator tube with several other crew for a trip up to what seemed to be a dedicated floor, as everyone got out on the tenth. Leta first helped Mirabelle to her room, or rather rooms, at the end of a hallway. Mirabelle unlocked the room and Leta hefted her bag through after her. Then she nearly dropped it in surprise at the opulence before her.

It was an entire apartment: A sitting room, a high-end kitchen, and a door through to a bedroom. The suite was at least as opulent as Mirabelle's rooms at Autumnwood Manor had been. Everything was ultramodern and sleek: glass and gold coffee, side and dining tables; forest green velvet lounge suite with matching ottoman; black leather dining chairs; even a glass desk with an executive chair. But the most eye-catching feature of the room was the floor-to-ceiling, wall-to-wall window made of three vast panes, affording a view of the city. Even though they were only on the tenth of forty floors, they could see all the way to Lake Astmere and the hills beyond to the south.

"Oh my gosh," said Leta.

"Even if your room is smaller, I imagine your view is similar. I don't suppose you've yet had much of a chance to enjoy accommodations such as these. Why don't you go look at your room? Enjoy the luxury."

"I'll do that," Leta replied in a breathless voice. She put Mirabelle's bag down by the door and turned to leave.

"Oh, just a moment," said Mirabelle as she poked at her aethervoicer.

"Yes?"

"I'd recommend learning the route to the contestants' rooms, and also to Jack's suite. When I ask you to deliver dailies, I do not want you to get lost. The contestants' rooms are between 1105 and 1117, and will be labelled with their names. Jack's room is higher up the tower, at 2032."

Leta nodded. "Understood. I'll scope it out." She picked up her own bag and backtracked until she found room 1024. It wasn't as impressive as Mirabelle's, but if she hadn't seen Mirabelle's first, she would have thought it was the fanciest hotel room she had ever seen. She took her boots off, though she knew it wasn't necessary in a hotel room. She just couldn't bring herself to traipse her dirty old boots through a room so fancy. With no one else around to see her being strange, Leta knelt down and ran her fingers over the rich, soft black carpet.

She had a tea and snack nook rather than a kitchen, and no separation between the living and sleeping areas. But she still had a glass desk and coffee table with an aetherweb globe on it, a spring green velvet two-seater sofa, a large bed with a velvet headboard that matched the sofa, and a bathroom with a massive tiled shower the size of a small room. And just as Mirabelle had surmised, Leta also had a floor-to-ceiling, wall-to-wall window, hers a single unbroken pane. The view wasn't the same as Mirabelle's because her room was facing a different direction, but if she went up to the window and looked hard to the right, she too could see the lake and the hills.

Despite the opulence, though, she was going to miss nature up in this room. It didn't even have an opening window for her to breathe the night air before bed as she liked. If nothing else, the room could have done with a potted plant.

Leta sat on the sofa and linked her aethervoicer with the aetherweb globe on the coffee table. She flicked away the hotel room service menu. A series of news headlines came up on the globe. Prominently displayed was a headline that read '*Goddess Found*: All you need to know about the latest developments.' She shouldn't look, she shouldn't look…

She opened the article.

Drama abounds on the set of Goddess Found! *If you hoped that one of the eight beautiful, talented contestants would stand out straight away as likely to be our Goddess Incarnate, you'll be disappointed right now as none of them seems more likely than the others. We have a way to go, though, so who knows how the aethercast will play out?*

So far, so bland. Leta started skim-reading.

...God Incarnate Jack, who seems more standoffish this year than he did last time...

There was truth to that. Leta thought it was because he was disillusioned, rather than him being any more anti-social than he had been.

...some truly talented mages. Perhaps some of these young ladies will grace the halls of the Geald Council one day?

Yeah, they probably would.

...and of course, we can't omit that Jack seems, if anything, more attracted to some random busty assistant than any of the contestants. Maybe he's been working out his frustrations with some extra-curricular activities? Wink, nudge.

Leta slapped her hand down on the globe, powering it down. *Nope. Nope. Big mistake. I should never have read that!*

Once again, she felt for a worry stone that wasn't there. Leta glanced around the room, looking for a distraction from her thoughts. *Some random busty assistant... argh! As if I'm just just a floating pair of disembodied boobs!* She stood and put her boots back on. Instead of torturing herself, she ought to do the task Mirabelle had set for her.

There was a floor-to-ceiling strip of mirror near the door. She paused, one boot on and one boot off, and looked at herself. *Some random busty assistant... damn, that's accurate.* She was wearing an old corduroy skirt, fluffy tights, and a home-knitted jersey. The juxtaposition between her and the room should have upset her, but she just found it funny. *Hunter and Harvester; why is anyone even paying me any attention at all? As if!* For a moment she considered putting one of the fancy blouses and the blazer on again, but she put that thought aside. It didn't matter today because the auto-aethercasters hadn't arrived yet. And maybe if she were herself more often, people would stop speculating.

She took the stairs up to the next floor and located rooms 1105 to 1117. They included all the rooms in one spur of hallway except the one at the far end, 1118, which ought to be a larger suite like Mirabelle's. Then she took the elevator tube up to the 20th floor and found Jack's suite 2032. She guessed other rooms nearby were allocated to the important aethercast people, perhaps Marcus, but nothing was labelled.

For some reason, she reached out to knock on Jack's door. It was as if her hand moved all on its own, and she watched it move in slow motion. What a silly thing to do. Though he wouldn't be here yet, surely. He would have been too busy to go straight to his room. And if he was here, why was she bothering him? Her heart hammering in her chest, she turned to run down the hallway back to the elevator tube, but it was too late. The door swung open. Jack had answered the knock.

THE FIRST THING Jack did when he got to his suite was change into his comfy evening clothes: old track pants, a t-shirt, and a cardigan his mum had knitted him years ago. He sighed in relief, mussed up his hair to get the tension out of his scalp, and looked around. There were twenty-four hours until the auto-aethercasters and the contestants arrived and it would be back to the work grind. He'd been looking forward to this break for days, to this opportunity to stop worrying about what he looked like and what people thought of him. But what else was he to do except lounge around watching the aetherweb globe? Jack considered going back to his apartment for the night, as it was only a half-hour walk away. But he didn't even like that apartment much: AllAether had found it for him.

And how often in his life would he have the chance to stay in a suite like this, even with his new position? He was in one of the fanciest suites in the fanciest hotel in all of Gealdland! It was full apartment-sized, with an immense expanse of windows showing a view of half of Astmere. Expensive velvet and glass furniture abounded. The kitchen not only had a stocked fridge, but also a stocked wine fridge! Which he didn't have to pay to make use of, because the charge-back was going to AllAether.

No, he would stay. He would stay and make the most of his freedom. If only he knew what to do.

A knock sounded on the door. He sighed and answered it, expecting to be called in for something and lose his freedom. Instead, he found Leta on his doorstep. A daily, already? Didn't Mirabelle get a break?

"Oh! Hello, come on in," he said, and swung the door wider, stepping aside for her.

A strange expression crossed Leta's face: one part horror and one part embarrassment. She dithered in the doorway. Jack wondered if his appearance was shocking in his comfy clothes. He gestured again for her to come in. "Don't worry: it is in fact me and not an impostor."

Leta stepped over the threshold. In case the auto-aethercasters came, Jack closed the door behind her so she wouldn't be spotted. Once he had done so, though, he realised it would look worse if anyone saw her leaving. Oh well.

Leta stood inside the door and looked around the suite, her jaw slack. He watched in amusement, wondering if he'd looked like that when he first arrived. She jolted and looked at him, her eyes running over his tatty old clothes. The look was appraising, but not judging.

"It's a fancy suite, isn't it?" he said, breaking the lengthy silence. "I don't know what to do with myself here."

Her look turned quizzical. "You're the God Incarnate," she said.

Did that mean she expected him to be in environments like the hotel? He hadn't ascended long enough ago to be used to it yet.

"I didn't always know that," he said. "I thought I was nobody." He shook his head. *Please see me for what I am*, he added silently. *Please see just a person.* But he'd hoped that before, since ascending, and had been disappointed. He didn't want to get his hopes up for her. "You have a daily for me?"

"Um, no," she said, and blushed. "I meant to find your room so I would know where to bring the dailies. I don't know why I knocked."

He raised his eyebrows. She just... knocked? Without meaning to? Jack understood her hesitation at the door. She had no real reason to be there, no assigned work tasks, if she was wandering. Jack thought of Ander's advice, to spend more time with people who he liked. And hadn't he been looking for something to do, anyway? "You on the clock?" he asked. "Because there're all kinds of booze in this room and the charge-back goes to AllAether. Would you like a drink before you go?"

He'd surprised her. She looked more agog at his words than she had at the suite. But her eyes flicked to the kitchen, then to the clock. He could see the temptation taking hold. "I'm more of a beer drinker than a fancy sparkling wine drinker," she said, pointing at the wine fridge.

"Ah!" he said and went to the normal fridge, padding across the kitchen tiles on his socked feet. He fetched two bottles of beer from the stock he'd found earlier and held one out to her. "*All* kinds of booze. Do you want it in a glass?"

She gave a wry smile, meeting his gaze for the first time since entering the suite. "Why? It's already in glass."

He couldn't contain his grin. "A lady after my own heart."

Jack found the bottle opener and cracked both the beers, handing one to Leta as he walked back into the sitting area. He sprawled on the sectional sofa, stretching his legs out along several seat cushions. He indicated Leta could take a seat too. She didn't seem as comfortable in his presence as he was in hers. She perched at the far end of the sectional sofa, her feet (now sans boots and shod only in cupcake-patterned socks over her tights) up on the edge of an ottoman.

"Cheers," said Jack, raising his bottle to her, and took a long swig of the beer, wincing as he found it to be stronger and more bitter than what he usually drank.

"Cheers."

"I'm sorry you've come across me looking like I'm in the middle of a lazy holiday," he said to Leta, who was already taking a second swig. "I figured I'd use this rare moment of downtime to relax." He pointed up at the ceiling in various directions. "Look! No auto-aethercasters!"

Leta looked up too, though he felt sure that she would have already noticed their absence. She had been so uncomfortable when she was pushed into the aethercast. "Fogarty is still at the manor, isn't he?" she asked.

"Yup. He'll come down with the contestants tomorrow, and then I'll be back to ignoring when my arse needs scratching. And certainly no sitting around in my underwear watching trashy 'casts." Jack froze, wondering if he'd been too comfortable and crude. But Leta snorted and covered her mouth. "I'm serious!" he doubled down.

Leta's eyes twinkled. "I'm sorry. Am I interrupting your plans? Should I go?"

"Will you be offended if I scratch?"

"No."

"Then, by all means, stay."

"I'm not sure I could handle you in your underwear, though."

He could tell she hadn't been aware of her innuendo until after she'd said it. While a dawning horror still encroached on her expression, Jack grinned and waggled his eyebrows at her. "No?"

Leta flushed bright red and hid her face behind her beer bottle. "Oh, my God! I didn't mean it like that. Hunter and Harvester, phrasing!" She was too adorable in her embarrassment.

Jack laughed despite himself. "You don't have to be so formal."

Leta looked up, puzzled.

"'Oh my God'?"

That did it. She was too embarrassed and annoyed at him to remain standoffish. "Oh! You!" She looked around as if for something to throw at him, but the cushions were a part of the sofa and she only had a beer bottle to hand. She shook her fist instead.

He chortled and took another drink. "Thanks for stopping by, even if you didn't mean to," he said. "No one jokes around with me anymore. Ander did the other night. But most people just see what I am now." He hadn't meant to sound so wistful, but there it was.

Leta's annoyance cleared, and she gave him a more sober look, her stormy grey eyes near piercing through him. "Mirabelle said she thought you might be lonely."

His face fell; he hadn't expected to be so easy for her to read. "Yeah, I guess. There are always people around, but…"

"Maybe not the right people?"

"Something like that." Jack sighed. Leta had seen right to the heart of the matter.

Leta raised her bottle in another toast. "Here's to finding the right people."

"I can drink to that."

THE EMPRESS
UPRIGHT

Delight in sensory experiences: touch, taste, smell!

General notice:

Please keep noise to a minimum and ensure you do not disturb the non-aethercast guests at Emerald Marquise Tower.

All crew with aethercasting talent, whether first, second, or third tier, are required to inform their line manager of their abilities. Failure to do so will lead to instant dismissal.

AllAether Executive Team

*W*hat in all the waters is happening? How am I here? That morning, if someone had told Leta that she would spend the afternoon socialising with the God Incarnate, she would have laughed at them. But there she was, perched on the lounge suite, drinking beer. Talking about Jack's feelings, as if this was all something that made any sense for her, Leta Wildwinter, to be doing.

"I don't know much about you," said Jack. "Where are you from?"

He wanted to know about her? No one usually bothered to ask. "I'm from a village called Little Ockstead."

"And what do you do when you're not doing contract work for aethercasts?"

Leta snorted. "This isn't something I've done before. I had a job at a bakery, but it went under. I've been having trouble finding a new job since I don't have enough magic to put on my CV."

"I had trouble with that before I ascended."

"You?" she asked. If he was the God Incarnate, surely he'd had magic?

"I had some kinetic magic, enough to do some landscape gardening. Moving soil around, building walls... that sort of thing. That's what I would have done." He paused, and his cheeks flushed. "Actually, I had a dream. I wanted to be a landscaping business owner, so it wouldn't matter that I wasn't so strong. I could hire people to do the heavy lifting."

It sounded a lot like her own dream. "I didn't realise that you were on the lower end of the spectrum," said Leta. "I thought... well, I guess I didn't think. You have more magic now?"

He took a sip of beer. "A bit more, but only passive stuff. I can see magic in action."

Leta took a sip of her own beer. She had no idea what to say about his magic that wouldn't sound either insensitive or ignorant. "My Mum has kinetic magic," she said. "She's a travel tube operator."

Jack drew air in over his teeth. "Wow, it takes a lot of magic for that."

"Yeah, she's strong. No idea why I came out the way I did."

Jack shrugged. "Who can say? But we should stop assigning so much value to magical strength, and more value to kindness and personality. It's all meaningless now in this age of aether storage and direct harnessing of the aethersphere."

Leta nodded along. He was voicing thoughts she'd had herself many times. Most mages were unnecessary these days, or at least one mage could do the job of twenty with the help of machines. Why did all job listings still expect magic?

"How about your father?" asked Jack.

Leta was quiet for a long moment, wondering how to answer this thorny question. "I don't know him," she said when she decided Jack had shown no signs of being uptight enough to care about what that implied.

"Oh, sorry," said Jack. "OK, hm." He snapped his fingers. "You once mentioned that Mirabelle called you a 'butterfly's wings'. Do you know what that's about yet?"

189

"No, but I haven't been thinking about it that much. I've been too busy. Mirabelle encourages me to talk to you more. Maybe my being here makes it more likely you'll find your goddess? But I don't understand how."

She could have sworn that Jack looked momentarily gob-smacked, but then he shrugged. "Ander said something similar, in a way."

"About me?"

"About people. That I should talk to more people, and when I feel close to someone, even if that person isn't the Goddess Incarnate, they could teach me more about what I'm looking for."

"So I'm here to give you a clue about the identity of the goddess?"

"Maybe."

"Like, what? She's a redhead? Or she wears glasses?"

He shrugged. "Or she drinks beer straight out of the bottle. Who knows?"

Leta nodded. "Well, if I can help you, I'll be happy with that."

He pointed to the kitchen. "You want some food to go with that beer? There's some stuff in the fridge."

She *was* a little hungry, but she didn't want to steal his food...

"I can see you're tempted. Come on."

Leta followed him to the kitchen. Jack dug around in the fridge, muttering to himself. He pulled out an armful of packages and dumped them on the black marble bench top. "This isn't the type of food I usually eat, but I'm sure something's nice." The packages were expensive deli goods: packets of marinated olives, fancy cheeses, a wrapped salami, a jar of sun-dried tomatoes. "Do we throw these things in a sandwich, or...?"

She smiled. "I suppose, but I think the olives and the tomatoes would make the bread soggy. It's all for making an antipasto platter. Are there crackers around too?"

"I think there's some stuff up here." He opened a cupboard and revealed a row of packets of crackers and breadsticks, and also some chocolate biscuits.

"They've given you enough rich foods to make you feel looked after, but not enough to avoid ordering room service for proper meals."

"Of course."

Leta started to feel the rhythm of the kitchen, the intention behind its design. She located a marble serving platter with gold trim and absent-mindedly pushed Jack aside to get the right type of crackers down. She opened packets, found a knife and chopping board, and got to work. Jack hovered over her shoulder. After a few minutes, she presented him with the assembled antipasto platter and gave a small curtsey. Jack took the platter and gasped. "Wow, so neat. Like a restaurant," he said under his breath. "How did you make the salami look like roses?"

Leta hadn't even thought about it: she'd been in charge of party spreads at her old bakery, so she'd done it all on autopilot. "This is nothing. I just put it on a board. You make it sound like I cooked you an entire meal." Leta wrapped the unused portions of all the food and put them away. "I want to learn more about food prep on a pâtisserie course, so I can own a bakery business. Right now, I'm saving up for the course fees. I'd have to start out small from home, with stuff like this along with pastries. Morning tea trays to be delivered to businesses. That sort of thing."

"I think you'd be great at it," said Jack. "Maybe catering for aethercasts? Did you speak to the catering staff at Autumnwood?"

"Yep. They gave me some great tips. I even did some of the baking you would have had while you were there. Catering for a large group sounds daunting, but lucrative. Maybe I could work up to that." She grinned at him as she was about to close the fridge. At that moment, he reached around her to grab another couple of beers. For a moment, their heads were way too close. He looked sideways and smiled. A dimple showed on his cheek. A dimple? Utterly unfair! Ridiculous, handsome man! While some strange magic, or more likely her own libido, froze Leta, he disappeared with the beers and the platter back to the sitting area.

Leta took a moment to collect herself before following him over.

"Does beer go with this food?" he asked when she got there. He had an eyebrow raised in a way that showed he already knew the answer.

"You're supposed to drink wine with this sort of thing. But who's watching?"

Jack grinned and pointed up. "Definitely not the auto-aethercasters!" He slapped a slice of cheese onto a cracker and topped it with quince paste, and ate the stack whole. "Mm, you know your way around a kitchen!" he said.

Leta shrugged. "This is all basic stuff. It's practised knife work, and I've had a lot of practise."

"Yeah, but you *dance* while you're in the kitchen."

Her eyebrows shot up. "Excuse me? I wasn't dancing!"

He shrugged. "It's like a dance."

She shook her head. What dancing?

"Thank you," he said.

There was sincerity in his eyes. It was just an antipasto platter, yet he seemed to think she'd done something special for him. "You're welcome."

He waved her forward, inviting her to eat. Leta shuffled along the sofa so she could reach. She took a cracker and a slice of cheese, and put a piece of sun-dried tomato on top. "That's good cheese."

"Yeah."

Leta finished the cracker and reached for another. Jack reached forward at the same time. Leta looked up into his eyes by accident and got caught there, food forgotten, looking at the subtle gold flecks in his light brown irises. She flushed. What would he think of a frumpy girl like her looking at him like he was as delectable as the antipasto platter?

She looked away, shrunk in on herself. "Sorry it's someone like me here with you today. I bet you'd be happier with one of the contestants."

"Why?"

"Because they're beautiful and talented."

Jack placed a finger under her chin and tilted her head up again. "So are you."

Leta heard static in her head. "Who, me?"

"Yeah."

"Fat and all?"

"Yeah."

"Glasses and all?"

"*Yeah.*"

There was a husky note in Jack's voice that at first she didn't recognise. She flushed bright red as realisation struck. "Oh. OH."

He broke eye contact with her for a moment to run his gaze over her body, giving her a moment of thinking time, although all she managed to think was, *What is happening? How is he interested in me?* The tension between them was like taut wires, and her body responded to it.

With the same crazy energy that she knocked on his door in the first place, she heard herself say in a breathy voice, "I can see you're tempted. Come on."

He grinned, recognising his own words thrown back at him. He slid a hand into her hair and guided her in for a kiss. She froze for a moment, then closed her eyes and leaned into the kiss, bracing herself against his shoulder. His lips parted against her own and she mirrored him. He tasted of quince paste and beer, not a favourite combination of hers, but it didn't matter. He felt *right*.

His free hand wandered, and they deepened the kiss. Leta was breathless, gulping in deep breaths of his petrichor scent. He was panting too. She had an urge to straddle his lap but didn't have the headspace for initiative. She gripped his thigh with her free hand, needing more support, more contact. His roaming hand tentatively brushed over her breast, testing out her reaction and boundaries. She moaned, and she felt his lips curve into a smile against her own. "I knew there'd be more to you," he murmured against her lips.

Leta jolted. He was wrong; there *wasn't* more to her. Her eyes opened, and the silver glow of his magic around her brought her crashing back to reality.

This was the *God Incarnate*. Who would soon find his goddess. There was no way she could even compare. This couldn't happen; it would break her heart.

She pulled away and stood up, trying to catch her breath. "Sorry, this isn't a good idea," she said.

He blinked up at her in surprise, his face flushed and his breathing ragged. His worn old track pants did nothing to hide that he was having a reaction of a more specific kind to their activities. She stepped back to avoid temptation. His foggy expression cleared. He looked hurt. "Sorry, did I misunderstand? If so, I'm sorry."

Leta shook her head. "That's not it. I'm not blaming you for anything. It's not a good idea, this idea we had? Bad. Bad idea. Um, I should go." She plonked her beer bottle onto the table, then scuttled over to the door and stomped her feet back into her boots.

"Wait!" he called after her. "Take some food! There's too much for me." He placed morsels of food into a glass from the bar cabinet, presumably because it was closer to hand than whatever bowls were in the kitchen. He held the glass out to her; it had wedges of cheese, olives, and sun-dried tomatoes in it. When she took it, he went back to wrap some crackers in a tissue and held them out to her too. "Just bring the glass back with the next daily reading."

"OK," she said, looking at the food in her hands and hoping no one would see her carrying a glass of snacks back to her room. It was a rather unconventional receptacle. She nodded. "See you later," she said as she opened the door. As she left Jack ran a hand through his hair, a complicated look on his face.

"See you later. Sorry for making you uncomfortable."

Leta nodded again, pointed along the hallway, and left.

JUSTICE
UPRIGHT

Be aware of your effect on others. You will be held accountable
for your actions. You may lose something if you act rashly.
If you rise above, you have nothing to worry about.

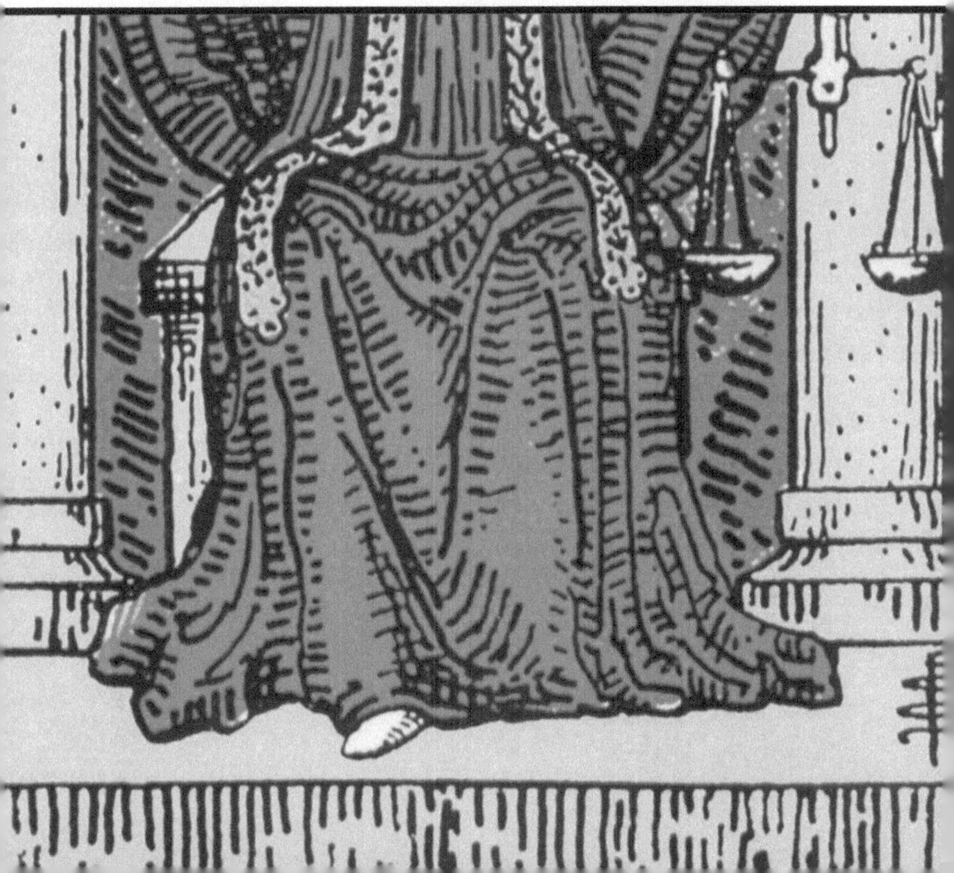

Tiffany,
  I know it's Mirabelle you usually get notes like
these from, but I have something to say.
  I had a vision that I think you need to hear about.
If Seer Mirabelle's assistant offers you something,
accept it. Let your actions speak well of you. Great
fortune will come of it.

Constance

p.s. Thank you for your help the other day. You are
not the kind of person I first took you for, and I'm
sure God Incarnate Jack noted your aid as well.

He was such an idiot. Jack spent most of his downtime beating himself up about scaring Leta off. Did that count as sexual harassment? He kept reminding himself that she *had* given him verbal permission. Had he misunderstood? Was she unclear about what he wanted, and she was offering something else? Because kissing her had been a mistake, judging by how fast she had run away. Though, hadn't she leaned in at first? Hadn't she put a hand on his thigh? But he knew people could change their minds even in the middle of something.

Or maybe his breath just stank.

Around midday, someone from Wardrobe visited and helped him choose a suit for the big evening event: welcoming the contestants to Emerald Marquise Tower. He also received information about the event: where he was to go, what he was to say, et cetera. It was more detailed than the missives he had received before, and more constricting. Along with the packet, he received a note: 'Someone will collect you for a meeting at 2pm. You'll be going to the ballroom from there.' Alas, the same messenger also gave him Mirabelle's daily viewing and, with a puzzled frown, the glass. "Thank you," said Jack, acting as if it was not at all strange to receive a glass with a letter. Then he sat down to read the daily.

Dear Jack,
   I had hoped to bring you new insights with the change in venue, but I must report to you that your reading is remaining remarkably consistent, even now. I am hopeful, even though confusion and loneliness remain with you. In my expert opinion, people with such consistent readings usually have a significant life event looming on the horizon. Reach out and connect with people. Beware betrayal. The goddess will make her appearance soon, but I cannot guarantee on what sort of timeframe 'soon' is measured.
   On a personal note, I received a message from an acquaintance who has similar advice for you. He is a man with particular expertise that must be regarded – Reach out to people. And, he says, take note if you find yourself looking at someone for a full minute with a silly grin on your face. He says he has thought more about instances like that and considers them to be of particular note.
               My warmest regards
               Mirabelle

There was no doubt in Jack's mind that Mirabelle's 'acquaintance' was Ander. The phrasing was exact. Jack sighed and slouched back in the sofa. *Take note if you find yourself looking at someone for a full minute with a silly grin on your face.* Yep, the exact wording. *Considers them to be of particular note.* Jack's eyes widened as the message from Ander, relayed through Mirabelle, came into resolution for him. Ander suspected Leta might be the goddess. That must be it. The reason that possibility jumped out at Jack is that, somewhere in the back of his mind, he suspected the same. Yesterday had been too quick and easy, the way they had hung out together like they'd known each other for ages. The way their words had sparked off each other. The way they had near fallen into each other as they kissed. It was a gravitational pull. Maybe she wasn't, and he just had the hots for her. But maybe she was. He had to consider the possibility.

Mirabelle said a vision told her to hire me. I'm a butterfly's wings, or something like that.

If she was the goddess, then Mirabelle knew. She'd engineered their meeting.

Mirabelle encourages me to talk to you more.

Yep, either she suspected, or she knew. Either way, Leta's presence in his life was Mirabelle's doing.

But: *She doesn't have enough magic to support ascension.* Marcus had said the specialists were sure she couldn't be. They were likely monitoring anyone in the crew who was young and female. Was that it, then? Or were they wrong? Were they basing their judgement off the wrong criteria? Did he trust AllAether to notice the goddess in their midst if she wasn't the type of goddess they thought she would be?

A knock on the door jolted Jack out of his reverie. He slid the incriminating letter — incriminating for Mirabelle — under the sofa and went to answer the door. A runner stood waiting on the other side. "This way, please," she said.

Jack followed the runner to the elevator tube. She was a young woman about the right age to be the goddess. Why was this runner sent to him, and not another, on a day when there were no auto-aethercasters? Was she also on the 'not the goddess' list, if there was such a thing? How carefully were they controlling who he saw in a day, even among the crew?

The runner led him up to the boardroom on the thirty-ninth floor and opened the door for him. Marcus sat at the large boardroom table, as did Evelyn Windrift. A grey-haired man Jack did not know sat at the head of the table, his fingers steepled. The man's eyes were hidden behind horn-rimmed glasses that shone with spells to Jack's vision. The backlighting from the window obfuscated his features enough that Jack wasn't sure he'd be able to pick the man out of a crowd later.

"Come in, Jack," said Marcus.

Jack waited to be offered a seat, but he wasn't, so he stayed on his feet. The man at the head of the table made no move to introduce himself, so Jack was left wondering.

"We've called you here today to make it clear to you how the rest of the season is going to go," said Marcus.

"If this is about Saturday, you already gave me a dressing down."

"New information has come to light," said Evelyn, nodding to Marcus as if he were the source of the information.

Jack firmed his footing. "Oh?"

"You were followed, Jack," said Marcus. "And that person saw you colluding."

"Colluding? Ander and I were chatting about our unique situations. He was giving me advice about being a God Incarnate."

"Not him," said Evelyn. "We know you're colluding with the seer."

Jack frowned. "Because Mirabelle visited the *one and only pub* in the village on the same night as I did, you think there is some sort of collusion going on? I went nowhere near her."

"Our informant says that her assistant relayed a message to you."

Jack snorted. "That's just silly. I ran into her near the loos, but so what?"

"You were seen talking to her."

"Yeah, just a common chat, like lots of people do in pubs. Anyway, AllAether kept throwing her at me at Autumnwood Manor to create drama for the aethercast. Isn't it only natural that I'd keep talking to her out of habit off site?"

Marcus sighed. "Oh, come off it. You expect us to believe you were having a friendly, flirty chat? After you ran off with a person you weren't supposed to have met before?"

What were they thinking? That he already knew Ander in this incarnation? That they were planning... something? He looked at all three of their stern faces; the silent man at the head of the table the most stern of all. "Yeah, I do. And I hadn't met Ander before that day. Not in this lifetime, at least."

"Why did you run off?" asked Marcus. "If Ander planned it all, how would he have even done so before he got here?"

Perhaps they suspected Mirabelle had helped Ander plan their escapade, and were trying to get him to implicate her. It would be better to steer the conversation away from her, but the only other person in play was Leta. "So you think an assistant on a short-term contract, one from a small village, somehow knows the God Incarnate of another nation? Marcus, you're not making sense."

"No: we think Mirabelle sent her assistant to you with messages to plan it," said Evelyn. "And we let it happen right under our noses, even giving her more opportunity to talk to you, because for some unfathomable reason you're keen on her."

Unfathomable? Jack wanted to stick up for Leta — he felt pretty sure it wasn't just him who would be keen on her. "We're here to find the goddess, right? Then instead of flinging around wild accusations of intricate plots, all for the sake of, what, a few pints of beer? Maybe you should pay attention to who I think is attractive, not who is popular with the populace in general, and use my preferences as selection criteria for the contestants on the aethercast."

Marcus snorted. "No one would watch an aethercast with a bunch of porky commoners trying to woo a fat chaser."

Jack took a deep breath in through his nose and exhaled through his mouth. He rarely felt the urge to commit violence, but he was in that moment. Leta's figure was a *gift*, not something to be derided. "You know, I can't believe it's taken me so long to realise what a nasty person you are, Marcus. How naïve was I?" He looked at Evelyn. "By the way, he's fucking one of the contestants. I won't tell you which one because with the power dynamic in play, it's not her fault. But he is."

Evelyn's face contorted with rage, and she let out a screech like a rusty door being torn off its hinges. Jack covered his ears and grinned. It looked like he'd been right about Marcus's mystery lady. A fey light gathered at Evelyn's fingertips and in her eyes as she clambered onto the table. Jack's grin dropped; he hadn't counted on her being a battle mage.

"You're doing WHAT?" she shrieked as she reached for Marcus.

Marcus let out a strangled squawk and toppled out of his chair. Beams shot from Evelyn's fingers over his head, and burned black scorch marks into the far wall.

"Babe, you're listening to *him*?" Marcus yelled, an edge of panic in his voice. A cold wind whipped up within the room, and it didn't come from Evelyn. It was Marcus's own weather magic.

"I'm going to cut your dick off and feed it to my dogs!"

The man at the head of the table cast up a glowing shield spell to protect himself, and another around Marcus, not a single iota of surprise or consternation on his face. "God Incarnate, you'd better go down to the ball-room and prepare for the contestants. You've done enough here. You'll be sans host, it seems. Have fun."

Jack, still unaware of who the man was, recognised the dismissal and the chastisement. Having to deal with the big event without Marcus's leadership would be tricky, and he supposed he deserved it, but he didn't re-gret his words. He felt exhilarated. And seeing Evelyn, her battle magic thwarted by the grey-haired man, jump down off the table onto Marcus and start slapping him around the head was more satisfying than it ought to be. Perhaps Jack had some soul-searching to do. It seemed he was a pettier person than he should be. "Sure thing," he said. "You'll get your event."

"We'd better, or you're in breach of contract."

Jack saluted and left the boardroom. Evelyn's shrieks were audible in the corridor. The now terrified-looking messenger was still standing out in the hallway.

"The aethercast will need to get through the rest of the day without Marcus, it seems," said Jack. "He is, um, in-disposed." Both the messenger and Jack jumped when a loud crash sounded from inside. "May I have your help to organise the arrival of the contestants? Unless you'd rather stay here."

The poor woman jumped to attention. "I would be glad to help, God Incarnate, sir."

THE EMPEROR
REVERSED

Consider the power dynamics of your life: are you taking advantage of others, or are you being taken advantage of? Does anything need to be adjusted? How can you step up?

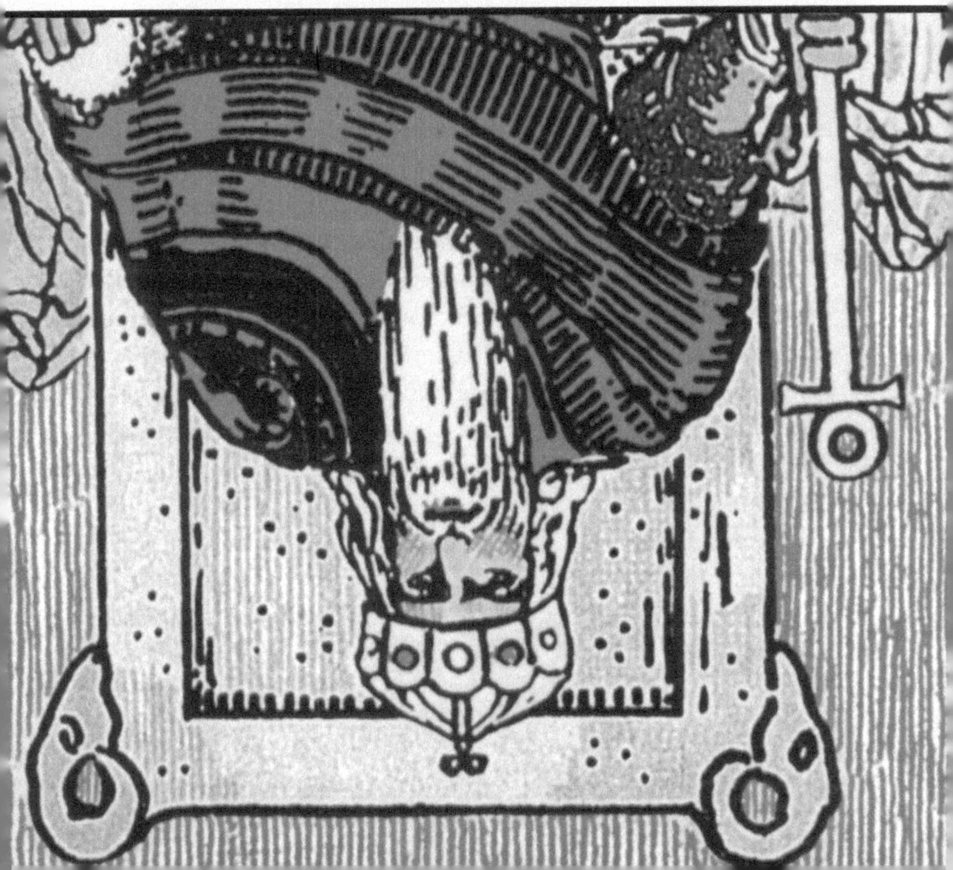

M,

We need to bring our plans forward. This place is a powder keg.

The preliminary results are promising. If you see an opportunity to set things in motion, take it.

G

M irabelle and Leta stood together on a mezzanine above the main atrium to watch the contestants arrive. Other crew gathered nearby. A few gave Leta tentative smiles, and a few others seemed to be whispering about her, which made her skin crawl: word had got out about how Leta had been used by AllAether.

Leta dreaded the auto-aethercasters' return. Although, since AllAether had decided she was too boring, Leta was more concerned about how Jack would fare.

"I wonder what's happening?" said Mirabelle. "I would have thought Marcus would be in position by now." Leta spotted a few concerned-looking crew members milling about below. A young woman, one of the work experience runners, jogged into the foyer to relay a message, which caused more concern. She looked about, and up, looking for someone, then sprinted for the stairs. Half a minute later, she bumped through the door from the café onto their mezzanine and ran to Mirabelle.

"Seer Mirabelle! The God Incarnate requests your help as soon as possible."

Mirabelle and Leta looked at each other in surprise. "Of course," said Mirabelle. "Please tell me about it on the way."

As they followed the runner, Mirabelle leaned on Leta's arm. Her cane thumped on the floor with every second step. "I'm not good with speed," she said in a low voice.

Leta nodded. "I understand. Lean on me as much as you need to."

"Marcus is, um, not available," said the runner as they walked to the elevator tube. "There's no host to welcome the contestants. The board told Jack to deal with the event, but he can't be in two places at once. The ballroom has already been set up as the place where he receives them. Someone needs to greet them in the foyer and send them to the ballroom. And Jack suggested you might be a not-too-unexpected person to do so."

"How much time do we have? And what is your name?"

"We've asked the drivers to take the scenic route. About half an hour. And my name is Ceresa."

They arrived at the elevator tube. "All right," said Mirabelle. "Here's what we're going to do: Leta, go up to my rooms and fetch my stationery set, the envelopes and paper. Also, get my bones. They are the quickest. Ceresa, take me to a quiet room as close to the foyer as you can find." Mirabelle handed her key to Leta.

Leta nodded. "I'll go to reception with the things."

"OK."

Leta made the round trip to Mirabelle's room as fast as she could. Ceresa was already waiting and ushered her down a corridor behind the reception desk to a meeting room for hotel staff. Mirabelle was there, and so was Jack, pacing by the window. He wore a tailored suit, the clean lines of which couldn't hide the taut energy around him. He looked up at her and flushed. Leta flushed too, remembering their last encounter. She hoped the perceptive Mirabelle wouldn't see that something had happened between them, something that shouldn't have happened.

Leta delivered Mirabelle's supplies to her and stood in the corner, out of the way. Mirabelle sat at the table and started a rapid-fire set of auguries with the bones, scrawling quick messages down on papers after each one. She also added to each note, 'Please head to the ballroom now. I will point the way.'

Jack drifted closer to Leta. *No, not now!* she thought. *Don't talk to me now!*

"That's impressive," he said to her, indicating Mirabelle at work.

Leta's shoulders relaxed when it became clear Jack was going to ignore the… incident. "Yes. She's good at her job."

"Can you *see* what she's doing?"

Leta shook her head. "I have little magic, remember?" said Leta.

"Of course," he said. "But now, I'm seeing a massive concentration of power around those bones and running through Mirabelle. I expect she's going to be exhausted after this."

"Thank you," said Leta. "I'll take extra care of her afterwards."

Jack nodded. "Um, about yesterday…" he said in a quieter, more hesitant voice.

Leta looked at him with wide eyes. "No need to say anything!"

"But…"

"No need!"

"I'm sorry I made you uncomfortable," he said, and then drifted away to look at what Mirabelle was doing.

Leta approached the table and began folding the dailies. Mirabelle paused her readings to address eight envelopes, then continued, leaving Leta to stuff and seal the envelopes.

A production assistant stuck his head into the room and said, "They're nearly here!"

"Go to the ballroom, Jack," said Mirabelle. "We will handle this end. Leta, can you go peek out into reception and tell me when you see the first car roll up?"

"Yes, sure."

Leta and Jack left the meeting room at the same time. "Good luck," she said to him as he left along the hallway in the opposite direction.

He turned and walked backwards for a few steps. "Thank you," he said, with more feeling than she expected. The tension around his shoulders was visible even at a distance. She didn't know what had thrown the day into such disarray, but it was stressing Jack.

He disappeared down the corridor, and she went to stand in reception.

While she stood there, trying to keep her face placid and unremarkable, she came to a rather devastating realisation. She was too late to pull herself away from him to protect her heart. She'd already fallen for him. And now she was preparing herself for several more weeks of watching rich, powerful, beautiful women throw themselves at him, and maybe even him finding his soulmate, the Goddess Incarnate.

What a fool she was.

She squared her shoulders. She couldn't have him for herself; that much was clear. He was too important for the likes of her, and pre-claimed by some unknown person. But she could help him. By how stressed out he had looked, he could use some more help. She would think about how later.

A car pulled up in front of the main doors, and an auto-aethercaster hovered above it, recording its approach. Leta turned and ran to the meeting room. She popped her head in and announced, "They're here."

Mirabelle was putting the last daily reading into the last envelope. "It is my time to appear on the aethercast once more, I suppose. How do I look?"

"As well-dressed as ever," said Leta. She wasn't just saying it: yet again, Mirabelle was wearing expensive-looking wool, with a silk scarf draped just so around her neck. Her makeup was perfect, as was her silver hair. She wouldn't look out of place.

"Well," she said, and used her cane to stand up. "Here I go. Feel free to return to the mezzanine to watch."

Mirabelle made her way to reception and then stood waiting where Leta had, her shoulders squared and her back as straight as possible for an old woman who walks with a cane. Before the contestants arrived, followed by a cloud of auto-aethercasters, Leta took the back stairs up to the mezzanine. She stood at the far end where she could see out the window into the forecourt below.

The cars had trouble getting to the door. A large gaggle of anti-incarnation protesters had gathered, enough that the security guards struggled to hold them back. One by one, the cars disgorged the contestants, who were all wearing fashionable dresses. The women did their best to ignore the chants as they made their way into the lobby to be greeted by Mirabelle and read their hasty dailies.

At one point, the crowd surged forward, threatening the car that had just pulled up at the curb. Leta's heart was in her mouth as she worried whether the occupant would be OK. The door opened and Destiny's red head emerged.

Leta's eyes narrowed as she remembered what she saw in the garden. The protesters rushed, and Destiny seemed to panic, shrinking against the car. It was only because Leta was watching so closely that she saw a protester tuck a piece of paper into Destiny's hand. No one else seemed to notice. Destiny hammed up her fear, and a security guard shielded her all the way from the car to the door.

Keeping a closer eye on Destiny was something else Leta could do.

Once the last contestant was being handed her daily, Leta returned to the meeting room. Soon after, Mirabelle re-entered the room and sagged against the door. Her face was grey and drawn-looking, and she looked like she had little energy left. "They're all on their way to the ball-room now. Our work here is done."

"You look like you need a rest. I'll carry your things."

In the elevator tube on the way up, Leta told Mirabelle about what she'd seen.

"Most interesting. Thank you for telling me, Leta. This is the second time you have spotted Destiny acting suspiciously."

"What do you think it's all about?"

"After you saw her the last time, I made some en-quiries. It appears her branch of the Brightbornes is in a bit of grief with the rest of them and has been 'cut off,' so to speak. I do not know why."

"What does that mean?"

"It means, dear Leta, that you have likely discovered why the anti-incarnation protesters keep finding where we are before AllAether announces our location. I imag-ine Destiny is not as rich as she would have people believe."

"And she's taking bribes?"

"Most likely."

In the end, Leta also half-carried Mirabelle along the hallway to her suite. She got the older woman cosy on the sofa with a blanket, a cup of tea, and a room service order on the way. Then she left her in peace to eat and nap until her energy returned.

"Thank you, Leta," said Mirabelle before she left. "You're a kind young woman."

Leta smiled. "Just get some rest, please."

ALTHOUGH ASSISTANTS BUSTLED around doing last-minute checks, Jack felt alone. He didn't want to be doing any of this. He wanted to spend more time with Leta to figure out if Ander's, and his own, suspicions were correct. What a waste of time all of this was if she was the goddess! Or not, as he had met her because of the aether-cast.

Also, maybe she didn't want to spend time with him. The way she had shied away from him in the meeting room, he had messed up even more than he thought he had. But she had taken the time to wish him luck, so perhaps she didn't hate him.

Eight large armchairs sat in a semi-circle in front of the ballroom's small stage. The intention had been for the contestants to show off their magical abilities yet again, this time in more detail. But Marcus was the one who knew what everyone had planned and how to segue into their demonstrations. Also, Leta's shame at not having useful magic was niggling at him. Why wave around the contestants' powerful magic and make the viewership feel inadequate when, as Jack well knew, powerful magic wasn't relevant to ascension? So, to tie their arrival to the welcome from Mirabelle, Jack altered the plan on the fly.

He was going to get in so much trouble. Maybe. It wasn't a radical idea he had, just one that he hadn't run by anyone else, and now he didn't have time to do so.

The assistants left, and then soon after, the fleet of auto-aethercasters entered the ballroom over the heads of the eight contestants. They looked around, surprised to see only Jack. He stood and paused a moment for the auto-aethercasters to capture his best angle, just as Marcus had always drummed into him, and then held his hands out.

"Welcome to Emerald Marquise Tower. I hope your journey from Autumnwood Manor was pleasant. Please, take a seat."

When they were all seated, Jack took his seat too. "I thought we would start the afternoon with a bit of a round-table discussion," he said. "You were welcomed to the tower today with a new set of viewings and insights from Seer Mirabelle. Ever since you arrived at Autumn-wood Manor, you've received daily viewings and divinations, and weekly in-person card readings. Very few people have such access to a seer's advice. I suspect that some of you have, like myself, found her viewings to be enlightening beyond the scope of this aethercast. So far, our interactions have been mostly one-to-one. But we're a team here, bringing this 'cast together. So, in the spirit of team-building exercises, let's discuss the signifi-cator cards that we've used for our readings, and what they've taught us about ourselves."

At the term 'team-building exercises', many of the women's gazes glassed over. *Tough*, thought Jack. *I'm in charge, and I think the original plan of showing off everyone's powers is tasteless.*

"I'll go first," he said. "The significator card I've been using is the Page of Swords. What I've learned through this card is that I'm very new to being the God Incarnate. I have a whole life ahead of me in this role, but very little behind me. I think I can bring a fresh outlook to Gealdland, but I don't know what that is yet. No matter what, I need to move forward. But I think this card also calls out some of the less admirable parts of my personal-ity, such as the ability to be two-faced when needed, or calculating. I'd like to work on that. Would anyone else like to share?"

They seemed shocked at his openness, but Jack didn't regret it. The country could either learn to accept him as he was, or not. He was tired of pretending he had any control over who he was.

He wondered whether anyone would voluntarily share, but then Tiffany put up a hand. "I've been using the Queen of Swords. I could go on about how the card makes me think of clear communication, and sticking up for myself, or something like that, but I suppose what it has taught me is that I can be a bitch sometimes. There was a situation the other week where I was being bitchy to someone without getting my facts straight, and that person was kind to me, despite the way I was acting. I need to do better."

Jack nodded. "That is insightful. Thank you for sharing. I think this situation they have thrown us into has highlighted for many of us where we could do better. It's difficult to admit, though. Tiffany, you're very brave. Does anyone else want to share?"

Destiny's hand shot into the air. "Mirabelle selected the Knight of Swords for me. I don't agree. I should have been a queen, not a knight, because I'm a woman. But the Knight of Swords, I looked it up, and it's all about ambition. I'm a very driven person, I work hard, and I'm glad that the seer could see that." She smiled as she completed her analysis.

Jack suspected there was more to the Knight of Swords than just ambition, but Destiny didn't seem the type to admit her faults. He wasn't familiar with all the cards, but he thought the Knight of Swords also meant arrogance, or something like that. "Thank you, Destiny. Anyone else?"

One by one, the contestants shared their significators. Nellie said she used the Queen of Pentacles and talked about the importance of a pleasant home, which gave her preoccupation with furniture context. Jess said she used the Queen of Cups, which she claimed meant that she followed her heart. Jack thought she could do with following her heart a little less, since she was partly responsible for the domestic happening upstairs. Chrissie said she used the Page of Cups and tried to claim it was because she was such a smoothie fanatic. Jack left it at that; there was no way that was the reading that Mirabelle had intended.

As his impromptu segment continued, Jack felt more confident in his choice. The aethercast would have a lot of capture to use that would give the audience at home an insight into who these people were. That would interest many viewers. It would also interest the selectors for the Gealdr Mentorship Programme, so how could AllAether complain? Some of these contestants were using the opportunity he had presented them to show themselves in a good light, which was no doubt what most of them wanted. Sure, they all hoped that they might be the goddess, or someone in their life hoped they might be. But they also all wanted attention for themselves to sustain them. The contestants would ride on the coat-tails of the aethercast for a while, being guests at events, setting themselves up as consultants, etc. Their magic was a given, but who they were would go further. He'd been covering his own arse when he came up with this idea, but he had probably won a lot of loyalty from them.

The door at the back of the ballroom cracked open, and Marcus stuck his head in. He mouthed, *What are you doing?* at Jack, but Jack kept listening to the contestant who was speaking. He couldn't respond to Marcus without drawing everyone's attention to the back of the room.

The last contestant finished giving her take on her significator. Jack stood up and said, "Thank you, everyone, for your insights. I've learned more about all of you. I hope you've learned more about each other as well."

He had been intending to call for the porters who would escort them to their rooms, but Marcus chose that moment to sweep into the ballroom and wrest back control of the aethercast. He walked across the ballroom to their circle, giving a slow applause. Jack was pretty sure that he was wearing thick concealer and foundation on his face. That was… worrying.

"Thank you all, and thank you, Jack," said Marcus. "A most enlightening discussion." He walked through the circle and stood near Jack's chair. "And welcome to Emerald Marquise Tower. In this second half of our aethercast season..."

Jack tuned out again as Marcus spoke at length about the hotel and hinted at upcoming events for the aethercast. Something about a boat ride on Lake Astmere? Something about a series of romantic dinner dates in the city? Standard fare. Instead of listening, Jack eyed the bruises visible under Marcus's makeup. What had Jack done? His guilt sat like a rock in his stomach. He vowed to never again drop someone into trouble the way he'd done to Marcus that day. Or, if he did, to do his best to mitigate the harm instead of just walking away.

Who was he if he couldn't do even that much? Not a good person, that was for sure.

Marcus announced the end of the welcoming event, and the porters led the contestants away. Jack and Marcus stood together, watching them go. Jack tried his best not to let on about the tension between them. Soon they were alone in the ballroom. Jack took a deep breath. "I know I'm probably the last person you want to hear this from, but if she treats you like that, then getting out is a good idea."

Marcus pivoted towards Jack. "You're right. I don't want to hear it from you. You're the one who made her angry at me, you piece of shit."

"I didn't know she was a battle mage, and certainly not one willing to use her magic on you. I'm so sorry. Call me what you want. But stay safe. Get out." Jack then walked away. It was better for both of them if they kept their distance from one another.

Jack trudged back to his suite. He collapsed onto the sofa and ran a hand over his face, and then rolled his shoulders, trying to get the tension out. He was debating taking a bath, both to help ease his stress and escape the auto-aethercasters, which had been programmed to not follow him into the bathroom, when someone knocked on the door. Jack sighed and hauled himself to his feet; perhaps it was Evelyn or that other board member he hadn't been introduced to, here to fire him and escort him off the premises? But instead, Leta stood outside the door, wearing another cosy jersey, this one grey-green, and clutching a daily viewing for him. He fought a smile as she held the envelope out.

"Mirabelle asked me to wait for a reply," she said.

"Interesting. Come on in." He took the envelope, waved her in, and closed the door behind her. He wanted to talk more about the day before, about what happened between them, but the two auto-aethercasters hovered nearby. They were treading on thin ice already, having her in his suite. If AllAether got any further sign he was keen on her, they might have another go at using her to cause drama with the contestants. He wanted to spare her. So instead, he ignored her as he opened the envelope. They stood a decent distance from one another, Leta staying near the door in a way that cried out, 'I'm going to leave again as soon as humanly possible.'

Jack unfolded the letter inside and angled it away from the auto-aethercasters. It wasn't Mirabelle's handwriting.

> To Jack,
> Things are looking very hard for you at the moment, and I'm worried about you. Is there anything I can do?
> Leta

She'd left a large clear area at the bottom for him to reply. Clever woman, using her position in such a way. Without looking at her, Jack went over to the desk, sat down, and laid his hands over the paper as he wrote in a way that further obstructed their correspondence.

*The reason today was such a clusterfuck was that
I had a big argument with Marcus, and I spilled the
beans to his girlfriend that he's canoodling with a
contestant (Jess, btw). Marcus's girlfriend is Evelyn,
and she's a battle mage. It didn't go well. At first I
was satisfied to see Marcus in trouble because he's
been such a git, but now I think back, it was awful. I
feel so bad. Burn this letter after you read it! I
shouldn't be putting this in writing!*

*I just want to go somewhere with no auto-
aethercasters for a while. A one-day break wasn't
enough. Yesterday was great, and I enjoyed our time
together. I'm sorry if I made you uncomfortable.
Maybe after this season of the aethercast we could
catch up?*

Your friend,
Jack

p.s. The green suits you.

He folded the letter again and stuffed it into its envelope, then walked over and handed it to Leta. He kept his
face neutral as he said, "Thank you for waiting."

Leta bobbed a curtsey and was gone again in mere
moments.

Jack sighed at his own manipulativeness — the two-
faced nature he'd admitted to in the ballroom. He knew
full well he was seeding an idea in Leta's mind that might
eventuate in the vision Constance had seen. He vowed to
keep Leta safe if she got in trouble for anything she did
for his sake. Just that day, he'd learned what happened
when he let people around him get hurt.

He also belatedly realised that he'd asked her to burn
a letter in a hotel riddled with smoke detectors. What an
idiot.

THE CHARIOT
UPRIGHT

T<small>AKE ACTION</small>. Y<small>OU CAN DO IT</small>!

Marcus,
My lawyer heard from your lawyer. Fuck you,
prick. Fuck. You.

Evelyn

It was an incriminating letter. No wonder he wanted it destroyed. Leta read Jack's letter several times over, lying on her bed. She had to hide her face in the duvet to re-equilibrate, both because of the compliment and the reminder of her brazenness the day before. What had she been thinking?

Actually, she knew what she was thinking. She was going to help him. Yes, she was considering giving herself a lot of extra work and stress for the sake of a man who would soon forget about her. Yes, she was setting herself up for heartache. But he needed help, that much was clear. He wasn't happy, and AllAether wasn't listening to him. But Leta was.

First, she had to get rid of the letter. He had said to burn it, but that wasn't a good idea in a hotel. Instead, she took it in the shower with her and tore it up into little soggy shreds and washed them down the drain. She thought all day Saturday and came up with a plan that she implemented on Sunday when she had some free time.

Leta took a deep breath and squared her shoulders as she stood outside the meeting room. She would need to be a different version of herself for this: a confident self, a

self who believed in her own ability to do something useful with her magic. And, fingers crossed, if she looked
confident enough, Fogarty wouldn't remember she was
the Mundane girl.

She knocked on the door. "Come in," came a bored-
sounding call. Dozens of glass globes, much like
Mirabelle's crystal ball, covered the meeting table, each
sitting on a plain wooden stand and showing a live 'cast
from an auto-aethercaster. They displayed all the contestants and Jack, some of them more than once from
several angles. Fogarty sat at the table, lounging in a re-
cliner chair and watching all the globes. His longish hair
looked like it hadn't been brushed in days, his clothes
were rumpled, and he had deep bags under his eyes.
Leta's hopes sank. This wouldn't work. He was much too
busy and tired to help her.

"Leave the message over there; I'll read it later," said
Fogarty.

"I don't have a message for you." She quailed when
Fogarty gave her a quick look.

"What are you here for? You lost?"

"I've been thinking about future employment opportunities. I'm on a fixed term agreement, so I'm learning
about types of magic that I could get into after this. May
I ask you a few questions about aethercasting?"

"Have you been tested and confirmed as an aethercaster?"

"Well, no, but…"

"Thousands of kids across the country have. They'll
get jobs ahead of you. You're wasting your time here." He
slouched further down into his chair and took a sip of
what looked like a cold cup of tea, the milk fat a solidified
scum on the top.

"What about hard work and perseverance?"

Fogarty reached into a box under the table and
lobbed something over his shoulder at her. She near fum-

bled the catch, but caught the object on the second attempt. It was an auto-aethercaster, its front globe dim and the propellers lying limp. "Can you turn that on?"

Leta turned it around and around in her hands, but couldn't see any way of turning it on.

"If you can't do that much, how would you expect to get into my line of work? Look elsewhere." He sounded very bored indeed.

Leta spotted a chip on the globe. "This one's broken. That's not a fair test."

"It still turns on; it just captures a bad image. You not being able to turn it on has nothing to do with its condition. Now, go away. I'm busy."

She'd wanted to figure out how the auto-aethercasters turned on so she could turn off the ones following Jack. But with Fogarty watching the capture in real time at all hours, that wouldn't have worked, anyway. But she had an idea. "May I keep this, since it's broken? You know, to practise on."

"Sure, whatever. I was going to throw it away. Spend all your free time trying to turn it on, see if I care." Then he swore. "Blast it, another one's down. Where did AllAether buy these pieces of crap?" He ignored her, instead tapping at a crystal ball that had no image in it.

Leta left the meeting room, her new acquisition in hand. If she could get it turned on and capturing, what a boon it would be! But even if she could get it flying, she might be able to use it to help Jack. She didn't care about image quality. Maybe she could sneak a non-operational auto-aethercaster in to watch Jack while Fogarty was distracted and give Jack some downtime.

Leta still had one other avenue of inquiry regarding aethercasting. Had Leta won Tiffany over with her assistance that day? Could she convince her to be of help?

Leta went back to Mirabelle's suite and asked for more stationery and an envelope addressed to Tiffany.

Mirabelle, who was on board with Leta's attempts to help Jack, obliged. "Best of luck, Lady Butterfly," she said.

Leta saluted, feeling awkward about the reminder that she was here to accomplish… something. Maybe Mirabelle was right. Maybe this was it. Then she went back to her room to write a letter.

> *Tiffany,*
> *   Sorry to approach you like this. Leta writing, by the way. Would you help me? I have a broken auto-aethercaster. I just need to get it flying, not capturing.*
> *   Leta*

She delivered the letter. Tiffany answered her door wearing a red silk dressing gown, even though it was the afternoon. Leta held out her letter. "Mirabelle has asked me to wait for you to reply," she said. "There's a question for you about your private viewing schedule in the letter."

Tiffany took the letter, opened it, and scanned it over. Her eyes widened. "Why don't you come in and have a cuppa while I respond?"

Leta stepped over the threshold. Tiffany's room was like Leta's, but the decor was teal and silver. It was surprisingly messy, considering that she had an auto-aethercaster in there with her recording the clothes thrown over the back of the sofa and on the foot of the bed.

As soon as the door shut, Tiffany gestured at her auto-aethercaster and it fell to the carpet.

"Ok, what's up? Why do you need to get a broken auto-aethercaster flying? Why would you even need to do that?"

Leta blinked, her brain still trying to catch up. It fell. Just like that. "Do you do that much? Is Fogarty getting suspicious?"

Tiffany grinned. "I think he is, but he's overworked and underpaid, and I suspect he doesn't give a shit. So, out with it."

"I want to replace Jack's auto-aethercaster with a non-functioning one."

Tiffany took a step back and crossed her arms. "You want me to help you get private time with the God Incarnate? Why wouldn't I get that for myself if I could?"

Leta sighed. This again? "It's not like that."

"Really? Because it sounds to me like you're trying to find the space to pursue Jack."

Leta flushed. Why did everyone keep jumping to that conclusion? Was she making lovesick eyes at him? *Oh no,* she realised. *I am making lovesick eyes at him. That's why everyone keeps thinking I'm pursuing him!* She flushed even hotter.

"I won't deny that I like him," she said. "I guess that's pointless. But I'm not trying to buy him time to spend with *me.* I'm trying to buy him time to get away from the 'cast for a bit. He looks stressed out, and the schedule isn't leaving him any time for himself."

"Right-o. You're smitten, sure, but you're intending to do that selfless thing and help him out, and what, then, pine?"

Leta shrugged. "Whatever. Can you help?"

"You mentioned a broken auto-aethercaster. I don't know where to get one of those, but I do know how to get someone out of the hotel undetected. It's not so difficult that you need something like a spoof auto-aethercaster."

"Oh, but I have one." Leta held out her daily spoils.

Tiffany inspected the small machine. "How did you get this?"

Leta shrugged.

"For fuck's sake, Constance is terrifying," she said under her breath.

"Constance?"

"She told me to accept anything you bring me. I thought she meant the dailies and was like, 'well, duh'. But this… OK, tell you what: Let's make a deal. You give me this, which will be useless for you anyway, and I'll help you enact your crazy 'free Jack' plan, OK?"

"What do *you* want that for?"

Tiffany shrugged. "Spying, of course."

Leta shook her head. Tiffany was so forthright about her corrupted morals. "Fine, that sounds fair, I guess. Provided your help is useful."

"Oh, it will be." She grinned. "There's a lounge where we've been given permission to hang out, right? And Jack can use it too. But no one's been using it much. Anyway, there's a small corridor behind the lounge that has some public toilets and a service elevator tube."

Leta frowned. "I don't see how this works."

"I may have *acquired* a staff elevator card. Also," she pointed to her auto-aethercaster lying dead on the floor. "If I knock them out at the right moment, by the time Fogarty restarts them, he thinks I've gone to the loos, and doesn't pay much attention. He's too busy to care about a contestant taking a while to piss. Meanwhile, I've taken the elevator tube down to the underground carpark and had a leisurely cigarette behind a pillar, with no eyes on me at all."

Leta was nodding along. She could see it now, the shape of the plan. "That could work. You knock out the auto-aethercasters, he borrows your card to ride the elevator tube down…"

"Hm, what do *you* do?"

"I run the messages. And I have another connection who will be useful. Is it OK if I bring this possibility to his attention and see what he thinks?"

"Sure, go ahead." Tiffany held out her hand for the broken auto-aethercaster and wiggled her fingers. Leta handed it over. No sooner had she done so than the dormant one on the floor lit up. Leta went to stand by the door, and Tiffany rushed to the desk in her room and busied herself writing something on the letter. She folded it up and put it back in the envelope, then held it out to Leta with a bored look. "Take this to Seer Mirabelle, please," she said.

Leta scuttled over and took the letter. "I will. Thank you for your quick response." She ducked out of the hotel room and returned to her own room. She opened the envelope to read what Tiffany had written for her.

> *Be careful. You might lose your job if you get caught.*
>
> T

A warm feeling filled Leta. She hadn't expected any of the contestants to care about what happened to her. But perhaps she'd won Tiffany over somewhere along the way.

JACK READ THE NEWEST letter from Leta, this one also disguised as a letter from Mirabelle. Leta stood near the door, waiting for his reply. He sat at the desk, re-reading her plan to get him out of the tower for a day. He shouldn't. It would throw so many things out. But he needed the break. Constance had said he should. And he was the one who seeded the idea in Leta's head. The aethercast schedule hadn't slipped yet, not even when he skived off with Ander. They could afford to lose a day, surely. He put pen to paper.

> *Let's do it.*

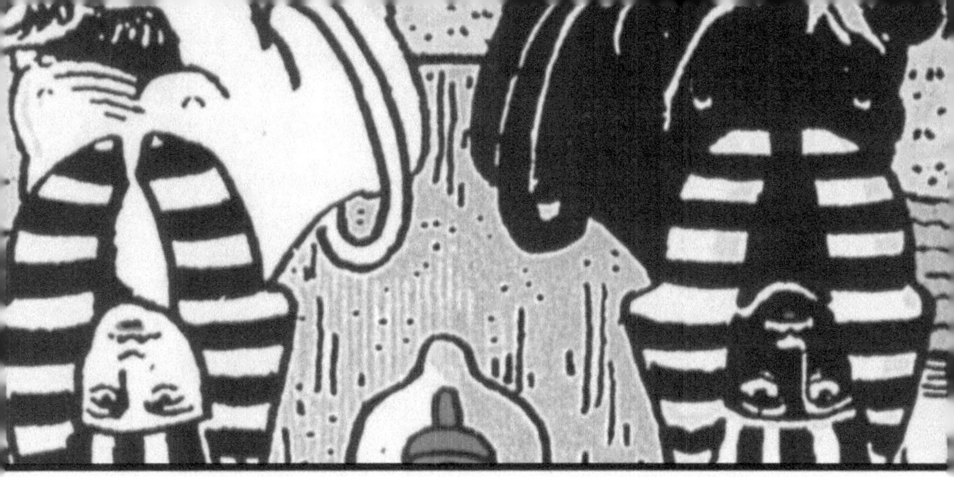

THE CHARIOT
REVERSED

Let life happen to you for once. Sit back and enjoy the ride.

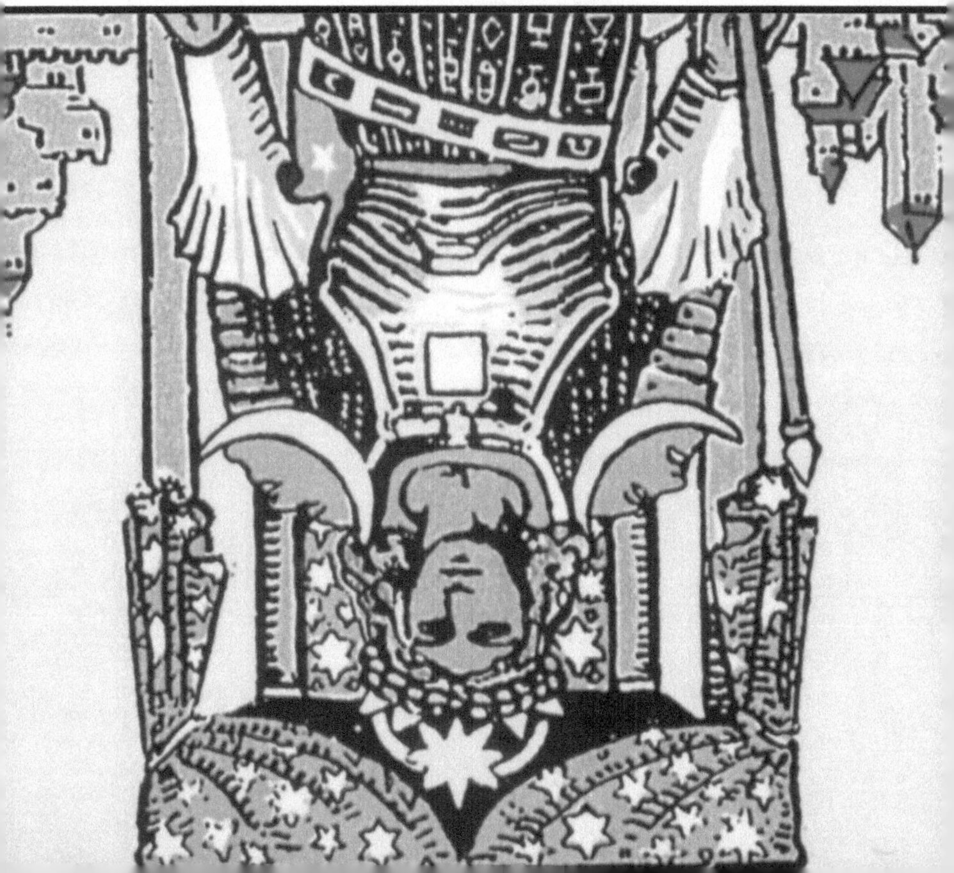

To the AllAether Executive Team,

This is an informal notice regarding the ongoing aethercast capturing on our hotel premises. We have received several noise complaints, particularly from penthouse guests on the 38th floor below the boardroom. Please keep noise within acceptable limits to avoid bothering our hotel guests, or we will have to send a formal notice requesting a revisitation of our agreement.

Johannah Blytheworth
Hotel Manager
Emerald Marquise Tower

The duffle bag hung heavy with implications in Leta's hand. She hastened through the hotel as if she was on a mission, which she was, and met Tiffany in the public loos near the lounge. "Are you sure this'll work?" she asked.

"I've done it several times already since we arrived. It'll work."

"Several times? Already? We've only been here a few days."

"Yeah, but my friend lives near here."

"You've gone to see your friend several times?"

"She is a *very good* friend." Tiffany winked.

Leta shook her head. She didn't want to know about Tiffany's love life.

"Go down the elevator tube now, while I'm here in the loos. There shouldn't be an auto-aethercaster there to see you. Toss the card back into the hallway before the doors shut. I'll go pick it up, signal to Jack, and get ready to break him out. All you need to do is drop that bag in the carpark and go find a taxi. Easy." It seemed Tiffany had already worked out that Leta would go with Jack to facilitate his escape. She probably had her mind in the gutter again about the turn of events, but Leta was going for practicality's sake. Also, if she went, then she would get something out of all of this effort too.

The duffle bag contained a woolly hat and Jack's fuzzy cardigan. They didn't want him being obvious to the security 'casters in the carpark.

"Thanks for this," said Leta. "I'm surprised you didn't dob us in."

"Not at all. I'm finding all of this *fascinating*. So much more interesting than following the rules."

"Before I go, may I ask: Why are you a contestant on the aethercast?"

Tiffany snorted. "Thought it might be fun. I thought I could make some friends. I tried to early on, but they were a bit too back-stabby. And to be honest, I quite liked the aethercast last year, and thought Jack was a bit of all right, and it would be awesome if I was the goddess. But, after talking to him, I'm sure now I'm not."

"Hence the meeting up with the *good friend*?"

"Yeah, Jack's not for me, so why not?"

"Why are you letting me spirit him away?"

Tiffany leaned against the vanity and shrugged. "Honestly? Because he's willing to go with you. Sounds odd, maybe. But he's a God Incarnate. If he wants to go, he should go."

Leta nodded. "He should go. This aethercast isn't doing right by him. AllAether either needs to let him go or rethink their strategy."

"Yeah. While he's gone, I'm going to have fun trying out my new toy. Maybe I'll overhear some of the background drama. Or maybe I'll just hear the other contestants cussing you out for stealing Jack."

"Why is everyone thinking along those lines? What kind of face am I making when I look at him? Am I that thirsty?"

Tiffany grinned. "It's more the face that he makes when he looks at you. Now, go." Before Leta absorbed her words, Tiffany was pushing her out the door of the loos.

Leta shouldered the bag, checked that there were no observing auto-aethercasters, and tagged open the service elevator tube. She tagged the control panel inside, and when she felt the magic of it come to life around her, she pushed the button for the carpark and threw the card back out into the corridor. On her way down, she mulled over what Tiffany had said. Jack was giving her looks other people were picking up on? Well, it had been obvious the other day that he was attracted to her. It stood to reason that people would have noticed. Did the auto-aethercasters catch any of those looks? The thought made her flush red-hot.

She didn't have time to worry about it. A short ride later, she alighted between two banks of rubbish bins. The smell was... different from inside the hotel, that was for sure, and the air was chill and damp. Leta left the bag behind the closest rubbish bin and walked out of the carpark up the ramp to the street level and hailed a taxi. She clambered into the back. "Could you wait here, please? My friend will be along in a few minutes."

"Tch!" said the driver, a nondescript middle-aged man who looked tired enough to be near the end of his shift. "I don't have all day."

"We'll pay more."

He sighed. "Fine, fine. You pay what I charge, OK?"

"Within reason," said Leta. "You try to fleece us and we won't be happy. We're not that desperate to avoid walking." She hoped she came across as firm and confident enough to keep the taxi driver in line. He waited without further complaint.

Before long, a tall figure in a cardigan emerged from the gloom of the carpark and headed straight for the taxi. The glow of his god powers was still visible if she squinted, but between it being a sunny day and the distracting woolly jersey, it wasn't too noticeable. He climbed in without a word and slouched down in his seat, making himself look smaller to someone looking in.

"Central Tube Station, please," said Leta.

"All right, your highness," said the taxi driver, with rather too much snark. "Off we go!"

Leta met Jack's eyes. A smile was threatening to break free, but he was holding it in.

Leta took out her aethervoicer and tapped the picture of her mum on the glass. She picked up the 'cast on the second ring. "Leta? Is everything all right? I'm at work, Honey. Is something wrong?"

"I'm glad you're at work, because I need a favour. Sorry about the short notice. Didn't want to be over-heard. I'm heading to Central Tube Station right now with a guest. I need a secret, untraceable transport. Can you catch us and, you know, not log it?"

There was a pause. "Yes, Honey, of course. Just get in a capsule. Don't tag on. I'll know it's you. I'll get it all sorted. See you soon."

The taxi driver charged them about double what it normally would have cost to get to the tube station. Jack took care of it without hesitation. They headed straight in and joined the queue for a west-ward travel tube. Between them, they only carried the one mostly empty duffle bag. Leta wouldn't need anything, and Jack couldn't have taken anything more than fit in his pockets without looking suspicious. Soon they were at the head of the queue and took a small four-seat capsule. The door swooshed shut behind them and they took seats opposite one another.

"Please scan your aethervoicer," said an automatic an-nouncement. "Please scan your akkkkkkkkksssssttttt."

The light flickered off and on again, and then the cap-sule rose and entered the travel tube. Leta grinned. "All good," she said. "It's a one-hour journey from here."

Jack sighed and slid down in his seat, his legs splaying out and his body seeming like jelly in fuzzy wool. His feet were close to her own.

"Do you feel relieved?" asked Leta.

He sighed. "I feel better. I can't help but worry about the fallout, though."

Leta's stomach roiled. They were going to be in so much trouble! "Yeah, me too. But let's try to worry about that tomorrow."

Jack smiled over at her. "You're going out on quite a limb here for me. I appreciate it, but are you sure this is OK with you? I didn't want to cause you this much trouble."

She considered lying to him, talking about trying to be a good person, trying to do what's right. But he'd probably had enough of half-truths. "It's OK. This feels like the right thing to do, though I don't know why. Because I have sympathy for you? Because I'd quite like a break too? Because I'm a foolish woman thinking with the wrong bits, getting in trouble for the sake of a hot guy?"

It was Jack's turn to flush. Between that and her woolly hat on his head, he looked something other than high and mighty. He looked far too much like someone she could get used to having around.

"Thank you," he said. "I know it sounds trite, but I appreciate it. And I'm sorry."

"Why?"

"Because we're going to be in so much trouble."

"I know."

"And, uh, sorry about your bits."

"I beg your pardon?!"

He laughed. "That came out so wrong! Um, I mean," he ran a hand through his hair. "I don't know what I mean." He sighed. "It's all a lot, isn't it?"

She wasn't sure what about the whole situation he was talking about, but she said, "Yeah," anyway.

"I mean, before I ascended, I would have just asked you out for a meal, kissed you, then — actually, we kind of did that, eh?"

"I suppose." He was right. They had.

"Then I guess we would have had a shag and figured out from there if we wanted to see each other more?"

"What? I'm not that sort!"

"No? Would I have had to take you out for another meal first? Or to the aetherhalls to see a 'cast?"

"Both! I am a firm believer in the three-date rule."

"OK. How about if we'd gone drinking at a club?"

Leta shuddered. "I don't like clubs."

"Me neither. I always thought I was supposed to, though." He sighed. "You know what I think the best date is? Something out in nature. Like a hike."

"Or a picnic."

"Yeah! Or fishing?"

"A bit too boring for me."

"Yeah, now you mention it…"

"A hike up a hill and a picnic near the top, sheltered under a tree."

He grinned. "Yesss. I haven't been out like that for so long." He sounded wistful.

Leta squirmed a bit in her seat, fighting the urge to speak her thoughts. "The one situation I'd consider skipping the three-date rule." She couldn't look at him after the words were out, and instead looked at the magical night school poster on the wall beside her.

He leaned forward in his seat. "Oh?" She didn't respond. "Like, outside?" She looked even more resolutely at the poster. "Like, on the picnic blanket? Then you'd get extra het up?" She clicked her tongue in faux annoyance, hoping he wouldn't comment on just how red her face was. But he just leaned back in his chair. "Interesting."

She thought he was going to drop the topic and breathed a sigh of relief.

"Can I kiss you now?"

Her eyes snapped back to him. "My mother is carrying this capsule! She'll sense it!"

"I'm getting hot under the collar, though." He fanned his face with his hands.

"Kissing wouldn't help! Pretty sure it would just make that worse!"

He shrugged. "You're not wrong."

For a few minutes, the rhythmic swoosh of the tube sections flying past outside was the only sound they heard.

"Hey," said Leta, interrupting the quiet. "Now that no one can overhear, I have a bit of intel for you."

"Oh?"

"Remember how I saw someone shady meeting with Destiny back at the manor?"

"Sure do. Marcus questioned her. She said a reporter accosted her and she ran him off."

"Yeah, well, I saw one of the anti-incarnation protesters slip Destiny a note when she arrived at the hotel. I told Mirabelle, and she passed it on. Mirabelle says Destiny's branch of her family has less money than people think, and she may have taken a bribe to let the protesters know where the locations are."

"So that's how they keep getting ahead of us."

"Yeah. I just thought you should know."

"Thanks. No one told me."

Leta shrugged. "They don't want you biassed against any of the contestants."

"True. Well, the aethercast won't be moving again, so it doesn't matter now, anyway."

They waited the rest of the journey mostly in silence, just checking in with each other about the logistics of their trip. The silent stretches were less awkward and more companionable than Leta would have guessed. He was a comfortable presence to be around.

The capsule jiggled in a familiar way: they were approaching their destination, and Leta's mum had taken a firmer hold of the capsule to prepare it for catching. Leta felt her mother's magic close in around her like a warm blanket and smiled.

"We're nearly there," she said.

Jack sat up and clasped his hands together, looking more nervous as Leta felt less nervous.

The capsule clicked as it settled into the cradle. It was a smooth catch: they had a lot of her mother's attention. Leta was on her feet before the door whooshed open, letting in the particular smell of home: the nearby woods, the stream, the sheep farm just out of the village, the... *history*, somehow, of her particular village, travelling through time and making itself known in the present in unexpected ways.

Leta hurried over to the small stationmaster's office and yanked open the door. Her mum was already out of her chair, but with a finger raised in Leta's direction and her eyes still on the glass before her.

"Your guest out?" she asked.

Leta looked over her shoulder and checked that Jack was out of the capsule. "Yep."

"OK." Her mum lay her hand on the glass and closed her eyes. The capsule lifted out of the cradle and eased back into the travel tube. "I've sent it back where it came from; I'll wipe the logs when it gets there." Leta's mum turned then and swept Leta up into a big hug, squeezing her tight. Leta squeezed back. Her mum pulled away again. "Now, care to explain?"

Leta nodded, her eyes a little misty. "It's complicated, but essentially someone needed a break, and AllAether wasn't giving him one. So I may have done something that will have got me fired. Sorry."

Leta's mum peered around her. She frowned at first, ready to tell off whoever had got her daughter in trouble.

But then her eyes lit up with recognition. "Oh! Oh, um. Yes, right. Well, the next capsule arrives in ten minutes. You'd best make yourselves scarce, just in case. See you later, Leta."

Leta smiled. "Thanks, Mum." She headed for the door out to the street. "This way," she said to Jack. "Let's get you out of public spaces."

He paused, and called back, "Sorry for the inconvenience, Leta's Mum."

"No problem! No problem at all!" Leta recognised that note in her mum's voice. It was the 'there's a boy talking to Leta! How exciting!' note. Except this time, there was also an edge of her excitement over the damned aethercast, and star-struck-ness. In retrospect, perhaps she should have been more worried about her mum meeting Jack.

THE HIGH PRIESTESS
UPRIGHT

You already have the answers you seek. Trust your intuition.

Marcus,

I am sorry that I missed your call. I was deep in a reading, and I completely missed the chime. I sent my assistant to acquire more stationery, so she was not able to alert me either.

From your expletive-laden message, I take it you have temporarily misplaced our boy Jack? I am sorry. I have no idea where he is. Have you checked the hotel gym? How about the rooftop pool?

Mirabelle

Jack followed Leta down the main street and along a side road to her mother's place. It was a house much like others in the street: semi-detached, brick, with a small front garden that was heading for winter dormancy. The door scanned Leta's aura and let her in. She toed her boots off and hung up her coat. "Would you like a cuppa?" she asked.

Jack hung the hat up on a hook and then looked around at the hallway that was over-stuffed with coats, scarves, and umbrellas. "Yeah, that sounds great."

Leta showed him to the lounge. It was also smaller than the contents would have liked, in a way that was reminiscent of his parents' house. He settled onto the sofa and looked around with interest at shelves of books, worn armchairs and an aetherweb globe on the coffee table.

"How do you take it?" Leta asked.

"Hm?"

"Your tea."

"Oh, milk, no sugar."

She disappeared into the kitchen. The sound of clinking mugs and boiling water soon followed, making him feel even more at home. He inspected the books on the shelves: gardening books and cook books took pride of place, but there were a lot of novels too. There seemed to be two distinct collections of novels, no doubt Leta's and her mother's: one of them read a lot of crime fiction and the other read a lot of fantasy and had an impressive collection of mythology texts. Jack stood and leaned closer. He hoped the fantasy novels were Leta's, because he had a lot of the same books.

The kettle finishing its boil drew his attention. He peered through the doorway into the kitchen and watched Leta. There was no one — or more to the point, no auto-aethercasters — around to notice how his eyes dropped to the curve of her hips as she bent down to get something off a low shelf. As delightful as it was to peruse her curves, he saw something else too. He hadn't realised just how much tension she had been carrying in her body while working on the aethercast. Here in her own home, she was a different person: she moved with ease around her kitchen, her movements a well-practised dance. She was smooth and graceful on her socked feet. She caught sight of him in the doorway and smiled. "I'll be through in a moment. I found a sponge cake. Would you like me to cut a slice?"

"I feel more comfortable in a kitchen than waiting to be served in a lounge. Can I help?"

"I'm almost done, but if you want to take a seat here, that's fine."

Jack sat at the kitchen table, and a moment later, Leta handed him a slice of cake on a small plate, not having waited for his answer. A large mug of tea followed, and then Leta sat across from him at the table with a slice and a mug of her own.

"Here's to mental health," she said, and raised her mug.

"Hear, hear." Jack clinked his mug with hers and then took a cautious sip. The tea was still too hot for him, so he let it sit and took a bite of the cake instead.

"I think she just bought it from the supermarket," said Leta after a large bite of the cake, "so it's not great. If we had time, I'd bake a better one."

"This is fine, but I would love to have the chance to try your baking some time."

Leta smiled, but the smile soon faded. "Not sure we'll ever have time for that."

"You sound like you think we'll never see each other again," said Jack. "No matter what, I'd still like to be friends after all this." The thought of his time with Leta being limited was uncomfortable. Painful, even.

Leta patted the back of his hand. "I'd like that too, if possible." She took a long drink of her tea, nearly finishing the cup. "I need to do some shopping to be able to cook dinner for all of us this evening," she said, with the air of someone changing the subject on purpose. "Mum has only single-portion easy meals at the moment, since she wasn't expecting anyone else. I'll go alone, for obvious reasons. Would you like me to pick anything up? Toothbrush? Deodorant?"

"Oh, yeah, if you could, that would be great." He gave her a list of things he would need, keeping it to the absolute minimum so as not to be a bother.

Leta then activated the aetherweb globe for him so he could watch it if he wanted. He carried his tea with him into the hallway to see her off.

"You'll be OK here?" she asked. "I'll be as quick as possible."

"Yeah, I'll be fine." He raised the tea in her direction. "This will keep me occupied."

"OK. If you need some fresh air, we've a bit of a garden out back. The fences are high, so no one will spot you."

"Thanks, will do."

Leta then stomped back into her boots, threw her coat on, and went out the door with a shopping bag.

When she was gone, Jack padded around the small downstairs of the house, tea still in hand, and had a bit of a nosey. Downstairs were the two main rooms, the lounge and the kitchen dining, but there was also a small laundry and a loo under the stairs. He guessed there were just the two bedrooms upstairs and a bathroom, but he resisted the urge to snoop. When he finished his tea, he put the mug in the sink, then fetched the hat and his shoes. He stepped out the back door from the kitchen and stopped in amazement.

Leta had said that they had a bit of a garden, but that descriptor did not do the space justice. Although narrow, the garden was long, and it was well arranged and maintained. Other people might have a lawn, maybe a tree. But the Wildwinters had a magazine-worthy garden, one that seemed productive food-wise. Who was the gardener: Leta or her mother?

Jack felt sure that it was Leta. It seemed like her.

A garden path ran down one side, beside a bed of flowers and shrubs. Those seemed to be the only pure ornamentals. The rest of the garden was divided into growing zones along its length. Near the house was a rocky herb garden with each herb bush — not plant, bush — labelled with a small wooden sign that gave the species and the common name.

Next lay a vegetable garden, which looked dry and weedy, but Leta had been away for weeks. He supposed it confirmed that this was her garden rather than her mother's. Behind the veggie garden, a glass house opened onto the path. It also contained veggies, including laden tomatoes and bell peppers. He hadn't known it was even possible to grow tomatoes this late in the season in Gealdland. What a green thumb she had! Those veggies looked well watered, probably because of the irrigation system he spied, but the plants were overburdened with fruit, some of which were withering on the vine.

He continued down the path. Behind the glass house was an area covered with bird netting. He recognised strawberry plants and blackberry plants, and he thought the upright browned canes held up by a wire might be raspberries, but all the fruit was over for the year, so it was hard to tell. Beyond the berries was a garden shed and a compost bin. Right down the far end of the garden, behind a little hedge, Jack found a small leisure area. An apple tree stood at the end of the garden, with rotting apples littered on the surrounding ground, a bench underneath that in summer would surely be nice and shady. There was a little area of grass nearby, the only grass in the garden. It had tracks in it that looked to Jack like it was cut with an old blunt push mower, but to be fair, if you had an area of grass this small, why would you bother getting a mower with an aetherconnection?

He kicked the apples off the bench and sat on a spot that had no pulp on it. He could imagine Leta sitting down here on slow Sundays, reading a book and drinking a cup of tea. His kinetic magic itched, though. The area along the fence behind the tree looked perfect for a raised flower bed. Maybe one of those with the wide edge, to make it easy to sit and weed. Sure, he bet the apple tree looked lovely in spring. But she deserved flowers at other times too. If he made her a flower bed, what would she plant?

What am I even thinking? I am getting so far ahead of myself!

Even without a flower bed, this little area was a perfect private grotto, hidden not only from the neighbours but from the house too. If it were a warmer day, Jack would have stretched out on the grass and taken a nap. He settled for looking up at the red and yellow leaves of the apple above and zoning out.

He wasn't sure how long he was sitting there, but eventually he heard footsteps, and then Leta came around the end of the hedge. "There you are!" she said. "You had me worried."

Jack smiled up at her. Her walk to the supermarket had brought up a lovely flush in her cheeks and some of her hair had escaped her braid to waft around her face. "You have a lovely garden, Leta," he said. "It's so peaceful here."

She flushed a deeper red. "Thank you. This is my hobby. I love growing things I can cook."

"Do you make jam?"

"Yes."

He pointed up. "Cider?"

"Had a go once. I need to refine my method."

"Was it bad?"

"It was *strong*."

He laughed. "So, depends on what you want out of it?"

She smiled. "Yeah. Mum liked it."

Jack stood up and brushed himself off. "Could you take me on a garden tour? I wasn't sure about what everything was."

On the return journey through the garden, Leta told him not just the species, but also the cultivars selected, whether they were early or late season, how they tasted. She tutted at how many of the tomatoes and bell peppers were going to waste, muttering about her mother 'ignoring the 5-plus a day rule', and then picked a tomato for him to try. It squirted when he bit it, and the juice flowed into his mouth, the taste fresher and deeper than any tomato he'd ever bought at the supermarket. It reminded him of summers at his grandfather's house when he was a kid, and he almost choked up at the thought. His grandfather had died many years before, and he hadn't thought about those tomatoes in years. He turned to the veggie plot beside the glasshouse to hide his emotions. "What about these?"

"Sure! Out here, I like to grow leafy greens. I think they taste better when they've weathered; they're too mild if grown in the glass house." She pottered about, showing him the different veggies, telling him what else she would have in the garden in summer, things that she had already pulled out. While she did so, she absent-mindedly weeded, throwing the weeds to the side of the patch. He stood and watched her rather than the veggies; saw her knowledge, saw her passion. And more, far more.

She thought she was without magic. She'd said so to him more than once. But here, in her garden, and with the sight that was granted to him when he ascended, he saw how wrong she was about herself. How wrong society had been about her. Her magic was all around her, twisting as fine green threads, connecting her to every plant in her garden, and to her house, and to the land, the water, the air. Connecting her to...

Jack drew a deep breath, realisation hitting hard. People didn't see a magical aura around Leta because it was *too big*. If someone was standing near her, they were already inside her aura. And stretched as far as it was, it was almost impossible to see, so faint was it upon the world. So faint, so connected. To the land.

No wonder AllAether's testers hadn't noticed her potential.

Ander had been right. His own instincts had been right. She *was* the Harvester Incarnate. His goddess, right here, in front of him, weeding a vegetable patch and looking happier than he'd ever seen her. Looking like she was home. Looking *like* home. A home for him.

What if his calling in life wasn't to be on aethercasts, to be famous? What if it was just to make her a garden, a bigger garden than this one, with lots of space for her to work her magic? To show their country how to slow down, to grow food, to reconnect with the land? How much had Jack himself been missing nature? He'd felt uncomfortable ever since he'd moved to the city and taken on the lifestyle the network wanted him to lead. This, here, was mind-opening. Here in Leta's small garden, he could finally see his future.

A future with Leta. Because they were meant to be. Somehow, he'd always known. He'd just had trouble daring to believe it.

He would have the pleasure and privilege of getting to know her over time; the parts of herself she kept hidden. Caring for her, and being cared for in return. Because that's the kind of people they would be. She would have time to bake for him, and he would do anything for her in return. Anything. And he would be free to do so because his contract was now over. All he had to do was…

… All he had to do was out her to the people who had exploited him. He couldn't do it. They would do to her what they did to him. Get hooks into her. Have her followed by paparazzi, do their best to get exclusive deals… She had the right to have her identity released to the public in her own time. He couldn't use her identity as a way out of his contract, not without hurting her.

"Are you all right?" Leta asked.

Jack startled. He hadn't noticed how much he'd zoned out into his thoughts. Leta had already moved on to the herb garden, and he hadn't followed. "Yeah, sorry. I'm just tired, I guess."

Leta looked concerned. "Sure, of course. Would you like another cuppa?"

"That would be great."

They went back into the kitchen. Jack attempted to help with the tea, but Leta pushed him towards a dining chair. He took a seat and watched her again. Here in her kitchen, too, he saw her magic at work, now that he knew how to look for it. There were remnants on all the kitchen appliances and tools that she used. A jar of biscuits in the pantry shone to him. She'd made those by hand with love, he was sure. No wonder he hadn't noticed, or at least been unsure, at Autumnwood or Astmere: her magic was tied to place, to home, to the things within it.

He hadn't even heard of a magic like this before, which was why she had always tested as non-magical. There was no standard swatch for this. It was likely that many other people were like Leta: possessing a subtle magic that helped them with tasks the testers didn't rate, and so their magic remained unnoticed and unremarked. It didn't help that Leta's magic seemed to be location- and activity-based. She was a shadow of herself when elsewhere. Even with his ability to see magic, he hadn't perceived it until now. He wasn't sure how to tell her about all of this, but his excitement was building up as he prepared to do so.

"You think Mirabelle is covering for us back at the hotel?" asked Leta.

Mirabelle. Oh no, Mirabelle.

"Yeah, maybe," he managed to say, but inside Mirabelle's words were suddenly echoing around in his head. *If you do find your goddess, make sure to protect her.* Protect. Yes, he would do that. Which meant it wasn't just AllAether who mustn't know she was the goddess: Leta couldn't know yet either, because Mirabelle's crystal ball had shown him she might be in danger when she ascended. He would tell her she was the goddess after the season ended and they were far from potential dangers such as the anti-incarnation protesters. He could come here and tell her in private, without the world watching, and without her needing to go back amongst the people looking for her in the wrong way the very next day. Yes, he could do that to protect her.

He thought back to the rest of that first viewing and reading he'd had with Mirabelle, and the subsequent ones that had reflected the same messages. Mirabelle's work was good. She'd been right about the betrayal: Marcus had betrayed him to the network in various insidious ways. And she'd been right about the descriptor of the goddess. Now he knew, it was clear the description she had given was of Leta.

"Here you are," said Leta, as she put another cup of tea on the table for him. This time, she didn't take a seat; instead, she started taking things out of a kitchen cupboard. "I wasn't sure what kind of food you like to eat, but I remembered the savouries, so I thought I could make a pie? Is steak OK?"

"Absolutely!" he said with relish. "But it's only early afternoon."

"I'm going to cook the filling as a casserole, so it's tender," she said.

While he drank his tea, he watched her turn the oven on, pan-fry some diced beef and onions, put them in a casserole dish. She then made a sauce with the meat fats remaining in the pan and various other ingredients that she didn't seem to need to measure at all, and poured that sauce over the beef in the dish. She then put the dish in the oven. "It's a two-step process, but oh, so worth it. There's nothing worse than chewy beef in a pie. Normally I'd slow-cook from morning, but this will do in a pinch."

Already the meal smelled lovely. It was going to be a long wait until dinner.

"Ok, what would you like to do?" asked Leta. "What haven't you done enough of while working on the aethercast?"

Kiss you. "Maybe blob out and watch aethercasts or read a book. *Other* aethercasts."

Leta led him back into the lounge. They sat together on the sofa and browsed for something to watch, but found nothing interesting. Instead, Jack started looking for something to read.

"Oh, sorry about my books," said Leta. "I know they're kind of nerdy."

"Are you kidding? If you're nerdy, then I am too."
Jack held up one in particular. "My favourite book from
two years ago."

Leta gasped. "Really?"

And that was how they ended up spending the afternoon talking in excitement about their favourite authors.

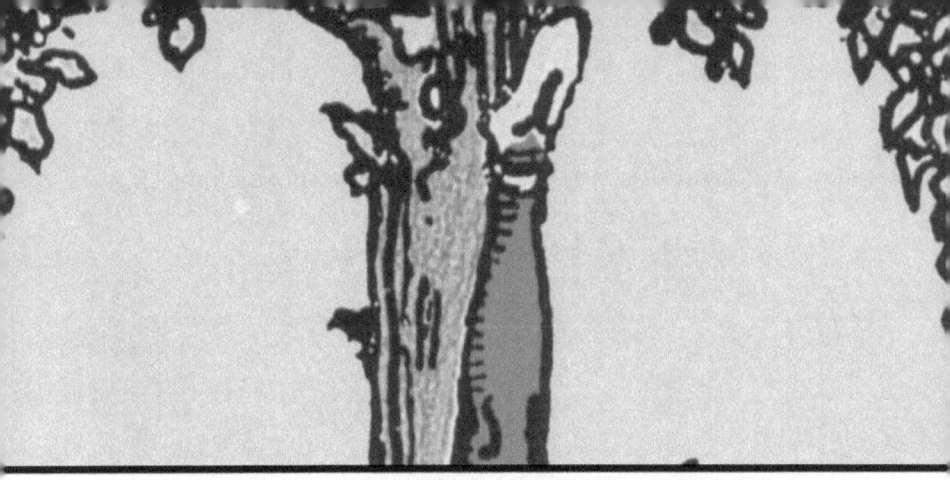

THE HANGED MAN
UPRIGHT

SURRENDER AND LET GO OF YOUR EXPECTATIONS. IF THERE IS A HOLDUP IN
YOUR LIFE, TRUST THAT IT'S NECESSARY.

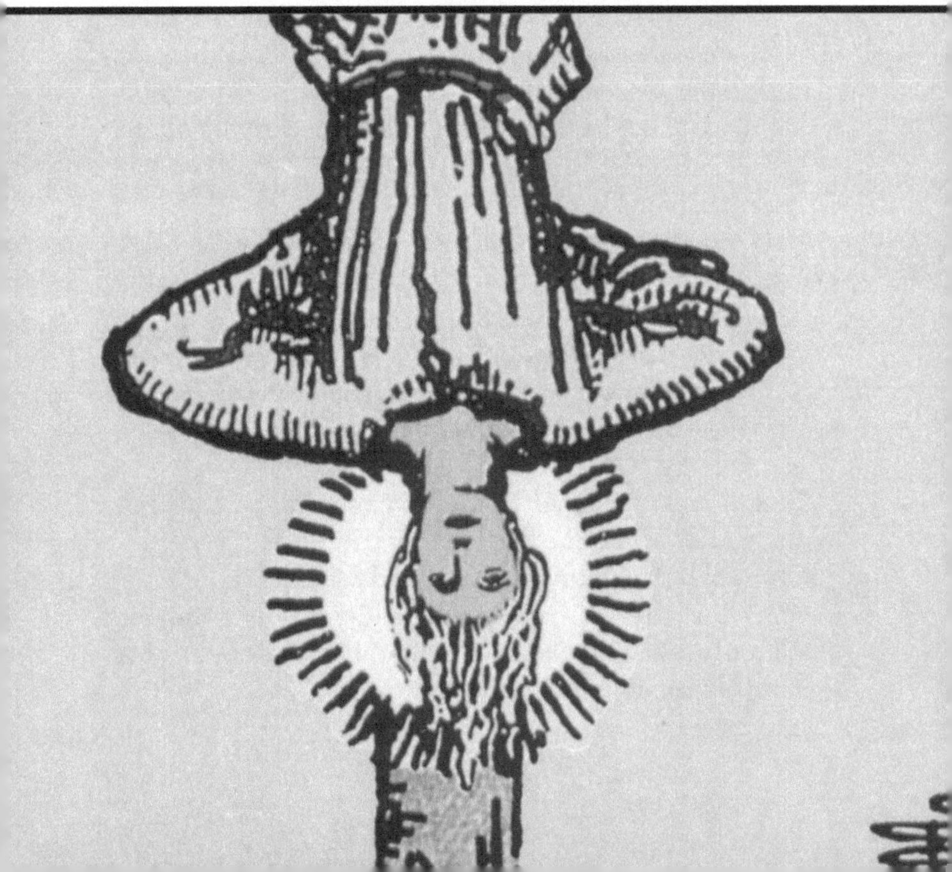

G,

An opportunity has presented itself. I'm going to present our case to the board in one hour. Let me know immediately if you want me to abort.

They talked so long that Leta lost track of time. She jumped when the door clicked open, like a teenager caught making out on the sofa. And yet, they'd only been discussing books.

Her mum's head poked around the corner, the kind of grin on her face that made Leta worry. "Hello," she said, drawing the word out a fraction, then moved in to the room to extend a hand to Jack. She was nearly levitating with excitement. "Nice to meet you. I'm Leta's mother. You can call me Carol."

He stood and took her hand. "Hi, we met earlier. I'm Jack."

"Oh, I *know*."

"Mum!" hissed Leta.

"I'm sorry about all this bother," said Jack. "Things were tense on set. Your daughter kindly offered me a break."

Leta's mum grinned. "I take it from the secrecy your break wasn't sanctioned?"

In reply, Jack hung his head and sighed.

"A word, please," said Leta and dragged her mum into the kitchen, shutting the door behind her. She opened her mouth to explain, but she was beaten to it.

"He is so *much more handsome* in real life!" her mum said in a whisper.

"Mum! Focus! Yes, that is the God Incarnate in our living room. But he needs a break from all of that for a bit. Can you please treat him like a normal person? Please? He's stressed out, and I doubt that fawning all over him will help."

Her mum nodded. "Sure, sure. I can do that. But first, why is he here, of all places?"

Leta shrugged. "Because I knew you could get us to Little Ockstead without leaving travel logs, and since we're in the village, why have him stay at the grotty inn when he can stay here?"

"Where are we going to put him? We don't have a guest bedroom. Are we going to put the *God Incarnate* on the camping cot in the lounge?"

"Maybe. Or he could have my room, and I take the lounge. I think he'd be fine with it. He was a normal person before he ascended. I don't think he's that used to the life of luxury yet."

Leta's mum raised an eyebrow. "Mm-hmm. Is this one of those situations where you pretend for me you'll be in separate rooms, but then you sneak around after I go to bed and end up in the same room? Are the rumours... based on something?"

Leta slapped her forehead with her palm. "Mum, don't be silly." She flushed. Were those rumours still circulating? Surely the episode where Destiny outed her as a Mundane would have 'casted by now? Nope, she didn't want to know. Luckily, she was saved from any further embarrassing questions by the oven timer going off. She turned away to finish dinner. She had the pie cooling on the oven top and some veggies in the steamer when she noticed her mother's absence. The murmur of not-quite-heard conversation from the next room terrified her. What was her mother saying?

Leta hurried into the other room to find her mother showing Jack, of all things, her *childhood album*. "Here she is on her fourth birthday. And here she is out in the garden. She enjoyed gardening even back then."

"Wow," said Jack, paying far too much attention to the album.

"Dinner's nearly ready! Go wash up!" interrupted Leta.

"Just a minute, Honey. I'm showing your friend some pictures."

"MUM."

Her mum sighed. "We'll have to continue this later," she said to Jack.

Jack nodded and went to the downstairs loo. Leta's mum headed for the stairs, picking up her work bag on the way. Leta glared daggers at her. "What?" said her mum with a shrug. "You said to treat him like a normal person. This *is* how I treat normal people."

Leta shook her head and went back to the kitchen to serve the meal.

The dinner that followed was one of the more awkward ones that Leta had ever experienced. Her mother oscillated between trying to ask Jack fannish questions about the aethercast without seeming like that was what she was doing, and making the embarrassing type of comments that parents often made when their kids brought home friends of a gender they were interested in. Leta burned with embarrassment. She had wanted to give Jack a break, not a Parental Inquisition.

"So, Jack, how come you've ended up here, of all places?" asked Leta's mother. "Have you two become... quite good friends?"

Leta choked on a mouthful. Jack gave a weak smile. "Sorry if I upset your evening plans, if that's what you mean?"

"Oh, it's not at all what I mean. You two must be close

for Leta to bring you here."

"Like I said, Mum," interrupted Leta, "there were practical considerations."

"Yeah, but, Jack, you must trust my daughter to come here."

"Yes. She's very kind."

Leta tried her best to hide her flush of embarrassment at his quick praise.

"Have you two been spending a lot of time together on set? Other than what I've seen on the globe, of course."

"Not really," said Leta.

"Not enough," said Jack.

"Hmm," said her mum, a shifty look to her.

When they finished the meal, Jack stood and started collecting plates. "Let me do the cleanup, as a thank you."

"Oh, you don't have to do that," said Leta, but he took the dishes to the sink anyway and started filling it with water.

Leta's mother winked at her and said, "One of us had better dry and put things away, because he won't know where they go. Oh, my favourite aethercast is on soon. Could you do it, Leta?" She left the kitchen and turned on the aetherweb globe in the lounge.

Leta picked up a tea towel and smiled at Jack, who was frothing up the bubbles with the dish brush.

"I'm sorry about her," said Leta. "That was a bit much, I know."

Jack sagged over the sink. "She's nearly as subtle as my father." He stopped the tap and began washing the glasses.

"Oh?" asked Leta, spreading the towel out to receive the first glass.

Jack glanced at her sideways in a considering way and said, "Yeah, once before a school ball, he handed me a condom. Right in front of my date."

"Oh no."

"Yep." The remembered mortification was thick in his voice.

"Mum once announced to another parent at the school gate that I wasn't interested in boys yet. Right in front of the boy I had a crush on."

"Oh no."

"Yep."

They both sighed, lost in remembered traumas.

"If I ever have kids, I'll never do that sort of crap to them," said Jack.

"Neither. I love my mum, but there are times when she has demonstrated to me how not to parent." Leta put the first glass in the cupboard. "Do you get the time to talk to your parents much?"

"Not really. The aethercast keeps me too busy. And I don't call them much because I'm not certain AllAether hasn't tapped my aethervoicer. I just send messages. You know, proof of life."

Leta winced. What a reality Jack was living! "Do you want to call them from here before we go back?"

"That would be great. Yeah, I want to."

"OK, we can do that later."

They continued doing the dishes in companionable silence for a few minutes. Jack was an efficient washer, and Leta was busy keeping up with the drying.

As he neared the end of the washing, Jack said, "I'm sorry if I've caused you a lot of stress today. I didn't consider how this lark would affect your family. I should have."

Leta smiled. "Nah. Mum doesn't care about people coming to dinner on short notice. Her only actual concern is where we put you for the night. We don't have a spare room. She's embarrassed about putting you on the camping cot in the lounge. If that's too cramped, you could take my room and I'll take the camping cot."

"I wouldn't dream of depriving you of sleeping in your own bed when you've been away for weeks already. The lounge is fine for me."

"If it's uncomfortable, come find me, OK?"

He grinned at her. "And what: sleep with you?"

Leta flicked him with the tea towel.

"Oh, my, my; am I interrupting?" said Leta's mum from the doorway.

Jack cleared his throat. "Not at all. We're just finishing up here."

"Well, OK," said her mum, holding her hands up as if blocking the sight of something she wasn't supposed to see. "I'm just getting a beer from the fridge. Don't mind me."

"I'm going to set Jack up to call his parents," said Leta. "I'll set him up in my room so he can have some privacy. Don't bother him, OK?"

Leta took Jack up to her room. She could only hope that she hadn't left anything embarrassing lying around, like her underwear. It had been weeks and she couldn't quite remember how she'd left things. She'd packed in a hurry, after all.

She waved the light on and breathed a sigh of relief: All her clothes were put away and the bed was made. Her plants were all looking good, although the auto-feeder bulbs looked close to empty, so she should refill them soon. She drew the thick green curtains and tidied away the books and stationery on her small desk to give him room to sit and 'cast to his parents.

"Would your parents accept a 'cast from an unknown ID? You want to avoid using your own aethervoicer, right?"

"If possible."

She turned off the biometrics of her own aethervoicer so he could use it. He went to look at her house plants while she did so.

255

"Why are all your plants up here?" he asked. "There's none in the lounge."

"They seem to do better up here, for some reason. Maybe the light is better." She handed her aethervoicer to him. "Here you go. I trust you."

He chuckled.

She went downstairs and sat beside her mother on the couch. She was watching some horrendous aethercast about pretending to live in the pre-ascendent times. "He upstairs?" her mum asked.

"Yup, 'casting to his parents."

"Hm."

"I'm probably going to get fired, Mum."

"Eh, whatever. It was only a temporary job."

"It'll go on my employment record."

"Nah. You don't need to say on your CV why you left a job."

"Still. I'm going to be in so much trouble."

"It'll be fine. Though, may I give you some advice?"

"You're going to, anyway, right?"

Her mum patted her on the head. "Ignore my teasing from before. I was just excited to see you making friends with a guy roughly your age. Don't sleep with him. It'll break your heart when he finds his goddess and can't stay with you."

Leta sighed. "I know, Mum. I'd already thought of that."

Her mum wiggled her eyebrows. "Really? You've been thinking along those lines?"

"Oh, Mum! You know what I mean! Just watch your aethercast." She huffed and went to find a book to read.

THE AETHERVOICER RANG for only a short time before his mum Brinna picked up. He'd chosen a full 'cast so she could see him. "Good evening, Brinna speaking," she said in a bored voice. Then she too switched to a full 'cast and her face popped up on the crystal. "Jack, it's you!" It wasn't the greeting he usually got when he called, and she sounded worried.

"Has AllAether contacted you?"

Unease etched lines in her face. "Yeah, they were looking for you. Said you'd done a runner."

"Nah," he said. "I'm taking a break for a day. I'll go back. Don't tell them I called, though. Let them wonder for a bit."

"What's going on, matey?" said Jack's dad Pierce as he stepped into view. His dad had grown greyer since Jack had talked to him last.

Jack sighed and ran a hand through his hair. "I should never have signed that contract, Dad. This wasn't the right way to go about things. I was so naïve."

"We were worried as soon as we heard you were the God Incarnate," said his mum. "This is a tough time to be born into such a role."

Jack raised an eyebrow. "You never said anything."

"We didn't want to worry you."

Of course not. It wasn't the first time they'd tried to help him by keeping things from him, but it never worked.

"Anyway," he said, "I wanted to let you know that I'm fine, and all will be well."

His dad peered behind Jack. "Whose aethervoicer are you calling from, and where are you? You look like you're in a girl's bedroom. Jack, are you seeing some-one?"

"I don't want to say where I am in case they've tapped the aetherconnection to your house."

His mum smiled. "The corner of your mouth turned up when your Dad asked if you're seeing someone. Just by the way. Have you *found* her?"

"There are many things I can't talk about right now, Mum."

"Right you are, dear." She tapped the side of her nose. Damned mothers.

"Anyway, I'd better go," said Jack. "Take care of yourselves."

"You too, sweetheart. Take care of yourselves!" said his mum.

"'Selves'?" asked his dad.

His mum shook her head and sighed. Then she cut the 'cast.

Jack headed downstairs to the lounge. He paused in the doorway and looked at the cosy scene before him. Leta's mother was stretched out on the sofa watching something on the aetherweb globe that she had clutched in her hands in personal viewing mode. Leta herself was curled up in a large armchair, her feet tucked beside her against one armrest and her elbow on the other, engrossed in a thick novel. She had taken her hair down, and it trailed over her shoulders in soft auburn-red waves.

Carol shifted position, catching his attention. She was giving him a sly smile. She pointed towards the kitchen and got up and walked that way herself. Jack went into the kitchen from the hallway door.

Carol took two bottles of beer out of the fridge and offered Jack one. It was a screw top. They both stood with their backs leaning against the bench and took long drinks. Carol was quiet for a moment, but not long.

"I can see you mean my daughter no harm," she said in a quiet voice. "But that doesn't mean that no harm will come to her because of you. What are you going to do about it?"

Jack sighed. "I've been worried about that myself. I shouldn't have got her caught up in my drama, but she was the only one kind enough to look past everything and offer to help. If she gets fired and I can't stop it, I'll pay for that course she wants to do."

"Know about that, do you?" Carol nodded. "I should say that as her mother, I'll pay for that, but I've still got enough mortgage on this place that it would be tight. So thanks for the offer. Even though you're young, I see you have some wisdom."

"Maybe it's the whole reincarnation chain. Maybe it's wisdom from a past life. After all, I have a lot of those. I don't feel like I've earned it, and it seems to come and go like the tides."

"Now, *that* is an interesting fact. They should cover more of that sort of thing on the aethercast."

"I have many opinions on what they should and shouldn't include on the aethercast. But I've never been able to influence the content. I'm just the freak show attraction, not the ringmaster."

Carol snorted. "There's another matter I wanted to ask you about."

"Yes?"

"The way you looked at her just now."

Jack felt his stomach drop. He wished Carol wouldn't also do the mother thing and figure out the truth. He wanted Leta herself to be the first person he told about her status. "How did I look at her?"

"Very fondly. Very fondly indeed."

Jack fought a blush. "Well, she's nice."

"She's an impressionable young woman, and you're the God Incarnate. You'll find your goddess one of these days, and then what? Will you break her heart?"

Jack held in a relieved sigh. Carol hadn't figured it out yet. "I won't break her heart. And she's not as impressionable as you think. She's already told me to keep my distance for that reason."

"And yet you're here in our house. Giving her gooey looks."

"I won't break her heart. I promise." Jack held up a hand in the 'I swear' gesture.

"You'd better not, or else." Carol took her beer with her back into the lounge and left Jack there in the kitchen to brood.

THE SUN
REVERSED

You don't have to be so serious all the time. Let your hair down! Have some fun!

General notice:

All cast and crew must receive permission from the AllAether Executive Team, via Marcus, before speaking to anyone outside the aethercast, until further notice. This includes hotel staff, with the exception of bare minimum communications regarding food and accommodation issues. Failure to comply will result in instant dismissal.

AllAether Executive Team

L eta only noticed how much time had passed when she finished a chapter of her book. She figured it was time to put out the camping cot. She was halfway through hauling the folded cot into the living room when Jack approached from the kitchen.

"Let me help you," he said.

Between them, they got the creaky bed set up and dressed. They had to shunt the coffee table towards the sofa to make room. Leta's mum lifted her feet up out of the way and kept watching her aethercast.

"I'll go find you something to wear to bed," Leta said. "Our washing machine dries too if you want to pop your, um, anything in for a wash overnight." Leta found an oversized t-shirt from a supermarket giveaway and her old PE shorts that had a tie waist. It was not a chic look, but they should be OK for sleeping in.

"Good night, Honey," said her mum, passing her on the stairs.

"Good night, Mum."

Leta found Jack sitting in an armchair, looking lost. She handed him the clothes. "Sorry about these. They're not the best, I know, but I didn't think you'd want to wear one of my nighties."

He laughed and took the clothes. "They'll be fine, thank you."

"Goodnight."

Leta turned to go, but Jack caught her hand. His brown eyes were earnest as he looked up at her. "I just wanted to say thank you. Thank you so much for everything you've done for me today."

She shook her head. "I didn't do much."

"You did. You did so much. And if there is anything you ever need from me, just let me know. OK?"

Leta nodded, not trusting her voice. Jack brought her hand to his mouth and kissed her knuckles. "Good night, Leta. Sweet dreams."

Leta ascended the stairs to her room on shaking legs. After that, she wasn't sure that her dreams were going to be *sweet*, exactly, but they were going to be good.

JACK COULDN'T SLEEP on the camping cot. It was narrow, short enough that his feet hung off the end, and it creaked with every movement. He got up and tried the sofa, but it was also too short. By 2 am, he took a break from trying. He flicked on a lamp, found a book, and sat in an armchair to read.

About half an hour later, he heard a creak on the stairs. Someone went into the kitchen and ran the tap. A sliver of light shone from under the door. The light flicked off again, and footsteps moved back into the hall. Somehow, Jack knew it was Leta out there and not her mother. He expected her to go back up the stairs, but she instead knocked on the door from the hallway.

"Come in," he called, trying to keep his voice level, though his heart raced.

The door clicked open. She was without her glasses, her hair in a loose braid over one shoulder. She wore a nightie that looked like an extra long t-shirt with a black witchy cat print all over it. He smiled. She hadn't tried to wear anything sexy because he was in the house; she was just being her adorable self. Though her adorable self was plenty sexy even without her trying. The curves of her thighs beneath the hem of her nightie taunted him with temptation.

Unaware of the direction of his thoughts, she blinked, perhaps half asleep still or perhaps having trouble seeing. "Why are you up?" she asked. "I saw the light."

"I couldn't sleep," he said.

"It was too cramped, after all. You should have just come up and asked me to swap."

"I don't want to deprive you of your bed."

She looked at him for a long, long moment, as if wondering what to do with him. Then she put the glass she was holding down on the sideboard and walked over to him. She took the book out of his hands and put it to the side, open pages down. He held out a hand to her, expecting to be led somewhere, but instead she sat on his lap, straddling him, and grabbed the sides of his head. Before he could process what was happening, she pulled him into a deep kiss.

Overwhelmed by sensation, his reason departed him and he wrapped his arms around her, pulling her in closer and giving as good as he got. She moaned into his mouth and ground herself on his lap. He gasped, his body catching up with the situation. She pulled her nightie up far enough that it wasn't trapped between them, an unspoken invitation to fondle. He obliged, moving his hands up her lush thighs and over her rounded belly. She broke the kiss and leaned back, giving him better access, her panting breath sounding loud in the quiet room. Her nipples tightened under the light brush of his fingers and she squirmed more. His fingers travelled down and brushed her underwear, finding them wet. Too wet. They hadn't been at this long enough.

"Leta, were you dreaming?" he asked.

"What?"

"Are you fully awake?"

"Mmm," she said. It wasn't a clear enough response for him. He took his hands out from under her nightie and instead took hold of her hips, scooting her back enough in his lap that they couldn't grind together anymore. "Wha?" she muttered, trying to move closer.

"You wake up fully and tell me you want this, and I will oblige. I will fuck you any way you like. But so long as you're half asleep, let's keep it to dreamland, OK?"

"Why?"

"Because I don't want you to do anything you regret."

That seemed to get through to her. The haze lifted from her eyes and her arms dropped to the side, no longer trying to draw him in. "You know what?" she asked, her voice husky.

"What?"

"You're a great guy. Does anyone ever tell you that anymore?"

"No. At least, not unless they are angling for something."

"Then I'd better make sure to do it now and then, so that you remember."

"You don't have to do that."

She smiled at him, and his heart fluttered. "I want to." She stood up and shimmied her nightie back into place. Then she pointed at the door. "Go, try my bed. You need the sleep more than I do. That's a demand, not a suggestion."

He sighed. "Fine, fine. I'll go." He lingered in the doorway, watching her pad over to the camping cot and turn down the blanket. To walk away in that moment, with only a mere taste of what he knew was to come, but she was still ignorant of, was excruciating. She looked up at him, a question in her eyes.

"Good night, Leta."

"Good night."

He escaped up the stairs before his resolve to wait for the right time faded.

WHEN LETA WOKE UP, she wondered why she was in the lounge — she'd gone to bed in her room, right? With a jolt, the events of the middle of the night came back to her. OH NO.

She sat bolt upright on the cot, making it squeak. "No," she whispered in horror. She'd done... things. Bold things. *Stupid* things. She pulled the blanket up over her head. "No!"

I don't want you to do anything you regret.

He'd sensibly rejected her. Thank God. Then she remembered that in a way he *was* her God, and she started laughing under the blanket. "Fuck my life." She sighed and got up to put the kettle on. It was 8 am, so Carol was already at work. She'd left a note by the kettle.

> *I popped in to say goodbye to you this morning, Leta, and found you'd switched rooms in the night. Oops! He didn't wake up, at least. Neither did you. How hard is that aethercast working you? I'll have a capsule ready for you to take back to Astmere whenever you get to the station. Eat whatever you want before you go; I'm going to the supermarket tonight, anyway. Don't get sidetracked gardening! Love you, and see you when you come through the station!*
>
> Mum
>
> *p.s. Don't check the news!*

Leta's fingers tingled at the mention of gardening. It had been wonderful to spend some time gardening the previous day while she showed Jack around. She had missed it so much.

266

The news... she hadn't been intending to check the news, but now her mum had mentioned it, her curiosity got the better of her. She sat by the aetherweb globe and flicked open the entertainment news. What she found was a surprising relief. AllAether was keeping mention of Jack's disappearance quiet. There was nothing about him leaving the hotel, or any sign of drama or fallout. She wondered if that would hold until they made it back to Astmere.

She also found an article discussing her. The episode in which Destiny had outed her as a Mundane had 'casted. The article was about how she couldn't be the goddess, and that she must have been a false lead put in the aethercast. The writer of the article had even guessed Leta was a crew member who had been used, and was sympathetic to her situation. The comments below the article were mostly people agreeing that Leta wasn't an important person in the aethercast, and instead talking about which contestant they thought was the goddess. She smiled, seeing a path back to anonymity before her. For the first time in her life, her lack of usable magic was of benefit to her.

Damn her mum. She must have known Leta would read the news if she was told not to, but wouldn't have read it if she was told to.

She returned to the kitchen, put the kettle on, and started mixing up some pancake batter. The sound of her knocking around must have woken up Jack. He soon appeared in the kitchen doorway, looking sleepy and with a shocking, yet endearing, case of bedhead.

Leta flushed, remembering her behaviour the night before, but decided to push through it, act as if it wasn't an issue. "Let me guess: you didn't sleep well in my room either?"

"Sorry, it was a lot better. I got some sleep."

"Good. You want a cuppa?"

He nodded and plonked into a chair at the kitchen table. "About last night…"

"You want pancakes?" she interrupted.

He blinked up at her for a moment, and understanding dawned in his eyes. He nodded. "Yes, thank you." He drummed his fingers on the table. "So, what's the plan for the day?"

Leta relayed what her mum had said about the travel capsule. "So the only two remaining questions are: when do you want to head back to face the music, and is there anything you want to do beforehand?"

"Not too late in the day," he said with a sigh. "If there are meetings and scoldings, I don't want them to run too late into the night. And as for what I want to do, you're already providing. I just want a lazy, comfy morning, no stress, and pancakes and tea sound perfect for that. Maybe another walk through your garden."

Leta nodded. "OK." She went to the stove and set it heating, the familiar hum of its aetherconnection sounding like the background of her entire life. When she had the first pancake on a plate, she asked, "What do you top yours with?"

"I like sugar and lemon juice."

Leta grinned at him. "Me too. There's a small lemon tree in the glasshouse. Could you go pick one?"

"Sure." He fetched his shoes from the hallway and went out the back door, wrapping his arms around himself against the cold and scurrying along the path. Leta watched him out the window from the corner of her eye and smiled. Her perspective of Jack had changed over the last day. Yes, she knew he was the God Incarnate. Yes, she knew he was a gorgeous man. But more and more, he seemed to be a normal person. That was both better and more dangerous.

He returned and asked for the juicer, then cut and juiced the lemon himself.

After breakfast, they washed the dishes together again, then Leta told Jack to have the first shower. Leta waited until she heard him go into the bathroom before she went up to her room. The running shower echoed through the wall. He'd already stripped the bed sheets off her bed and put them in a pile to take to the laundry, and he had left none of his few possessions in the room. It was hard to tell that he'd stayed in her room at all. But there was a small piece of notepaper on her dresser with the words "thank you" written on it. She picked the paper up, smiled, and tucked it into her special notes journal.

Leta chose an outfit for the day while she waited for her turn in the shower. She decided to shake things up a bit and wear jeans and a stretchy black boatneck top. She didn't feel like armouring up with a jersey and corduroy any more. She'd already been forced to wear her heart on her sleeve, so what was the point? Jack hadn't been complaining about her ample curves. In fact, he seemed to enjoy them. She had already decided she didn't care what the contestants thought, and who else was even paying her any attention? She'd been too boring for fake drama, even! For good measure, she threw a few more comfy tops in a bag ready to take with her.

When she finished her shower, Jack wasn't in the house, so she grabbed her coat and shoes and went to look for him in the garden. He was at the far end, sitting on the bench seat with one cup of tea in his hands and another on the bench. He held the spare cup out to her. She took it and sat beside him.

"What should we do when we get back to Astmere?" he asked. "Do you want to try sneaking back into the hotel? Maybe they won't know you came with me. Mirabelle may have been the only one who noticed you were missing."

Leta looked up through the branches of the apple tree to think. "What do you intend to do?"

"I'm going to walk through the lobby, bold as any-thing, and take it as it comes."

Leta nodded. "I might try a quieter entrance, if that's all right. Not that I'm trying to avoid paying my part of the consequences! I'm sure I'll catch that. But maybe your bold entrance would work better if you just strode in all casual and all alone. Make a grand entrance?"

He nodded. "Yeah, maybe. Although, if you can get away without consequences, I'll be thrilled." He leaned his elbows on his knees and inhaled the steam from his tea. "I think our little jaunt is at an end, huh?"

"Yeah."

He grinned at her sidelong. "It's been great. Thank you so much."

"You're welcome."

THE LOVERS
UPRIGHT

BE HONEST AND OPEN. YOU KNOW WHO YOU ARE, AND YOU KNOW WHO
AND WHAT YOU LOVE.

Thanks for finding that security capture of Jack in Little Ockstead. Don't bother sending someone down to fetch him just yet. We don't want to cause a scene. Small town like that, all the gossip. Let's give lover-boy until the afternoon to come back on his own. We can go get him by night if he doesn't.
                    Marcus

J ack watched as Leta hugged her mother goodbye. She let go and stepped into the travel capsule. Jack gave Carol a formal bow, which made her grin, and then stepped into the capsule after Leta. They took their seats as the door slid shut. A short while later, the capsule rose and whooshed as it entered the travel tube.

"Neither of us slept well last night," said Jack. "Maybe we should try to nap on the way back."

Leta flushed. So she *did* remember what happened during the night. "Yeah, we should," she said.

They sat in companionable silence, lit to Jack's eyes by the light in the travel capsule and also by Carol's magic that surrounded the capsule and propelled it on its way. Soon, Leta had nodded off, her head lolling back onto the headrest, but Jack never slept in transit no matter how tired he was, so he just sat there gazing at Leta.

Sometimes, he thought there was an 'aethercast' version of him and a 'real' version of him. He saw a similar difference in her. While working on the aethercast, she'd been tense and uptight. She'd shifted over the last day to what he assumed was more like her normal self. She'd even chosen a different sort of outfit to wear: jeans, and a stretchy top that clung more to her figure than the jerseys and skirts she had been wearing until now did. She looked great. Well, the librarian look still did it for him big time, but casual Leta was also great. The clothes displayed her lush curves. He crossed his arms and hid his hands against his sides, lest he be tempted to reach out and touch her again.

He regretted going back to an environment where he wouldn't be able to spend as much time as he wanted with her. But she was the Goddess Incarnate, he was sure of it. This period apart would be temporary. Then they would have as much time together as they wanted once she knew. They would have forever. An irrepressible grin broke out on his face. He would have to be careful to guard those smiles back at the hotel, or someone would guess that something was up. They should finish the season of the aethercast before anyone else knew. He didn't want her to have to go through a public revelation. She would hate it.

By the time they approached Astmere, although the happiness was still there, worry had taken forefront in his mind. He shook Leta awake. "We're nearly there," he said.

She stretched and opened her eyes. "OK. We should go in different directions straight away. I'll go get a coffee, you get a taxi."

Jack took his cardigan and the hat off and handed them to Leta, who stuffed them into her bag. She leaned forward and kissed him on the cheek. "Good luck."

The capsule settled in the cradle with a clonk. "Thank you. Same to you, Leta." As soon as the door swung open, he strode away, trusting Leta to make her own way, and not wanting anyone in the station to make any connection between them.

He took the stairs up to the taxi rank two at a time, which was a common sort of pace here in Astmere anyway, and hopped into the first one. Not because he was in a hurry, but because he was cold. "Emerald Marquise Tower, please."

He thought the taxi driver recognised him, but decided to say nothing. "Sure thing, sir," he said, then engaged his magic and swung the taxi out into the flow of traffic.

It was a short and much cheaper ride than the one from the hotel to the station had been. All too soon, he stood before the main doors to the hotel, ready to make his grand entrance. He hoped. He squared his shoulders, willing himself to not hunch against the cold.

The anti-incarnation protesters were there, of course. They spotted him right away.

"There he is!"

"Fake god!"

"What use has Gealdland for a fake god who shirks his responsibilities?"

"Admit it: you're in it for the money!"

Well, they clearly knew he'd been missing for a day. They also weren't aware how little money there was in being a God Incarnate.

He looked around at the small yet loud crowd. He spied a familiar head of red hair in need of a re-dye. Why did that woman look familiar? Ah, at the pub. So that table had been anti-incarnation protesters! No wonder these people knew too much. They were engaging in espionage. Though the suspicions about Destiny had already confirmed that, so was this news?

This wasn't the time to deal with the situation. He already had one fight ahead of him that day. But as soon as Leta had ascended, they would need to convince these protesters to stop. They were getting inconvenient and dangerous.

Jack walked past the protesters without acknowledging them and strode through the doors of the hotel. All eyes were on him as he strode across the lobby. Jack ignored them and headed straight for the elevator tubes. Before he had even reached them, two auto-aethercasters swooped down from the mezzanine above and followed him into the elevator tube. Jack turned to face the lobby. He smiled and waved at the onlookers, who were still watching him as the doors slid shut.

He keyed open the door to his suite, picked up the envelope on the floor just inside the door, and then went to sit on the sofa. The envelope was a daily from Mirabelle. He wondered who had delivered it. He opened it with a flourish, performing for the auto-aethercasters, and read Mirabelle's note.

> Jack
>   All methods available to me indicate that something big has changed over the last day of your life. They also indicate that the strife that has been on the horizon for all of your readings this season looms ever closer. Guard what is important to you.
>   Mirabelle

As soon as he finished reading the letter, a knock sounded on the door. He rose and answered it. On the other side stood a runner who had been working with the aethercast since the year before. She handed Jack a letter, bowed, and left without saying a word.

> Jack
>   You are required to attend a meeting at 6 pm. A runner will come to collect you. Until then, stay in your suite and don't do anything stupid.
>   Marcus

Jack shrugged his shoulders. Marcus wouldn't be fond of him at the moment, so the brusque tone of the letter didn't phase him. But being told to stay in his room rankled a bit. He tidied up the letters and then went to the kitchen to make himself a cup of tea. He hoped Leta had made it back to the hotel safe and sound, and had avoided trouble.

NO ONE PAID any attention to Leta when she returned to the hotel. She made it up to her room and hid Jack's cardigan at the bottom of her suitcase for now. She intended to go to Mirabelle's suite to let her know she was back. Unfortunately, when she emerged from her room, Marcus stood there, his arms crossed.

"So, she returns," he said.

"Can I help you?" said Leta. "I was about to check in with Mirabelle."

"She tried to hide that you had left the hotel at the same time as Jack, but we figured it out." He pointed towards the elevator tube. "Come along."

"I need to talk to Mirabelle," she said. "She's who I'm attending to."

"And you've sure done a good job of that, huh? You can see her later. On your way out." He pointed at the elevator tube again and started ahead of her.

Leta sighed and followed him. As much as Jack had said he wanted to protect Leta from this kind of fallout, she had known it would happen.

"Why fetch me yourself?" she said when she caught up. "Why am I getting the special treatment?"

"You've started enough rumours amongst the crew. You want a runner wondering why you're having a meeting with me?"

Leta supposed not.

While they waited near the elevator in uncomfortable silence, footsteps sounded along the corridor. Leta's heart rose at the accompanying sound of a tapping cane. Marcus waved a hand through the call signal twice more, as if that could somehow hurry the capsule.

Despite Marcus's attempts, Mirabelle rounded the corner and approached them. There was a stern frown on her face. "Marcus, are you trying to take my assistant somewhere without my approval?"

"A disciplinary meeting is in order, don't you agree?" He affected a bored expression.

"It isn't your place to hold such a meeting with Leta."

"Then come along, if you think that would be more appropriate."

"I shall do that."

The elevator capsule arrived, and Marcus stepped in first. Leta gestured for Mirabelle to go ahead of her, and Mirabelle smiled at her as she passed.

They all rode in silence to the thirty-ninth floor. Marcus then led them along the hallway to a conference room. He didn't match his pace to Mirabelle's and looked annoyed when he turned around to find that they were still half-way along the corridor.

No one waited in the conference room. Leta eyed the scorch marks all over one wall. Was this the evidence of a fight between Evelyn and Marcus over his affair? The marks and their significance made her feel sorry for Marcus. Of course, he immediately dumped cold water all over her compassion.

He took a seat at the head of the table, then before either Leta or Mirabelle had taken seats, said, "Your services will no longer be required."

Leta helped Mirabelle to a seat, then sat beside her. "I beg your pardon?" she said.

"Your services. They will no longer be required."

It was what she had been expecting, but even so, her stomach dropped.

Mirabelle cleared her throat. "May I remind you, Marcus, that Leta did not sign a contract with *Goddess Found*. She only signed an NDA. She signed a contract with *me*. And I still require her services."

Marcus rolled his eyes. "Who exactly she signed a contract with isn't important."

Mirabelle spoke as if to a small child. "I rather think that every single lawyer in the country would disagree with you on that point." She turned away from Marcus and to Leta. "I am quite happy to have you work out the remaining time until the end of your contract, Leta. I understand that after the stress certain people have put you through over the last few weeks, you wouldn't want to work on the aethercast next season anyway. If there even is a next season."

"And what do you mean by that?" asked Marcus in a combative tone.

"As I understand it, Jack's contract only holds until he finds the goddess. As soon as he does, the aethercast is over. So if the goddess is here this season, it will be the last season."

"Well, we have rights to an exclusive follow-up 'cast…'"

"Yes, if the goddess is a contestant, sure. But otherwise, he is free as soon as he finds her."

Marcus waved a hand, warding off her words. "We're getting really off topic here. We're not discussing Jack; we're talking about your assistant."

The full scale of the injustice done to Jack finally became apparent to Leta. He couldn't leave the aethercast until the goddess ascended, but he wasn't free to go find her on his own schedule. Which was no coincidence. Her anger burned away any reticence to put her head up that she would normally have. "Except we are talking about Jack, aren't we? Because what are you trying to punish me for? Noticing that he was super stressed and needed a break before *he* broke, and arranging for him to have a day off. A day that you should have thought to schedule for him."

"He had one last week when we moved here."

"It wasn't enough. He's working away fulfilling a contract that he knows is taking him farther away from his purpose, and instead of being supportive, you're taking out your own stresses on him."

Marcus stood up. "What stresses? What did he say?"

"He said nothing," said Leta in a calm voice. "You're just easy to read."

"As are you. You're just a gold-digging girl who caught the attention of a powerful man by being a slut."

"I beg your pardon!" said Mirabelle in a sharp voice. "What did you call her?"

"You heard me. You do know that they ran off to her home for the day, probably spent all their time in bed. *That's* the kind of person you've hired to be your assistant. Seems your auguries failed you, seer."

"I assure you, they did not. And even if Leta slept with Jack…"

"I didn't," said Leta with a blush.

"Even if you did, dear, it wouldn't bother me. What are we expecting here, Marcus? That our national God Incarnate has come unto us a fresh, untouched virgin? How ridiculous! Have you *seen* the lad? I'm fairly sure he's had women before."

Leta felt a small twinge of jealousy at that thought, but Mirabelle was right on that point: who would expect Jack to be a virgin? Nobody.

"You're not angry that Jack may have canoodled with someone, Marcus," she said. "You're angry that he may have canoodled with someone who is *fat*. You're not worried about emotional entanglements; we all know that at soon as he meets his goddess, he'll see no one but her. Nothing will come between them. You're worried about the optics, if some reporter got wind of him spending time with someone who looks like me. You're worried about unflattering tabloid captures."

Marcus sat down with a sigh. "Finally, you get it."

279

"Yeah, I get it. Certain people around here are *so sure* that I must be tricking him to get him to spend time with me. You know what you should do instead of harass me? Cast fat women and red-heads for next season! Because if he is at all attracted to me, that's a big fucking clue of who you should look for, don't you think?"

"He said something similar."

"Then why aren't you *listening* to him? As far as I can tell, all you're doing is hiring women *you* want to fuck!" She raised an eyebrow at him. By the thunderous look on his face, he got the message.

Marcus shook his head. "I'm just trying to understand what's going on here. This has all been out of character for Jack. He's usually a great guy. We weren't expecting any trouble from him. Then you showed up, and it all went pear-shaped."

"What's going on here," said Leta, "is that Jack and I hit it off as friends, and I helped him out because of that friendship. That's it, that's the whole story. Now he's back here, less stressed, and less hungry, too, since I fed him proper meals. And he's ready to push through with the rest of the season, and do all he can to find his goddess. You're welcome." Leta stood and offered a hand to Mirabelle. "I think we're done here. Is there anything I can help you with this afternoon, Mirabelle?"

Mirabelle took Leta's hand and let herself be helped to her feet before taking up her cane and walking to the door. "I am half-way through preparing daily readings for the contestants. I would like your help to deliver them, please."

"Sure, let's go."

Once they were in the elevator capsule, Leta sagged against the wall. "Did I just stand up to Marcus?"

"He said some horrendous things to you, Leta. You were well justified in getting angry. I am so, so sorry I couldn't shield you from that."

"I don't care as much as I thought I would. He's a petty man. Jack has told me some stuff. I mean, it sounds like he's a victim too, but also a perpetrator of shitty things. His opinion of me doesn't matter in the slightest."

Mirabelle smiled. "You've grown a lot over the weeks you've been working with me. I hope you have gained something valuable out of this experience."

"I have," said Leta. "I haven't unpacked what it is, but I'm sure I have." She sighed. "I'm sorry about the trouble I've caused along the way."

"Not at all, dear," said Mirabelle. "I've been in my profession long enough to know what it is like to bring a butterfly of fate into a tense situation like this aethercast. I knew what I was doing by hiring you." She smiled at Leta, and Leta couldn't help but smile back. Mirabelle's words helped a lot: Leta was what she was. She didn't need to apologise for existing.

JUSTICE
REVERSED

You aren't taking full responsibility for your mistakes.
Own up to them.

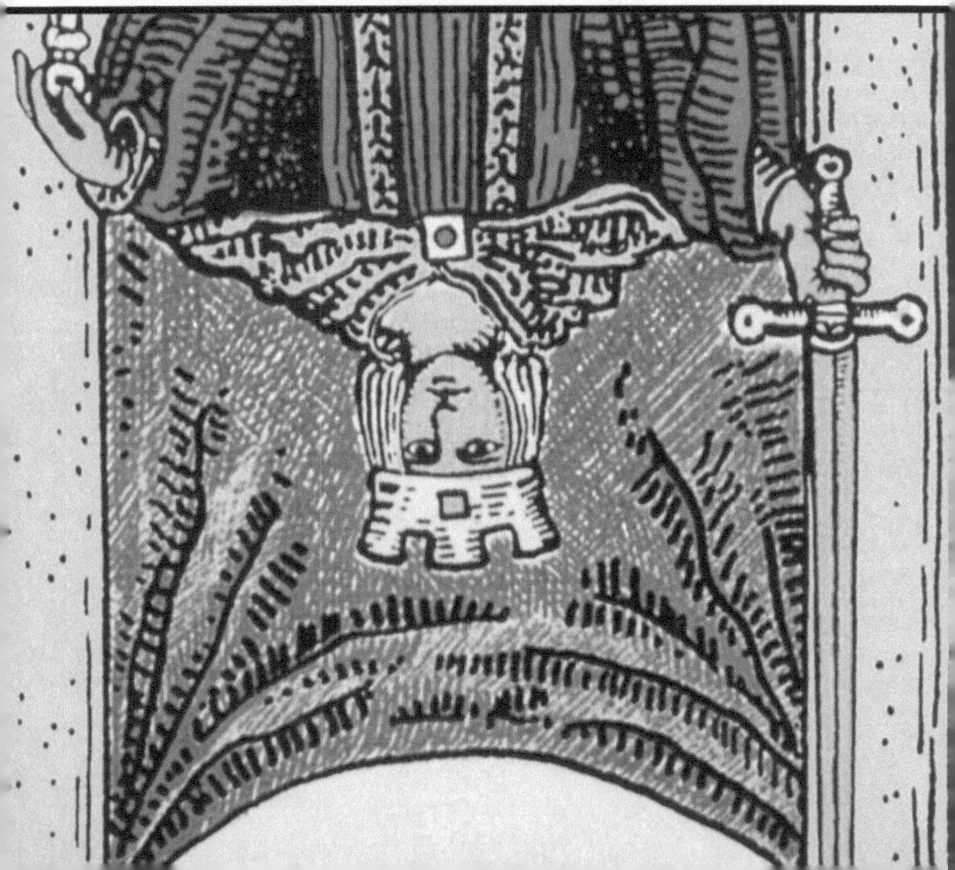

M,

They've approached me with your (our) idea.
Good work. We're going to make a difference.

G

The thirty-ninth floor was eerily quiet. Jack had expected more... something. Bustling, stressed-out people? Shouting, maybe? He entered the conference room at 6 pm on the dot. The auto-aethercasters following him waited outside. Marcus was the only one sitting at the table; he had his feet up and was eating a burger out of a takeaway box. His blond hair was dishevelled, and the smell of cigarettes lingered in the air. Jack raised an eyebrow but said nothing. Marcus usually adhered to the strict aethercast-star diet, but Jack thought a nice juicy burger might do the man some good. The cigarettes, not so much.

"Sit down," said Marcus around a mouthful. "The board members aren't here, so it's just me you need to face tonight. Lucky you."

"You mean Evelyn still doesn't want to be anywhere near you? I think you're much better off without her."

"Maybe, man. You're still an epic arsehole for how you spilled the beans."

"And you're an epic arsehole for cheating on her with a contestant. And *she's* an epic arsehole for turning her powers on you. We're all arseholes, OK?"

Marcus shrugged.

"How're your bruises, by the way?"

"Better. Had some captures taken, sent them to my lawyer. You know, as leverage if she tries to tank my career."

What a horrible existence. "Good for you."

Marcus put the rest of his burger back in the box and wiped his fingers on a napkin. Then he swung his feet down from the table and leaned forward.

"Ok, so, let's get started. If you're worried about your girlfriend, Mirabelle protected her. She stays until the end of her contract, but then she's gone. Sounds like she wanted to go, anyway."

"Yes, she just needed a job to tide her through a spot of unemployment."

"Hm. Whatever. I hope you know she was a temporary feature in your life and you got whatever you wanted from her already."

"I don't think of people in those terms, Marcus."

"Don't fool yourself, Jack. We all do."

"Spoken like a true narcissist."

Marcus chuckled and shook his head. "Moving on — your little stunt caused some bad publicity. The media got wind of your disappearance, and also your unannounced return today. We think the protesters outside leaked the info, though we're not sure how they knew. Mirabelle said Destiny told them, but she had an alibi, so it wasn't her. Anyway, the board has decided you're on your very last chance. If you don't do exactly what we tell you to do, your contract will be in breach and you can kiss your kinetic magic goodbye. We'll be powering the elevator tubes at headquarters on your magic for the next month." He paused, smirked. "Or maybe closer to a week. Do you understand?"

"Oh, perfectly." He would remember this moment for the rest of his life. He *would* let them know he remembered, some time in the future.

285

"So, here's the situation. We've had reports that the ley lines are indicating something big. Some researchers have been looking into how the ley lines behave around ascendants, cross-referencing data from Agranos with that from... Avanui? Is that the place?"

Jack frowned. That research sounded familiar... "Ander said he knows a researcher who's been researching him. You talking about that?"

"Yeah, sounds right. Anyway, the guy who was here the last time we called you up?"

"The guy I was never introduced to?"

"Yeah, *him*. That was Gregory Hallowborne."

Jack whistled. "Well, *shit*." The Hallowbornes were a Geald family, the closest the country had to a monarchy like some other countries had. They were supposedly the family that magic was first granted to in Gealdland by the Hunter and the Harvester, the randy family that spread magic to the rest of the country over the past few millennia via intermarriage and illegitimate children. Pretty much *everyone* had to be distantly related to the family, but only a select few carried the name. And Gregory Hallowborne was one of the very top mages of the country, although reclusive, and his face not known to most.

"Yeah, *shit*. That's who you acted like a shithead in front of."

Jack shrugged. "May as well start treating the Geald families as I mean to go on."

Marcus shook his head. "Gregory is a multi-talent, of course, and he's told us that the ley lines are behaving very much like the reports from before you ascended during your midnight bender in, what, religious ruins? Is that how it happened?"

Jack shrugged. "I guess."

"The researcher from Agranos has backed up the claim. So AllAether is working under the assumption that one of the contestants is the goddess. The fact you haven't noticed she's there is, frankly, an indictment of how seriously you have, or haven't, been taking this."

Jack hoped that Marcus wouldn't read the truth in Jack's face. "We'll have to see whether their assumption is right or wrong, won't we?"

Marcus sat back further in his chair. "Oh, we will. Tomorrow."

"What? How?"

"They've finished analysing what happened with the ley lines when you ascended. It was a different sort of signal than they got when Ander ascended; it seems different gods do things different ways. But they've figured out what signal the goddess would make, and Gregory has reverse engineered it."

"For the layperson, Marcus?"

"We've started the advertising campaign for a big event tomorrow. The network has decided this is all too much trouble; the publicity, you running wild, the anti-incarnation protesters getting in the way, all of it. They want to recoup their losses with a big aethercast event tomorrow. The whole country, and many from beyond, will be watching."

"Watching what?"

"The reveal of the goddess. Not that they are sure that's what they are getting tomorrow, but that's what will happen."

Jack ran a hand through his hair. "How?"

"Gregory is going to trip the ley lines in such a way as to force the goddess to ascend, live on the 'cast."

Jack hoped he didn't look too panicked or pale. "He can make it so that, wherever she is, she ascends tomorrow?"

"Eh, if she's in the hotel, maybe?"

Jack restrained a sigh of relief. Leta still had a hope of escaping the madness. "But isn't the aethercast lagging the capturing? How can we switch to a live event?"

"As we speak, a mega marathon is running, catching the viewers up to the present. The aethercast editors had to stay up all night putting it together. You'd better write them a thank-you note."

"OK. So, big event tomorrow, try to trip the ley lines, then what?"

"Then you get what you want, right? Which I think is far more than you deserve. But you get out of your contract, and you find your soulmate, all in one evening. Fucking good for you, you arsehole. Bravo."

"And the network gets what?"

"Ratings, viewings. And the follow-up cast next year to see how you and your lady-love are doing."

And the chance to get their hooks into the goddess. He wasn't naïve anymore. He knew that what AllAether wanted was another exploitable star, since they were finding Jack intractable. 'Recoup their losses'? He'd already made them heaps of money!

"Fine," said Jack. "Thanks for the update. I'll be ready and waiting."

"You bet you will. We'll make sure of it."

"Oh, come on. As you said, this is everything I've been waiting for. This is the best outcome for me. I'm super keen, and fully on board. How could I not be?" He hoped like hell that his face was convincing. Leta's privacy depended on it.

"Good," said Marcus. "You're dismissed. I want to finish my dinner." Jack rose and headed for the door. "Wait a moment," said Marcus. Jack paused. "It's been bugging me. Why *did* you run off with that frumpy girl in the middle of looking for your goddess? I'd almost think she was the goddess herself, the way you've been fawning over her. But as I already told you, there's not enough magic in her to support ascension."

Thank the Hunter and the Harvester the testers hadn't been testing for the right kind of magic. "Then why are *you* so obsessed that I made a friend? Just drop it and get your mind out of the gutter."

Marcus held his hands up. "Fine, fine. I mean, maybe I didn't go about it right. You're right to call me out on the things I've said about her figure. Slap on the wrist; naughty naughty. But I've felt like you two are going to break each other's hearts. I've seen shit like this on other 'casts, and that was with stakes much lower than this. I know this is the pot calling the kettle black, but you should never have got close to a woman who isn't the goddess. Especially one who is an assistant. That's a crappy power dynamic, and it never works out well."

Jack's eyebrows rose. At core, Marcus's reasoning wasn't bad. He'd been looking out for Jack, after all. But somewhere along the way, their relationship had broken down, and it had all been expressed poorly. By both of them. "You're right," he said. "And you shouldn't have been sleeping with a contestant."

"Yeah, yeah, I know." Marcus sighed. "I know."

"At least we both know where we went wrong."

Marcus sighed. "Yeah, I guess. I've made an appointment with Kellan, the counsellor, for you. He'll come see you in your suite. Talk some shit out or something. Get yourself together for the end of the aethercast. Oh, and I'm sorry I have to do this, but AllAether wants me to confiscate your aethervoicer. You'll get it back after the event."

Jack hesitated. He needed his aethervoicer. He really, really needed it. He didn't know Leta's room number; he had thought it would be too tempting. But if he was kicked out of the hotel for noncompliance at this point, how would he warn Leta? He nodded and placed the aethervoicer on the table. He would have to give his warnings in person.

He left Marcus to the rest of his burger and headed back to his suite. He held it together until he was in his suite bathroom, where the auto-aethercasters wouldn't follow. Then he sat on the toilet and put his head in his hands. Mirabelle's readings had been saying for weeks that he would need to protect the goddess if he ever found her. This forced ascension must be the situation she had warned him about. What was he going to do?

A KNOCK SOUNDED on Leta's door. Fearing yet another stressful summons, she put aside her room service salmon dinner and answered the door. As soon as it was open wide enough, Tiffany slipped through the crack and shut it behind her. "I've found something I don't know what to do with," she said.

What was Leta getting caught up in now? She was still mired in the last drama to occur on the aethercast set. But Tiffany looked worried. Leta waved her further into the room. Tiffany flopped onto her stomach on the bed and held out the inactive auto-aethercaster. "I got it working," she said. "Found some dirt. Had lots of fun, have an opportunity to make some serious money after the aethercast is over. You handed me something very useful. So I feel like I owe you. Also, I heard the rumours about you running off with Jack."

Leta sat down in the chair. "'The rumours'? Tiffany, you were the one who broke us out."

"Yeah, but I didn't know you were going to run off with him for a whole day. You've got steel ones. Anyway, you need to see this." Tiffany turned the auto-aether-caster on, then with a gesture projected something it had recorded onto the aetherweb globe on the coffee table. Leta moved to the sofa to watch. It was a recording of a mirror in a familiar style seen all over the hotel. The mirror showed a group of people huddled around a corner having a conversation. "That's a creative angle," said Leta.

"Shh."

Leta could hear audio, now she paid attention. A whispered conversation. There were three distinct voices in the conversation. Leta was pretty sure they were Nellie, Chrissie, and Destiny. It certainly looked like Destiny's back in the mirror: her red hair was visible.

"It's because of Jack disappearing for a day. The executives are mad," said Destiny.

"But why take that out on us? That's not fair!" said Chrissie.

"What do you mean, take it out on us?" said Nellie.

"I don't know about you, but I'm here for exposure. If they end the aethercast now, that cuts short our time to shine. Why did we get chosen the year they find the goddess?"

"I don't think they've found the goddess. They're guessing," said Destiny.

"But then how can you know if the aethercast is going to end tomorrow? It only ends if Jack finds the goddess, right? So when they force-ascend her with their ley line thingie or whatever that is, the 'cast only ends if she's here, right?"

Force-ascend, wondered Leta. *What does that mean? What's going to happen?*

Oh. It was going to happen tomorrow. Jack was going to find his goddess, one way or another. She made herself keep listening despite the sadness welling up in her.

"Yeah," said Nellie. "Either she's here or she isn't, and how can anyone know if she hasn't ascended?"

"Most likely she isn't," said Destiny. "Since none of us contestants have got close to Jack. But that's how you two come in."

"I'm listening," said Chrissie.

"You want fame, right, Chrissie?" said Destiny. "And Nellie, you want money. I want to be announced as the goddess."

"You're the goddess?" asked Chrissie in an awed voice.

"No, I don't think so. But does it matter if the country thinks I am?"

"I don't understand," said Nellie.

Destiny sighed. "What I want is for the three of us to combine our magics to make it look like I've ascended at the special goddess-revealing event tomorrow. At this rate, the real goddess may never be found. Wouldn't it be good for the country to have something to believe in for now? In return for your help, and your silence, I will reveal some very important knowledge I'm holding to the two of you. Connections I have through my parents, and some upcoming policy announcements that are going to affect the stock market."

Tiffany cut the 'cast off with a wave and powered down the auto-aethercaster.

"Is that the end?" asked Leta.

"No, but the next bit I want to keep for myself. It's my prize."

"The information Destiny gave them."

"That's it."

"So you get to keep the information that will make you rich and famous."

"Yes. And you have the plot that Destiny is brewing against your boyo, and the warning you need to save him from a life of thinking that *Destiny* is his, well, destiny."

"Ugh," said Leta. "And that's an even split, is it?"

Tiffany shrugged. "I don't think so. You're a fool for getting involved with someone like him, given the circumstances. But you want to save him, right?"

"Can we show this 'cast to the execs?"

"Do you want to explain how we got it?"

Leta sighed. "No."

"He's got special magic that can see what others are doing, right?" asked Tiffany. "All he needs is a heads-up, and he'll be able to save himself by being all, 'Um, that's fake; that's not a real ascension.' It would have the bonus of embarrassing her in front of the nation. The 'cast of the big event tomorrow is going out *live*." Tiffany gave an evil chuckle. "You can warn him. I bet you have his aethervoicer number by now. And if not, haven't you already been passing him secret messages? I'm assuming that's how the two of you arranged your escapade."

Leta wouldn't risk calling Jack. He feared AllAether had tapped his aethervoicer; they would glean all sorts of secrets from such a call. But she could arrange a note. "I can do it. I'll warn him. Thank you." Leta sighed. "Destiny's sharing info with the anti-incarnation protesters, too. It's being kept quiet for now because she can't do any more harm now, and to avoid bad publicity."

Tiffany shrugged. "Yeah, she seems the type to play both sides. It doesn't surprise me." She rose to her feet and stretched. "You're all right, you know. Sorry I read you wrong, back at the beginning. I wasn't nice, because I was just thinking of me. I mean, mostly I still am. But you looked out for me even when I was being a jerk. You're a good sort, Leta. All the best."

"Thanks, Tiffany. I read you wrong at the beginning too. Thank you for all of your help." At the beginning of the aethercast, Leta had assumed that all the contestants would be awful to her. The assumption was borne, she was ashamed to realise, of internalised misogyny. Tiffany's help buoyed her heart.

"Don't mention it." Tiffany opened the door a crack, peeked out, and then slipped away.

Leta wolfed the rest of her dinner, then went to Mirabelle's suite. The seer was finishing her dinner and watching a historical drama. "Sorry to bother you this late, Mirabelle, but I need your help."

The older woman patted the sofa beside her. "Come, tell me."

Leta outlined the problem as thoroughly as she could. "All I need is to warn Jack. He can deal with the plan from there, I'm sure. May I write him a letter and deliver it to him as if it were an extra daily from you?"

"Absolutely, dear. Help yourself." She pointed to the desk where the special writing paper and envelopes were laid out.

Leta went to the desk and wrote up what Destiny's plan was in a letter.

Please, keep safe, Jack. I hope everything works out well for you.
Love, Leta

She sealed the letter, brought it to Mirabelle to address, and bowed to her. "Thank you so much for your help, Seer Mirabelle."

"Not at all, dear Leta. Off you go. Save the boy."

Leta went up to the twentieth floor. Two burly security guards stood by Jack's suite door. That was new. "I'm Seer Mirabelle's assistant," she said to them as she approached. "I have a daily viewing to deliver to Jack."

They stepped close enough together that she wouldn't be able to fit between their shoulders. "No one can see the God Incarnate," said one. "Marcus's orders."

"I don't need to see him. I just need to slide this envelope under the door."

"You can't do that."

"It's my job," said Leta. "The seer has important advice for the God Incarnate about tomorrow's event."

"If she comes here herself with Marcus supervising, she can go in and deliver her message. Otherwise, she'll have to wait. Now, off you go, girlie."

Leta left, heading back to Mirabelle's rooms. What was she going to do?

WHEEL OF FORTUNE
REVERSED

NEGATIVE FORCES ARE SWIRLING ABOUT YOU. YOU FEEL HELPLESS, BUT
YOU ARE NOT. WHAT CHANGE CAN YOU MAKE TO BREAK THE CYCLE?

For immediate release:

Goddess Found *live aethercast extravaganza!*

Tomorrow evening, tap in for a special event on your favourite aethercast, Goddess Found. We will be bringing you a special live event direct from Emerald Marquise Tower. You won't want to miss this special occasion!

To catch up with the exciting events of the week so far, tap here.

AllAether. AllYourFaves

End media release

That evening, after the counsellor Kellan visited him, Jack received a nasty surprise. When he tried to leave his suite to warn Leta, he found two sketchy-looking security guards stationed outside his rooms. They would not let him leave. 'Marcus's orders,' they said. Fuck Marcus. If he wanted to see anyone, he would have to call Marcus and ask him to escort them to his suite.

He couldn't call Leta. There was no way he could get Marcus to escort her to his rooms. And if Marcus were there, he couldn't warn her without letting him figure out who she was, so that wasn't a goer.

Then he remembered his suspicion that Mirabelle knew who Leta was. She was likely aware, and hadn't said anything to anyone else yet. If that was the case, he might get the message through in hints without letting Marcus figure out what exactly he was talking about. Asking for a visit from the seer was also easy to justify. And it wasn't as if Mirabelle didn't have experience 'guiding' things along. Most importantly of all, Mirabelle had never seemed particularly close with people like Marcus and Evelyn.

He called the connection he'd been given for the executive suite from the room's aetherweb globe. It was currently the only connection he hadn't been locked out of. Marcus answered.

"I've received your present," said Jack.

"Oh?"

"Yeah. They said I can't leave the suite and they won't let anyone in unless you escort them in."

"You're not going to get me to escort your girlfriend in for a visit, are you? I don't wanna see that."

"No. I want a viewing with Seer Mirabelle. I need advice."

"Don't you ever," said Marcus. "Fine, I'll see what I can do. In the morning."

"But—"

"Come on, man; be reasonable. It's getting late. The old biddy is probably in bed by now."

Jack tried to distract himself with the aetherweb that evening, but he couldn't sit still. He could have sworn that he didn't sleep that night, just tossed and turned and fretted. He must have slept at some point, though, because he dreamed of monsters; of dark things; of needing to go to a school exam, but he'd lost his trousers. And worst of all, of Leta disappearing under mountains of emerald silk, never to be seen again.

He woke in the steel-grey dawn, convinced that Marcus would not follow through on his words. But to his surprise, Marcus came by with Mirabelle in tow after breakfast. She carried a large bag of her paraphernalia, and Marcus wasn't trying to help carry it, despite how it made Mirabelle struggle with her cane. Jack rushed over and took the bag, placing it on the coffee table for her.

"I know you like to do your readings one-on-one, seer," said Marcus. "But you'll just have to handle having me in the room. Our boy here can't be trusted at the moment. He's been behaving badly."

"That's fine," said Mirabelle, the strain of carrying the bag along the corridor still in her voice. "Now you will get to see what a reading is like." She settled in a chair and sighed.

"Can I get you a cup of tea, Seer Mirabelle?" asked Jack.

"Oh, yes, please," she said.

"Milk, two sugars, right?"

While Jack made her a tea, but not one for Marcus, Mirabelle set up her paraphernalia. The augury bones, the cards, the crystal ball... and a crystal pendulum?

Jack delivered the tea and sat on the sofa. Marcus took a seat on the other length of the corner sofa and crossed his arms.

"Jack," said Mirabelle, after taking a sip of her tea. "Which method would you like to start with today?"

The pendulum flickered to his eyes as Mirabelle engaged and disengaged her magic from it. He appreciated the hint, but he'd caught onto her intentions. "The pendulum, please," he said.

"All right," said Mirabelle, picking it up as if this was a part of their routine. She held it by its string over the table and spun it with a finger. "Please look into the pendulum," she said.

As Mirabelle's magic surged in the pendulum, Jack looked in its direction but unfocussed his eyes and looked beyond it. Marcus, apparently, did no such thing, because he suddenly slumped to the side as if he had fallen asleep.

"We have mere minutes to speak freely," said Mirabelle as she put the pendulum down.

"I have a message for Leta," said Jack.

At the same time, Mirabelle said, "I have a message from Leta."

Jack blinked. "You go first."

"Leta has uncovered a plot by Destiny to make herself announced as the Goddess Incarnate this evening." Mirabelle sketched out the details. "You have the power to stop her, even if she starts her little trick: just interrupt

her and say what's going on for the viewers at home.
Don't let her finish before revealing her intentions, and
no one will believe her."

Jack sighed. How stupid was this? It was a complica-
tion he didn't need. "Thank you. And please thank Leta."

"I will. Now, your message?"

"Don't let Leta be here later today. Send her home for
the day. Give her a night off."

"Why?"

"Come, now. I think you know why. You want her to
ascend in a live 'cast? You want that pressure on her? I
can just tell her who she is later, in private. Keep the
slavering money-grubbing AllAether away from her."

Mirabelle smiled and sat back in her chair. "Well,
well. I didn't know you knew."

"I do. And she deserves better than this." He waved
his hand around, indicating the hotel, the aethercast, everything. "So send her away while Gregory does his
thing. She can come back after."

Mirabelle nodded. "Understood. I will encourage her
to take a day in leave." She eyed Marcus. "My spell is
wearing off. I'm going to wake him with a jolt. If we start
off exactly where we were, he might not figure out he's
been asleep for a few minutes. He might think he lost concentration for a second. Are you ready?"

"Yep."

Marcus jolted awake, and they kept talking about the
readings as if nothing had happened. Mirabelle did a fake
reading for Jack with the pendulum, not pushing any
magic through it at all and instead just rehashing things
she'd read for him before in the auguries. Then she continued through auguries, cards and crystal ball with a real
reading, apparently boring Marcus as he yawned a few
times.

The auguries and the cards gave the same message as
before. The crystal ball was interesting, though. He saw a

flash of light, emerald green silk, danger. The desperate need to *push, push*. But this time, he recognised the particular shade of Leta's auburn hair in the vision. It was Leta he had been seeing in danger all these weeks. Somehow, they were still on the path to that vision.

He reassured himself it was something that he could worry about another day, because the danger she faced could not happen at the event that evening. It must be a future danger, one closer to the time when she would ascend. He'd already saved her from ascending that day. Mirabelle would pass the message on. After Ander, after knocking Marcus out just now, after all the times she had been at odds with AllAether, he believed in her. She would save Leta from being outed as the goddess at the aethercast live event.

LETA COULDN'T SIT STILL and wait while Mirabelle went to relay her message to Jack. She'd go crazy if she didn't release her nervous energy.

She wrapped herself up against the cold and stepped out of the hotel into a morning that smelled of the lake and the forested hills beyond. A mist from the lake lingered in the grim morning air, chilling the tip of Leta's nose in mere moments. Despite that, protesters still loitered on the forecourt, though they were quieter than usual. Why hadn't they been moved along already? They were an inconvenience for the hotel. Did AllAether want them there for the drama?

Leta strode past the protesters, intending to take a turn around the block to stomp out her nervous energy. Round the corner, and another corner, the sound of her boots muffled by the damp air. Then…

Déjà vu.

There were two figures in the mists, lurking in the shadow of a service entrance behind the hotel. One of them was Destiny, wrapped in a fine green woollen coat.

Leta knew how this would go. It wasn't the first time Leta had come across Destiny acting shady. But she'd had enough. She strode forward. "What's going on here, then?"

The nondescript man talking to Destiny startled and then did a runner. It was the same guy she had seen her with at Autumnwood.

Destiny stood her ground and let Leta approach. "It's none of your business," she said.

"You're not very sneaky. This is the third time I've caught you communicating with the protesters. Were you telling them about this evening's event?"

Destiny sneered. "So what? Are you going to tell on me?"

"Naturally."

"Who'd believe you?"

Leta smiled, showing her teeth. "You have no idea. You think people don't know you're in financial trouble and taking bribes?"

Destiny's face contorted. She stepped into Leta's personal space and loomed over her. "They're not using me; I'm using *them*. They're so stupid. They think I'm one of them, but I'm descended from divinity. This is my *birthright*."

Leta gaped. Of course. Destiny's family name was Brightborne, and several incarnations ago... before the Sudburys... the God and Goddess Incarnate of Gealdland had been Harold and Mary Brightborne.

Birthright. It looked like Destiny thought she had more of a right to the status of Goddess Incarnate than the actual Goddess Incarnate.

Destiny smirked at Leta's confusion. "I won't bore you with the details. Plus, with no magic, and no goodwill from AllAether, what are you even going to do? Tah tah!" Destiny waved with her fingers and then slipped back into the hotel through the service door.

Leta watched her go. If she said anything further, Destiny would know that Leta knew about her plan, and Leta would lose her advantage. So far, the woman thought Leta was still sniffing around, several steps behind, and too late to do anything.

But Leta knew Destiny was planning to steal the ascension spotlight. And now she knew she was going to be using the anti-incarnation protesters as part of her plan, as well as Chrissie and Nellie.

But Jack didn't know that part. Leta would have to make sure she was there to look out for them on his behalf.

She returned to Mirabelle's suite to wait. It wasn't long before the seer returned, a smile on her face. "I warned him," she said straight away.

Leta breathed a sigh of relief. "Thank goodness. I didn't think I could get the warning to him. Thank you so much, Mirabelle."

"Not at all. If they announced the wrong person as the goddess, I would feel like I had failed. I very much want the actual Goddess Incarnate to be found and announced."

"Could you pass on anything more to him? I've learned something new." She outlined what she had learned from her conversation with Destiny.

"I'm afraid not, dear," said Mirabelle. "Marcus is busy now. However, I have another solution. For tonight's event, they are hoping for a big 'crowd' of onlookers in the ballroom. Apparently, any crew or hotel employees not working at the time who can round up suits or fancy dresses can be a part of the crowd. Most likely, Destiny's protesters will be intending to infiltrate the crowd. Would you like to go? Between us, I am sure we could keep an eye out for them and draw Jack's attention to them if needed."

"Oh, yes! But I don't have a fancy dress..."

"I'm not doing any private viewings today because the contestants are getting ready for the event. How about we go shopping?"

"I don't have enough money for—"

"Leta, I'm offering you as your patron to buy you a dress. And me a dress too. I want a new dress. So, let's get ready for the ball. I want to make sure that you can attend."

THE TOWER
UPRIGHT

You see the web of lies around you, the harsh truth. But if you
are wise, your truth is revelation, not devastation.

General notice:

All crew and hotel employees who are not working necessary roles at the time of the Goddess Found *live event and who can access formal attire may attend the event as crowd fillers. Young women under the age of 26 are particularly encouraged to attend.*

The wardrobe department has a limited selection of ball dresses available to borrow for the event. Tap here for details. Limited sizes; first come, first served.

AllAether Executive Team

The day inched by interminably. Jack could leave his rooms only when it was time to go to the gala. He had dressed in the sharpest suit in his aethercast wardrobe and waited like a good little boy for 'permission' to go to work. He visited the makeup station where they dusted him with stage foundation, then went to the ballroom, auto-aethercasters in tow, to watch the final preparations being put in place. Workers were dressing the room with silver bunting and balloons. Maybe it would look good to viewers at home, but in person it looked more like a school ball run on too small a budget.

Jack hoped Leta was well away from the hotel by now, perhaps relaxing at home with her mother. That was his number one priority, but he was also running through how he would phrase his shoot-down of Destiny's spoofed ascension. He wanted to be firm and clear, but he didn't want to humiliate her.

Jack offered to help hang some bunting — after being cooped up inside his suite for a whole day, he was happy to do anything — but the workers waved him away with scandalised looks. Instead, Jack took a seat on the edge of the stage and watched. Not long after, Marcus and

Gregory Hallowborne, the man he'd met that day in the boardroom, arrived. They noted Jack's presence, then ignored him while they walked around the ballroom, Gregory looking into a palm-sized crystal ball as they did so. He stopped a little over to the left of the centre of the room and cast a light mage spell to place a glowing X on the floor. Then Marcus waved an assistant over and gave some instructions. That assistant began measuring from the cross and made their own magical lines, designating areas for different groups of people to stand. While Marcus, Gregory and Jack watched, the assistant sectioned the ballroom off into a crowd area, a clear path to the door, a contestant area, a mage area with a table, and the head stage.

Jack hopped down from the stage to talk to Marcus and Gregory. "Is that where you're going to do your thing, Gregory?" he asked, pointing at the cross.

"You've got some balls, eh?" said Marcus. "Your bad behaviour is why we're all here working our backsides off."

Gregory pushed his spell-glinting glasses further up the bridge of his nose. "Now, now, Marcus. Something you aren't appreciating is that our boy Jack here has what the rest of us don't: vague senses and memories of past lives. He makes more sense if you think of him as an old man. A crotchety old man who doesn't care who he offends, and who has lived too long for this bullshit."

"Finally, someone who gets me," said Jack. "I don't care. I just want to find the Goddess Incarnate."

"Given any luck, we'll do just that this evening. Mirabelle seems to think it's likely, and I've been working with her for twenty years, so I know she's good."

Jack felt a chill right in the core of him. "Mirabelle? You work with her?"

"Yes, for a while now," said Gregory. "We've been looking for you and your counterpart. It's been a pet project of ours for some years, because it's high time Gealdland has both of its incarnates again. Not only for the land, but because people are forgetting what's important. Take those protesters outside as a case in point. Gealdland needs its spiritual leaders, and it needs them working well with the Geald Council. Anyway, Mirabelle had a reading that indicates the goddess might be close by. She couldn't guarantee that she's a contestant, though. That's why we've arranged for as many staff and crew to be present as possible, so we have the best chance of catching her."

Gregory continued, talking about how this was all sold to AllAether as the best possible option considering that they weren't sure that the goddess would be nearby for long, but Jack barely heard him. This had been Mirabelle's idea. Mirabelle, who knew that Leta was the goddess. Mirabelle, who was more buddy-buddy with the Geald Council than he had known.

Mirabelle, who he had asked to warn Leta to stay away.

He'd been such a fool. He'd assumed her not getting along with Marcus meant she wouldn't be on his side. But it had all been much more complicated. By what Gregory was saying and what he didn't know, she had even manipulated him. She'd manipulated them all.

Betrayal, Mirabelle had forecast for him. Promised him. The one who had betrayed him was Mirabelle herself.

"Please excuse me," he said and started for the door. He had to find Leta and warn her.

"Where do you think you're going?" said Marcus. "You can't leave!"

"I'm not going far," said Jack over his shoulder. "I just need to piss!"

Well-dressed people were already filing into the ballroom and milling about in the designated crowd area. He walked against the flow, looking about for a familiar head of auburn hair and a glint of light on glasses. He went out into the crowded hallway. Assistants were giving the crowd instructions on where to go once they were in the ballroom, and what to do. People were jovial: most were hotel or aethercast workers, and being guests at an event like this was a novelty. He recognised some near-familiar faces too; perhaps the families of the contestants.

Many both recognised him and took notice, which was hindering his search. People moved closer, tried to talk to him. He said, "Please excuse me; I'm looking for someone," so many times the sounds of the words became arbitrary on his tongue. Thankfully, he was tall enough to see over most people's heads, and going up on tiptoes gave him a view of who was in the hallway flowing past.

Finally he spotted her: she stood with Mirabelle, the two of them farther up the hallway and over to one side, letting people stream past them, waiting for a lull so Mirabelle could walk with her cane safely. Jack waded through the crowd, scattering apologies. Mirabelle spotted his approach first. She had the decency to look guilty and glance away from his no doubt thunderous expression.

He drew close enough to get a good look at Leta. She was beautiful. Stunning. He stopped for a moment and just looked at her. Her hair fell in silky curls down her back, and makeup enhanced her features. He was glad to still see her freckles through the foundation. She wore a flowing dress, demure but still elegant. She held her own against the rich people in the crowd, with their wardrobes that cost as much as a normal person's house, and she shone amongst the hotel staff and aethercast crew who had only limited funds to 'fancy up' for the gala. He'd seen her means at her home. He guessed Mirabelle had purchased her a dress. At least she'd done that much for the woman she had engineered to be announced as the goddess on live 'cast with no warning. And she must have had no warning, because she would have ascended already otherwise, and he would have felt it.

Leta caught sight of him and looked up at him with a mixture of surprise and pleasure. "Jack," she said. "Good evening."

He stepped closer and took a hold of her arm, pulling her closer to the wall to have a quiet word.

"What? What are you doing?" she asked.

He paused a moment to gather his thoughts; he would have to phrase this carefully. One wrong word and he would force-ascend her, right here in the middle of this crowd that was no doubt filled with reporters and watched from every angle by omnipresent auto-aethercasters. Force-ascending her right now would be about the second-worst way of it happening. She raised her eyebrows at him.

"You're not supposed to be here," he said at last. "You have to leave."

"What?"

"I told Mirabelle to warn you. You're not supposed to be here!"

She looked up at him in confusion, and dawning hurt. "You don't want me here? Why? Because your goddess will be announced?"

"Yes."

She drew her shoulders back. "I can handle it. What, do you think I'm going to cause a scene?"

He did, but not in the way she seemed to think. With a sinking feeling, he realised she thought she was being treated like the 'other woman,' who had to be hidden. "It's not like that. You're not safe."

Not safe. It dawned on him what colour her dress was. Emerald green. The same colour he had seen in his crystal ball visions many times. She was on the verge of ascension, and on the verge of locking in whatever danger the crystal ball had been warning him about. He took her upper arms in his hands. He had one chance left to move her off the path. "Leta, *please*. They won't let me be close enough to save you. You'll be in danger!"

She scoffed. "Me? I'm no one. What about you? What about Destiny?"

"That doesn't matter!"

Her face was overtaken with sadness. "I understand. Don't worry about me. I won't interfere."

"You *don't* understand!" He wished he could just tell her, but there were auto-aethercasters hanging over his shoulders right now, ready to send their captures to AllAether. He didn't want her ascension to go this way.

She pulled out of his hands and joined the flow of people into the hallway. "I'm going to see this through to the end," she said over her shoulder. "I don't care how hurt I am. And look out for anti-incarnation protesters. Some might be here waiting to cause trouble." With that, she was gone.

He couldn't stop her, not without making a scene. He turned to Mirabelle, who had been watching the whole conversation. "You had better stick with her, and make damned sure that she's safe. This is going to be hard on her, and I can't shield her. You engineered it; you make it as easy as you can. And look out for someone who wants to do her harm."

"Why are you so sure she's in physical danger? She will soon be able to protect herself better than I ever could. We've done it, Jack. We have brought her safely to her ascension." Mirabelle beamed at him as if everything had already worked out for the best.

She didn't get it. She had no idea what he was worried about. He stabbed a finger in her direction. "*You* were the one who told me I wasn't allowed to tell you what I saw in the crystal ball. Well, now you're operating without all the information." A different voice welled up from within

Jack, one that he knew carried more weight than normal. "Stay on guard, seer. Your aid will be required."

Mirabelle's face paled. Perhaps she recognised the Hunter speaking through Jack. "Oh," she said. "Oh, my." She hurried after Leta. Jack followed and walked down the aisle to the front of the hall. The pieces were now in their places, despite his efforts. He had no choice but to play the game.

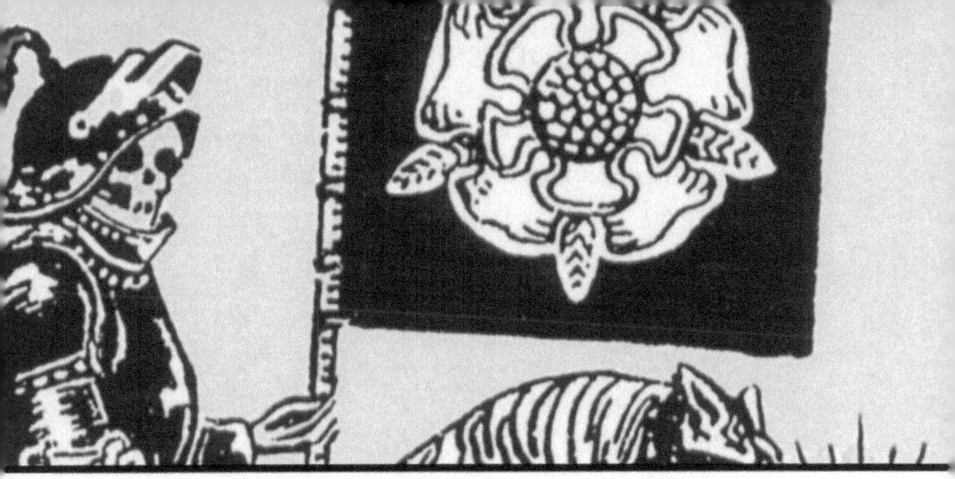

DEATH
UPRIGHT

Step through the doorway. Something better awaits you.

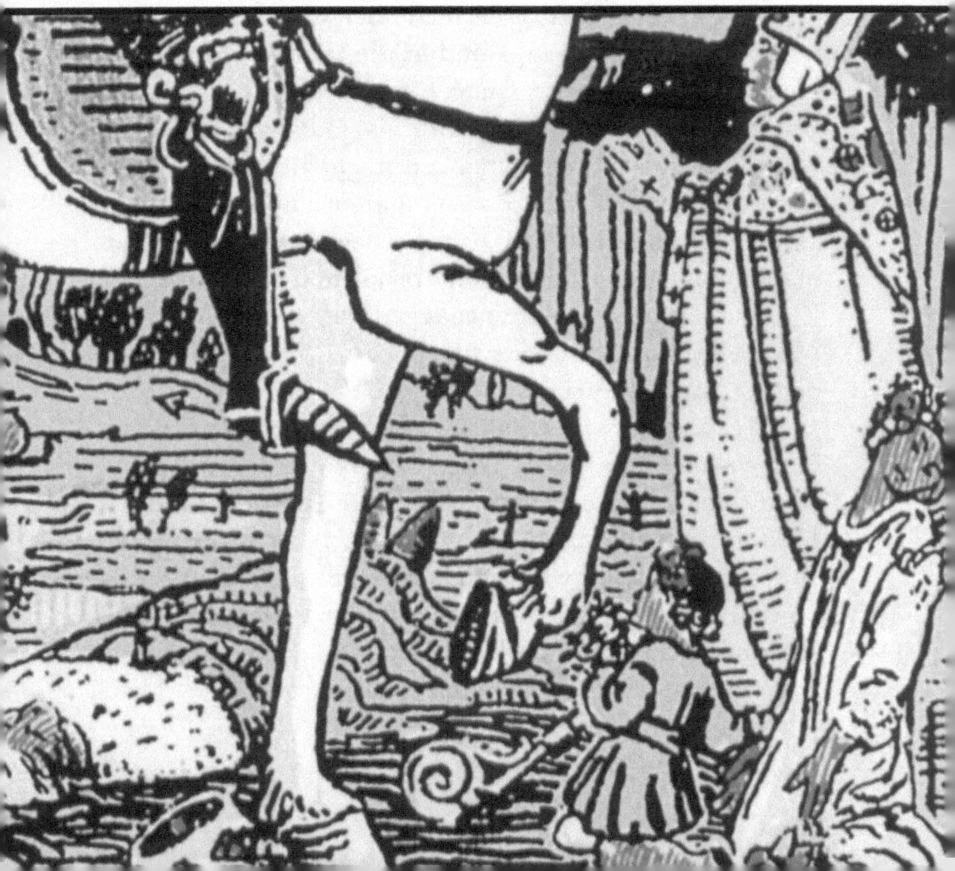

GODDESS FOUND

You are coming to the event, aren't you, father? Please. It's important. I've found a way to fix everything.

Destiny

Crowds were usually the bane of her existence, but she didn't care at that moment. Leta stood in the ballroom, numb to it all, the effervescence of the crowd failing to lift her mood. Even the close buzz of dozens of voices that often made her want to run away was nothing more than sound at the far end of a tunnel. He'd tried to hide her, to push her away. Did he think she would sabotage his joining with his goddess? A goddess who he seemed to be convinced might be Destiny after all, if his comment of 'it doesn't matter' implied what she assumed it did. Sure, she'd got her feelings all tangled up in everything, but that was her problem to deal with.

A touch on her elbow snagged her attention. It was Mirabelle, looking at her with concern. "Are you all right, dear?" Mirabelle asked.

"Yeah, sure, why wouldn't I be?" She looked around. "Do we have any way of telling where Destiny will be? I want to be as close as I can to her in case I'm needed." If Destiny was the goddess, she'd just have to accept it. Maybe that was why he'd got a bit confused and attached himself to her, because they were both redheads. But if Destiny wasn't the goddess, Leta wanted to save Jack from that fate, even if he didn't appreciate it.

"Leta, that is not your responsibility. Jack can deal with it. Let us search for the anti-incarnation protesters."

Ah. Them. Leta should have given Jack more details when she had the chance, but she'd been distracted.

"We can do both," she said. "Better if someone the auto-aethercasters aren't watching deals with Destiny. Less fuss for everyone involved."

"What are you planning to do?"

"I don't know; shoulder-barge her or something? That would break her concentration."

Mirabelle pursed her lips. "It might be a wiser move to target either of her co-conspirators. What do you think? How about Chrissie? She seems the most foolish of the three."

"Yes," said Leta. "Let's get closer to where the contestants will be standing."

They pushed through the crowd. Some people seemed annoyed about being jostled until they saw Leta helping Mirabelle, and Mirabelle's cane. Some people gave Leta odd looks. With a sour feeling she realised they recognised her from the Autumnwood Manor episodes of the aethercast.

As they passed through the crowd, Leta kept her eyes peeled for anyone she'd seen in the gaggles of protesters, but it seemed they were not foolish enough to send in the same people who had been outside the hotel. That was both to be expected, and worrying. There must be people who had connections with the protesters who hadn't made an appearance yet, either because they didn't want their faces shown, or because they had jobs to go to and couldn't afford the time.

What if there were protest sympathisers amongst the hotel staff? How had AllAether selected this crowd? She knew a lot of it was hotel staff, aethercast crew, and families of the contestants. The crowd seemed bigger than that, though. Who else was here?

Eventually, they stood at the front of the crowd, near an area that seemed to be sectioned off for the contestants. Leta looked up at the stage at Jack, who had already spotted them. He looked angry and afraid. He was staring daggers at Mirabelle. Since when had he not liked her?

She remembered his words out in the hallway. Not everything he had said had registered at the time. Now, with more time to think, she had a burning question.

"What did Jack mean by 'I told Mirabelle to warn you'?"

Mirabelle didn't answer at first, long enough for Leta to worry. "Jack had a vision during our viewings. After you walked away, he said something about what he had seen in the crystal ball. But those kinds of visions can be misleading. Maybe you were going to target Destiny and get hurt, because she is a fire mage, and could do a lot of damage to you in retaliation. But Chrissie is a light mage, and all her magic can do to harm someone is blind them for a moment. Maybe we have already thwarted whatever vision he had."

Leta's stomach flip-flopped. She had misunderstood Jack's intentions in the hallway. He hadn't been trying to hide her; he had been trying to protect her. She looked at him, sitting on his chair on the stage, dressed like someone famous, someone untouchable. But he was looking at her, worry etched on his face. She mouthed 'I'm sorry,' at him. He read the words on her lips and mouthed the same back to her.

"So, I might be in danger after all, despite being no one important?"

The long stretch of silence from Mirabelle spoke volumes. "If I have brought you into danger, Leta, I am so sorry. That wasn't my intention. Shall we go?"

Leta considered it; considered leaving, going back to her room. But she couldn't. Despite what she had heard, something was keeping her here. Perhaps it was stubbornness. Perhaps it was foolishness. Perhaps it was hormones. But she felt like she was exactly where she needed to be. "No. Though you can if you want to."

"I promised Jack I would protect you."

"Mirabelle, you're a seer, not a battle mage, and you walk with a cane. Pardon me for saying so."

"Not like that. I know I cannot protect you physically. But my name and reputation are a shield of a different sort."

"You mean, if I get in trouble for helping Jack, because Destiny causes a fuss?"

"Yes."

A production assistant calling out with a magically amplified voice interrupted their conversation. "And we're live in 5, 4, 3, 2, 1."

Marcus jogged down the aisle from the back of the hall to cheers from the crowd. "Good evening, viewers at home!" he shouted as he jogged, keeping his voice even and looking at the auto-aethercasters flying backward just above and in front of him. "We're coming to you live from Emerald Marquise Tower! We have a special event lined up for you tonight. A little bird has given us a big clue that we just can't help but follow up on! Seer Mirabelle, where are you? Come on out!"

To Leta's surprise, Mirabelle stepped out of the crowd and into the special 'magic' area marked on the floor, around a small table covered in implements. Marcus jogged over to meet her. "Can you tell us what we are all here for this evening, Mirabelle?"

"Yes, Marcus, I can," said Mirabelle. Leta's jaw dropped. What was going on? Where had all of this come from? She glanced up at Jack, but he only looked grim and stiff, not at all surprised. "While divining for the aethercast, I had an important vision in my crystal ball," said Mirabelle, talking to the auto-aethercasters. "While nothing is at all certain in my profession, as the tides of fate may change at short notice, all indications are that the goddess is nearby, right now!" A murmur passed through the crowd like the ripples of a pebble dropped in a pond.

"So one of the contestants is the goddess, after all?"

Mirabelle shrugged. "We'll just have to wait and see, won't we?"

"Yes indeed; and that brings me to our guest for the evening. Viewers at home, we are blessed with a most illustrious guest this evening. Please welcome Gregory Hallowborne!" The ripple of gasps was even more pronounced at this new announcement. Gregory Hallowborne was almost a myth, the greatest mage in the original Geald family. A recluse, an institution. He was *here*? *Why*?

A greying man in a navy suit and horn-rimmed glasses stepped out of the crowd and approached the table. "Thank you, Marcus. While I can't quite say it is a pleasure to be here, because I'm not a fan of crowds," he paused for a nervous titter of laughter from the crowd in question, "it is a great privilege. Few have the chance to witness what we will tonight, if Mirabelle is right, and no one I know of has ever instigated it."

Marcus grinned at him. "Could you please explain? Put our poor audience out of their misery?"

"Absolutely, Marcus. When our new God Incarnate, young Jack, ascended a few years ago, an unprecedented amount of data was collected on the nature of ascension and the signals it gives off into the aethersphere, because of an experiment that was running at the same time in a nearby research post. A colleague of mine in Agranos has compared the data with that from the ascension of Ander Palomo, the God Incarnate of the Agrani, some years ago. I've been collaborating with him on the research. We believe that if I trigger a ley line nexus point in just such a way, then the goddess, if she is nearby, will ascend without the normal, less reliable or more fraught triggers that can hasten the process, such as mortal peril, heightened emotions, communion with a god — whether intentional or unintentional as our Jack did — or being told by another incarnate who has recognised them, a process that takes a long time."

"Yes, which is why we let Jack get to know our contestants well, because it can take a while for incarnations to recognise one another. So, is there a nexus nearby?"

Gregory pointed at the ground. "There's one right here."

Marcus looked up at the auto-aethercasters. "How fortunate!"

It impressed Leta how accurate the rumour mill had been, even though it was so surprising and nothing like anyone had known would be possible until yesterday.

She looked around at the surrounding crowd to see if anyone looked angry at the news instead of awed. Through the crowd, she spied a familiar head of lank blond hair. She'd seen that guy amongst the protesters before. Should she move towards him or stay where she was? She started to move, but then looked up at Mirabelle. The seer gave her a tense look and shook her head. 'Stay there,' she mouthed.

While Leta had been looking at the crowd, Marcus had hopped up the stairs to approach Jack, who was now standing. "What do you think of all this?"

Jack paused while the crowd applauded him. "This all feels surreal."

"I'm sure it does! You might very well be meeting the Goddess Incarnate in mere minutes!" Marcus clapped him on the shoulder. "Please try your best to contain your eagerness."

"I'll try," said Jack. He didn't look eager at all. He looked like he was going to be sick. Why? If this was the case, shouldn't he be happy? Did Jack know something they didn't? Wasn't it going to work? Or was he preoccupied with Destiny's plot? Had she ruined what should be a happy moment for him?

"Without further ado, let's welcome our contestants!"

The contestants filed into the ballroom. Each was dressed like they were expecting to win acting awards. They waved to the cheering crowd. When they had taken their places, standing on the opposite side of the aisle from the mages' table, Marcus dragged the 'cast out by talking to each contestant to ask who they thought the goddess was.

Leta used the time to work her way through the crowd until she was behind Chrissie and close to the front of the crowd. The blond-haired protester, meanwhile, went to the other end of the row, near Destiny.

Chrissie giggled when Marcus questioned her and said she was sure they would find the goddess. She didn't have any subtlety. Nellie blushed and shrugged. She would be a terrible cards player. Destiny demurred with a false wise take: "As Seer Mirabelle said, the fates are fickle; how can any of us say for sure what will happen this evening? I hope with all my heart that Jack is happy with this evening's outcome."

Since Leta knew what Destiny was going to do, she could see how Destiny was positioning herself in the viewers' minds, and she didn't like it one bit. Leta looked up at Jack to see if he looked excited to see Destiny. Did he think she was the goddess, after all? But no, he looked tense, with a vague hint of annoyance. Leta had got the wrong end of the stick out in the hallway. Why, then, had he been so keen to hide Leta away?

Constance was blunt. "It's none of us," she said.

"None of you?" asked Marcus in surprise.

"Yeah, none of us are the goddess." She didn't elaborate further. But Constance was a clairvoyant. Did she, too, have more information than others?

Tiffany backed Constance up. "Yeah, Constance has the right of it. We've all spent heaps of time with Jack, but none of us held his attention. If the goddess is here, maybe she's in the crowd?"

"Here in the crowd?" asked Marcus. "Oooh, that's an exciting idea."

"Yes, I know. It could be you! Or you!" She pointed at different people in the crowd. "What about you?" A woman who Leta had seen at the reception desk jumped when Tiffany pointed at her and then fanned her face. The crowd laughed. Tiffany had changed the mood in the ballroom. She had the crowd in her thrall. People starting pushing forward, jostling Leta from behind. It could be *anyone*. Anyone who was born after the previous Goddess Incarnate died. Finally, some excitement leaked into Leta. Jack did like her company. It could be *her*.

...Nah, no way.

Marcus returned to where Gregory and Mirabelle stood. "Are you ready, Gregory?"

While everyone had been distracted, Gregory had prepared his paraphernalia. And also, apparently, he'd been having a quiet, friendly conversation with Mirabelle. She was *friends* with Gregory Hallowborne. Leta had never realised just how enmeshed with the rich and powerful Mirabelle was.

Gregory stepped to the glowing cross on the floor, a glass knife in one hand and a bottle of blue powder in the other. "I'm ready, Marcus. Shall I proceed?"

Marcus jumped up on the stage again and stood beside Jack. "What do you think?" he asked.

"I want nothing more than to find my goddess."

"That sounds like a yes to me. Contestants; shall we start?"

Several of the contestants cried out, "Yes," or some variant thereof.

"Audience, what say you? Yea or nay?"

"Yea!" cried the audience as if in one voice.

"Then, Master Hallowborne, please proceed!"

No fewer than five auto-aethercasters trained themselves on Gregory as he poured the powder from the bottle in a circle around the cross. Leta hadn't seen magic performed with such consumables in years. She wondered if it was necessary or, as most people thought these days, it was just showmanship that the mages of old had clung to for far too long, looking outside themselves for control of what was innate. She supposed most of the audience was writing it off as showmanship too, but there were always those who preferred this style of magic, and thought it was more 'proper'.

When the circle of blue powder was complete, Gregory knelt with a slight grunt and cut the circle outwards at the four compass points with the glass knife. He laid the knife on top of the cross, held his hand over it, and closed his eyes. Then he sang.

It wasn't a song by modern standards, but rather a chant. Gregory pushed his voice high for it, nearly reaching falsetto. While Leta had seen magic performed with consumables before, she had never seen someone working with chants, the original Gealdrspeak that their country was named after. She hadn't thought that anyone even knew how to anymore. It was an *ancient* method.

Leta looked around the ballroom. It seemed as if everyone had stopped breathing as they watched and listened. The auto-aethercasters flying around the room in arcs, capturing the crowd, were the only thing that moved. Leta looked up at Jack again. He shielded his eyes as he looked at Gregory and winced as if he were trying to look at the sun.

Leta turned her attention to where it should be: Chrissie. She had a hand wrapped up in her voluminous navy skirts. It looked like she was twisting it nervously, but Leta suspected otherwise. She moved to the edge of the crowd, pushing two women aside, who both gave her dirty looks but otherwise said nothing. Leta then made her move. With everyone concentrating on Gregory, she didn't need to do much. She reached out across the line on the floor and tapped Chrissie on the shoulder. When Chrissie looked behind her, Leta caught her eye and shook her head. Chrissie frowned.

"She's using you," Leta whispered to Chrissie. "She thinks you're gullible."

Chrissie looked at Leta for a long moment, the frown still her face. Then she glanced over at Destiny, who was looking at them with a thunderous expression, her hand also clutched in her skirts, hiding some magic gestures of her own.

Leta didn't know if she'd inspired Chrissie to rethink whether she should associate with Destiny, but she had at least delayed her. Had she delayed her enough? Gregory still knelt on the floor, mid chant. He wasn't done. If Chrissie could still do whatever it was she was going to do, perhaps make Destiny glow like Jack…

Leta lost her train of thought. That glass knife… it… *sang.*

The words differed from Gregory's chant. Richer, deeper. What? What was it saying? If only she could focus. She was closer to it than she thought she was. No. She was walking. She'd shouldered her way past Chrissie at some point. The crowd was loud around her. Behind her. Why? She stopped and looked around. She stood all alone, halfway to where Gregory knelt. Auto-aethercasters circled her. Ahead, by the table, Mirabelle grinned. Behind her, the crowd was a cacophony she feared to look at. "It's her!" "I knew it! Didn't I tell you? He was so into her!" "It's that assistant!" She looked up at Jack…

He had glowed before, but it was nothing compared with what she saw now. He shone so brightly he was hard to look at. Jack stared straight at her, not glancing anymore. He looked afraid. Then she looked down at her own hands. She glowed too, in a rich copper hue.

"Oh," she said. "That's new."

She looked up at Jack again, but he was looking beyond her. Leta felt a prickle on the back of her neck and spun around. The blond-haired protester had pushed himself free of the crowd. He was looking back and forth between Destiny and Leta. Everyone was looking at the man, wondering what was going on, but Leta looked at Destiny and saw her surreptitiously point towards Leta. The man blinked, and ran at Leta. "Down with fake gods!" he screamed.

Destiny shrieked. "He has a knife!"

Leta's eyes snapped back to the man. So he did. He didn't look confident using it; rather, he looked sweaty and ill. Nevertheless...

Knife.

Pointed at Leta.

By a man running straight at her.

Oh, fuck.

"No!" cried Jack. Leta felt power whip past her to either side. The man slowed and slipped on the floor. He still held the knife towards her. Then he wriggled out of the hold of Jack's kinetic magic and charged again.

"Leta!" cried Jack again. He sounded so afraid. Leta felt like she was stuck in treacle. Everything was happening so fast. The man was mere steps from her.

Destiny leaped into action, coming up alongside the protester. The woman's skirts and hair whipped with the wind of her magic-assisted leap, and her clawed, outstretched hand glowed. A beam of battle magic shot from her hand and knocked the knife away. It spun across the floor into the base of the stage. The man was still barrelling towards Leta, his eyes full of fear and desperation. Magic now gathered at his fingertips, crackling like lightning.

What? thought Leta. *What the fuck?*

While she was still trying to figure out what the hell was going on, a deep well of power rose from beneath Leta's feet. It flooded her, *filled* her. It came from all directions, a fresh, green power, smelling of the forests and the fields, the rivers, the crisp mountaintops. *Protect*, she thought. And did so.

The man reached out, and lightning arced from his fingertips. Weather magic. It shot towards her...

... and around her, missing both her and Jack. The lightning then ceased to exist.

Leta knew she had done it. She even knew it had been easy. She didn't know how, though.

Destiny slammed a battle shield up around the man, trapping him. That was the second time she'd used battle magic. Hadn't she been a fire mage? It seemed Destiny was a multi-talent like Tiffany. Who knew? Destiny stood up straight, brushed her hair out of her eyes, and beamed at the crowd. As close as Leta was to the woman, she could see her eyeing up the auto-aethercasters, turning to show a good angle.

The new flood of power in her overwhelmed Leta's senses for a long moment. When she came to, she was being held up by a strong pair of arms and a band of silver magic. Jack, keeping her from fainting onto the floor. He steadied her on her own feet again. Leta looked around and saw Mirabelle gazing at her with wonder, relief, and no surprise whatsoever. The crowd beyond her was going nuts.

A rustle of fabric drew Leta's attention to the ground before her. Destiny knelt there. "Goddess, I am glad you are all right." Behind her, hotel security was already taking charge of the protester.

Leta looked down into Destiny's calculating face. She had done a good job of putting on a relieved mask. But the irritation in the woman simmered beneath the surface.

Leta had never been this good at spotting people's inner thoughts before. Was this something… new?

She thought back to when the protester had looked between Destiny and Leta, and saw the full shape of Destiny's plan and how she'd pivoted on the fly. She had been going to make it look like she had ascended, then be attacked by a protester, then save herself with her hidden multi-talent powers, which would make it look like she had received new powers as Jack had. But when Leta had ascended, she'd pivoted to make the best of the new situation. It was as if a voice whispered in the back of Leta's mind, telling her the whole story.

Leta squeezed Jack's arm and then stood free of him. Saving her with his kinetic magic had been his battle. This was hers. Would she expose Destiny's manipulation, or let the lie stand?

She looked out over the crowd again. They had settled. Hundreds of pairs of eyes now watched her to see what she would do. *If only I could ask someone for advice.*

Take the subtle path, said a voice within her mind. *You don't have to denounce her to have things not go her way.*

The Harvester. Oh, shit. That was the Harvester. No time to think about *that* development.

Leta smiled and looked back at Destiny. "Thank you for your help," she said.

"I'm at your service," said Destiny with a demure lowering of her head. No one but herself and Jack would have seen how tight Destiny's face looked to be bowing to Leta. To a Mundane.

"In that case, would you be able to render more assistance? You noticed the danger quicker than anyone. Could you go with security? I'm sure the police will be here soon. Could you tell them everything you saw? They'll want to find whoever put the stooge up to attacking. He looks terrified; he was surely working for someone." It felt *so good* to tell Destiny what to do.

Destiny's face paled. "Certainly, Goddess Incarnate."

Leta walked around Destiny to where the attacker stood restrained by two security guards. Up close, the snarl of anger and bravado on his face did nothing to hide the fear in his eyes or the quaking in his legs. "And you. I see pain in your eyes. Something has happened to make you susceptible to manipulation." Something about her voice seemed off, as if the words were not her own. "I am very sorry the world has been cruel to you. I forgive you, though you'll still face consequences for your actions. My advice is to tell them about the man who put you up to this." Leta knew exactly who had manipulated this poor man: the nondescript, dark-haired guy. The sweaty blond-haired guy before her stood straighter, and his knees stopped shaking. He looked awed.

Leta gestured to the security guards. "He's all yours. Destiny, could you go with them?"

"Wait a minute," said Marcus, striding forward to join them. "You can't send one of the aethercast contestants away."

"Marcus, there is no aethercast," said Jack. "We found the goddess. It's over." Leta could hear the grin in his voice.

Destiny followed the guards as they took the man away. Tension was visible in every line of her body.

A man who looked like an older version of her stumbled out of the crowd. "Now, see here," he said. "You can't send her away: she's a Brightborne! She deserves to be here more than anyone!"

Destiny shook her head at him. "Not now, father."

"But we're not just any Brightbornes; we're the descendants of the God and Goddess Incarnate themselves! If anyone should be the goddess, it's you, Destiny! It's always been you." At his words, Leta had a faint memory of a house. A manor. Brightborne Manor… she'd lived there once. She remembered a particular pink chaise lounge.

Destiny gave her father a sad look. "It's over," she said.

"But... I was so sure that... I—the money."

Destiny shook her head and kept walking.

"Perhaps you could go with her, sir," said Leta.

Brightborne senior looked at her, swallowed, and followed his daughter.

Leta couldn't bear the attention of the crowd any longer. She turned and looked only at Jack. He took her hands. "Are you OK?" he asked.

"Yes. I think Mirabelle saved me. I wanted to stand near Destiny, but she said I should stand near Chrissie. If I was next to Destiny, I would have been so close that..."

Jack closed his eyes and gathered her into an embrace. "I'm go glad you're safe," he whispered into her ear.

"It's me, isn't it?"

"Yes."

"You knew, didn't you?"

"Yes."

"Why didn't you tell me?"

"Because as soon as I did, you would have ascended. I've hated every public moment of all of this. You deserved to go through it in private. I was going to come tell you after the season ended."

"Oh fuck, the whole nation is watching us right now." She said the last directly into his shoulder, doing her best to hide her face.

Someone tapped Leta on the shoulder. She looked up to see Tiffany grinning at her.

"Goddess Incarnate, we can take it from here," she said. "Go on."

Jack grinned. "Thanks Tiffany," he said. Then, "Wanna make a run for it?" he asked Leta.

"How?"

"Literally run."

"They won't forgive us."

"We're the incarnations here. They should beg our forgiveness for using us as a spectacle."

"OK, here goes."

They grabbed each other's hands and ran up the aisle.

"Where are you going?" cried Marcus, and the crowd erupted in confusion and cries of shock. Some people jostled forward, reaching out, trying to grab them. But they held on tight to each other and ran, Leta holding her skirts up and not caring how undignified she looked.

Behind them, Leta heard Tiffany's voice raise above the din. "And there you have it, folks. Gealdland has its Goddess Incarnate at long last. There they go, riding off into the sunset. Isn't love beautiful?"

They ran from the crowd, from Marcus's protests, from Tiffany's grand gesture. Most of all, from the auto-aethercasters. They ran to the doors, threw them open, and pelted along the hallway, through the lobby, and out the main door into the cold evening. Jack found a taxi, and they tumbled in. The taxi driver jumped and threw his magazine to the side.

"Whoa, why are you in such a hurry? Is the High Hunt after you?"

"You could say that," said Leta.

"Just drive, please," said Jack.

"Where to?"

Jack gave Leta a side-long look, then gave the driver an address.

THE STAR
UPRIGHT

GENEROSITY, CALMNESS, HOPE. YOU HAVE FOUND WHO YOU ARE.
DARE TO DREAM!

Congrats, my friend.

A

Once he had brought Leta into his apartment, he second-guessed himself. He hadn't been there in weeks. What if there was something mouldy in the fridge? It certainly smelt musty. But she didn't seem to mind. She stood by his bookcase, inspecting his reading tastes, while he whipped about, opening windows a crack, closing any blinds that were open (because he was sure the media would start staking the place out soon and he didn't want them to get zoomed captures through the windows), turning on the heating, and checking the kitchen and bathroom for emergency cleaning jobs.

"Cup of tea?" he offered. "Sorry, I don't have any milk. I wasn't expecting to be back here for a few more weeks."

"Yes, thank you."

When he had made two black teas, they both settled on the sofa.

"This is where you live?" asked Leta.

"For now."

"I hope you don't mind me saying so, but it doesn't quite feel like you."

Jack looked around at the plain grey curtains, the exposed brick walls, and the cold, soulless kitchen.

"AllAether found it for me. It's the kind of place the network expected me to live in."

"They wanted you to be someone you're not."

"Yeah. And I was afraid they'd do the same to you."

Leta leaned forward to sip her tea to avoid drips on her glorious green dress. "My head is spinning trying to catch up with everything," she said. "I'm the Goddess Incarnate?"

"Yes."

"And you knew."

"Yes."

"That was why we kept being so comfortable with each other."

"We've known each other in past lives."

"More than known each other." She blushed.

"Well, yeah. We've been married in many lifetimes."

She stared at the tropical print on the wall, lost in her thoughts. "Mirabelle must know too. That's why you were mad. She made sure I would be there tonight."

"Yes. I felt like she betrayed us." He sighed. "I think things may have been more complex, though."

"Did you see how buddy-buddy she was with Gregory Hallowborne?" Then she waved her hand to ward off her own words. "Let's think about that tomorrow." She put her cup down. "Also the whole being attacked thing. Tomorrow. And Destiny playing everyone. Tomorrow. And the nation watching everything. Tomorrow?"

"Tomorrow," he said. He put his cup down too and took her hand instead. "Are you OK?"

She looked into his eyes for the first time since arriving in his apartment. "Yes? No? I don't know."

He stroked her hand. "Take as long as you need to sort your thoughts."

"I had power."

"You *have* power. More than me. My powers since ascension are passive, but yours seem active. You knocked the lightning bolt away as if it was nothing. I've never seen anything like it."

"It was more defensive than active."

"In a country full of mages, we're not needed to be powerful, per se. Just useful. Negating magic is an excellent choice of power for the Harvester to instil in you. It complements your own magic."

Leta laughed. "I don't have magic. Or rather, I didn't before tonight."

"Yes, you did. I can see magic, remember? You have gardening and cooking magic. No one recognised it in you because it's subtle and they're tasks that are seen as, well, mundane. But I saw your magic throughout your home and garden. It wasn't you that was the problem; it was how the world was seeing you."

Leta bit her lip. "Oh," was all she said.

Jack's thoughts returned to the ballroom. He couldn't help but remember the sight of the knife-wielding fanatic charging at Leta. His hands shook.

Leta brought his hands to her mouth and kissed them. "Are you OK?"

Jack gulped. "If I hadn't got some kinetic magic practice in at Autumnwood, I don't think I would have been quick or strong enough to stop him."

"But you did," she said, and kissed his hands again. "You saved me."

Jack's pounding heart beat more steadily, and tension eased out of his shoulders. "You saved yourself," he said, accepting that the danger he had been waiting for had passed. The nightmare was over. He edged closer to her. "May I give you a hug?" She leaned into his side and he wrapped an arm around her shoulders. "It's a lot, I know."

"Yeah."

"I'm here with you."

"I know."

Just then, Leta's aethervoicer chimed. She looked at the screen. "It's Mum."

"She'll be in a tizzy. You'd better talk to her. I'll go call my parents too." Jack stood and patted Leta on the shoulder as she answered the call.

"Leta! Oh my god, Leta!" Carol was a fright in the small crystal. She looked like she'd been crying.

Jack walked around the sofa and loomed over Leta's shoulder. "Goddess," he said. "She's your goddess." He waved and then headed into the kitchen, the sound of Carol's excited talking filling up the living area. She was barely letting Leta get a word in.

He wondered if he should check in with AllAether. Give some sound bites, maybe. But no. He decided that, going forward, AllAether, and the rest of the media, would get his time when he was ready, not when they forced the issue. His contract was over now. He was free. And they never had Leta long enough to lock her in.

This was part of the message he was supposed to bring. He was certain of it.

LETA'S MUM HAD FINISHED freaking out and was now, for some unfathomable reason, giving Leta a live running commentary of AllAether's feedcast. They were showing reruns of all the times they had caught Leta and Jack interacting during the aethercast. Leta cringed, reminded once again of the fire drill incident.

"Why did all of this have to be so *public*?" Leta complained. "This is what Jack was trying to protect me from."

"Protect you?"

"He knew who I was, but he kept it a secret. He wanted to tell me after the aethercast season finished so that all of this wouldn't happen."

"He knew when he was at our place?"

"Yeah."

Her mum rubbed a hand over her face. "I owe that boy an apology. Bring him home again soon."

"Will do."

"Where will you two be living?"

"Oh crap, we've got to think about that!"

"Sorry, sorry, Honey. Didn't mean to stress you. There's no hurry. But if you're going to be staying with him for a while, I understand. Don't worry about me."

"Oh, Mum," said Leta, realising that being announced as the goddess meant to her mum that Leta was moving away and she would be living alone.

"I said don't worry! Maybe now I can bring hot guys home from the pub."

"I don't want to hear it!"

"I bet you don't. Now, go deal with your own hot guy, OK? I bet he's shaken up too. He nearly lost you, you know? That guy nearly got you."

"OK. Speak to you later."

"Bye, Honey. Love you!"

When Leta hung up the call, Jack appeared at her side with a plate. "Something to eat?" he asked. "Sorry, it's nothing like we had that day at the hotel." The plate contained crackers, other crackers, and a few particularly shrivelled raisins. "The kitchen is near bare, sorry."

She selected a cracker. "Thank you, this is fine. I don't have much of an appetite right now."

Jack sat beside her. "Are you OK?"

"Not really. Are you?"

"Your Mum said I might still be shaken up." He put the plate down and took her hand. She looked up into his light brown eyes and saw more than worry there. She saw genuine fear. "I did nearly lose you, and that terrified me."

"I'm sorry."

"Don't worry about that." A thought seemed to come to him. He reclaimed a hand and rummaged in his pocket. "I just remembered. Hold out your hand."

She frowned and did so. He dropped something warm and smooth into her palm. It looked like her old worry stone. No, wait. It *was* her old worry stone. "Where did you get this?"

He grinned. "You left it at the temple, didn't you? As an offering. You don't need to leave offerings at the temples, Leta. So I'm returning it to you."

Leta remembered when she'd left the stone as an offering, sad at its loss after so many years. Jack must have been there after her. And the Hunter must have directed him to take the stone back for her. Otherwise, how could he have even known it was hers?

"Thank you," she said, at a loss for how else to express her amazed gratitude. She wouldn't need to use the stone as a crutch any more. It'd been a while since she had reached for it. Even so, it felt right in her hand, like it was where it was supposed to be. Was she also, now, where she was supposed to be? Needing reassurance of a different kind, she touched Jack's arm. "Is this OK? I mean, me being the goddess. Do you feel let down?"

"No!" He tilted her chin up. "I'm thankful and ecstatically happy. Did you not notice my feelings? I mean, I thought I'd had no subtlety."

Leta blushed. OK, he had been obvious.

He laughed. "I can read your mind. You threw yourself at me while wearing nothing but a loose nightshirt and knickers. Did you expect me to take that in my stride?"

"I didn't think I would ever make anyone feel that way."

Jack shook his head. "I take it there have been people who've knocked your confidence. May I look them up and give them a good hiding?"

"Let's leave the past in the past."

"Yeah. It's the future that's important. And although we've only just found each other, we'll have plenty of time together to look forward to." He shifted closer, his thigh close against hers. "I want to make myself clear. For weeks now, I've been drawn to your personality, your kindness, your beauty. That you're the goddess is the icing on the cake. You were always my type."

Her heart felt two sizes too big for her chest. "Me too. I know everyone raves on about your looks, and yeah, I agree with them. But I've never felt as instantly close to anyone as I felt to you. I could sit for hours in the same room as you, us both reading books, and feel nothing but comfort." She giggled and looked down again. "That sounds weird. It's as high a compliment as I can think of, though, for how my brain works."

He chuckled. "I get it, I do. Other people grate when you're trying to read. But to be comfortable in silence." He stroked her cheek. "It would thrill me to read in silence with you again."

"Again?"

"Because I'm sure we've done it before, in past lives."

A phantom sensation of an old, worn leather armchair with riveted arms surrounded Leta for a moment. A chair she had never seen, but knew so very well. "Yes, I think so too."

"Me on the sofa and you on a leather chair by the fire."

"Yes."

They looked at each other in wonder. "Wow," said Jack. "I felt a bit of recognition when I met Ander, but you..."

"We've only just begun to experience this."

"We may have small, shared memories like that for the rest of our lives."

"The rest of our lives..." Excitement built in Leta. This was so big; her mind couldn't see the shape of the change that had happened in her, even as she lived through it.

"Of course," said Jack. "Do you need me to get down on one knee and propose?"

"Half of me wants to say, 'it's too early for that!' And the other half wants to say, 'why bother? We've been married before.'"

Jack grinned and wound his hand into the hair at her nape. "Yeah, we have. We don't need to stress about the details, do we?"

In response, Leta pulled him in for the kiss that he wanted to give her. There was no more hesitation. They both deepened the kiss, confident in how much each other wanted that connection. Leta wound her arms around Jack's neck…

And froze when her stomach let out a massive rumble.

"My love," he said against her lips. "You may not have an appetite, but your stomach has other ideas."

"I'm so sorry," she said, pulling back.

"No, no; I'm the host here. Shall we order pizza?"

Jack ordered them some food. While they waited for it to arrive, Leta watched in bemusement as he shunted the coffee table out of the way and dug around in a cupboard, looking for something. "Aha!" He emerged with a folded bundle. He shook out a green and cream woollen blanket and spread it over the floor. He then lit a pillar candle and put it on the coffee table. Finally, he fiddled with his aetherweb globe until it projected a star scape on the ceiling.

"You cheeky bastard," said Leta.

"I beg your pardon?"

"You remembered my words!"

He grinned at her from where he knelt on the floor. "Of course I did. I'm not expecting, well, you know, if you don't want to. But you must like picnics for you to have said that, right?"

There was a buzz on the aetherweb globe and an image of a pizza popped up. Jack went to accept the delivery and returned with a pizza box and a few small boxes of sides. He lay them out open in a row on the blanket. He'd bought wedges and dipping sauce, and crumbed something, and a box that he left closed for now, but something smelled sweet and chocolaty. Leta looked down at her dress. "Do you have a sheet or something I could cover my dress with? I don't want to drop cheese or sauce on it."

Jack looked up at her. "That would be a travesty, because you look stunning in that dress. How about you take it off? It's warmed up in here."

Leta flushed. "Take it off?"

"I'm going to. I'm tired of being trussed up like a Yuletide roast." He turned the lights off so they were lit only by candle, fake stars, and a faint glow of streetlights through the curtains. Giving her a saucy grin, he took off his suit jacket, a little slower than necessary, and threw it over the back of a chair. He undid his tie, and it joined the jacket.

"Oh my god," said Leta when he unbuckled and unzipped his trousers.

"Yes, indeed," said Jack. He grinned and dropped his trousers, but turned away as he kicked them off and draped them on the chair, moving in a more workmanlike way, perhaps noticing that Leta was getting overwhelmed. He took his shirt off and, wearing navy boxers, a white singlet, and socks, he sat cross-legged on the blanket. A little chest hair poked out the neck of his singlet. He had just the right amount of muscle to him: enough to show that he was strong, but not too much.

He jiggled the pizza box, looking up at her expectantly. The food smelled divine, and Leta was starving, and, well, under the circumstances...

She reached up and undid the button behind her neck. Then she turned around, knelt, and pointed up at her back. "Could you get the zipper?"

A long, intense pause later, one hand pressed her back and another slowly undid the zip. He dragged his fingers close as he passed her arse. When he let go, she stood again and shimmied out of the dress, not allowing it to drop to the floor. She stepped out of it and draped it on the chair with Jack's clothes. She turned to face him, her cheeks flaming. He was wide-eyed and slack-jawed.

"Is something wrong?"

"Hell no! That's, wow."

Leta flushed hotter. The black shapewear she was wearing was opaque, hiding her from the tops of her thighs to above her breasts, but it was lacy, and it had stocking suspenders and, well, it was racy. She was glad the sales assistant had recommended it to keep the lines of the dress smooth, because otherwise she'd be wearing granny panties and a ratty old bra. She knelt down near the food and cleared her throat. "May I?" she asked.

"Mm?" He was looking at her with heavy eyes.

"Food?"

"Oh, yes. Dig in."

Leta tried the crumbed thing. "Deep fried cheese?! You know the way to a woman's heart."

"Isn't it men's hearts that can be won with food?"

"We all eat, no matter our genders. We're all susceptible." She took another bite of the cheese. "Mm, so trashy; so good."

"Deep fried cheese is the food of the gods," said Jack, taking one for himself.

"Is that the message we bring to Gealdland?"

Jack snorted. "Maybe. But I had an epiphany at your house. I was at peace there in your kitchen, in your garden. Maybe that's a key part of what we are supposed to do. I've hated this fast-paced city and aethercast life. It's felt so wrong."

Leta took a slice of pizza. "But a quieter life?"

"Making things by hand."

"Keeping older, simpler knowledge and pastimes alive?"

"Yeah, something something vegetables, something something baking bread, something something making cider that's too strong."

"Something something."

"Yeah. If I've learned anything since I ascended, it's that I don't need to worry about the details. I just have to be me. And you just have to be you. And, well, if that's who you are…"

"And if that's who you want to be…"

He grinned at her. "Yeah. I think we have a vague heading to start out on?"

"I think so."

They lingered over the meal, sharing small talk and passing side dishes. Leta kept stealing glimpses of Jack, and she was pretty sure he was doing the same. For once in her life, she felt worthy of those glances, and it wasn't the fancy clothing or the makeup; it was him. The situation, maybe. Fated lovers means surety.

When they were finished, Leta stretched out on her back on the blanket and sighed, looking up at the projected stars on the ceiling. "I'm pretty full now," she said. "I'm wishing this shapewear wasn't so constrictive around my belly."

Jack lay down beside her. "I'm trying hard not to say the obvious," he said.

"You mean telling me to take it off?"

"Yeah. I mean, I wouldn't complain."

Leta seriously considered doing so; that's how comfortable she was with Jack. But she was stuffed, and that seemed like too much effort. "I'll need help. I'm like a sausage in too tight a casing."

"What a lovely turn of phrase. Ever so delicate."

"I hope you're not expecting me to be a delicate flower of a wife."

He propped himself up on an elbow and looked down at her. "High Hunt take me, no. I'm expecting you to be the kind, strong, capable, and fun person I've known you to be, no matter what opinions I or anyone else hold about you. In other words, I expect you to be you, no more or less. I hope those are OK expectations."

"I can be me, yes." She grinned up at him. "And I expect you to be you; the you that people have been trying to gloss over, to shape, to change — I want you to be free to be that person."

"Free to eat deep fried cheese?"

"Yes."

"Free to wear a t-shirt and shorts in summer?"

"Sure."

He smiled. "Free to grow a beard, wear gumboots, and get grubby using my kinetic magic to put up glass houses and sheds and whatnot?"

"Yes."

"Hm, I guess we'd still need to do some incarnate stuff in there somewhere. The Blessings tours are essential, at the very least."

Leta smiled. "The tours sound quite nice. Making people's land grow better crops, their cows produce more milk. I can get behind that."

"Yeah. The tours I've been on so far have been great."

"Sounds perfect."

He stroked her cheek, his smile turning softer and sillier. "Will you marry me?"

"Yes. Now, why are you still so far away?"

He grinned and leaned down and kissed her. No longer patient with interrupted kisses, Leta pulled him to her and wrapped a leg around him, pulling him on top of her. He felt right there, his weight comfortable on her and his height aligning them perfectly. He propped himself up on his elbows for a short while, alternating between kissing her and looking down at her in awe. Then he gave up on all pretence of holding back and came down to join her fully. They ran their fingers through each other's hair, and learned the contours of each other's faces, the lines of their backs, the sounds they each made when kissed on the ear, the neck, the chest. Before long, Leta was letting Jack peel her shapewear off. He knelt between her legs and stripped his singlet off, throwing it to one side. She sat half up and ran a hand down the trail of hair to his boxers, aiming for the growing bulge within.

"Wait!" he said, catching her wrist. "Are you on any pill or spell or anything?"

"Oh! No."

"Just a moment." He disappeared into the bedroom and came back with a box. He flushed as he checked the expiry date on the bottom. "Don't tell anyone I had to check that; it will ruin my reputation as a hot guy who girls throw themselves at."

"What if that's exactly the reputation that I want to ruin?"

He grinned. "Fair enough." He took a condom out of the box and put it within reach. He knelt back between her legs. "Now, where were we?"

"At the showing me the goods stage."

"Ah, yes."

He showed her, in more ways than one. Several times.

THE WORLD
REVERSED

It's time to let go of the past. You are not that person anymore, and the change has been good for you. Trust you are who you were meant to be.

I can't hold it in anymore. I'm so happy it wasn't me.

I love you. I love you.

I don't care about anything else anymore.

Morning light streamed around the edges of the still-drawn curtains. Jack was making tea in the kitchen, wearing only a pair of trousers he'd grabbed on his way to the shower. He looked up and felt a thrill to see Leta, glowing softly with ascendant goddess light, sitting in his apartment. She was catching up with the news on his aetherweb globe, wearing one of his sweatshirts and her knickers, which they'd had the presence of mind to throw in the wash overnight, or she would have nothing to wear on her bottom half at all. His sweatshirt covered her upper body fine, but it kept riding up over her hips, giving him a lovely view. She'd lost the last vestiges of her shyness around him overnight, so she didn't seem to care. She seemed worried about what she was reading, though, a frown marring her forehead.

He brought her a cup of tea and, when he leaned down to put it on the table, kissed her on her forehead frown line. "What's the matter?" he asked.

"We'll be going back to a huge mess. We caused a lot of drama to unspool in our absence."

"Or consider this: we don't actually have to go back at all."

She looked up at him. "Jack, I don't even have clothes, except for a ball dress. I'll be doing the walk of shame out of here. I at least need my suitcase. Do you need yours?"

"Point taken. Also, I'd like my aethervoicer back at some point. But why don't you call Mirabelle and get her to organise your suitcase to be delivered? You said she saved you, but she still orchestrated a lot of this, and she owes us. A lot."

"I guess I could. I should call her anyway."

Jack nodded. "If you feel you must."

Leta took out her aethervoicer and talked with Mirabelle, explaining her predicament and her location. Then Leta and Jack had a breakfast of tea and cold pizza, and discussed, well, them. The things that couples knew about each other, but which they hadn't had time to learn yet: which side of the bed they each preferred (thankfully, not the same one); their go-to comfort meals and aethercasts; what kind of pet they wanted; whether they prefer morning or evening showers.

The aetherweb globe chimed. Jack fetched a shirt and a blanket from the bed, then threw the blanket to Leta to cover her lower half and shrugged into the shirt while he walked to the door. He was expecting to see some messenger from the aethercast on the other side, but he found Mirabelle, accompanied by both of their suitcases. He stared at her for a moment, his anger from yesterday returning to his mind. Then he eyed the suitcases. "You didn't carry them up yourself, did you?" He hoped not; the woman walked with a cane.

"Of course not," she said. "I had my driver help me, then sent him away. Your aethervoicer is in your suitcase. Oh, and by the way, the media are lying in wait outside."

"We know." He moved the two suitcases into the apartment. He raised his eyebrows at Leta. "You want to talk to her?"

Leta nodded, and so Jack waved Mirabelle into the apartment. Mirabelle stepped in, but had the grace to seem scandalised to be there.

"I'd get up, but I won't be decent until I've got things out of my suitcase," said Leta.

Mirabelle nodded and stayed standing, leaning on her cane. "I see Jack is still angry with me," said Mirabelle. "Are you?"

Leta met Jack's eyes, and he saw reticence there. "Yes and no," she said. "I don't like being manipulated, and I think you have an aim that you haven't let on. But I don't think you were being malicious, and you tried to help when you discovered that you'd misjudged things."

"May I sit?" asked Mirabelle.

Jack waved her to an armchair. He sat beside Leta, close enough to provide comfort.

"You are right, I misjudged, and for that I am truly sorry," said Mirabelle. "I knew you were the goddess all along, Leta. A vision led me to you, but the vision was more informative than I implied. I—" she looked back and forth between them. "I was willing to let AllAether get the coup of having you ascend on their aethercast. But I didn't know that would lead to you being in physical danger."

"Why?"

Mirabelle folded her arms around herself. "I'm more enmeshed in the group behind the aethercast than I let on. I have a financial stake in AllAether. That being said, I don't have a deciding role in how it is managed, and I disagreed most heartily with the approach to finding the contestants. So we took things into our own hands."

"We?" asked Jack.

"Gregory Hallowborne," said Leta.

Mirabelle nodded. "Yes. He considers himself to be a caretaker of the ascensions of our country, because of family history. We worked together to acquire the vision that led me to you, and he worked to find the means to secure the ascension."

"Because you are close."

"Yes."

"Are you of the Geald houses too, Mirabelle?"

Jack hissed. Of course. It was obvious in hindsight.

"Yes," confirmed Mirabelle. "My family name before marrying my late husband was Gealdward."

Jack and Leta looked at one another. He saw his comprehension reflected in her face. The Hallowbornes and the Gealdwards had been close allies for centuries. They considered themselves to be the true caretakers of Geald-land's magic.

"So, was it more about family power and influence or more about money?" asked Jack, his voice sounding numb to his own ears.

"I admit the gala was pitched as my idea, and therefore I get a bonus. But Gregory and I have been working towards our goals of guiding and aiding the newly ascended gods for decades, since before you were born, I merely wanted to continue that—"

"That won't be necessary," said Leta.

"Leta dear?" said Mirabelle, sounding confused.

"You're just another one of the elite, thinking that we're your possessions, your mascots. I very much doubt that's what our deities ever intended. For our message to be conveyed, we need to be left to fly free, and be ourselves. Otherwise, how can we fulfil our purpose?"

"But the incarnates always work with the Geald Council, and as a seer I can—"

"No. Just because it has always been done that way doesn't mean that it has to continue."

"I only have your best interests at heart—"

"I know you've been kind to me the last few weeks, and I appreciate that. But it's clear you always had an ulterior motive."

Mirabelle looked first shocked, then pale, then wry. "You have gained much wisdom overnight, Goddess Incarnate Leta."

Leta gave Jack a quick smile. "It's helped that I've heard Jack's concerns and seen his struggles for weeks now. The path that you're guiding me towards is the same one that Jack was placed on, but since it's not been working for him, it won't work for me either, will it?"

"You will have to do something," said Mirabelle, panic colouring the edges of her voice. "Both of you. Gealdland *needs* you. I know you feel free of your contract, Jack, and you are, I suppose. But Gods Incarnate can't just go out and get normal jobs. You will need money to maintain this lifestyle. AllAether or any other number of companies will be here to help."

"Who says I want to maintain *this* lifestyle?" said Jack.

Mirabelle looked at a loss. "And you, Leta? You've had a taste of what the higher echelons of society can offer." She gestured at the dress, which was still draped over a chair. "You enjoyed the hotel, at the very least."

Had she enjoyed it? It was awe-inspiring, but Jack knew that she hadn't felt at home in Emerald Marquise Tower. And as for the clothes... "I now understand how you always look so fashionable and fancy," said Leta. "Because you prioritise it, and you spend a lot of money. It was nice, I admit, to shop in a boutique for once. But I'd be happy with that sort of thing being a rarity in my life."

Mirabelle looked exasperated. "Well, what about the message you are supposed to convey? How are you supposed to do that without pursuing fame?"

Jack shrugged. "We'll figure something out."

Mirabelle threw up her hands. "Neither of you are behaving anything like I expected you to. This isn't what the country expects."

"We aren't supposed to be what the country thinks we should be," said Leta. "We're supposed to be what the gods want us to be. Who are we to question them?"

"Your divinations can only ever take you so far, Mirabelle," said Jack. "You see the general shape of the future, not the details. You may have forgotten that, and inserted some of your own wishes into your predictions."

Mirabelle's mouth became a thin, displeased line. "Well, I suppose I shall leave you two to it, since you have everything sorted out. But I will always be available to you for advice, if you ever need it. If you want it." She stood, and Jack walked her to the door.

He leaned against the door after he closed it and sighed, giving Leta a wry look. "Well," he said.

"Well."

"That was awkward."

"It sure was. Awkward encounter number one of how many over the coming days, I wonder?"

Jack sighed. "Another cuppa?"

"THANK YOU, GODDESS INCARNATE WILDWINTER, for your statement. I am no longer aethercasting this interview to the records." The police aethercaster, a small, dark woman with a headscarf, gave Leta a seated bow across the interview table. Leta had finished giving her statement to the aethercaster and the interviewer, a lanky, balding police officer.

"You're welcome," said Leta. It had been hard recounting the events of the ballroom, because everything had been so quick, so busy, that it was hard to pick out a clear narrative. Also, she hadn't been given a lot of notice to go to the police station to give her statement.

"Do you have any questions for us before you go?" asked the interviewer.

"Can you tell me who that man was and how he got into the ballroom?"

The aethercaster and the officer gave each other un-uncomfortable looks. "We can't give too many details, be-cause it's an ongoing investigation," said the officer. "But, the short of it was that he gave a false name at the door, one that was on the list of guests and not claimed by any-one else. He didn't seem to be connected to the aethercast or the hotel otherwise."

He must have claimed to be a relative of a contestant. That was why they looked so uncomfortable. Had he claimed to be one of Destiny's relatives? No, she was smarter than that. Maybe Chrissie's, as he was blond like her. Which meant Chrissie could be in the firing line too. She deserved better. "I would imagine that whatever false name he gave was not connected to the actual leak in the aethercast. Whoever it was would have used someone else's family name to hide their identity."

The officer's eyebrows rose. "You think there was a leak?"

It was Leta's turn to raise her eyebrows. They hadn't got that far yet? "Right from the beginning, sure. Some-one was leaking information from the aethercast to the anti-incarnation protesters all along. You should ask AllAether about it. They were investigating." There, that might lead back to Destiny. It was up to her to wriggle out of it if she could.

Leta found it satisfying to nudge this investigation. The officers weren't dismissing her. They were listening and considering her words. She could advise, and things would happen without her having to strive so hard for them. Was it just the investigation? Or would her life be more like this from now on?

"May we turn the recording back on for a moment, get you to repeat that?"

They added the extra information to her statement. Really, they should have asked questions like that during the interview. "Is that all for today?" she asked.

"Yes, thank you for your time," said the aethercaster, and opened the door for Leta.

As she was leaving, the interviewer cleared his throat, and Leta paused. "May I ask… just for interest's sake? Did you have any idea that you were the Goddess Incarnate before your ascension at the hotel?"

"None whatsoever."

"But I did." Jack, who had been waiting outside, leaned against the doorframe.

The police officers gave each other surprised looks. "Why did you keep looking, then? On the 'cast, I mean."

"A vain attempt to protect her from a public unveiling."

Leta patted him on the shoulder. "Thank you for trying."

"You're welcome." He held out an elbow. "Are you done? Shall we get going?"

She took his arm. "Yes. Let's."

They were passing through a corridor intersection when they, with the most awful timing, ran into Destiny, who was being escorted by a policewoman. She was dressed to the nines, with dark sunglasses covering her eyes.

"God Incarnate Jack! Goddess Incarnate Leta! How wonderful to see you!" She had a beatific smile on her face. "Congratulations."

Leta smiled in return. There was no need to be petty. She had faith that things would turn out well. "Good morning. Are you still here, or here again?"

"Back again." Destiny tilted a hand forward in an 'it's nothing' gesture. "They had a few follow-up questions, is all. Don't worry, Goddess Incarnate. We'll get to the bottom of what was going on. I cannot believe that man had a knife! He must have been so desperate!" There was a sheen of sweat on Destiny's upper lip, and a slight wildness to her eyes behind her shades.

A strange feeling welled up from within Leta, like someone leaning over her shoulder. But Jack stood beside her, not behind.

She looks like someone whose plans went awry, said a voice within her mind. The voice was not her own, but similar.

As the words came to her, she saw Destiny in a new light, and all the details about her slotted into place. Leta had never had this kind of wisdom before, and she knew exactly where the insights came from.

Destiny *hadn't* expected a knife. She *hadn't* thought everything through. And there was her father's brief mention of money… She was desperate about something, and she was on the verge of learning an important lesson. Did Leta want to walk away from the aethercast still thinking back on those 'bitchy' contestants with disdain? Or should she learn a lesson too and do her best to root out that internalised misogyny? After all, she had been wrong about other contestants. Why not Destiny too?

She regretted leaving that crumb to lead the police to Destiny. But if she hadn't, they might have started looking at someone else, perhaps Chrissie.

All she could do now was nudge Destiny as well, so that everything was fair.

"May I have a private word?" she asked. She looked at the police officer. "May I borrow her for a moment?"

"Please, be my guest, Goddess Incarnate."

Leta gave Jack a look, asking him to stay where he was, and led Destiny into a small alcove that had a chair and a drinks machine.

"Can I help you with something, Goddess Incarnate?" asked Destiny in a low voice. There was trepidation in that voice. Leta bet she was regretting being so bold about her activities behind the hotel.

"Please be at ease," said Leta, as she thought through her strategy for this conversation. "I'm not here to tell you off, or say mean things, or anything like that."

"But, I was cruel…"

"You were. I can't deny it. But I've also jumped to conclusions about the type of person you are, with only evidence from a strange situation that doesn't let people be who they truly are." Leta took a deep breath. They weren't close enough to talk about topics like this. She kept her voice low so they wouldn't be overheard. "I know what you were planning, and I'm not in favour of it. I know that guy was a stooge, and I don't like how I won't be able to keep him from taking the fall for a situation he was coerced into. But he had a knife on a live aethercast, and it looked like he was going to use it. It's out of our hands now. You will have to live with the guilt of whatever punishment he receives."

Destiny hung her head. Her lip trembled.

"As will that other guy, the ringleader. The one you were talking to in the gardens at Autumnwood."

Destiny looked up in surprise. "I'm sorry, Goddess Incarnate. I shouldn't have got mixed up with them. I just… felt so powerless."

Leta nodded. "I figured. Can you tell me why? I don't understand what led you down that path."

Destiny sighed and glanced at Jack, who was studiously looking at his aethervoicer and not paying attention. "My father's an idiot. A gambler. I'm used to going around behind the scenes and fixing things up in his wake. I collect information and influence, claw back the money he's lost the family… then he goes and loses it again."

The influence and information that she'd shared with Nellie and Chrissie as a bribe… and which Tiffany had overheard. Leta sighed. It had never occurred to her that rich people could have money troubles too, but of course the rich were better at spending — and losing — money than common people. "Ah," she said. "What happened this time?"

"You remember I said I'm descended from a pair of incarnates?" She snorted. "Which I guess makes you and Jack my great-great grandparents. Anyway, my father got it in his head once I was selected as a contestant that I was certain to be the Goddess Incarnate. To his mind, it couldn't be a coincidence. So he told everyone that I would be goddess soon, of course alienating a lot of the family and his friends in the process, and he bet on the outcome. He bet damn near everything. And then, the first day I arrived at the manor and looked up at Jack… I knew it wasn't me. I felt nothing, no particular connection to Jack. I know it's supposed to take a while to figure it out. But I knew."

Leta thought back to the first time she'd met Jack. She'd felt a pull to him immediately, like he was a magnet and she a pin. She'd put it down to base attraction for so long, but it had been there from the very first moment. She believed Destiny could tell. Even so… "You don't think he's gorgeous?"

That faint smile appeared again. "He's alright, I guess. But I like my men a bit more…" she mimed something around her shoulders, her chest. "I like being squished by a big, hairy bear of a man, to be honest. Your Jack's too slight for my taste."

Leta thought Jack was just right, of course, but each to their own.

Destiny flushed and cleared her throat. "Anyway, I panicked, because I realised there was no way I could dig my father out of the hole he had got himself into, unless it ended up looking like I was the goddess… at least long enough for father to collect his winnings. It didn't even occur to me the real Goddess Incarnate would be there. He wasn't vibing with any of the other contestants, either…"

"And you didn't notice he was vibing with me."

"No. Sorry."

Leta nodded. Of course. She was used to being invisible. She sighed. What a tangle. "Presumably the problem stands."

"I don't know what I'm going to do." Destiny held onto her left elbow with her right hand and stared off into the distance.

Instinct welled up from within her. The advice she had to give would be a bitter pill to swallow. "Don't do anything," she said.

"Pardon?"

"Your father's an adult. It's not your place to save him from himself. Give him compassion, of course. But the problem is his to fix."

Destiny gaped at Leta. Then she bit her lip. "It's my money too, though."

Of course. She probably had a credit line from the bank of Daddy. "No, it's not. And you don't need it. Sounds to me like you're resourceful and can take care of yourself. Start looking after yourself, making your own money. It's not beneath you — taking care of yourself is below no-one. You'll be fine."

Destiny nodded, considering her words.

"If you do not let your dependents try to stand on their own, they will never know that they can," said Leta. She frowned: that didn't sound like the way she talked. "I think that was advice direct from the Harvester, by the way."

Destiny blanched and dropped a curtsey. "Thank you, Goddess Incarnate Leta."

"You're welcome. But I also have a confession. I've given the police a crumb that will lead them to learn about how you were leaking information to the protesters." Destiny opened her mouth as if to protest. Leta held up a hand to forestall her. "I had to, because you'd left clues that would lead back to Chrissie, who was mostly innocent, right?"

Destiny dropped her gaze again. "I suppose so."

Leta shrugged. "Look, I won't give them any more. The rest is up to you. But if you deflect their attention, don't do it by dropping someone innocent or misguided into it."

"Would you count a manipulative bastard who radicalised a bunch of people, was willing to bribe me, and then buggered off before anything could trace back to him as a person who is too innocent to pin things on?"

Leta gave Destiny a feral smile. "No, I would not." She stepped away from the other woman, back towards Jack. "Farewell, Destiny. Do better in the future. You have it in you."

Destiny dropped another curtsey. "Thank you, Goddess Incarnate. Farewell."

Leta rejoined Jack, and they walked out of the building together.

"You all right?" he asked her. "I know you and her don't have the best track record."

Leta took his hand and smiled up at him. "Thanks for your concern. I have it all sorted, though."

"But she was the one who—"

"Yeah. She was. But it was more complicated than it looked from afar. I won't be singing her praises, to be sure, but I hope she gets herself sorted out."

Jack brought her hand to his mouth and kissed the back of it. Right there, on the pavement, where anyone could see. Leta blushed. "It's always complicated, isn't it?"

"Yeah. You know, I kind of expected some sort of showdown with Destiny. To get vengeance for how she treated me and what she tried to do."

"But you reached out with compassion instead."

Leta looked up into Jack's eyes, which were glowing with admiration. "Yeah. And it feels good. Light, as if all of my stress about it dropped away. This was the right way to go about it. Just trying to understand where she came from made all the difference."

"You're wise."

"No, but the Harvester is."

"Had your first one of those moments, huh?"

"Yep."

"They take a bit of getting used to."

Leta smiled at him. Of course, he knew exactly what she was feeling today. Exactly. "Right, where to next?"

Jack grinned. "I have a very important errand to run. One that's a bit scary. Will you be my backup?"

"Always."

JUDGEMENT
UPRIGHT

The journey has been long, but you're not the only one on the
path, not the only one who is changed and born anew. Who has
been travelling with you? Support one another, for your journeys
are in parallel.

Boom!
Resignation letter attached.

Jack wouldn't have thought it possible for them to sneak past a pack of reporters into AllAether's headquarters if they hadn't just done it. It helped that they both wore nondescript clothes that day; Jack in jeans, his woolly cardigan, and a woolly hat, and Leta in her jeans and a hoodie she'd borrowed from him, with the hood up. They got past the reporters, through vast glass auto doors with inbuilt aetherweb connections showing advertisements, through the marble-floored atrium and to the smooth sweep of the reception desk before anyone figured out who they were.

"Good morning; how may I help?" asked the sleek-haired receptionist, seeming polite but bored.

Jack leaned his elbows on the desk. "God Incarnate Jack to see whoever involved with *Goddess Found* is available. I have a contract to terminate."

The receptionist started, gave them both a double take, and then bowed. "Of course, God Incarnate Jack. Please take a seat."

Mere minutes later, Evelyn Windrift herself appeared at reception. She cut an imposing figure in her sharp tailored white suit and patent leather red heels. She looked tired and irritable, exactly what one didn't want to see in a battle mage. With one hand, she gestured to the elevator tube. "This way, please." She didn't greet them.

They rode up with Evelyn to the fifteenth floor. She led them along a bright corridor of offices. "Goddess Incarnate, please wait here," she said, gesturing to a tearoom. "Help yourself to the coffee machine."

"I'd rather accompany Jack," said Leta.

Jack thought that was a great idea. After all, if Evelyn lost her temper, Leta was the one who could counter battle magic.

Evelyn gave Leta a wry smile. "I see where you're going with that. No, I won't harm him. In the end, he performed the actions required by the contract. It's not anyone's fault that things didn't go the way AllAether expected."

Jack gave Leta a reassuring look as he followed Evelyn into her office.

It took little time to make the change to his fortune that he'd wanted for several years now. Just one signature and a few initials on the bottom of several pages of the termination document, and the weight of the legal binding spell lifted from his shoulders, weight that he had forgotten he bore. "There: all done," he sighed. "And there are no stings in the tail?"

"None," said Evelyn, who was lounging back in her executive chair behind her desk. "We're disappointed, of course. But that's on us. You met the terms of the contract, so you're free, other than a follow up—"

"No," interrupted Jack.

"What?"

"No follow up 'casts."

"But the contract states—"

"That there is a follow up 'cast if a contestant ascends. Leta wasn't a contestant."

Evelyn narrowed her eyes at him. "Fine. You're right, that's what the contract stated."

"But you just wanted to see if you could slip one by me?"

Evelyn shrugged, her dangling gold earrings swinging. "Whatever. I'm too tired for this shit." And she did look tired.

"Go take a holiday," said Jack. "Take your dogs to the countryside. Get some fresh air. Let them chase some rabbits."

Evelyn raised one thin eyebrow at him. "Excuse me?" There was a warning note in her voice.

"Advice from the Hunter," said Jack, knowing his words to be true.

A thread of fear passed across Evelyn's face. Did she only just realise the truth of who he was, and what that meant? She gulped and regained her composure. "Well, I expect you'll have other things to do. Shall I escort you out?"

"No need: I know the way." He rose, and Evelyn did too. "Don't worry," he added. "I won't cause trouble. I already got what I wanted." He tapped the termination document on her desk. He waved over his shoulder as he left her office. "See you again, perhaps, never?"

LETA TRIED NOT TO BITE her lip with worry as she fussed with the coffee machine. To her surprise, she had no trouble with it. It must be the ascendency magic.

She nursed her coffee alone for a few minutes until two people entered the tearoom. It was Tiffany and another of the contestants, Constance. Leta grinned at Tiffany. "Hey! Good morning! Thanks for your help yesterday!"

Tiffany saluted her as if she were a general in the Battle Mage Corp. "I heard you were here. What a show you put on!"

Leta raised an eyebrow. "It wasn't a show for me. It was my life."

Tiffany grinned and went to the coffee machine. "We're here for a debriefing," she said over her shoulder. "Constance wanted to speak to you."

Leta looked at Constance, who was standing, back straight and hands clasped, by the door. Leta hadn't spoken to Constance before, but she'd seen enough of her to remember that she'd never seen the woman look anything other than indomitable. "May I help you?"

"Goddess Incarnate Leta, I have a confession to make."

"Oh?"

"I knew you were the Goddess Incarnate early on. I didn't tell anyone, though."

Leta indicated she should take a seat at the table. Once Constance had sat down, she asked her, "Why didn't you say anything?"

"I saw you and Jack interacting one day in the kitchens. There was a phantom glow around you visible through my clairvoyance magic. I didn't want to tell anyone because I didn't know who would do right by you, other than God Incarnate Jack, and I wasn't sure he should know while the 'cast was still going. I'm sorry that this is the first time I've spoken to you. I was afraid my knowledge would show on my face and I might trigger you to ascend before you were ready."

Leta nodded. She supposed Constance had known in the same sort of way that Mirabelle had known. "It's OK. I can see why you would make the choice to bide your time."

"I didn't wait," said Constance. "I sent Jack your way. Or, rather, I set the seed that became the day you both left the 'cast. I heard you got in trouble for that. I'm sorry."

"That's all right. We needed to take that trip. That's when Jack figured it out."

Constance raised her eyebrows, but said nothing in response.

Tiffany took a seat at the table and placed down two coffees, one for herself and one for Constance. "Me too, right?" she said. "You sent me to Leta to help. You said it was for my own benefit, though."

"It was, wasn't it?" said Leta. "We both benefitted from working together."

"That we did." Tiffany raised her coffee in a toast and then took a sip. Then she pulled a face as if the coffee wasn't to her taste. Fair enough. Leta thought her own was merely passable. "So, how are you feeling today?" asked Tiffany.

"Tired."

Tiffany smirked and then hid her mouth behind her coffee. "I bet," she murmured.

Leta flushed. "I didn't mean it like that!"

"Oh!" said Constance. "You're referring to sex."

Tiffany, who had been mid-sip, spluttered and choked on her coffee. "Constance! Please develop *some* social graces."

"I see everything like it is: I say everything like it is."

Tiffany sighed and jabbed a thumb in Constance's direction. "Can you see why this one kept her mouth shut while capturing the 'cast?"

Leta chortled. "Yes, I think I can."

"Listen," said Tiffany. "Considering everything, you might think I only ever helped you for my own gain. And maybe that's fair. But if you ever need anything, just ask. Things are going to be different in your life from now on, and you're going to need people on your side whose agenda you're at least aware of."

Even with all the qualifications, Leta was touched. "Thank you, Tiffany. I'll keep that in mind."

"Me too," said Constance. "We don't know each other, but I've never had anything proper to use my magic for, other than party tricks. I would be honoured to convey my visions to you, Goddess Incarnate."

Leta smiled. It was nice to know that not all the contestants hated her. "Thank you."

JACK WATCHED LETA from the doorway. He'd been expecting to find her sitting alone, but she was chatting with two contestants, the two who had helped him at one point. He smiled. Since they'd helped, they were in his good books. It seemed they were in Leta's too. That was great. She deserved as many friends as she wanted to have.

They were talking in low voices, so he didn't know about what. But when all three caught sight of him, Tiffany giggled, Constance raised her eyebrows, and Leta flushed red. He decided he did not want to know.

"Are you finished?" asked Leta, changing the topic as soon as she could.

"Yeah, I'm a free man!"

Leta grinned and stood. "Shall we go? Oh, my mug…"

Tiffany gave her a shove. "We'll sort it with ours. Go be with your man. See you again sometime!"

Leta waved to the women and then linked her arm with Jack's. He smoothed her hand over his forearm in another one of those gestures that he was sure came from a previous life. "Let's go," he said. "Shall we get lunch at the station?"

"Sounds like a plan."

They headed for the elevator tube. Ahead of them, two other people exited an office, two people who were also arm-in-arm, talking and giggling together. It was Marcus and Jess. Marcus held a box of possessions under the arm Jess didn't have a hold of. Marcus stopped as soon as he saw Jack, and Jess looked around in surprise.

"You're leaving?" asked Jack, stopping in the hallway with Leta at his side.

"Yeah," said Marcus. "Time for something new."

"Were you pushed, or did you jump?"

Marcus smiled wryly. "I jumped. Mostly. I guess you walked me to the cliff edge? As did Jess here." He nudged her with his shoulder, and she blushed, looking up at him.

If they were being so lovey-dovey here in the hallway, the break with Evelyn was clean. "Good for you," said Jack. "I think you'll be a better person away from here."

"Yeah, I hope so. For what it's worth, I think you will too. Did you have to run off yesterday, though? I didn't want to have such a stressful last day on the job. You left me in the lurch."

"Sorry," said Jack. "But, yeah, we did. That place wasn't right for us."

Marcus nodded. "A few days ago, I wouldn't have understood. But maybe I do now." He looked at Leta. "Sorry about all the trouble earlier, Goddess Incarnate," he said to her. "And congratulations on your ascension."

Jess also murmured her congratulations.

"Thank you," Leta said in a polite voice that didn't betray her dislike of Marcus.

"Well, we'd best be off," said Jack. He walked past them, and Leta followed. He patted Marcus on the shoulder as he passed. "All the best."

"All the best to you too, Jack. You'll do great." Marcus clicked and shot his patented finger guns at Jack, just like he used to do when the two of them had been on better terms. Jack acknowledged the imaginary shot with a wave.

Jack and Leta both sighed as the door of the capsule slid shut. "Was that the bulk of the awkward encounters?" asked Leta.

"We can but hope."

They hopped straight into a taxi outside the building.

"Central Tube Station," said Leta to the gaping driver. It was where they had left their suitcases, and where

Leta's mother would pick them up from in a travel capsule so they could visit for a night before heading north to Jack's parents' place for a visit.

"Yes, ma'am," said the driver, and engaged his magic into the engine.

Leta and Jack held hands throughout the ride.

As they pulled into the taxi rank outside the station, the driver asked, "Sorry to be a bother, but the wife would kill me if I didn't. Do you have any wisdom to share? Any guidelines?"

"I never know what to say when people ask," said Jack.

"How about, 'Follow your heart, and eat good food'?" suggested Leta.

"Good!" said Jack. "Also, 'reduce, recycle, reuse.'"

"Not to look a gift horse in the mouth, but those are common pieces of advice," said their driver.

"Yes," said Leta. "Common, average, practical. Exactly what we're supposed to be."

Soon they were ensconced in their travel capsule, along with their suitcases and café-bought filled rolls. Jack sighed, stretched out, and grinned. "Common, average, practical. I love it."

Leta smiled. "It feels right, doesn't it?"

"That it does." He nudged her with a toe. "Are you *sure* your mother would notice if we canoodled in the travel capsule? Because I'm feeling a rather common need right now."

"Jack! Behave!"

THE WORLD
UPRIGHT

You are in the right place, doing the right thing at the right time.
You have found your place.

After several years, they were still not comfortable inviting interviewers into their cottage, but they were getting better at it. If nothing else, it amused them to see the confusion on people's faces when they discovered that, yes, Jack and Leta really did live in a smallish house outside a smallish town, near Leta's mother, with a productive garden and kitchen. They served visitors home-baking, and tea in mis-matched cups. There wasn't anything remarkable about them, other than the whole conduits-of-divine-powers thing.

The country had expected them to be celebrities. Instead, they owned a bakery around the corner from their house, with an outdoor seating area, landscaped by Jack and planted by Leta. The 'mobile caterer to raise capital' plan hadn't worked because their notoriety had got in the way, so they'd done the minimum sort of paid interviews necessary to raise the capital instead. They still did some to keep cash coming in, and they earned more from their biannual Blessings tour stipends, and writing the odd column. The columns — which were not what Gealdland had expected from them but they were learning to deal with it — were their way of fulfilling their obligation to pass on what they felt to the people of the country, and hope that it constituted what the gods had wanted them to convey. The magazines had hoped for juicy gossip articles from them, but instead got regular recipes and gardening tips, and advice about slowing down. Advice that they had recently taken for themselves when they hired a bakery manager to help run their business.

They were still in contact with some contestants from the aethercast. Tiffany and Constance had remained friends with Leta. Some of them had done very well out of it all, too. Chrissie's indie smoothie 'cast had been syndicated, and she was now a famous influencer. Nellie had broken away from her parents' expectations and become an in-demand interior designer. Georgina had won a placement on the Gealdr Mentorship Programme and was now a powerful university mage. Jess and Marcus were married and lived in marital bliss while Marcus worked for a different aethercast network and Jess volunteered for a whale rescue organisation. Tiffany had founded an influential media company of her own, backed by certain members of the Geald families. Leta wasn't surprised in the slightest, considering what she knew about the information Tiffany had left the aethercast with.

The chap who had attacked Leta had ended up with psychiatric help. When he had improved, Leta met with him. She'd felt sorry for the guy in the end. He'd just been someone who'd lost his job and who had been preyed upon. The man who had organised the protesters hadn't been found. Yet. Leta was confident that he would face the consequences of his actions one day, though.

Destiny came through it all well enough in the end. Leta had heard through the grapevine that she had done some community service, but otherwise she had cut a deal with AllAether. She'd pulled away from her father and was now working as a socialaether guru for some other celebrities, and was married to a rather strapping footballer. Leta hadn't seen her in person since the police station, though she still wished the complicated woman the best.

That was all in the past now, though. Today, an interviewer was visiting for one of the semi-regular 'Let's interview one of the incarnates and see if we can shake some gossip free this time' interviews they fielded. The interviewer sat in their living room with her aetherimprinter assistant, dubiously eyeing their over-stuffed bookshelves and the houseplants on every surface, while Jack and Leta bustled about in the kitchen, pulling together a tray of tea and ginger bread.

"You got this?" asked Jack.

"Yeah, this one's harmless, I think. She'll ask about married life and whatnot." The interviewer had only asked for Leta, as she was from one of the women's magazines, and as a married man, Jack had graduated from being featured constantly in their pages.

He carried the tray into the lounge and placed in on the coffee table. "Please enjoy," he said. "I'll be outside." He kissed Leta on the way out of the room and patted her on her the bottom in a friendly manner. The interviewer blushed and busied herself with her tea.

Leta took a seat across from the interviewer, ignoring for the moment a flutter in her belly. "Shall we get started?"

They interviewed her for an hour, asking about her home life and her plans. Nothing unexpected. Occasionally, Leta was distracted by the sight of her husband weeding the front garden. Partially by the sight of his arse as he leaned over, and partially by her fear he would pull the wrong plants by accident. He didn't have the instinct for it that she did.

The interviewer caught her looking out the window and smirked. "That's quite a view you have from here, isn't it?"

"Uh…"

"I mean the distant hills, of course."

"Of course."

When they finished, the interviewer, aetherimprinter, and Leta went out into the garden. They had her sit in front of one of her flower beds and took a few imprints for their article. Then the interviewer shook Leta's hand, and they started down the garden path towards the gate. "Thank you for your time, Goddess Incarnate Leta," the interviewer said as she left.

Leta stood next to Jack, and he paused his weeding as they linked their arms and waved their visitors good-bye. When they had walked down to the end of the road and turned towards the local travel tube station, Jack smiled at Leta. "So, how did it go?"

"As expected. The same sort of fluff as usual."

"Did they get the big gossip?" he asked.

"You know what? I don't believe they did." Leta toed Jack's weed pile.

"You're not going to grade my work, are you?"

"Wouldn't dream of it. Especially not after you drank that whole batch of cider without complaint."

"It wasn't bad."

"It wasn't good either. I don't think my magic covers making booze. You might need to take over that task."

"How about we don't bother with the booze for a while, and I make you a gazebo instead? After all, only one of us can drink it at the moment." He eyed Leta's belly.

"A gazebo would be nice. Although, I'm going to need you to take up the potting and composting tasks for the next few months, because of the risk of legionnaires."

"I can do both. I'm pretty sure you're usually a lot more productive than me. Time for me to pull my weight." He flexed an arm.

"Speaking of things you need to do," said Leta, swatting him on the chest. "You have that live aethercast thingie with the uni students in an hour. You'd best go have a shower."

Jack wiped his face with the hem of his t-shirt. "Oh, yeah; care to join me?"

Leta shrugged, then started walking back to the house. She looked back at him over her shoulder. "You coming?"

He grinned. "Yes, ma'am."

THE END

ACKNOWLEDGEMENTS

Many people have helped and supported me while I brought this book into being.

My thanks go to Camille and Kim, who gave me the beta feedback that helped me whip this book into shape. I also wish to thank Stef, who made such a fantastic cover.

The BookTok community helped me believe people would actually want to read my book. I am ever grateful for your enthusiasm.

As always, my Kiwi writing buddies have my back. It is a true blessing to know you all.

Last but not least, thank you to my family, who put up with me being a total stress bunny while finishing this project.

ABOUT THE AUTHOR

Calanthe is a writer from Aotearoa New Zealand. She lives with her family and a very fluffy cat. She likes growing food more than flowers. She enjoys cooking and baking, and she watches K-dramas. By day, she is a parent and freelance editor.

Calanthe is a pākehā (white settler) who lives and works on the ancestral lands of the Kāi Tahu iwi.

Find out more at www.CalantheColt.com

www.ingramcontent.com/pod-product-compliance
Lightning Source LLC
Chambersburg PA
CBHW031421240626
47154CB00001B/140